The Land Was a Wild, Untameable Thing!

Somehow Jason staggered toward the house, squinting against the lightning, defying the roaring, rolling, exploding earth, taking its jolts through legs, body, jaws, teeth. Blessedly, at last, there was the figure of his wife in the doorway, shrieking, and holding the bundle that was his son.

"Throw him!" roared Jason. "Throw him to me!"

She shrieked on, sinking with the house as it wafted crazily toward the earth's ravening mouth.

"You damn fool!" Jason roared, his voice rending his ears, riding above the sounds of the clamoring earth. "Throw him, you fool . . . throw him . . . hard. Then jump . . . jump like hell!"

Books by Sailee O'Brien

Beelfontaine
Blood West
The Bride of Gaylord Hall
Captain's Woman
Shadow of the Caravan

Published by POCKET BOOKS

Saliee O'Brien
BLOOD WEST

PUBLISHED BY POCKET BOOKS NEW YORK

Another *Original* publication of POCKET BOOKS

POCKET BOOKS, a Simon & Schuster division of
GULF & WESTERN CORPORATION
1230 Avenue of the Americas, New York, N.Y. 10020

ISBN: 0-671-81765-5

First Pocket Books printing March, 1980

10 9 8 7 6 5 4 3 2 1

POCKET and colophon are trademarks of Simon & Schuster.

Printed in the U.S.A.

For Thurlow Benjamin Weed

my son

ACKNOWLEDGMENT

To Peggy Ryder and staff of the Hollywood,
Florida, Public Library.

BLOOD WEST

Chapter 1

Mild weather lay warm upon the land. It glowed from the village sky and from the forest sky, its sunlight shimmered on the Mississippi, bathed the log houses of New Madrid in that part of Louisiana which was to become the Missouri Territory, and filled the air with languorous richness. It brushed the skin, stroked the hair, warmed the heart; it enticed the mind away from home and lured it on into dreams.

Jason Blood, long rifle in hand, padded along in his hand-sewn deerskin moccasins, crossed the last stretch of clearing into forest, his eyes searching ahead and around as they always did when he came to hunt. When they caught no flick of deer, no surge of turkey, they were neither impatient nor disappointed, but remained quiet and keen and certain of success before the day was ended.

He moved noiselessly among the trees—the tall pines and white hickory, sweet and black gum, winged elm and white ash, long since stripped for winter on this day of December 15, 1811. In other seasons, instead of brown undergrowth and crumbling leaves, poppies, golden seal, white baneberry, and beech drops bloomed.

1

Prickly gooseberry also grew here, and in season he gathered the hard, sour green little fruits, from which Massie Ann stewed a sweet sauce to eat with bread and butter or made a deep and succulent pie.

Behind him, though he couldn't hear so much as a rustle, Jason knew that his hunting companions, Tench Coghill and the young Pole, Samuel Janas, were matching him stride for stride, eyes as quick and probing for game as his own.

Now Sam spoke, his voice a deep, quick bass which still surprised Jason for its contrast with his short and wiry build. "No sense pussyfootin' too much yet," Sam said. "It's plain to see the game's deep in somewheres this mornin'. Anyhow we kin talk some, if we hold it down."

"What's there to talk about?" asked Tench. His voice was high-pitched for his near six-foot muscular body. Tench was thirty, brown-haired, brown-eyed, his face weathered and pockmarked.

Sam was always outspoken, being young and of hot Polish blood. He retorted brashly. "Hell, there's allus somethin' to talk about! Show me the day there ain't! Right then I was wonderin'—Jase, how'd you git out of lettin' old man Cremer come along with us?"

"Sam," chuckled Tench, "didn't your pappy teach you respect?"

"That he done!" agreed the young Pole cheerfully. "With a strap and with a club. And behind the plow. Only I got shet of straps the day I took off fer Pittsburgh and left him his other seven boys to beat into good Christian men."

"Just the same," Tench reminded, a touch of gentleness tempering his words, "you ain't but twenty, and Fred Cremer's a good forty or more."

"Forty-three," put in Jason, a flicker of apprehension flashing through him because one day he, too, would be, not twenty-one, but as old as Cremer, who was his father-in-law.

"Aw, cut off yer pesterin', men," protested Sam, still cheerfully. "Old man Cremer's too much like my pappy to suit me. Neither one of you likes to hunt with the varmint, way he tromps and crashes and scares the game off, and you might as well own up to it."

"Man his age has got to be respected some," Tench insisted. "Though I can't misagree about him scaring off the game."

"He doesn't rightly appreciate the way he is," Jason told them. "He means to walk careful when he's hunting, knows a man's got to, and he does start out that way. Then he forgets himself and goes headlong to get the job done. And as a result, comes home with nothing, often as not."

"Like the ones unlucky enough to be with him," Sam snorted. "He's got it good, you bringin' him meat. That how you got around him this trip, promise to bring him a deer and a brace of turkey?"

"No, young Fred decided to hunt with the Duval boys," Jason replied, telling only that part of the truth his companions needed to know.

The unpleasant scene had taken place in his father-in-law's abode late yesterday. The cabin had been, as always, so filled with stench that Jason had wondered if slicing his hunting knife down the air would leave a visible trail. There had been the smell of the dirt floor, unswept and lacking clean straw, annointed and soaked by the dripping clouts of the endless succession of babies, ten of them since Jason's wife, Massie Ann, had been born. That was the basic stench, which embraced also the years of grease and cabbage and onions frying and boiling, which retained the sour-milk odor, both today's and that of yesteryear, with everything, food and offal and baby-stink so mixed and mingled and ground in that, Jason was sure, the only way to eradicate it would be to burn down the cabin and build afresh.

The family had been at supper when Jason spoke from the doorway. Fred Cremer, who stood five feet seven, all breadth and brawn, a bull of a man, had sat at the head of the table, facing the doorway. His gray-

ish eyes had shot a look at Jason out of his square face
and his fair eyebrows had dipped in a stern frown.

"Vhy bist du hier?" he had growled, chewing. "Der
grub ist on der plates. None left."

"Massie Ann's cooking our supper," Jason had told
his father-in-law, trying to endure the stench.

"Vhell, komm in!" Hatt Cremer had ordered. She
had been at the foot of the table, her wide, billowing
back to the door. "Ich vant nobody to shtand behind,"
she had continued in her shrill, scolding whine.

Reluctantly, Jason had moved into the cramped
room, which served for living, cooking, and even sleeping, having a crude bunk against the wall opposite the
fireplace. He had come to a halt midway into the room,
from which point he could see into his mother-in-law's
vast, fair-skinned face.

She was easily the fattest woman he had ever seen,
being Massie Ann's height, one inch over five feet,
weighing better than two hundred pounds. Everything
about her surged. Flesh looped from her shoulders,
down her arms, rolled bracelets around her wrists,
cushioned and padded and dimpled her tiny hands.
Flesh hung in softly springing wreaths beneath her chin,
swelled and leapt into a vast and overwhelming bosom,
girdled her waist, molded her hips and limbs into but-
tresses and columns. Her hair, once white-blond, was
darkened and lank. Only her blue eyes remained pretty,
though in color only, any size they once had now
shrunken into the spread sea of her face.

Her gobbling young were seated along the table,
their dingy blond heads over their plates, five to her
right, four to her left. She had been holding the youngest
on her enormous lap, his clout stinking, his elbow digging into her belly, where already she carried his successor, his mouth opening and closing as she spooned
some dripping, greasy mess into it from her plate.

As often as he'd been here—though that was only
when he must come—Jason had felt a shudder go down
him. It had still seemed impossible that human beings
would live like hogs, worse than hogs, for, left to run

free in the woods and forage, hogs were clean enough. It was only penned up that they wallowed in mud. Mud, Jason had thought, is clean compared to this, and the stink not nearly as bad.

Even young Fred, eighteen and a year younger than Massie Ann, had been dirty, his hair unkempt. Massie Ann, emancipated from this cabin, was always telling her brother to take a bath, was forever washing and ironing his clothes, but despite her efforts he managed to remain almost as dirty as the rest of his family.

From where he had been standing, Jason could see into the other room. It held only bunks, one against the end wall, one against the south wall. On these bunks nine Cremer young slept crosswise, though young Fred's feet must protrude considerably.

"Vhell?" Cremer had growled. "Du vergass how to talk? Vhat iss?"

"It's about the hunting trip tomorrow," Jason had said, carefully measuring his tone, holding it normal and assured and definite.

"Vhell? Ich habe mein rifle, ich habe mein lead und powder."

"He don't want you to go, pa," young Fred had put in, his mouth full. He had swallowed noisily. "He wants to go with that loudmouth Pole and that Pittsburgh boat builder, that's what he's here fer, and he don't know how to tell you."

Jason had felt the quick flush of red up his rugged face, through his eyebrows and into his scalp, had felt it really burn beneath that one tawny wave of hair which swept back from his brow. Young Fred had hit squarely on the truth, and now there was no diplomatic way to deal with the situation.

"Iss true?" Cremer had demanded, his scowl thick.

"Yes," Jason had admitted. "Tench stopped by after I got home and asked me to go with them. I told him you and I were going out, and Tench said for you to come along with us."

"Mit him, ja," Cremer had growled. "Aber nicht der Pole."

"No need fer you to go at all, pa," young Fred had put in. "You was mouthin' about wantin' to fish, so fish. I need yer rifle tomorrow anyhow. Anton and Pierre want me to go out fer deer with them. I'll bring in the meat ma wants."

"Vhe-ll," Cremer had speculated. "Zo . . ."

"Nicht zo," Hatt had scolded, fiercely spooning into the baby to hush the wailing he had set up. "Wenn du fish, ve don't essen but mush until Freddie mit meat gets hier. Du fish."

Cremer's scowl had thickened until it had constituted layer after layer of anger. Just as it had verged on rage, it had reversed and gradually assumed its normal character—a mixture of disapproval and general glowering.

"Zo," he had grunted. "Tell der Pole Fred Cremer don't hunt mit him. Du hear?"

"Yes," Jason had agreed, thankful to get off so easily, understanding anew why Massie Ann had been so frantic to escape this household. "Another time," he had added, given an inclusive nod at the table, and departed.

Today, walking with his hunting companions, he felt a tinge of guilt over his relief at being spared the company of his father-in-law. Cremer had no friends, and he, Jason, had these two good friends. It hardly seemed just that the man had not even his eldest daughter's husband in friendship.

Now the others overtook him and they walked abreast, at ease with one another. All three were dressed in the habitual garb of the country—tow shirt, coarse homespun trousers, leather leggings. A leather belt held up the trousers, and from it were suspended the knife, powder and shot pouches, and sundry other articles in regular use.

"Well," Sam resumed as though he'd never ceased to speak, "there's one way you kin be shet of the old man, Jase, once and fer all."

Jason smiled to himself. He'd heard this before, and so had Tench, but it was Sam's favorite topic, and there was no way to persuade him from talking about it. He was merely using Bremer as an excuse.

"Sure, Sam," Tench said, giving his chuckle. "We know, we know . . . go up the Missouri."

"You bet!" Sam seized the cue as if for the first time, his deep voice excited, booming softly, yet still almost a murmur so as not to disturb any possible game. "Go up the Missoura and take up land, real honest-to-God land! That's the way to git ahead, to know what you've got and what yer goin' to have! Not grub away in this place, raisin' beans and a little grain and huntin' and fishin'!"

"We trap some, too," Jason reminded.

"Yes, but the country up the Missoura ain't trapped out!" Sam retorted.

"This here ain't either," Tench said. "Trappers started New Madrid, don't forget. There's still plenty out from here."

"Sure," Sam argued, warming to his subject, "that's jest it! Out from here! They started it off fer a tradin' post fer furs when there wasn't nothin' here but the Delaware village where I got Yeller Flower from, and some other Injun villages. And all these years folk've been comin' in and trappin' and farmin' . . . I tell you, it's time far-seein' people moved on, up the Missoura, where they kin git eight hundred acres fer forty dollars!"

"Where are any of us going to get the forty dollars?" Tench demanded. "We've sunk what we had into our places here."

"Sell out, take the money, and go!"

"Who's going to pay for our places when they can come in and settle cheaper, the way we did?" Jason countered.

"We kin leave 'em fer sale, go up to St. Louis and trap out of there fer our money, then move up the Missoura," Sam insisted. "We ain't none of us old . . . yer strong as a bull, Tench, even if you got the edge on us in age."

"Maybe I don't think as young as I used to," Tench

said soberly. "I've got Medary to consider. I brought
her out west in hopes the change would strengthen her
so she won't miscarry every time."

"But it didn't," Sam pointed out. "She lost the last
'un, jest the same."

"All the more reason I can't go dragging her up to
St. Louis, then up the Missouri," Tench said.

"Her and Massie Ann'd stay in St. Louis whilst we
trap," Sam argued. "She'd rest and git to be fine. And
up the Missoura, no tellin' how strong she'd git to be."

"I doubt that Massie Ann would take kindly to the
idea of going into the wilderness," Jason offered, knowing full well how violently against it she would be.

"It ain't a woman's place to say where a man'll make
his livin'," Sam declared. "That's one thing about
Yeller Flower. That's the fine advantage to havin' an
Injun squaw . . . she don't never open her mouth ag'in
you. She jest does what she's told, and does it top-
notch."

It still made Jason uncomfortable that Sam had
hunted himself out an Indian girl even before he'd set
ax to tree. And that he'd let the girl build them a lodge
to live in while he raised the cabin. He wondered what
Hendrik van Delft, back in New York City, would say
it he heard that his foundling apprentice was consorting
with what he would term a squaw man.

He smiled grimly. He didn't give a damn what Hendrik van Delft would think. He was his own man now,
product of the stern and bookish Dutchman, but his
own man nonetheless.

"This argument'll never end," Tench said. "We're
deep enough into the woods. We'd best separate, don't
you think? I'll go off to the south half a mile or so,
work south from there. How about you fellows?"

"I'll go to the north," Sam decided, "keep workin'
north."

"I'll stay centerways and work west," Jason said.
"See you both at the village, if not before."

They nodded and turned, each in his own direction.
Jason stood and watched them go, marveling at the

silent swiftness with which they vanished—as though they'd never been there. Then, with the same careful skill, he moved deep into the trees, going west, thinking he'd try first for turkey. One of them would last himself and Massie Ann several days, the other, should he be able to bring down two, supplemented with hot bread and potatoes, would last Fred Cremer's family a full day.

Turkey gunning never was a pastime for children, he thought, as he drifted through the stand of pines. Only by penetrating their haunts with stealth and guile could those sly creatures be taken.

He chose a spot beside a stream which he knew to be one turkeys used for water in their travels. He fell to the ground, sinking a bit into the brown carpet of pine needles, a big fallen log right in front of him. Here he knew he must make himself as much as possible like a bump on that log, must not move, cough, slap at any flying insect or scratch its bite.

His eyes and ears must multiply their powers, for about the only difference he'd ever seen between turkeys and shadows was that turkeys wore feathers. They might come trotting or flying or pussyfooting along, stopping to search the ground for food, at a speed so torturously slow that he'd go tense with anxiety, over and again, before he dared chance a shot.

Thus, as he waited, every sense alerted for turkey, his thoughts slipped back to Sam's fervor for the Missouri and what lay up its reaches. Then they went to his own life here on the Mississippi, to his cabin, his infant son, his young wife.

Massie Ann wasn't the sort he'd planned to seek out for wife, not at all, having had in mind one of those New Orleans girls with dark and flashing eyes, long black swinging hair. And dancing feet making her silken skirts swing and rustle, betraying some enticing ruffle inside the hem, as he'd once read in one of the books he'd found hidden away in Hendrik van Delft's library. Anyhow, she'd be a girl he'd know and recognize the instant he saw her.

Well, that New Orleans girl was a storybook wife, and Massie Ann was real. She kept his cabin as clean as her parents' cabin was dirty, and somehow she had learned to cook deftly and, as far as Jason knew, perfectly.

Yet he luxuriated in hunting, in waiting and watching for turkeys, however long it might take. And he dreaded going home, wanted to put off the moment when he'd have to face his clean, obese wife, hear her wants, endure her intensity and the streak of viciousness which sprayed out now and again from her core.

Only when she sat at the table to feed upon her own cooking did she grow calm. At such times she was still quite pretty. The boy, the infant, was quiet and healthy. It was as though he drained his mother of placidity as he gulped and swallowed from her strutted bosom, leaving in her only dregs—the bitterness and resentment she visited upon Jason for putting her so soon into childbed, and the accusation that he meant to put her there endlessly, as her pa did with her ma.

Jason wondered if ever Hatt Cremer had been young, had been clean, had been like Massie Ann. What if childbearing made them both into what Hatt is now? he wondered. What if Massie Ann gets to be like her mother, exactly like her?

His mind sheered from the prospect and shot back in time to childhood, to New York, to the first moment he could remember seeing Hendrik van Delft. The Dutch scholar, watchmaker, farmer, who had beaten him and taught him and worked him and sent him forth at last to become his own man.

Chapter 2

Before Hendrik van Delft there was the foundling
home, a bare, drafty structure which would have echoed
had it not been filled up with unwanted children, the
abandoned, the doorstep babies. They walked the bare-
board corridors, ate at the long tables in the naked
dining hall, filed in a silence foreign to childhood up
the stairs to the rows of cots in the great, creaking
rooms.

Yet the woman in charge, the matron, had not been
unkind. Her name was Mrs. Allis, she was comfortably
fleshed, knew where each child was at all times and
what he was doing. Her face wore a slight frown which
never left it, a frown born of her many responsibilities
to the children.

She saw that the boys learned to chore, the girls to
cook and clean and sew. She made sure that each child
learned to swim the creek which ran at the back of the
wooded property and to fish and garden. She taught
them from the Bible, taught them to read and figure.
Every one of them learned courtesy and proper de-
portment in the presence of his elders.

She was kind enough the morning the man came who

was to apprentice Jason, to give him a home and training for all that lay ahead, the unknown and frightening
future. They sat together in the parlor, waiting. This
was a formidable room with a bit of dark red carpet,
bits of dark red at the windows, and severe wooden
furniture. The parlor was used only when visitors came
or when a child went out for adoption or apprenticeship.

Mrs. Allis sat at one side of the small square table,
which held only a white candle in a wooden candlestick. Jason sat in the chair on the other side.

"You're ten years old now, Jason," she began.

"Yes, ma'am," he responded, as he had been taught.

"You're going to live with Mr. Hendrik van Delft,"
she continued. "You will be obedient and industrious
and courteous toward him at all times. In return, he will
give you a sound upbringing. You're very fortunate that
Mr. van Delft is taking you. He is a respected and
learned man."

"Yes, ma'am," Jason muttered. He was uncomfortable, unused to such grown-up talk.

"As is our custom at the home, I've supplied Mr.
van Delft with all the information we have concerning
you, Jason," Mrs. Allis said. "At this time—when a
child leaves the home to be apprenticed—we also tell
the child what we know if the information is suitable
and decent. Do you understand?"

Jason nodded. "Yes, ma'am," he agreed, though he
didn't understand, not at all. Decent was to keep your
ears clean and your voice down, to use proper table
manners, to make your cot up tight and smooth, to keep
your boots polished and worn with care so as not to
wear them out before it was your turn to have a bigger
pair. He wasn't sure what "suitable" meant at all.

"I'm pleased to hear that," Mrs. Allis said. "Now,
as to how you came to the home." She drew a sheet of
folded paper out of her pocket. "You were found on
the doorstep here at six o'clock in the morning, January first, 1790. You were newborn, wrapped un-
clothed in a blanket, laid on a pillow. This letter was

tucked into the blanket. I answered the knocker myself. It was cold and icy, with a strong wind. No one was there. Only you and this letter."

"Yes, ma'am," Jason half whispered. His eyes felt like they were stretched so wide they couldn't go any farther. His ears were throbbing. He tried to swallow, but he couldn't, his mouth and throat were so dry. He could hardly even breathe. All the boys and girls at the home made up stories about where they'd come from, but he'd not made up any, not to tell, just dream stories about a pretty woman who was his mother and a laughing father who would come home to supper. Now there was this, and it was real. His heart was knocking. He'd never felt like this before, not shaking exactly, but everything somehow in him gone wrong.

Mrs. Allis unfolded the letter. " 'Dear Matron,' " She read. "'My baby's name is Jason Blood, and this is the name to which he has a right. Please keep him and please find him loving parents, for there is no breath of shame attached to his birth, only tragedy. My husband has died, I am worse than penniless, and forced to return to my childhood home."

Mrs. Allis folded the letter and regarded Jason. "It isn't signed," she told him. "So, while it may seem you don't know much about your family, you know the important things. You have a name of your own, a strong name—Blood. You have your true birth date and, on the evidence of this letter—the handwriting and the wording—you will later understand that your mother was a woman of some intelligence and education. I'll entrust the letter to Mr. van Delft. When you leave him, he will give it to you." She waited, then asked, "Is there anything you wish to say, or have me explain further, Jason?"

"N-no," he faltered. Actually he wanted to know why nobody had ever adopted him. He'd always wanted to know that, as did the others who watched, big-eyed and envious, when some favored little girl orphan with dark curls, or one of the handsome little boys, was taken away by a brand-new father and mother.

Mrs. Allis seemed to know what was in his mind, for she said, her voice crisper than usual, "It's nothing against you that you've not been adopted, Jason. It's not your looks, which have always been rugged and manly, and it's not your ways. I've shown this letter to people, but in one case they decided to take a girl, and in the other the gentleman persuaded his wife to settle on an infant. You were five at the time. You never need feel that you weren't good enough. It was rather that there are so many of you in the home, and so few adopting parents, that most of you are left to grow up here. I will say this—the apprenticeship for you is the best we've ever arranged. Mr. van Delft is an exemplary man who has never married but who feels kindly toward children. In fact, he has a nephew your age in Holland, a boy he's never seen, who is to be his heir. Yet you have the privilege of growing up under his guidance. You're fortunate indeed to go to Mr. van Delft, Jason."

He hadn't felt fortunate but simply frightened when the tall thin old man with gray hair and keen gray eyes, with even a gray look to his sharp features, took him away in a polished carriage. They rode a very long time, Jason staring all around at the great buildings, some of which were shops and others that looked to be foundling homes. The thought struck him that maybe families lived in some of the houses, but he dismissed it as impossible. Surely they were foundling homes, being so big and tall. He glanced sidewise at Mr. van Delft to see if his face might reveal the truth about these houses.

Van Delft caught him at it. "Never been so far before, eh?" he asked.

"N-no, sir."

The keen eyes went thoughtful. Then van Delft gestured, indicating the street. "New York's the biggest city in America," he said. "Don't forget that, Jason."

"N-no, sir. I won't, sir."

"They taught you to say 'sir.' That's one thing I won't

have to drill into you. Never forget to say 'sir' to me. I tell you this once, but not again."

"Yes, sir," Jason said, swallowing against the knot of breath in his throat. "I won't forget, sir."

"So. Now this . . . while we ride . . . take it all in now. You're not going to be riding around in the carriage every day. The town has grown up along here . . . this is Bowery Road . . . and it's grown a few blocks out. Beyond that is my place. And the population— know what 'population' is, Jason?"

"N-no, sir."

"It's the number of people living in a place," his master explained. "When you were born, there were thirty-three thousand people living in New York. Now the population has gone to over sixty thousand. Think of that. It's more than doubled in ten years. That's phenomenal. 'Phenomenal' means extremely surprising, never before heard of. Can you remember that? Can you add it to your vocabulary? 'Vocabulary' means the words you can understand when others use them in speaking, and which you yourself can use. Can you remember these new words and use them, Jason?"

"Yes, sir," Jason replied, his heart lightening. He'd always liked to learn. "I-I like to read, sir," he ventured.

"Don't think you're going to spend much time reading," van Delft said sharply. "For ten years you do what I want. My outside man, Billy, will train you to take care of the horses and cow and hogs and the stable. He'll train you to farm and hunt and trap and build. What you learn from him will enable you to feed and house yourself, no matter what. You're my apprentice, which means I'll train you to build and repair clocks in my workshop in the house. When you get so you can turn out your work, all of it, in proper time and do it the best it can be done, then and only then will you read and study. In your spare time I'll teach you, if you're bright."

"Yes, sir." Jason felt overwhelmed by all the things

he must learn and all the work he must do. He wondered how ten years, long though that was, could be enough time. He didn't know how to tend a horse, how to milk a cow, how to plant a crop. His chores at the home had been cutting wood and carrying water and growing vegetables. And clocks were rare things in the home. He believed Mrs. Allis had one upstairs, but he'd never seen it. He didn't even know how to tell time. To think of actually building a clock left him speechless. From that moment he looked upon reading as his refuge, his place of safety, because it was the only thing of the many expected of him that he knew how to do, even a little.

But he learned. Taught by middle-aged, wispy-haired, slow-witted Billy, who demanded perfection in a kind and stubborn manner, he learned. Working until his strong little body was tense with soreness, he learned how to clean the stable, curry the horses, oil the harness and mend it, polish the carriage, milk the cow, slop the hogs, clean the duck shed, gather the eggs. He learned to plow and plant and harvest, to trap and hunt and fish, to repair and build.

From van Delft he learned to hold the delicate parts to the inner workings of clocks in his fingers, though clumsily at first. He learned to help take clocks and even pocket watches apart, he learned how to clean them, repair them, put them back together. He learned to take pride in this work, though he never learned to like it.

What he liked was to read, to plant and harvest, to hunt and fish. And he liked to build whenever his master wanted any carpentry done.

He was eleven when he got his first beating. He'd done his stable work, helped with the cow, tidied the workshop. After supper, though his growing legs and arms were a network of soreness and fatigue, he lit a candle and went to the room called the library to read, as he was allowed to do.

He didn't know his master had come into the room

until the keen voice pierced him. "What are you doing, eh?" it demanded.

"I'm reading, sir," Jason said, springing to his feet, laying aside the volume of *Robinson Crusoe*. "Do you want me for something, sir?"

"Have you finished your work, Jason?"

He thought swiftly, naming the things over in his mind—stable, milking, tidying the workroom. All done. "I think I have, sir," he replied.

"The walnut clock belonging to the widow van Buskirk," the sharp voice accused. "You didn't wax it. I told you it must be waxed, and now she has sent her son to tell me she wants it first thing in the morning. And I find you reading."

"Y-yes, sir."

"Why didn't you do your work?"

"I don't know, sir. I'm sorry, sir. I'll wax it now, sir."

Actually, he hadn't understood that his master expected the work to be done by candlelight. Until now, waxing had been done in a clear north light. But he dared not speak these things to his master.

"Step over in front of me, Jason."

That was the first he noticed the leather strap dangling from the long-fingered hand. The hand moved, and the strap swung gently.

That knot of breath came to Jason's throat and that awful dryness. He couldn't speak, could only step, as ordered, to stand before the strap.

"You have got to learn to do one thing at a time, Jason Blood," van Delft said, his voice as cutting as any knife. "You have got to learn to do first things first—to do your work, every small task, before you indulge yourself in the joys of the mind. Since my training has failed to instill this principle in you, I must resort to this." Again his hand moved, and again the strap swung, not gently this time. "It will impress so you'll not forget. Later, you'll be grateful. You'll become a man, you'll be able to meet life because you have learned here, month by month, that life is a hard thing to live, that it makes demands which must be met. Bend over. Take your beating like the man you are to become."

The strap whistled as it came at him. It cut down, burned through his trousers, cut down again, harder, across his shoulders, tearing his shirt, biting into his flesh, searing him with sharp and sudden pain. He clenched his fists as the strap came harder yet, over and again, endlessly. He held his breath, endured the blows, the cuts, locked back the screams, even the moans. Tears were in him, hot and stinging as sharp-pointed knives, but he didn't let them out. Not even when the beating was ended did his breath betray him by so much as a quiver. Later, when van Delft gave him lard to smear on his stripes and cuts and welts, he refused it stoutly. And still he held back the tears.

There were other beatings, but the months lengthened between beatings as he remembered his lessons. He came to know that his master was more pleased than displeased with his progress, but the vigilance on both their parts never let up, nor the constant drilling nor the frequent reminders of how fortunate Jason was.

Despite the reminders, Jason didn't feel so fortunate. It was no fun being a bonded servant or an apprentice. He missed the boys at the home, missed playing ball with them and racing. He even missed the Sunday morning hymns. There was no occasional joy here, such as Christmas dinner at the home. He comforted himself with the reading.

On his sixteenth birthday, van Delft presented him with his own copy of *Robinson Crusoe*. This was the only gift Jason had ever received in his life.

He felt tears deep inside, but there they would remain. He held the book in his hands, a treasure. "Thank you, sir," he said. "I'll keep it always."

"You feel like jumping into work today, eh? Your birthday?"

"Not especially, sir," Jason replied.

"But you're willing to work?"

"Yes, sir."

"Do you remember the day I took you into my stable for Billy to train?"

"I remember, sir."

"And you remember what you've been taught? All of it?"

"Yes, sir."

"Recite it."

"I am your indentured servant, sir. I must work for you until you are repaid."

"Yes. Continue."

"I owe everything to you, sir."

"Why?"

"I was an orphan, sir. You took me in, gave me food and bed and clothing. You taught me to work hard and industriously."

"Go on, go on."

"You have never beaten me except when I am slow or slovenly, sir."

"That I have not, Jason."

"You taught me to read and write and cipher further, sir."

"As the law demands."

"Yes, sir. But because you are kinder than most masters, and have greater perception, you recognize that learning is to my mind what water is to the mouth of a man dying of thirst, and you permit me to read, sir."

"Yes."

"Because you are an uncommonly kind master, sir, you also apprenticed me and taught me clockmaking and watchmaking so that I may earn my living at it when I am a free man, sir."

"Yes."

"You have taught me to speak like a gentleman, sir, and you have taught me courtesy."

"You are courteous, Jason."

"I try to be, sir."

"Only sometimes your eyes talk back. As now. See to it that they watch their words. Around me, that is."

"Yes, sir."

"As to others, remain courteous, Jason. But firm. For if the boy doesn't have spirit in him, the man never will. I've taught you that. Remember it."

"Yes, sir."

"And when you leave me, what then, Jason? Are you going to be a clockmaker in New York and steal my customers?"

"Oh, no, sir. I'll leave New York."

"And where will you go?"

"To the Ohio River, sir."

"You know about that, eh? And what will you do at the Ohio?"

"I'll get on a boat, sir. One of those keelboats, and go far down the river, to the Mississippi, to a village that is new, but not too new, and there I'll stop, sir."

"What then?"

"I'll live there, sir. I'll be a free man, and I'll have my own land with my own cabin on it. I'll root myself into the new country, have my own family, my own blood. I'll be an equal of all other men, and I'll look squarely into the eye of each one of them and call him by name, and never say 'sir' to a man again."

Hendrik van Delft seized his leather strap off the wall hook then and beat Jason Blood for that, flogged him until welts stood the length of his body, and as always not the first sound did Jason let escape. When the thrashing was finished, he glimpsed what could be tears in the Dutchman's eyes, but he would never know for van Delft went outside, got into his carriage, drove away and did not return until late at night. While he was gone, Jason scrubbed the floor of the workroom, cleaned the stable, cut wood for the fireplaces, did everything else he could find to do until all he had strength enough for was to drop into his bed in the slant-roofed room off the kitchen and go instantly to sleep.

The stinging, burning stripes on his body did not rouse him. Nor did the book, *Robinson Crusoe*, which lay on the table next to him.

Chapter 3

Though he later apologized to his master for his defiance, Jason was never to entirely rid himself of regret that he had chosen that particular moment, when Hendrik van Delft had just presented him with his only gift, for asserting his future independence. The apology was accepted and the incident never again mentioned.

During the next years, on rare occasions, van Delft took Jason to various sites so he could learn about the great city, saying he must appreciate the modern world and think carefully before he buried himself in the wilderness. "This corner is where Broad and Pearl streets meet," he told Jason on one such excursion. "That's Fraunces Tavern yonder . . . the kind of place you're to shun wherever you go."

On another occasion he pointed out a section of pasture land which had a barricade of untrimmed trees to keep the animals from straying. "Over there is Wall Street," he said. "The wall is gone now, but it once stood when a war broke out between England and Holland, and the city feared there might be an invasion from New England. Presently, a body of men meet working days under that buttonwood tree. They devote their entire time to the buying and selling of securities. Some years ago twenty-four of them entered into a formal agreement with respect to their business methods. They're going to be important to the city, to the nation."

"Yes, sir," Jason responded. "What are 'securities,' sir?"

"They are what one might term a system of investment of money other men earn," van Delft explained. "It isn't a method I use, but many substantial men are investing on Wall Street, and for the most part, they seem to prosper."

"Yes, sir," Jason said, bewildered. He'd never had any money, and couldn't imagine parting with it in such manner should he acquire some. Why have the money at all, he wondered, if you were going to hand it over to someone else? How would you get it back if that person didn't choose to return it?

Interested though he was in all van Delft took him to see, Jason saw nothing he would regret leaving, nothing that held the pull the far, unknown West exerted upon him. Thus it was with eager rather than sad heart that, the ten years of servitude done and Jason twenty, he stood at the door one early morning taking leave of his master.

He was wearing the new coonskin cap, the gray cloth shirt, the knee-length leather breeches, and the stout shoes that were his due. He was carrying a small pack slung from one shoulder, and holding eagerness from spilling out of him.

"Well, Jason," Hendrik van Delft said in a voice as old as his face, "the time is here."

"Yes, sir."

"You've got your start in life. You've got fifty dollars gold, your clothes, and books you took in place of gold. You're got your mother's letter. You have earned it all."

"Yes, sir. But you gave me my opportunity."

"You're sure about the books? As part of your pay."

"I'm sure, sir. The Bible, *Pilgrim's Progress, Poor*

Richard. And the *Robinson Crusoe*. I prefer them to gold."

"You can still reconsider. You can take land instead. It would be worth more."

"No, sir. Thank you, sir."

"Then only our handshake remains."

Their hands met briefly and strongly. Then Jason turned and began his long walk to the Ohio, and the days strung out, one fastened to the other, as he walked the land.

When he strode, at last, into Pittsburgh, smoke lay in the April sky, blacker than the sky, darkening the cold evening twilight. It made a living roof over the borough, and at the far edges were streamers and feathers and tiny geysers of smoke that stirred with the breeze from the two rivers. These were the Monongahela and the Allegheny, which came together at Pittsburgh to form the Ohio, which, in turn, led to the Mississippi, where he was bound.

Here on Liberty Street, and the streets leading off on either side through the borough, which must number some five thousand souls, no corner lamps burned as in New York and no night watch patrolled to cry the hour. But already, in windows along here and along Plum Alley and Wayne Street and Garrison Way, along Strawberry and Virgin alleys and St. Clair and Pitt streets and Perry, showed the yellow point of candle flame or the glow of sperm lamp.

He gazed at the houses he passed. They were built in a jumble of styles and materials, their situations erratic, some facing the street, others shouldering gable ends or corners at those who passed. All were streaked with soot which looked like gray and black shadows in the dusk, and were at this moment laying down fresh soot from their smoking chimneys.

At Marbury Street, which bordered Fort Pitt, he turned away from the square structure of earthworks and logs which looked, in this gray light, almost black. He made his way to Water Street as he'd been directed,

followed it eastward toward Suke's Run, and continued
in that direction after the footway ended and the
borough lay behind. Here he came upon one of the
temporary villages occupied by immigrants awaiting
the breaking of the ice and the spring floods which
would float them down the river.

Some of these immigrants were living in wagons they
had driven from beyond the hills, some in flatboats
they had built ashore and pulled over the now-vanished
snow to spots where the rising water would float them,
others in clumsy huts and tents. Their chickens were
penned in coops and their horses and cows in flimsy
lean-tos or staked in the open. Poorly dressed children
and skinny dogs ran everywhere.

Though Jason had been told of these winter villages,
he hadn't imagined their starkness or given the travelers
who inhabited them a thought beyond appreciating
their eagerness to go into the new country. Now the
trusting innocence of the playing children who must
have every sort of parent—dreamers, doers, adven-
turers, even cruel abusers—struck him with hard, deep
concern. What would happen to these children out
there in the West where he himself meant to seed his
own children?

He swept his gaze over the darkening scene, the
wagons with men gathered to pass a few words while
their women bent over outdoor supper fires, the boats
tied up at the bank, an occasional figure moving about
the deck. There were rafts loaded with merchandise, and
flatboats of various kinds: Kentucky and New Orleans
boats, so named after their intended destinations; broadhorns named for their wide-bladed sweeps; arks for a
fancied resemblance to the first such river craft, which
featured a steering oar at both bow and stern.

Jason eyed the flatboats closely, thinking that if he
had a family it was the only way he'd choose to travel.
These boats varied in size, the smaller ones looking
to be about twenty feet in length and twelve in width.
They were built on sills or gunwales of heavy timbers,
and the bow of each was raked forward to offer less

resistance to the water. The decks were variously roofed. On some boats almost the entire deck was covered with one big cargo box. On others there was a cargo box at each end, one for the family to live in, the other to hold supplies and tools. One of the sturdiest of the flats was equipped with a brick fireplace chimney and had a glass window in which one of the shoreside fires was beginning to reflect. The others, Jason knew, used boxes filled with sand, or kettles as cabooses, in which to keep their fires.

Steering was done with a thirty- or forty-foot oar made by fastening a board to the end of a long pole. The oar was pivoted in a forked stick fastened to the roof or to a porthole in the stern. At least two sweeps, or broadhorns, similarly pivoted on the sides, were used to keep the boat in the current.

His attention came back to the flat with the chimney, and he began to move toward it purposefully. He had to make inquiries somewhere, and the man who had built this sturdy boat, or had had it built, must be a solid and sensible person, a man who meant to take his family downriver in both comfort and safety.

He went across the gangplank and onto the deck between the cargo boxes. He felt the boat move on the water, felt the vibration and the thrill of anticipation fill his body. This was the first time he'd set foot on a boat, and it seemed to promise at first touch to take him where he must go, take him joyously. Another thrill fled through him, one of recognition—that he wanted from life not only his roots in the wilderness and blood of his blood, but the joy of them which he would somehow win as well.

Now he became aware that there someone was squatting against the wall of the windowed cargo box, next to a rain barrel at one side of the door. The figure rose, and Jason could see that it was a very young man, slightly built and wiry, dressed in the same sort of garb he himself wore.

"Howdy," the fellow said, his voice deep and quick. "Lookin' fer somebody in perticular?"

"Yes, I am," Jason replied. "My name is Jason Blood. I've just arrived from New York. I take it I'm speaking to the owner of this boat."

"Not right now, you ain't," said the fellow. "I'm Sam'l Janas, from down towards Philadelphia . . . Sam fer short. Pleased to meet you, Mr. Blood."

He stuck out his hand and they shook.

"I'm not used to being called 'mister,' " Jason said, and grinned.

He could just make out Sam's grin. " 'Jase,' then," Sam said. "Suits you better."

"Who is it, Sam?" a woman's voice called from inside. The voice was light and somehow just missed brightness.

"Feller name of Jason Blood, lookin' fer the owner of the boat, fer Landers," Sam called back. "Landers ain't at his waggin, even, went up to Strawberry to help Tench fetch yer truck."

"Invite him in, Sam," the woman said. "Supper's almost ready."

Sam gestured and led Jason through the door.

Lamplight lay across the wooden floor of a tiny compact room. Facing the door was the brick fireplace fitted with iron vessels, one of which was emitting a mouth-watering aroma of meat. On one wall was the window, beneath it the table, laid for a meal, and plain chairs. Slat-front shelves of dishes and cooking supplies lined the inner partition on either side of a door leading to what was presumably an extremely small sleeping accommodation.

A woman of near thirty came through that door and regarded Jason with hazel eyes which were bright with sadness. And then he lost sight of the sadness at the impact of her long and silken shawl of blazing red hair. She wore it, at the moment, tied with a black ribbon at the nape of her neck. Her skin was unbelievably white against that red; the cat's-mask of freckles she had across her nose, out to the cheekbone, seemed to take on a redness from the hair, and he noted but did not mind that her features—nose and mouth—were plain and that she looked worn.

Her pale lips stirred toward a smile, then quieted back into plainness. The sadness of her eyes brightened further. "Please, Jason Blood," she said in that light voice, "forgive my appearance." She indicated the colorless robe she wore, or perhaps it only appeared colorless because of her vivid hair. "I was resting. I've been ill . . . I . . . lost my baby."

"Sorry," muttered Jason, not knowing where to look.

"I'm Medary Coghill. My husband is Tench Coghill. He's a boatbuilder, just finished helping build a keelboat. He built this flat for Mr. Landers, who is kind enough to let us stay on it until we leave on the keel tomorrow. You see, we had to move out of the house we rented. Today . . . April first . . . is moving day in Pittsburgh . . . everybody who is going to move from one house to another does so on this day. So we had to leave in order to let the new tenants in, and the Landers were kind enough to offer us shelter."

"Yes, ma'am," Jason said. "I can wait outside for Landers, ma'am."

"You'll do nothing of the kind!" Medary declared, a hint of brightness touching her voice. "Sit down at the table. You, too, Sam. They should be back any minute. Do you live in Pittsburgh, Jason Blood?"

He leaned his rifle, which he'd bought for half his gold on his walking journey, against the wall. He sat across the table from Sam.

He told where he'd come from. In no time at all, Medary got it out of him that he had walked every step except for a couple of rides on wagons, and she marveled at that.

"Heck, Medary," complained Sam, a grin splitting his face, making his features a trifle less sharp. He pawed a lank fall of tan hair away from his pale eyes. "Heck, I hoofed it from Philadelphia!"

"But New York is so far away," admonished Medary, and this time she really smiled, and her smile set her face alight.

"You didn't have to hoof all them miles to see boats, Jase," Sam teased. "Way you was gawkin' at this one. New York's got a-plenty from what I hear tell. Even had a steamboat once. Did it really go? We've heard it did, and others after it, but it jest ain't believable that a boat'd go in such an outlandish way. No tide, no oars, no sweep, no poles . . . jest steam, like that a-comin' out of that kittle of Medary's stew!"

"That was Fulton's boat," Jason said. "It did go, and over two years back. I saw it myself."

"You did?" Medary breathed, her eyes beginning to shine.

Sam's mouth had fallen open and he stared, waiting.

Thus, to satisfy his unexepected audience, yet wishing to avoid seeming a braggart, Jason related what he'd experienced that August day. "Everybody predicted that Fulton's attempt to navigate his boat—the *Clermont*—by steam would fail," he said. "The vessel was a hundred fifty feet long, had a thirteen-foot beam, drew two feet of water, and was said to have a speed of four miles an hour."

"Impossible!" snorted Sam. "These flats don't average but four miles an hour downstream on flood tide! No boat kin reach any four miles under steam ag'in the wind and tide!"

"Well," Jason continued, "quite a few people gathered that day at the Hudson to watch. The man I was apprenticed to came with me."

"What'd this Fulton do first?" demanded Sam.

"His friends were in groups on the deck," Jason said. "They all looked worried. The signal was given, and the *Clermont* moved a short distance, then stopped. Everybody on deck seemed to grumble and shrug. I could even hear some of them say quite loud, 'I told you it was so!' and, 'It's a foolish scheme!' and even, 'I wish we were well out of it!'

"Then Fulton got up on a platform and said he didn't know what was wrong, but if they'd indulge him for half an hour, he'd either go on or abandon the voyage for that time. Of course they agreed. Fulton went below, and it is said he examined the machinery and found the cause, a slight one. In a short time it was righted. The boat was again put in motion. She continued to move. Everybody was incredulous. She moved steadily but slowly from the wharf, and when she turned up the river and was under way, there arose such a huzza you couldn't hear your own voice."

"It's a freak!" Sam declared.

"It could be they'll get it to work, Sam," Medary said.

"W-ell," he conceded, "may-be. You was a schoolmarm, and you read stuff. But I don't think none of us'll live to see that day!"

He had no sooner spoken than two men came in from the deck. The younger was six feet tall and all muscle, the older was over six feet and less muscular.

"This is my husband," Medary said, indicating the younger man. "Tench . . . Jason Blood, from New York City. Mr. Landers . . . Jason Blood. He's been waiting to speak to you."

Swiftly, even as he got to his feet, Jason took in Tench Coghill's weathered skin, his brown eyes and hair, his strong, yet kind features, his firm mouth. He was perhaps thirty, as was his wife. Landers was grizzled, a man of assurance and substance, but with farmer written all over him.

He raised one grizzled eyebrow at Jason. "Want to talk on deck?"

"No," Jason said. "It's not private. I want to go downriver, and thought I'd offer my help in getting a flatboat to its destination in trade for transportation and meals. Also, I can hunt and fish for the boat."

"It'd pleasure me to give you transportation," Landers said, "only I've got three grown sons to help me, and I've got my woman. We're crowded as it is."

"It might be you could sign on to a keelboat," Tench offered, "the flats being filled with families, as a rule. That's what we've done, Sam and me. I get my fare and keep as oarsman, and part of Medary's fare in place of pay. That's the main reason we're going west, to build Medary's health. Sam gets fare and some pay both."

"Say!" exclaimed Sam. "Why don't you try to come with us, Jase? We'd all hit it off real good, all of us could settle in the same place. We're polin' off tomorrow, but the patroon's bin havin' a time gittin' a crew."

"He must have a crew if he's poling off," Jason said.

"Matter of fact," Tench said thoughtfully, "Bull was doubtful of that river-roarer, that Wee Willie he talked to yesterday, the one that claims to be a pal of Mike Fink. Said he'd almost rather pole off shorthanded, seeing it's downstream and flood tide, than having that roarer making the trouble he's made on other keels."

"He looked like a snortin' good boatman to me," Sam said.

"He is," Tench agreed. "But it seems he fights more than common. There just might be a chance—you know how to set a pole, Jason?"

"What if he don't?" argued Sam. "Look at him— don't miss six foot by more'n an inch, the right weight to him, all muscle and hard-lookin' as rock. Give him one day and he'll be settin' pole as good as any boatman on the rivers."

Tench eyed Jason from head to foot, nodding slowly. Landers, too, was nodding.

"He'll be the handsomest boatman on the river," Medary said lightly. "Those rugged features barely save him, and even then, that tawny-gold hair with the wave . . . Jason, eat plenty of this stew tonight. Build strength to man that pole and to fight off the girls along the banks! Sit down, all of you . . . you, too, Mr. Landers. Your wife fed your family an hour ago. The least I can do is see that you don't go to your wagon hungry and cause her extra work."

Jason sensed that this was a glimpse of the real Medary, as she could be when not grieved over losing her child, when there was room in her for joy. He saw Tench's quick, eager look at her, heard the throb in his voice.

"You listen to Medary, Jason," he said, and grinned. "She's a judge of men. I have a notion that Bull'll take you on . . . he listened to a couple of my opinions when I was helping build his keel. He's as big a river-roarer as you can find, but I think he might listen to me again."

Chapter 4

At dawn, as the three of them—Jason and Tench and Sam—neared the keelboat *Bull,* they saw a group of keelers ashore opposite it, heard their loud discordant voices. There were five or six of them, powerful and tall, gaunt and big-boned in buckskin trousers, red shirts, and moccasins. The way they held their mighty bodies, the amazingly long stride of one of them, who surged a few paces away, then back to the others, flaunted their restless daring, their vicious drive to fight at the slightest provocation, their instinct to use prowess to counter any real provocation. From the deck of the vessel, their varied fellows, some six or seven in number, leaned against the cargo box and stared ashore.

"Bull . . . Bull Hecker!" Sam yelled at the group, his voice booming over theirs. "Kin we palaver fer a minnit? We got another keeler fer you!"

A burly figure wheeled and strode impatiently toward them. Bull Hecker, Jason thought, watching the patroon's great, thrusting strides, must be taller, bigger-boned, stronger-muscled, and more dangerous than any of his keelers. There was tremendous leashed power in his move, and in his cruel and craglike features. The

32

rough black hair which sprang back from his high, jutting brow bespoke power and violence. The notorious Mike Fink himself, river-roarer of fame and infamy, would need to fight to the death were he to challenge Bull Hecker.

"Whar's yer woman at, Coghill?" roared Bull. "I'm settin' pole on the tide!" He surged to a halt. His eyes, a blinding blue, flashed. "Wal?" he bellowed.

"Landers is bringing her and our truck in his wagon," Tench said. "Ten, fifteen minutes and she'll be aboard. This fellow here is Jason Blood. He wants to sign on for as far as St. Louis, New Madrid . . . wherever you take on more crew."

Jason noted, without looking, that the other keelers had stalked over to them in a few mammoth steps.

Bull's brows plunged. The eyes stabbed Jason to the bone. "Never poled a boat, did ye?" he roared.

"As of today I pole a boat," Jason snapped, met the blazing, accusing look full on, shut his lips so they made a line across his face.

A towering giant of a keeler, vast-shouldered and muscled beyond his mighty fellows, spraddle-legged himself in front of Jason and the patroon. He was second to none in black-browed ugliness. He stood at least six feet four inches, with bone and seething power which awed Jason.

He slammed his ferocious look at Jasen, black eyes murderous. "Don' horn in on me," he growled. "Ye wonder 'bout me, eh? Wal, me'll tell all ye puny rats that calls yerselfs rivermen! Me'll tell Bull Hecker, too . . . me'll show ye all! Me's the wildest mannee ever hatched, an' no mis-take!"

With a single move too swift to identify or actually to be seen, he was closer, standing over them, his great moccasined feet spread a mammoth distance, his trousered legs as strong and ungiving as the tallest, stoutest forest tree.

"This is *me,* an' don' fergit!" he roared, beating his huge fists against his great chest. "Me, Willie Screamer, Esquire, commonly called Wee Willie, the River-

Roarer. Me kin outroar, outsing, outwork, outbrag 'em ever' time! Me's all the way f'um the back of Hell, whur the divil hisself couldn't beat me! Me's a small sample, as ye see . . . on'y a yearlin', but goin' fer me peak, but damn me if me ain't the su-perior breed whut kin whup any mannee on any keel, in this section of the kintry, in any section of any kintry! *Whoops!* Won' one of ye wee mannees stan' up an' fight me? Step out, one of ye varmints an' die decent . . . me's Willie Screamer, the River-Roarer, fightin' pal of Mike Fink, an' me's *spilin'* fer a fight! Me ain't had one in Pittsburgh, an' if ye don' come out, anyone, me's crow-stripped fer a certinty! So stan' up to me an' try ter let fly!

"Mebbe ye don' know who Wee Willie is! Me'll tell ye: Me's a pore man, that's the truth, an' me smell's like a swilly hawg, but me's the i-dentical specimen that stared a hull crew of river-roarers down, an' made 'em unloose their fists an' slink off with their tails a-tween their balls, a-skeered to come near me big toe! *W-h-o-o-p!* Me's the in-dividual, too, that towed the biggest barge men ever see up the Mississap, up the Ohio, acrosst wood islands an' snags an' sandbars, a-tween sawyers so thick an' vicious they jumped up out of the river an' whacked the heads off the rest of the crew—fact, an' if anybody blinks his eye ag'in it, jest let him jump into his coffin! *Cock-a-doodle-do!* Mebbe ye never heerd 'bout the time the 'gator got me by the laig an' bust his jaw an' turned his belly up an' died an' me walked away laughin,' huntin' me a whole bunch of gators, but they was all lily-livered an' dug into the mud an' laid there an' shook, tryin' to shake the riverbed loose, but it was me feet, Wee Willie, the River-Roarer's feet, a-steppin' an' a-trompin' what caused the earthquake! If it ain' true, try to cut me up an' feed me to the 'gators . . . they won' touch a bit of Wee Willie . . . *w-h-o-o-p-s!* Oh, me's the toughest of the tough, me's the wildest of the wild, me's the very in-fant whut looked the divil in the eye an' got kicked out'n Hell because me made it too hot fer the horned bastard! Look at me . . . look hard!" he screamed, and smote his chest so hard it made a sound like a deep-toned drum. "Me's the gin'wine, unbeatable, unkillable Wee Willie . . . me's the Screamer . . . me's the River-Roarer, an' no mis-take, an' me kin outrun, outjump, outswim, outdrink, outwork any other mannee on earth! Me'll step back fer no mannee on no keel . . . me'll hold me fightin' till Noo Orleens . . . but then me'll kill any mannee riles me . . . me'll chew him up an' spit him out an' stomp him into dust! Me don' min' doin' it afore we pole off now, any mannee asks fer it! *Cock-a-doodle-doo!*"

He stood, chest working like a great bellows, black eyes showing a flash of red. The keelers behind him looked almost as wild as Wee Willie, eyes hard, fists at their sides, powerful bodies ready to spring.

"Ye had yer say, mannee!" Bull Hecker bawled. He glared violently at the river-roarer. "There'll be no fightin' here! Ye keep yer oar . . . but if ye slam a fist afore Noo Orleens, Bull Hecker personal'll tear ye apart, an' that's a promise! What ye do in Noo Orleens don't bother me a gaw-damn, ye kin kill ever' mannee on the waterfront there, but not on my keel, an' they kin kill you an' feed ye' to the river! Same fer all of ye," he said to the others, then yelled it to those aboard the *Bull*. "Bull Hecker's goin' to git his cargo, he's goin' to git his flour, down to Noo Orleens, chew on that! Bull Hecker's a river-roarer kin match Wee Willie, kin match Mike Fink, kin match the divil an' best 'em all at the same time with one finger! Now—" He wheeled on Jason. "See what yer up ag'in?" he yelled. "Kin ye handle yer oar, handle yer pole, keep yer fists out'n men's faces, along with such as Wee Willie . . . an' Shark an' Ripper an' Hammer . . . these mannees, an' the others aboard?"

"I'll put out the work," Jason said grimly.

"Hell, yes, he will," Sam put in. "He's as good a man as any of us!"

"Five dollars an' keep," Bull said. "No more . . . yer a greenhorn. Ye'll work yer ass off, er git it beat off."

"Suits me," Jason said, his mouth hardening. Why Bull considered him more of a greenhorn than Sam and Tench escaped him, but there was no room for argument. Either he took what offered or he remained ashore to seek other transportation.

Bull grunted and started walking off with Tench and Sam toward an approaching covered farm wagon pulled by an unmatched team. Landers was holding the reins and Jason caught the glint of Medary's red hair, then watched the keelers, led by Wee Willie, move toward the *Bull*. Their vast strides covered the distance in seconds, and the sturdy gangplank shook under them as they went aboard. He heard Wee Willie go into another roaring tirade, crowing his victory.

He eyed the *Bull*, judging it to be fifty feet long, nine feet in the beam. It was sharp at both ends. The middle section was covered by a long cargo box, which left a deck fore and aft. Medary, as passenger, would find shelter inside one end of the cargo box, and the keelers would use the other end for shelter when needed.

A cleated footway ran around the gunwales, and it was on this the crew walked to pole the boat. There were six seats at the bow for rowers, and a steering oar pivoted at the stern, where Bull Hecker, as patroon, would stand on a length of upended log. The figure of a slightly built man appeared on the top of the cargo box. He sat down, legs hanging over the edge, and began to tune a fiddle, the sound twanging thinly.

All up and down the river, craft were on the move. Well out in the stream, a skiff equipped with oars, setting pole and sail, bounced on the current. The man in the skiff waved at a keelboat which was laboring upstream against the current, a fiddler atop the cargo box playing a thready tune, but there seemed to be no passengers, and the crew didn't look toward the skiff.

A barge loaded with hogsheads was being poled upstream. A raft with a little cabin at the bow and chicken coops at the stern went floating downstream. Two children were running about the raft, falling and wrestling, and a woman stood watching them, laughing, the sound

floating back. A clumsy Kentucky boat went heavily
down the river, only her crew to be seen. A two-masted
galley of two dozen oars came smoothly upstream. Behind it, also Pittsburgh-bound, glided a packet, a large
bateau propelled by square sails and a dozen oars,
steered with a rudder.

"Lively traffic!" roared Bull almost in Jason's ear.
"It'll thin out downstream, us'll git ahead of 'em all!
We makin' it afore them cussed damned flats clutter up
the water, too! Come on, mannee, git aboard!"

Following the patroon, Jason went onto the *Bull*,
dropped his pack and rifle where the other man indicated. Feeling the river a fluid, living thing beneath
himself, he was suddenly impatient to shove off, to be
on his way. This is the start, his pulse sang in his
veins, this river is going to take me where I want to be!

"Watch that keel comin' upstream!" Bull roared,
swinging his arm toward it. "Ye'll see what ye got to do
when he hit shallow water an' have to pole out! An'
watch rowin', too. We row downstream; a-tween rowin'
an' current we git some speed to us!"

The men on the other keelboat were ranged eight
on each runway. "Set poles!" came their patroon's
shout, and they sank their poles to the bottom of the
river.

"Down on 'er!" sang out the patroon.

Each keeler placed the button of his pole against his
shoulder, bent and moved aft in a creeping walk, pushing the vessel slowly upstream, a boat length at a time.
As the first man reached the stern, the patroon yelled,
"Lift poles!" The fiddle squeaked, the keelers turned
and walked forward, dragging their poles in the water,
and stood ready to repeat the process, poles "tossed,"
held at the ready.

Now there was the small flurry of Medary's boarding,
with Landers, Sam, and Tench carrying her belongings
aboard and stowing them in the cargo box. And then,
with Jason and Sam and Tench as new hands ordered
to watch and learn, they were untying, were poling into
the current, were manning the oars and within minutes

were skimming along at five or six miles an hour. Jason felt the life in the boat as it rode the eager current. He listened to the river. It flowed and sucked as it carried the keel along.

By the time they passed Big Beaver Creek, which emptied into the Ohio from the right side fifteen miles below Pittsburgh, Jason thought he'd begun to get the feel of boating. Yet, after they'd passed Steuvenville, a village of several hundred houses situated on a high second bank of the right shore, he realized that there was bone-breaking work ahead, and that the trip, running day and night, rowing by day, using the current by night, was going to be grueling.

The first turn he had at the oars revealed that all the work he'd done for van Delft, all the planting and plowing and woodcutting, as well as the endless walking from New York to Pittsburgh, hadn't toughened him enough for this. New muscles made themselves known to him by their soreness and deep aching, until gradually they hardened. But even in a morass of soreness and fatigue, Jason was determined never to miss a stroke, never to give Bull Hecker or Wee Willie or Horse or Shark or any of the others cause to know how it was for him.

During rest periods, he lounged on the bow deck with the other three men who were also resting and listened while they traded yarns. Sometimes they sang wildly to the tunes the fiddler scraped out from atop the cargo box.

They sang what the fiddler told Medary was the keelboatman's classic, with a swinging chorus:

"The boatman is a lucky man,
No one can do as the boatman can,
The boatmen dance and the boatmen sing,
The boatman is up to everything.

"Hi-O, away we go,
Floating down the river on the O-hi-o.

"When the boatman goes on shore,
Look, old man, your sheep is gone,
He steals your sheep and steals your shoat,
He puts 'em in a bag and totes 'em to the boat.

"When the boatman goes on shore
He spends his money and works for more,
I never saw a girl in all my life,
But what she would be a boatman's wife."

Every day one keeler or another would roar and shout his boasting tirade as Wee Willie had done in Pittsburgh. But there were no fights, partly, Jason thought, because Bull was always ready to outscream any screamer, and ready to back it up with his fists.

These tales of unbelievable prowess went on until the screamers began to repeat themselves, and Jason began to seek Medary's company on the stern deck during his rest periods, as did Tench and Sam.

With Medary, Jason gazed out at the river, admiring its beauty and size. They spoke of it together.

"It's said to be four or even six hundred yards wide along the upper parts," Medary told him. On her lap she held an open copy of Zadok Cramer's *Navigator*, the river guidebook found indispensable by flatboaters. "I would have thought it wider," she commented.

Jason nodded. Sometimes the river did look astonishingly wide. Now, as far as he could see, both upstream and downstream, it was empty of boats. The water, in the April sunlight, was a clear and sparkling green as they passed a solid wall of forest.

"Look at all the different greens in the forest!" Medary cried. "The pines, that new leafage such a delicate yellow-green, and far back where you can hardly see, you'd think the leaves were black! And so many kinds of trees—pine, walnut, ash, hickory, oak and sycamore without end!"

Indeed there were more sycamore than any other. They were monster trees, surging to the sky, throwing unbelievably wide their enormous, broad-leafed branches.

Great stretches of grapevine appeared, and the vines were as tremendous, in their way, as the trees. They were almost a foot wide, grew so profusely and climbed so high they made a roof beyond which the tops of the trees were not to be seen. Huge vines hung as much as fifty or eighty feet from the tallest trees, never touching trunk or ground, so that they looked to have grown not from the earth beneath but from the unseen sky above.

"Someday," Medary said, "crops will grow along these banks between the forests and the hills. There'll be cabins, even houses."

"Yes," agreed Jason. "It's likely country here; there'll be those who'll want to stop and settle. They'll pasture their horses and cows so they can come down to the river to drink."

"Sometimes," murmured Medary, "I see this river as a silver chain leading into the wilderness, pulling Tench and me to where we're going."

To where I'm going, too, Jason thought. To where I'll stay.

They passed timbered islands. They saw a bear swimming the river, and later some deer swimming it. Sam spotted the first wild ducks, Medary the geese, and all of them noticed the many turkeys at the same time, and the flash of birds among the forest trees. And a few times Jason and Tench glimpsed red-skinned Indians melting into the greenery, but they said nothing about this to Medary.

She was thriving on the clean river air, eating well of the coarse, plain fare of the boatmen. This was based on the staples of corn, potatoes, hardtack, and meat, which Jason or Tench or Sam brought down with their rifles. They had fish caught by the keelers, wild greens and new berries found and gathered by Tench and Sam any time the *Bull* tied up for an hour.

They passed Marietta, a community of over one hundred houses built on high rugged banks on either side of the Big Muskingum. Boats were gathered to its shores, and more boats were arriving or shoving off, both upstream and downstream, making a busy traffic on both rivers.

With Medary strengthening, with Jason and Tench and Sam harder-muscled each day, they left behind the Little Hockhocking River, the Great Hockhocking, the Shade. They got safely over Letart's Rapids, passed Galliopolis, and a great salt lick farther down. They saw Limestone and Cincinnati, and glided on to Jeffersonville, a town of almost five hundred inhabitants, where they tied up at dusk. Jeffersonville stood above the falls of the Ohio, nearly opposite Louisville, which was twice as large.

Here Bull Hecker, surprisingly enough, took open notice of Medary. He even subdued his normal roar when he spoke to her.

"We're takin' on pilots to git us over the rapids," he growled. "Wastin' no time, the kin' git us over night er day. Ain't nothin' to be skeert of, ma'am . . . no need to scream."

"I shan't scream," Medary told him pleasantly. The *Navigator* was again open on her lap, and she touched a page with her forefinger. "The Messrs. Fite and Bowman, are they the pilots?"

"That's 'em," growled Bull.

"According to this book, there are three passes through the rapids, Mr. Hecker—Kentucky Chute and Middle and Indian. Are we taking Indian Chute?"

"Best in any water."

"And it's fully two miles long?"

"At least, an' falls twenty-two and a half feet."

Jason, listening, suppressed a whistle.

Both he and Tench stayed with Medary on the stern deck for the running of the chute. The crewmen took their places, and three figures appeared atop the cargo box, blurs in the dusk, merging into it. The sky was clouding over, making it near-dark.

Jason heard chains hit deck, felt the first long,

pushing movement and the slow turn of the boat. A gust of wind yanked his hair, pressed his shirt against his body. They were riding the current now, riding it swiftly. Suddenly the keel leapt into swifter water still, went sweeping along, and Jason reckoned that the current was drawing into the chute.

He peered at the acting pilot, standing spraddle-legged on the bow roof, facing downstream, arms held straight out.

His left arm dipped.

The *Bull* went veering ponderously right.

His arm lifted, straight, and the *Bull* surged forward. The wind drove a slant of mist. Around them, the river boiled and slapped and roared.

The pilot's arm dipped, lifted.

The boat veered right, straightened, plunged on.

The wind strengthened and gusted, bearing the misty rain. There would be a deluge before the night was over, Jason thought. He wondered about Medary, whether she'd best go inside, then dismissed the wonder. That was Tench's lookout.

The pilot was a living figurehead up there. The *Bull* literally shot along now, faster, on and on, hair-raisingly on, and downward.

Abruptly, its speed lessened. The pilot whooped, Bull's great roar cleaved the now dark sky, bursting through the wind, and the second pilot and all the keelers whooped.

Jason found himself breathing easier, and that was the first he'd known he'd been having trouble breathing. They were through the chute, riding easy water.

Downriver they went—past Shippingport, past Cave-in-Rock, the nefarious nesting place of the most murderous of the river pirates who captured craft of all sorts and killed and pillaged and raped. Past the little chain of rocks they skimmed, the great chain, and right on to the mouth of the Ohio.

There was a willow point at the junction of the Ohio and the Mississippi which was nearly in the form of a triangle, having sides from half to three-quarters of a mile in length, and it was covered with young willows or cottonwood. Bull Hecker said that two years ago this point was only a bar of sand and mud.

The Mississippi contrasted poorly with the Ohio because of the whitish, muddy aspect of its water, which eddied and swirled because of the mass of descending water. Bull roared for his oarsmen to stand ready for strong rowing, and Jason, at his oar, steeled himself. But the heavy boat was not affected by the swells and boils other than turning a little, and this the patroon controlled by active attention to his steering oar.

They tied up at New Madrid in late afternoon, Bull having decided to take on his new crewmen there and continue downstream. He settled up with Jason and Sam, paying them, roaring that Tench owed him on Medary's fare, biting the coin Tench gave him, then bellowing at them to get the hell ashore.

Jason led down the gangplank, pack on his back, rifle strapped atop it, and a valise belonging to Medary dangling from each hand. Sam was similarly laden, as was Tench, who would not permit Medary to help.

"This woman!" Tench complained cheerfully. "Reason we got so much truck ain't clothes! It's seeds for her vegetable garden and *flowers!*"

"Also the coverlet your own mother wove, Tench Coghill!" Medary retorted gaily. "That's heavier than all my seeds! *And* a warm quilt, as well as a few things to brighten our cabin . . . curtains and books and music, a tablecloth and napkins, and my own mother's six silver spoons!"

"Hell," Sam scoffed in high good humor, "I'd tote a cow if they was a cow in one of these bags Medary! I'm jest hopin' you'll in-vite me over to yer good cookin' here in Missoura, like you done in Pittsburgh!"

Laughing, she assured Sam that this would certainly come to pass. "You have a standing invitation, Sam!" she declared. "And you, Jason! The two of you are our first and only friends in this new country! We're fortunate we met you in Pittsburgh and traveled downriver together!"

Thus, laughing and joking, yet with a deep seriousness to their friendship, they came off the plank this eighteenth day of April, came into New Madrid, where they were to make their homes.

Chapter 5

The town of New Madrid was laid out on a rectangular plan extending four miles along the river. It looked like another world, a world of wood. The buildings were of hewn timber set upright in the ground, or upon plates laid on a wall, the intervals between the upright pieces being filled with stone and mortar.

Off to the left, as they trudged along the earthen walkway, were keelboats and arks and barges and even two flatboats tied up. There was some lading in progress, the scarlet shirts of keelers moving fiercely, tow-shirted inhabitants among them, their kerchief-wrapped heads making blue dots amidst the red.

Jason and his companions passed a mercantile and fur-trading establishment, a tavern, a hewn-wood shop where an open barrel of flour stood on outdoor display at one side of the entrance and a keg of pungent pickles at the other side. The moccasined feet of villagers trod the walkway, going in and out of the primitive shops. The men wore blue cotton trousers, striped cotton trousers, and usually the blue headkerchief. The women wore cotton dress, a mantlet and a Madras handkerchief around their shoulders. The older women wore headkerchiefs wrapped turban-fashion.

These were the first French people Jason had ever seen, and he observed with pleasure that their movements were sprightly and their black eyes quick and friendly. Without exception, the men nodded, and even the women glanced up in friendly, though ladylike, manner.

From down the street plodded a span of oxen yoked by the horns, pulling a two-wheeled wooden cart loaded with kegs. The driver walked alongside, popping a long-lashed whip every time the wooden wheels dropped into a rut, and the oxen pulled the cart laboriously out and along.

A small farm wagon, with a man and woman on the seat and a gaggle of small girls overflowing its bed, passed the cart, seemingly bound for the tied-up river craft. The horses hitched to the wagon were smaller than Jason had ever seen, but looked vigorous and tough and pulled their load smartly. The driver had no reins on the horses, but, wielding a whip with a handle about two feet long and a lash about two yards long, guided them as effectively as if he'd had the strongest reins. This family was not French, but blond and wide-faced and American.

"Hell," Sam said suddenly, catching up with Jason, "we kin spend all day jest gawkin'. First thing we got to do is find a place to stay whilst we pick our land and build."

"That's right," said Tench from behind them. "I want to get Medary settled. I reckon the thing to do is ask around. What you say, Jason?"

Jason agreed.

"I'll ask in here," Sam said, and went quickly into the nearest shop.

Jason and Medary and Tench stood in the wonder of this strange environment. At last in the great, new, free country of his dreams, Jason breathed the fresh springtime, let his nose inhale the smells of sun and greenery, of river and, somewhere unseen as yet, of new-turned land. He looked at everything going on around him and he felt himself fill with joy, standing in this place where he was free to do as he would.

Sam came hurrying out of the shop, his face beaming. "Ain't but one place takes in boarders and then only oncet in a while, 'cause don't many boarders show up. It's right down here a few buildin's." He led out so rapidly the others had to walk briskly to keep up with him.

He turned in at a long, low house with a porch in front and a chimney in the center, dividing it into two parts. A thin curl of smoke was drifting up from the chimney.

Sam knocked boldly on the door.

The man who opened didn't look to be French, though, except for the headkerchief, he dressed French. He was the smallest, thinnest man Jason had ever seen, and one of the oldest, having snowy hair and deep lines from nose to shaven chin.

His tiny hot black eyes sparkled as he look at them all—Medary and Tench, Sam and Jason—at their packs and their valises, and he nodded to himself. He smiled, and years fled. He was probably no more than sixty-five, seventy at the most.

"Ye just landed," he said, "and yer in need of a roof."

"That's right," Sam replied. "We was told this was the place to come to. 'See Azor Davis,' a feller told me."

"Come in," said Davis, and stepped aside. "Yer welcome in this house, ma'am," he continued, putting a gallant old hand under Medary's arm and escorting her to a tiny snow-haired woman who had risen from her chair. "Annette, beloved," he said gently, "these folks have come from upriver, and they're going to honor our home. You see, we'll have pleasure a-plenty now, folks to talk with, to exchange tales with and explore the joy of new friendship."

Annette Davis was as old as her husband, and resembled him enough to be his twin sister. She had the same black, hot eyes, the same deep lines and miraculous smile. which she turned upon the newcomers now. "Welcome!" she cried. "Yer names . . . we must know what to call ye!"

Sam, still taking the lead, introduced himself, then the others. "You got room fer us, ma'am? And if you have and are willin' to feed us, kin we meet yer price? We ain't rich settlers a-tall. We got to scrape to git along."

"That's understandable," Azor Davis said. "Our charge is a dollar a week room and board for each man. The lady . . . Miz Coghill, ma'am . . . if ye tidy the rooms we'll provide, and give my wife company and a bit of a hand as she cooks and bustles about the house, will be charged nothing in money."

"That sounds fair," Tench said thoughtfully. He glanced at Medary and she gave a small smiling nod. "I'm agreeable, then, if you two are . . . Sam . . . Jason."

Paying out money for keep would hit Tench the hardest, because he'd had to forgo his wages on the keel plus paying extra on Medary's fare. Still, he had some money from his work in Pittsburgh and should be able to manage.

The room in which they were standing was dining room, parlor, and principal bedroom. It was furnished with table and chairs, two oaken armchairs, an armoire and a double bunk on the wall opposite the fireplace. The floor was of dark waxed boards.

The second main room proved to be a kitchen, the fireplace fitted for cooking. Each of the rooms had a small chamber taken off its end, and it was to these cubicles that Annette Davis showed her paying guests. Tench and Medary were given the chamber off the kitchen, and Jason and Sam the other.

"It hadn't ought to take us more'n a month to git our land and git some kind of shelter up," Sam said when he and Jason were alone. Jason deposited his pack and rifle in the armoire, closed the door. "That way," Sam pointed out, "we won't be out so much."

After supper, they all sat in candlelight before the fireplace and talked. First, the old gentleman insisted that Medary and Tench relate where they were from and what they had done in that life, then Sam and Jason.

"Schoolteaching and shipbuilding," he mused. "Takes brains." He looked from Sam to Jason. "Sounds like yer pappy and that Dutch gentleman tried to give both of ye a useful raising."

Sam snorted, then half grinned. Jason, thoughtful, nodded.

Despite his twin-wife's gentle protest, Azor Davis launched into memories of New Madrid, tapping his lore of the place, his love for it sounding in every syllable. "Annette and I came from New Orleans at the start of New Madrid, more than twenty years ago," he said. "At the end of the Revolution, the American colonies came right to the boundaries of the Spanish territory. So, to keep the colonies from expanding, the Spanish settled on a plan. Settlers were offered land grants, the bottoms being well suited to farming, offered religious freedom, local government, and a port of entry so they wouldn't have to carry goods to New Orleans. There was a goodly Delaware village near, still is, and there was other Indian villages, all being good fer the fur trade that had already sprung up hereabouts."

"Sounds reasonable and attractive," Tench commented.

"It was. Colonel George Morgan, himself once of Pennsylvania, by the way, brought surveyors and carpenters and woodsmen—I was a carpenter—and commenced the settlement of a city whose plan wasn't to be outdone anywhere in the world."

"Azor, now," chided Annette.

"They need to know, my love," the old gentleman chided back, and plunged on. "The city was to extend four miles south and two west from the river and have Lake St. Annis in its limits. There were to be wide streets on its banks, planted with trees fer the health of the citizens. And there was to be a street on the river one hundred twenty feet wide, planted with trees. Twelve acres in the middle of the city was to be ornamented with trees and used fer public walks. There was to be forty half-acre lots fer other public uses, and one lot of a dozen acres fer the king's use."

He paused, the glory of those lost plans glimmering on his face. "Some folks did come and build, and today there's four hundred houses in our city. Morgan descended to New Orleans to obtain proprietory and honorary concessions, failed, never set foot here again."

"But the city did prosper," Jason put in quietly.

"Not as it could have. A Monsieur Fouché was sent by the governor general. He was here only eighteen months, but he did a great deal—divided out the country, regulated the land needed fer the village, built the fort. He laid out the work, went into the cypress swamps to select trees, walked with compass in hand to align the streets and limit the lots. While he was in command, there came the largest portion of the families still here, and it was he who attracted them here."

"Azor was very sad when Monsieur Fouché left," Annette murmured.

"As who was not, my love? His successor, Monsieur Fortell, wasn't a man of the people, though he had a good heart. He found the inhabitants at this post made up of traders, hunters, and boatmen, fer the most part. Trade was still fair, so that nearly everyone dealt in trade, and not a soul farmed. It was so easy, with a little powder and lead, some cloth and a few blankets on credit from the shops, to get themselves meat and suet to live on, and pay off their debts, or part of them, with peltries. A very few of them seeded, very badly, about an acre of corn, but all found time to smoke their pipes and socialize."

"It's always been a gay place," Annette smiled. "And we've gone to our share of balls."

"That we have, my love. And still do. Well, as time passed, game grew scarcer, the Indians moved farther off, and were seldom here with meat and grease and peltries to sell. The traders knew where to find them, but the inhabitants waited fer them in vain.

"A few Americans had risked farming and were prospering. Then, in one year, five galleys came up-river and passed the summer here. They caused such a run on food supplies that provisions had to be brought in from Illinois and Kentucky. As a result of this and other things, people turned more to the earth. Now we've been transferred to the United States since 1804 and have real prospects fer growth with people like yerselves coming in. I'm expecting more of you every year."

"This Medary child is tired," Annette said suddenly. "She can scarcely hold her eyes open. We'll have other evenings to talk, let's see that she gets some rest now—and you young men, too."

Thus, with his mind filled with tales of New Madrid, which was to be his home, Jason fell instantly asleep. He didn't hear Sam's rasping snores, nor did he dream.

Chapter 6

The first thing Jason did next morning, too eager to wait for breakfast, was to walk through the village and back. In that first solitary walk he saw that though houses and cabins for a full four hundred people had been built, there was room for more, many more. Each house, with its outbuildings, gardens, and orchards, took up a great deal more space than houses in New York City, and the entire aspect, though of different architecture, was similar to the farmyards he had seen on his long walking journey to Pittsburgh. He watched for unimproved building lots as he explored, noting that many of them took up an entire city block, favoring for himself a place this size rather than a farm because he was inexperienced in farming on a big scale, and situated in the village, he might get some employment from time to time. He speculated as to which vacant block he would make application for, and he studied the different kinds of houses and cabins, comparing them, considering which type he would build for himself. He had to be sure he was right before he started, for he would build only the one house on his grant, and in it he would live his years and die his death.

There were many French-style houses of logs on sills, the sills supported by stone foundations or wooden blocks, the spaces between the posts filled with clay and grass. The walls of these had a marked inward slope, were sometimes plastered, sometimes bare, and occasionally dazzlingly whitewashed. The porch, or gallery, built on one or all four sides, varied in width from four to eight feet, and looked so usable that Jason determined he would have a gallery no matter what the house.

There were many log cabins, some of unhewn logs, the ends of the logs projecting, and others of hewn logs, with squared timbers. There were houses like Azor Davis's house. Most roofs, whatever the house, were covered with hewn shingles.

On that first morning, though he didn't stop to talk to any of the villagers, as many American, it seemed, as French, he watched them going about their work on their places and lifted his hand in return to their friendly nods. They moved in a leisurely manner, leading a cow to its milking spot, driving cattle to pasture, plying their small implements of husbandry, setting wooden plows into the soil at the far end of a lot, turning rich dark furrows.

Jason's heart moved.

One day he, too, would have his full block. He, too, would work his land, as his neighbor would be doing, plowing his soil and laying his seed in its warmth, and he would tend his plants—ah, he would nurse them!—and when their fruit was ripe he would harvest it.

It was noon before he returned to the Davis home.

They chose their grants, paid their fees, set to work. Jason had taken two full blocks across the street from Tench's two blocks. Sam obtained a like situation one block farther south.

While Tench and Sam started putting up Medary's cabin, assisted by friendly villagers, among them two young brothers by the name of Anton and Pierre Duval, Jason began to plow with a wooden plow the three of them had bought in partnership. He camped on his homesite, slept in the circle of his walnut and elm and maple trees. He planted some crops on his own land and some on Sam's before he began work on his cabin.

By the second week of June, Medary was hanging her curtains, Tench was planting, and Sam and the Duvals came over to where Jason was cutting down the first tree. After shaking hands, the smiling, dark-eyed French boys set to work cutting trees and worked steadily.

"I aim to help ye build," Sam told Jason, "if ye'll let me stay on yer land, that is." His expression and his tone were half defiant, half sheepish. "Medary jest give me a reamin' out—in a lady's way, Medary couldn't be no ways else, but she ain't pleased."

"I don't know why you shouldn't be on my land," Jason said. "I can't think of any reason that could ever come up."

"Hell," Sam blurted, skin fiery, "might's well come out with it. I've took me a squaw."

"A squaw?" Jason heard himself say blankly.

"Delaware girl, sixteen years old. Yeller Flower. Me-dary says I ain't bein' fair to Yeller Flower. Hell, I don't aim her no harm. Man needs a woman, you know that."

Jason did know. There were times he had to work till he dropped to get his mind off it. A woman was something he couldn't have, he told himself, until he got things ready.

"Why don't you say somethin'?" demanded Sam. "Hell, she won't lack fer nothin', Jase."

"Well, I'm surprised," Jason said, thinking dumbfounded was a better word, refraining to mention the possibility that Sam would father half-breed children. "But it's nothing to wreck our friendship over, that I can see," he added.

"I'm relieved you feel that way," Sam said. He continued, the defiance replaced by worry. "It frets me 'bout Medary, though. She likely won't never have nothin' to do with me now, and I'll not only lose her as a friend but Tench, too."

"Nothing of the kind," said Tench, who had come noiselessly up behind them, carrying his ax, startling them. "I left off planting to help a bit. Medary was hit sudden and hard by your news, is all, Sam. Once she gets used to it and meets Yellow Flower and sees that you treat her well, she won't be bitter. Though I don't think there's any way she'll get used to the fact that you're living with a girl you're not married to."

"Marry . . . marry . . . marry!" grumbled Sam. "Why can't wimmin think of nothin' but marry? It ain't pesterin' Yeller Flower none. She don't feel *not* married, and her people look on her bein' my squaw same as married. It's honorable, accordin' to them."

They pushed Sam's lack of marital status to the background as they felled trees and trimmed logs. Jason's muscles were a mass of new sorenesses and aches, fully as bad as those he'd acquired on the keelboat. Looks like there's nothing a man can get for himself, with his bare hands, without working until he can't move, he thought half humorously. Oaring or poling a keel, breaking new land, cutting logs for his cabin, hoisting them into place, each thing seemed harder than the last, each set of screaming muscles seemed to tire him more. At first, he reminded himself, only at first. After a while, a man hardens to what he's got to do.

They were quitting for the day when a very dirty brawny bull of a man some forty years old came stomping across the grounds to the cabin site. He was followed by a youth who had the same build and gave promise of being, one day, as brawny. He was already as dirty.

"Ich vill vork auf haus," the man growled. "Ein dollar day. Mein boy ein dollar efry two days."

He addressed them all, his dirty-gray eyes swiveling.

Jason stepped forward. "I'm Jason Blood, Mr.—?" He offered his hand.

The man didn't take the hand. His eyebrows shot

down in a frown. "Cremer. Fred Cremer. Mein boy ist Fred auch. Du pay us?"

"I haven't the money," Jason told him. "I'm going to build my cabin myself, with the help of my friends here, Tench Coghill and Sam Janas."

They didn't offer to shake hands.

"And with the help of Anton and Pierre Duval . . . they've went home now," said Sam brashly. "And Pierre Labadie and Gabriel Racine and Jean-François Gascon and William Teper. They ever' one told me they'd be over to raise the walls and put on the roof. As friends and neighbors."

Cremer glowered, jerked his head at his son, and stomped off. The lad followed him, stomping in his own manner.

Thus, with the help of friends, old and new, Jason built his house in the French fashion, setting the logs erect in the ground, roofing it with large, hewn shingles laid on poles, held in place by battens of poles stretched across them, the ends fastened by wooden pegs to the corners and the frame. His house was twenty by thirty feet, with an inside partition splitting it, and a stone chimney through the middle so that each room could be heated. He put one window in each room, set with six-inch glass, hinged and swung like a door. His floor he laid of slats, and his gallery, across the twenty-foot front, he made eight feet wide.

His furnishings he set out to build alone, and it was while he was working on his bunk one day that a small sound at the door brought his attention up, and there stood a girl.

She was tiny, surely not ninety pounds. That was the first thing he noticed about her, and later he was to discover that when he held his arm out at shoulder height, she could stand beneath it. In spite of her tininess, he noticed, her bones were large and sturdy.

She was young, maybe eighteen, and there was a prettiness to her. She had very blond straight hair and fair blue eyes, her cheekbones were broad, and her features smooth and small, plainer than need be because of a mixed look of discontent and avid eagerness. She wore a very old, thin, patched clean dress washed to no-color. She was barefoot, and her feet were stained with fresh mud. She must have stepped into a puddle left from yesterday's shower, Jason thought.

Her skin was white and thin, with a rosy underglow so violent she must only recently have scrubbed herself with soap and water. The thought came to Jason that perhaps the reason her hair seemed to float palely about her face while actually caught into a knot at the back was that it, too, had been newly washed.

She kept standing in his doorway, and he remained idle over his work, feeling uncomfortable, as he had never been alone with a girl before.

She smiled widely and said, "You're the new man."

He laid down his hammer and smiled back. "I suppose I am," he said. "One of them, anyhow."

"I heard you was here."

"You did?"

"Ja. My pa told me. You rode the keelboat."

"The *Bull*. Yes, I did."

"You've planted, a'ready."

"Yes."

"Pa, he wanted to work for you. And my brother. Fred. He's seventeen. He's younger'n me."

"I remember them," Jason said.

"I'm Massie Ann. Massie Ann Cremer."

"I'm Jason Blood."

"Blood—what an outlandish name."

"It's my own. It's a strong name."

"Pa didn't say you was young."

"I'm not so young—I'm past twenty."

"I was eighteen yesterday."

"You've always lived in New Madrid?"

Her face clouded and she nodded. "Pa and ma come from Germantown when they got married. We live a long ways from you, clear at the north end." Suddenly her fair eyes sparkled around the room. "You got two rooms?"

"Yes."

"Two fireplaces?"

"And two glass windows." He was as proud of those windows as anything. They had cost him enough—five cents per light and each window had ten lights in it—and the floors had cost and his iron pots and his traps, but everything else had cost him nothing but labor, his labor and that of his friends. All his money was gone, but he was equipped. He'd trap and sell. In five years he'd make himself a trip to New Orleans and bring back a wife.

"You've got a wood floor," breathed Massie Ann.

"I'm building for keeps. A man has got to know what he wants and stick with it."

"We got dirt floors," she said, as if spitting.

He looked at her, and her whole face had changed. It had sharpened, the lips had thinned, the eyes were pinpoints, and her knuckles stood up from her fists.

"It's no sin to have dirt floors," he said.

Now her face took fire and she blazed at him, her words flicking out like hot, burning little tongues of flame. "It's the same as pigs!" she cried. "It's living in a hog wallow, that's what it is, and ma won't let me clean it!"

"Your father is a good man," Jason said. "He's a hardworking man. If he could give you better than a dirt floor he would."

His words, or perhaps his tone, served the same as if he'd thrown cold water over her. Her anger fell away, her face assumed its pleasant expression so fully that for a moment it looked stolid and even dull, then her mouth resumed friendliness, and her fair eyes regarded him softly.

"Ja," she said. "Pa works hard. He's got so many mouths to feed." Then, swiftly, all eagerness: "Can I see the rest of your house?"

He nodded, relieved at the change in her, and watched her go running lightly across the floor on her mud-stained feet, through the door and into the other room. She stopped in the center of the room and pivoted slowly, her eyes stroking the walls, the open glass window, the stones in the fireplace, the width of the mantel.

She drew a quivering breath. "You'll whitewash?"

"Inside and out."

"Ja . . . you must be so rich!"

"I'm not rich at all."

"But such a house!"

"The logs are free."

"But glass windows, yet! And the floor!"

"I had a little money from my apprenticeship. From being crewman on the boat."

"You see. Others come here like pa and ma—walking, talking like foreigners the way the Father learned me'n my brother different. They come horseback, too, and canoe, then horesback."

"I walked, too. I walked hundreds of miles. All the way from New York City to Pittsburgh. That's where the Ohio begins."

"You lived in New York City and left it?"

"Of course I left."

"Tell me how it was there."

"It was too big, and there were too many people."

"Rich people, with fine things?"

"I suppose."

"Ach, never did I have a fine thing! But I think to myself how it would be, a fine thing."

"It's not so different."

"Now you talk crazy. Tell why not."

"Well, take a person who buys something fine—like a clock. When it's new, he sets great value on it, and he examines it often, and calls attention to it. But after he has owned it a few years, and is used to seeing it in his house, he hardly notices it except to glance at the time. He spends no more thought on it than he does on some plain belonging."

"It is a rich person you are talking of."

"No. Any man, once he is used to his fine clock, won't ponder on its value unless he means to boast, or to sell it, or take it to a shop for repair. Then it becomes again his most valued possession."

"Not me! If I had a fine thing, I'd never forget!"

"Maybe not. But it is something I've noticed."

"About clocks?"

"And other things."

"Why did you say clocks?"

"I was apprenticed to a clockmaker."

"Was he rich?"

"I suppose he was."

"Then you will be rich."

Jason smiled. "How many clocks are there in New Madrid?"

"Some . . . you'd be surprised!"

"How many will be brought to me for repair in a month, in a year, even?"

"Enough . . . you'll see!"

He smiled again. "I'll still plant and trap and hunt," he said, "every year of my life. What a man works for each time it comes into his hands, he never takes lightly or forgets the value of."

"You talk like an old man!"

"I was apprenticed to an old man."

"You talk funny too, like the Father. Pa made us quit learning from him, me'n my brother."

"My master was no priest, but he was educated."

Now she smiled, a friendly, wide smile, and he returned it. She edged to the door, suddenly shy. "I got to go. Pa don't know. I ran off."

"That's not good."

"Ach, I always run off."

"Why?"

"Pa!" She spat the word.

"I see," he said, remembering the surly Bremer.

He saw, too, that other look slide onto her, as if she was used to it. Out of her thinned and twisted lips she flung a half-whisper, her eyes pinpointed and hot. "A girl is for work—to dig and hoe and chop and plow—always work!" The bad look fell from her face, leaving it almost blank, and an ache came into her voice and she said, "So. I run off."

"And when you go home?" he asked, tuned to her ache.

"Maybe he won't find out."

"But if he does?"

"He'll beat me. With his strap."

In the wink of an eyelash, Jason's own flesh shrank from the blows under which hers might soon cringe, took again the thump and thud and whack, the cut and sting and fire of the strap, pulsed with the lingering throb of welts and cuts and purpling bruises.

"This," he said tightly to the girl in his doorway, "is a free country. None of us are servants here."

"You don't live with pa," she said.

He had no answer for that.

Suddenly she was smiling again, pretty and friendly. and as before his answering smile came of itself.

"You know what?" she demanded.

"No—what?"

"You're—wonderful!"

She jumped across the threshold and went running as fast as she could from his new house in its circle of trees toward the north. He stood and watched as long as he could see her. He was grinning widely, and he was having trouble with his breathing.

Never before, in all his life, had anyone called him wonderful.

Chapter 7

She came back the next day.

He had just put the straw-filled bag of sacking onto the framework of his bunk when the small sound at the door reached him and he turned, and there she stood.

She was as painfully clean as before, and today there was no mud on her feet. She was breathing fast, smiling through the breathing, but her eyes were shy.

He said, "You're winded."

She said, "I ran."

"Ran away, too?"

She nodded, and laughed.

"What happened yesterday?"

"They was all working behind the barn. They never seen me come or go. I was to work inside. And I did, only fast."

"And today?"

"It can take care of itself. Can I look at your house?"

"It's the same as yesterday."

"I didn't see it all, not every log, every board in the floor, how they go. Last night, I couldn't remember."

He stared. "Are girls like that, remembering the separate boards?"

"I don't know about other girls."

"This isn't a fine cabin, you know."

"It is, even pa said! He's been past! Says it's foolishness for a man alone!"

"I never thought of it like that," Jason said.

"How did you think—with a wife?"

"No, not soon, anyhow," he replied honestly. "I thought of my needs, of what I want in a cabin now, and whether that will be what I want when I'm old."

She drew a long, quivering breath. She faced him from the doorway, and he saw her shoulders go square, and she said, "I want to know."

He looked into her unflinching eyes. "What do you want to know?"

"Iss there . . . a girl?"

His face burned. His tongue seemed to swell so he couldn't move it. He thought fleetingly of those New Orleans girls. He shook his head.

"Then I can help with your house," Massie Ann said.

"I can manage," he told her, not wanting her here.

"Not the prettying up." Her eyes wandered, touching, petting. "You'd spoil it."

"You can't come here," he argued.

"There ain't no girl to be jealous. You said."

'It's your father I'm thinking of."

"He won't find out."

"Even so, it won't do," Jason said. "You're a young girl, and you have to think of your good name. You'll have to leave."

"Can't I do something, just this once?" she pleaded. "I could wash the floor. I never scrubbed a pretty floor, not in my life. Can't I . . . please?" Her eyes and her voice and even the lines of her tiny firm young body were supplicating.

"Scrub then," he said, and stalked outside.

He turned to clearing underbrush, working in the open where he could be seen. Thus, if the girl's presence became known, it would also be known that he was not with her inside the house.

Sam found him at this work some twenty minutes later. "Yer tearin' at that like a damned wildcat," he said cheerfully. "Glad to see you this spry—I'm fixin' to start a cabin fer me'n Yeller Flower tomorrer. Tench an' the others is all set to come."

"You can count on me," Jason said grimly. He swung his ax, sliced a thorny bush to the ground, swung at the next one.

When he'd dealt with it, he looked up to see why Sam had gone dumb instead of talking a mile a minute. The young Pole was gaping toward the cabin, mouth slightly open. Massie Ann was standing inside, opening and closing the window slowly, as if it were a new and marvelous toy.

"Who the hell's that?" Sam demanded.

Uncomfortable, Jason told him.

Sam stared. "You gone plumb crazy, Jase? If ye got to have a woman, git yerself a squaw."

"It's nothing like that," Jason told him shortly.

"Don't talk to me!" Sam snorted. "A man needs a woman, but it don't do to take up with the first one he sees!"

Jason thought again of New Orleans. Sam was right. I could go down there as a keeler during the winter, he thought. Find me the right girl and get onto a keel for the upriver trip, work her fare, like Tench did for Medary.

"Don't get into an uproar," he assured Sam.

"Yer goin' to be the one that's in an uproar," Sam warned, "if old man Cremer finds out. He's a mean cuss, got that look in his eye, an' all over hisself."

When Jason made no reply, Sam glowered and said he'd see Jason in the morning. As he turned to leave, his eyebrows were bushed onto the top of his nose in a deep frown.

Jason put aside his ax, strode directly to his house. Massie Ann met him on the gallery, eyes shining, cheeks flushed. "The floors!" she cried. "They're the finest I ever seen!"

"You're going home," he told her. "I'm taking you."

She shrank, and her lips paled. In her desperation, she lapsed into German. "Nein . . . ach, nein!" she whispered.

"I'm going to tell your father I hired you to scrub. I'll trade him work or game in payment. Then you won't get a beating. And you're not to come back."

"Pa won't believe. If you hire a girl here, you speak first to her pa. He'll say I ran after you. He'll kill me!"

"Fathers don't kill their daughters."

That thin-lipped, ugly look took her face, and her words came out spitting. "Pa would—he *says!*"

Jason stood frowning, watching her. Under his look, she let the ugliness drop away, and her face went through that stolid transition into openness, though it remained unsmiling.

"Pa keeps his girls pure," she said.

"That's a natural thing."

"He beats us pure. He beats us if we don't work, and if we talk back, and if we don't kneel right at family prayer."

"You hate your father, don't you?" Jason asked, and a trace of his consternation sounded in his tone.

Her eyes flicked to his, dropped. "It's a sin if you hate your pa and ma. The Bible says."

"What your father does, according to his own lights," Jason said, "he means for your good." The memory of things van Delft had done for Jason's own good lanced through him.

"Ach, let me go!" Massie Ann cried.

"Go, then," he said.

She lingered to pivot slowly, as she had done yesterday inside, her eyes this time trailing across the gallery and seeming to memorize the very leaves on his circle of elms and walnuts and maples, and then she was gone, running.

Chapter 8

Jason returned to his work, started to build a table, which was to be free-standing, not hinged to the wall to save space. He kept thinking about Massie Ann.

She's as much servant to her father, he pondered, as I was to Mr. van Delft. Only she's not bonded or apprenticed, so there's no end to her servitude. Probably she'll have to marry a man her father chooses, and become a servant to him.

These thoughts depressed him, but as there was nothing he could do for the girl, he pushed her out of mind and concentrated on his table, planning what wooden trenchers and spoons he would later make. He saw no evidence of her having been in or around his place the next few days when he returned from helping raise Sam's cabin.

He'd met Yellow Flower, who as quiet and shy. She was a trifle stocky in build and very strong, even helping to put some of the cabin logs in place, lifting her end as Sam lifted his. She made her cookfire outside the Indian lodge she'd built for temporary shelter. There she roasted fish she'd caught early in the morning, baked potatoes and an Indian bread, and at noon the men feasted, washing it down with coffee.

"See what I'm talkin' 'bout?" Sam muttered to Jason. "A squaw like Yeller Flower knows how to take keer of a man. She's makin' me some Injun sandals, on top of it."

Jason smiled, studied the brown-skinned Delaware girl. She looked mature for sixteen, carrying her head more like a princess than a squaw. The hair was very black and shone in the sun, wound on her head in braids. Her eyes were very black, shining in her plain face. Her voice, the few times she spoke, was quiet and pleasing.

"I see," Jason muttered when Sam nudged him impatiently with an elbow. "But how many like her are to be had for the asking is another matter."

"Yeller Flower kin help," Sam replied. "All you got to do is say the word."

"Thanks," Jason said. "I'll keep it in mind."

But he'd never do it. He'd never take a Yellow Flower, whose only thought, only purpose, was to please a man with comforts of the body. For Jason there was the mind to be fed as well, and that required two people—both woman and man—to spark interest and nurture it and bring joy to their joined lives.

He'd scarcely given Massie Ann Cremer another thought until she appeared that first day he stayed at home to work on his table. But when she did pause in his doorway in that breathless manner she had, he could think of nothing else.

They quarreled again, and she stayed again, with him working outside and her within. So it went as often as she could slip away from home. Jason began to like her way with his house, to watch, from his outside work, for a glimpse of her fair head moving past door or window. Every time she left, he forbade her to return, and one day there she'd be again, refusing to leave.

If her father ever discovered she'd been gone, or if he beat her, Jason could not learn. She never stayed

long, never had much to say except to defend, violently,
her determined visits.

"Don't you like me?" she would demand.

"That has nothing to do with it. Someone will see
you. Talk will spread. Your father will hear it, and he'll
beat you."

"He beats me anyhow."

"But this would be my fault, Massie Ann."

"How could it be your fault?"

"For permitting . . . this." He would spread his
hands, including her, himself, the room, the half-built
table, the clearing.

"Let me stay, let me work . . . just half an hour!"
she would plead.

So she would stay a bit, and then she would flee,
running, heart thumping. He always told her not to
come again, but she willed that next time, beautiful
next time, after they had argued, he would let her stay.
It was worth any price to walk in those rooms, to lay
her palms on the rough newness of the fireplaces, two
of them in one cabin, to breathe in the sheer cleanness,
to pretend it was her own.

When she got home, if pa had missed her, or if one
of the brats had tattled that she was gone, or if pa
thought she hadn't done enough work and went for his
strap, she would cry out, because the merciless blows
hurt like death. But she didn't truly mind, because there
was the cabin, new and clean, and there would be tomorrow.

After her beating, she would glower at the two filthy
rooms of home. She would smell the years of defile-
ment and glare at the spread of ma's body and count
her whiskery chins.

Nauseated, she would shut her eyes, squeeze them
against the only surroundings she had ever known, and
chant in her mind like a song or a prayer, *I've got to
get out of here, get him to marry me . . . somehow, anyhow, before some other girl gets him! His house, no
other girl would scrub it like me, make it laugh with
being clean. I've got to find a way, got to!*

Now, on her forbidden visits, she took to watching Jason out of the corner of her eye. She talked to him shyly, talked pertly, hands on hips, smiled, batted her stubby blond lashes, blushed with the knowledge of what she was trying to do.

She couldn't tell whether he liked her that way. She didn't know how to make him like her. She couldn't fix herself pretty, for she had no dress to wear but the thin, faded, patched one, and she washed it so often that her ma began to rant.

"It vasn't dirty!" he ma screamed. "Und a bath, so quivck? Du vash like a bad girl to lay out mit ein mann! Ja . . . lay mit ein mann, und pa, he kill such eine tochter! Mit beating, yet!"

Beating, Massie Ann thought. Yes, beating.

She sensed that Jason had a deep-rooted aversion to beatings. Even that day he'd said pa was in his rights to beat her, he hadn't liked to think of the strap coming down on her. She had seen it in him, plain as talk.

So she pondered beatings. One midnight, wakeful in the midst of her sleeping, sweating siblings, it came to her—the idea, the method—and this, too, she pondered. When she had shaped a plan, she went to sleep.

Early next morning, after pa and Fred had tromped off to hunt, she washed her dress, washed her hair. After noon dinner, she scrubbed herself with soap and water, put on her dress, pinned up her hair. She let ma catch on to what she was doing, and when she slipped away, did it clumsily, so that ma saw her go. And every step of her way to Jason Blood's place she knew that her twelve-year-old sister, Wilhelmina, was following, keeping out of sight, and she was careful not to look back.

Chapter 9

Jason had never seen Massie Ann gay before. It made her really pretty, and he found himself darting secret looks at her. She wouldn't stay inside to work, but declared she had come to visit. She danced after him wherever he went, got in his way when he tried to whitewash the outside door, and laughed constantly.

"What are you up to?" he demanded once, grinning in spite of himself.

"Fun, silly—just fun!"

Everything was funny to her. Gaiety had her, and it was so catching he found himself grinning at her deep little chuckles, found himself laughing, the sound hanging like a bell tone in the circle of trees. He realized, as he laughed, that this was his first time, ever, to really laugh.

She began to tease. "Did you ever kiss a girl, Jason?"

"Of course not," he muttered, neck going hot.

"Why not?" she demanded, head cocked to one side. He grinned, found no answer.

"Ain't you going to ask me?" she demanded.

"Ask you what?"

"If I ever kissed a boy, that's what!"

"Girls don't kiss boys. It's the other way around."

"Go on, Jason, ask me!"

"Well, did you?"

"I never did!" she laughed, "not in my whole life, not yet!"

"That's good," he said, neck hotter now.

"What's good about it, silly?"

"Nice girls don't."

"Who says I'm nice?" she challenged, fair eyes dancing. He'd never seen her so pretty.

So embarrassed he didn't know what else to do, he scooped up a wood chip and flung it at her, laughing, and she dodged, stood with her arms akimbo, her eyes twinkling, and then she turned and ran.

Jason resumed his work, disappointed, for some reason, that she had gone so soon. He slapped whitewash onto the door and thought it was certainly time she got married. He frowned, hoping her father wouldn't marry her off to a man twice her age, a widower, with a family of growing children for her to slave over.

She'd no sooner got out of sight than Tench came walking across from his place, his face split in a grin which looked at the same time foolish and troubled. At first Jason thought his neighbor had seen Massie Ann on the gallery, and had in mind to warn him.

So he said, "She wasn't inside . . . she's gone," and grinned to show there was nothing to it.

Tench looked bewildered, then gestured. "I ain't Sam," he said, grinning. "It's just his way . . . if he's got something on his mind, he's right out with it. I came over to give you an invite to supper tomorrow. Medary's of a mind to celebrate."

Jason said, "Why sure. What are you celebrating?"

"Seems Missouri's lucky for us," Tench said. "Medary's health built on the keelboat, and now she's in the family way again and feeling so good seems she'll carry through this time."

"Well, say!" exclaimed Jason and seized Tench by the hand and began to pump. "Sure she will! That's the finest kind of news! How should I act? Like I don't know? I don't want to shame her."

"Medary's so proud of being in the family way again, and being so well and strong, she'd as soon get on top of our cabin and shout it out for everybody in New Madrid to hear!"

"What did Sam have to say about it?" Jason asked, the thought crossing his mind again that the young Pole might one day find himself father to a half-Indian baby.

"I'm going over to tell him now, and invite him to supper," Tench replied. "January, the baby's due in January!" He grinned again, then he turned and went striding away.

He'd been gone several hours, and Jason was white-washing an inside wall, when he heard the first sobbing wail and the muffled, light sound of running feet. He looked up, and Massie Ann was swaying in the door-way, her hair torn from its knot, her dress ripped, one eye puffed, red welts along her arms.

They moved together, him opening his arms, her staggering into them. She was tinier than she looked, wiry, yet amazingly soft. He held her, cupped his hand on the back of her head and murmured into her hair, which floated against his lips. "There . . . there . . ." And such a compassion rose in him he thought he could not contain it.

She sobbed, took a great, gulping breath. "Ma . . . she seen . . . me leave . . . sent my sister to follow me. Pa . . . he found out . . . when he came home. Ma, she told him . . ."

"Hush . . . shh . . . hush!"

"Don't let him get me . . . Jason . . . !"

"Shh . . . don't tremble . . . no need to tremble . . ."

"Never let me go, Jason!"

"Shh . . . shh . . ."

"Promise!" Her voice rose, winged through the open door, the open window.

"He won't touch you again," Jason murmured reck-lessly, to soothe, to comfort, to protect her.

"Promise . . . oh, promise!" she begged, sobbing.

She was so tiny, so helpless, with only his arms for refuge. "I promise," he heard himself breathe, and felt the hair at the back of his neck stir.

"Kiss me . . . love me . . ."

She lifted her head, tipped her young, bruised face to him, and his mouth came down on her quivering pink lips, and when the lips parted his tongue entered. He felt himself begin to caress her, felt his man's passion rise until, finally, there was no way to stop.

After he had lit a candle, he sat beside her on the bunk, ashamed, his arm around her, waiting for her sobbing to end. When it did, he held his handkerchief so she could blow her nose, and after she had composed herself somewhat, he began to speak.

"I hold myself to blame," he said.

"I th-thought you was a g-gentleman!" Her breath jerked. "Now, look at you!"

"I agree, Massie Ann."

"What you going to d-do about it?"

"I must think, we must decide."

"I'll have a b-baby!"

"You may not."

"I will, I know I will!"

"It takes time to know," he said. "If people rush into something, they're liable to be sorry for a long time."

"Y-you ought to of thought of that sooner!" she wailed.

"Yes . . . I should have."

"Pa'll kill me!" she wept. "He'll throw me out! If he ever f-finds out what you did to me, he'll k-kill me! You don't know what he's l-like!"

She flung her arms around his neck, pressed herself into his embrace and wept loudly. A sudden, thundering knock at the door brought Jason to his feet, his hands disengaging her clinging fingers even as he arose.

"It's pa!" she gasped. "I know it's him!"

"Probably," Jason said grimly, and went to the door.

The man who stood on the gallery looked, in the darkness, like a boulder. Then the boulder moved and Bremer stepped into the house and shouldered past Jason, his eyes boring at Massie Ann, who remained cringing on the bunk. From his fist dangled a leather strap.

"Ach, zo!" he growled. His fist moved, jerking the strap. "Already ich beat her for running hier, und now ich do it again."

"You'd better beat me in place of her," Jason said.

The dirty-gray eyes came slowly to him, and he saw their cold rage. Cremer's fist tightened on the strap until a bulge rose up his big arm. Then, imperceptibly, his fist loosened and he shook his head.

"Nein. Du ich talked mit. Du bist gut mann. Sie runs after in dein haus like a shlut, like mein schwester."

"That's an awful thing to say about your own daughter," Jason said.

"Aber, ist zo," growled the father. "Sie ist shtubborn und lazy. Tvice today sie runs avay, vonce ich vhip, und sie says to be gut. Aber, vhen gifs time to milk vhere iss sie? Hier. Sie lies, und runs off like shlut."

"Do you think beating helps?" Jason asked, holding his tone expressionless in deference to the German's seniority.

"Ihr ich raise, und others!" Cremer growled. "Ich learn them to be gut, to vork, to be like ihr ma und pa. Not like mein schwester." He moved a step toward the bunk. "Shtand up!" he bellowed.

Massie Ann cringed, got to her feet, shoulders folded inward.

Cremer walked slowly at her, the strap jerking at every heavy step. She waited, face dull. The sobs were frozen in her throat as the rage was frozen in her father's eyes.

He brought the strap up.

Jason stepped between him and the girl. "Wait," he said.

Cremer's arm stood in midair. He scowled, not looking away from his cowering daughter. "Vhat ist?" he growled.

"She has a right to be here," Jason heard himself say.

Now the icy eyes swung rigidly to him.

"We—had things to talk about," Jason said out of his guilt. "I—want to ask you for Massie Ann's hand. In marriage."

Cremer's arm dropped. The strap came to a standstill. "Vhy? Vhy du vhant to marry mit ihr?"

Jason swallowed. He could feel the warmth from Massie Ann's body, so close behind him she had moved, could hear her unsteady breathing, reminding him how recently she had wept, and why.

"Every man," he told Cremer now, "after he gets his land his house, needs a wife."

The German considered, nodded. He moved to a bench at the table and sat. He leaned forward and studied Jason.

"Ich haf to undershtand," he said. "Ich komm hier to vhip ihr, und ich tell du sie ist bad—me, ihr pa, tells —und du vhant to marry mit ihr anyhow. Vhy . . . after ich tell du?"

"I can see both sides," Jason replied truthfully. "You think Massie Ann is bad, and she thinks you are cruel. I don't agree with either of you."

"Vhat talk ist das?"

"Fair talk, I think. She doesn't want to work all the time, so she runs away for a while. Not to do anything wrong, but to have some freedom. You believe this is bad, and because she is your daughter, and you want her to become a decent woman, you punish her. For her own good."

"Ja. Ich habe right."

"Do you give your consent to our marriage?"

"Vhat ist dein rush?" Cremer stared pointedly.

"I need a wife now, not next year."

"Ja . . . ja. Vhy ihr . . . vhy not another girl?"

"I don't know any other girls."

"Vhen did du meet ihr, eh?"

"She came past once, and we talked about my house."

Cremer motioned Jason from in front of Massie Ann, and when he had stepped aside, stared at the girl. She was ashen, and her stiff-held jaw gave a quiver, but she endured his scrutiny.

"Du vhant?" he demanded.

She nodded. Her breath shuddered.

Cremer turned the stare on Jason. Spread his hands. "Efen gifs it bad mit du already," he asked, "vhy vould ich say nein? Now ihr ist dein vorry, nicht mein."

"We'll be married tomorrow," Jason said.

"Zo. Es ist ein hurry."

"You won't beat her tonight," Jason said.

"Sie ist mein tochter."

"Even so."

Cremer rose, not a flicker of expression on him. "Sie vill not be vhipped," he said, "until du vhip ihr. Ve go now."

Massie Ann threw one look at Jason, her face as expressionless as that of her father, then ran across the room and out the door. Cremer followed, his moccasined feet thumping.

Jason sat down on the bunk, heart roaring. What have I done? he thought. What have I done?

It was late before he undressed. It was dawn before he fell into fitful sleep.

It was newly dark again when he stood up with Massie Ann Cremer at a parson's house and took her to wife. Tench and Medary were there, looking stunned, and Sam, who for once had not a word to say. No Cremers were present.

Massie Ann was scrubbed and smelled of soap. She was barefoot and wore her same thin washed dress, which had been mended where her father had ripped it. Jason wore his usual clothes. The parson, whose name Jason hadn't caught, wore the customary French garb of cotton and so did his murmuring wife, though they weren't French.

Immediately afterward, the newly married couple said their stilted good nights to all. Jason declined when Medary repeated her invitation to supper, picked up the small bundle that held his bride's extra clothing, and led her into the sultry July night.

He walked in silence, her beside him, felt dust spring up his moccasins, breathed it. He looked beyond the motionless dark trees at the moon, which had stopped halfway up the sky. He tried to think of some pleasantry to say, failed, remained silent.

In his house he shut the door, put her bundle down, lit a candle. When he turned, she was standing in the middle of the room, that dullness on her.

He thought, Here we are, Mr. and Mrs. Jason Blood, entering our years, and it's wrong because we started wrong. A bride shouldn't be barefoot and speechless. She should be laughing and gay. She should wear a new dress and real slippers, and have music and happy tears at her wedding.

He said gently, because this, at least, he could give, "Welcome home, Mrs. Blood."

She whirled, her face suddenly fierce and alive. "Yes! This is my home! I'll never go back!"

"Of course not. You live here now."

"I mean never! Not to visit, or to a burying even! And I don't want none of them here, but my brother Fred, he can come! It's got to be like they was dead or moved away, clear across the world!"

He said, "You'll change."

"Never!" she cried, her voice a throb, an ache. "Take me away, Jason! You lived in New York, take me there! Then I'll never have to see them again!"

"I can't do that, Massie Ann. My life is here."

"Life is where you take it! They never want me but for work! And now you don't want me, not really!"

Tenderness surged up his throat and well nigh choked him. His voice came out uneven, but his arms were strong and eager as they lifted her. "I do want you," he said. "Yes, I do."

Chapter 10

She couldn't believe that it had really happened. Even when Jason, her bridegroom, pushed his empty trencher back at breakfast, said he was going to work in his vegetables, then go help Tench, it still felt like she was dreaming.

She jumped up. "I'll hurry with my dishes," she said. "I'll be ready."

"Ready for what?" he asked.

"To hoe . . . to weed."

"Sit back down, Massie Ann," he said gently.

She obeyed, a shiver down her back at his kind manner.

"We'll get one thing straight now, on our first day," Jason said. "I'll do the man's work in this family, and you'll do the woman's work. I don't want you in the fields. I want you in your house."

Tears smarted her eyes. She set her gaze and made her face still to keep tears back, nodded so he'd know she understood.

After he was gone, she stood bewildered, unable to realize that this cabin was now her own. She washed her wooden dishes and the iron pot. She made up the bunk, pummeling the straw mattress, covering it with the coarse sheet, and then she began to scrub her floor.

Even then, caressing the boards with soapy hands, feeling their smoothness under her knees, she couldn't believe it was true. She sat back on her heels and looked at the rafters, the walls, the open window, the fireplace, the tables and benches, back at the floor, the beautiful floor that she would keep so nice. She peered into the second room, which had no furnishings yet.

Her heart glowed as she pushed the suds along, some of them standing in white foam on the backs of her hands. Jason would take her to balls, and they would dance, here in New Madrid. She'd have a new dress, the prettiest one in the village. Jason would set up to fix clocks and get so rich that he'd take her to New York, and there, where nobody knew about pa and ma and their filthy ways, she would be somebody.

Jason would do this for her. She'd make him do it, even as she'd made him marry her.

She began to sing.

Jason, too, had a busy mind as he hacked at the weeds which sprang so fast out of this fertile soil. Carefully, he took stock of his situation.

Overnight, due to his own folly, he found himself married. He wouldn't have picked Massie Ann ahead of one of those New Orleans girls, but he had feelings for her. He liked her tininess and her cleanliness and she was a glory in the bunk. What he felt for her could well go into husbandly affection.

More immediately, he found himself with a barefoot wife who had for clothing two very old dresses, two patched chemises, and a man's worn blanket-cloth coat. He owned a log house and furnishings, but no winter covering except the blanket he'd brought from New York in his pack. Therefore, clothes for his wife and warmth for their bed he must provide within the next weeks, and by his labor, his money being gone.

It was midmorning when, spade in hand, he made

his way to the far end of Tench's place. Sam was there, helping to turn a new plot.

"Medary wants me to invite you and your bride over for supper tonight," Tench said without preamble. "Sam's coming. She's making it tonight instead of last night. She's having her fish chowder."

"Thanks," Jason said, "we'll be pleased to come." He set his spade into the grassy earth, put his foot on it, turned the soil, set the spade again.

They worked without talking, as they frequently did. But there was a constraint to the silence today, and Jason began to feel uncomfortable. He wondered if a man's being married changes his friends, makes them remote somehow.

It was Sam who blurted, in his rash manner, "Hell, Jase . . . what's goin' on?"

Jason stared at the young Pole, whose cheeks were an angry red. "What do you mean, what's going on?" he asked.

"Where's yer brain?" Sam demanded, his bass voice rough. "Gittin' hitched so sudden, takin' a reckless step like that, an' not a word to yer friends! Jest 'come to my weddin',' then standin' up afore the preacher, an' after that stalkin' off an' not so much as an in-vite to come an' drink yer health!"

Suddenly Jason realized his lack of manners. Caught up in the shock of the marriage itself, never having attended any wedding, he'd behaved in an ignorant fashion. He groped for words, for apology.

Tench spoke easily into the rigid silence. "Marriage hits each man different, Sam," he said. "I was so bashful, it was a chore even to mention Medary by name, her being a schoolteacher and all, and me— You, now, you'd tell the world if you was to get married. You told us right off about Yellow Flower. With Jason, it likely hit so sudden he didn't have time to think, much less talk. That right, Jason?"

"Yes," Jason replied.

He couldn't say, Look, I had to get married. I bedded the girl. Her father might have half killed her, and it would have been my fault. So he said nothing beyond, "Yes."

Sam glowered, grunted, resumed spading. Jason and Tench followed suit, and before long they were back on their usual footing.

Reluctantly, that evening, Massie Ann put on her better dress. She pinned up her hair, which slipped and flew about from its slippery cleanliness.

"That red-headed woman don't want me," she grumbled. "She only asked me because you married me. She didn't know I was on earth till now!"

"Well, that's true enough," Jason agreed, "but I don't see that it matters. I was a stranger once, but Medary's had me for meals a lot, and Sam, too. We're Tench's friends and we're her friends. Now you'll be her friend, too."

Her mouth thinned, and she jabbed pins into her hair. And she went trudging along with him, careful not to kick up dust and dirty her feet. Moccasins first, Jason thought, she has got to have moccasins before anything else.

Medary's table was in the center of their one big room. It was laid with a red and white cloth and napkins, wooden mugs, and trenchers. A silver spoon glittered at each place, and a small china bowl in the middle held yellow wild flowers Jason didn't know the name of.

Massie Ann was silent throughout the meal, murmuring the briefest of replies when she was addressed. She kept her eyes down, ate largely, and touched the handle of the silver spoon in a kind of wonder. The rest of them talked freely, with Sam spending considerable time describing how Yellow Flower was making him a fine deerskin shirt. Repeatedly, one or another of them tried to draw the bride into the conversation, and repeatedly failed.

It's that she feels out of place, Jason thought. She'll loosen up in time.

Afterward, the men sat at one end of the room while

the women cleared the table and washed up. Jason kept his ear out at them, anxious for Massie Ann to be more herself.

He heard Medary, who all evening had glowed with happiness, mention being in the family way. "I'm so proud, it's a temptation to tell everybody I see," Medary said to Massie Ann. "Strangers on the street, even. Lady or no lady, I want to tap them on the shoulder and say, 'I'm going to have a baby in January!' But I can't, of course. I've told only Mrs. Davis and her husband, and Tench has told Sam and Jason. Now you. And that's all."

"But why would you want to tell?" he heard Massie Ann ask, and this was her first unsolicited speech this evening.

"I suppose," Medary said, "it's because of the miscarriages, three of them. Tench got the notion that the Pittsburgh weather was causing it, all that smoke, too. That's why we came west. And I've been getting healthier by the day, and feel so good this time, not dragged out like the other times."

Massie Ann gave the red-haired woman a searching look, seeming to linger on that cat's-mask of freckles. Then, brushing aside the subject of the baby, she asked, "Who's this Yellow Flower?"

"She's a Delaware girl," Medary said quietly, and busied herself with her dish suds.

But Massie Ann persisted. "If she's making Sam a shirt, then she's his squaw, ain't she?"

"Sam seems contented," Medary replied. "He'd be good to any woman, it's not in him to be otherwise."

"Just the same!" Massie Ann sniffed, and after that scarcely opened her mouth.

But when she and Jason got home, she had things to say. "That Sam's a squaw man," she began. "Why didn't you tell me?"

"I never thought about it. It didn't seem to matter, still doesn't. She takes good care of Sam, I've seen that for myself, and he'll provide for her. I figure it's none of my affair what they do."

"I ain't having her in my house," Massie Ann said.

"I don't know that she'd want to come," Jason told her.

"Or him either. No squaw man comes here."

"Now look," Jason said firmly. "I'm the man of the family. Sam's my friend, and I'll not forbid him the door. If you don't want Yellow Flower here, that's your privilege. Medary hasn't invited her to their cabin either, which is her privilege. But Sam goes to Tench's, and he comes here."

She had that stolid look on her face, and her lips were the thinnest yet. But she accepted his decree.

"That Medary!" she snorted. "I never seen such a uppish woman! Moving that red head like she thinks she's so wonderful, bragging 'bout having a baby! She ain't a lady, for all of her schoolteacher talk . . . more like a cat!"

Jason glanced at his bride. Why, she's jealous! The thought slammed through him. Jealous of Medary!

"You'll come to like her," he said, gentling his tone. And as he spoke, he felt sorrier for her uncertainty and insecurity than he'd ever felt for the beatings she'd got from her father.

"She's a fool," Massie Ann said, with a flash of venom. *"Wanting* to have a baby! She ought to see my ma, she'd find out! She'd get down on her knees and give thanks for losing the ones she lost! She's got life easy and ain't got the sense to know it!"

Chapter 11

Jason got in his crops, mostly potatoes and beans and corn, for winter. He set his traps, though it was early for prime furs. He shot two bucks, skinned them, cut up the meat, and gave some of it to the men who had helped him build.

He gave an entire half buck to his father-in-law, taking it to his cabin without Massie Ann's knowledge. She had made good her declaration and saw only her brother, and him only occasionally. The remainder of the venison, with her help, Jason dried and hung from the rafters of their unfurnished room. After the skins were dressed, Massie Ann used one to make each of them a pair of clumsily sewn moccasins, though he'd bought her a pair earlier, and put the remnants aside for future use. The other skin Jason deposited at a village shop as credit against the dress goods, thread, and the woolen bed blanket he would buy later.

He learned to skin a beaver the first day he found one in his traps. He laid it on its back, slit it down the belly and inner legs, peeled off the hide and folded it, fur in, for the trip home. They ate the tail as a special supper treat.

They had eaten well almost from the start: potatoes and cabbage and squash from their garden, roasting ears and pumpkins from their field, fish from the river, and small game and fowl, wild berries and nuts from the timber. They had milk, too, from the cow Tench had bought.

Before a month had passed, Massie Ann told Jason there would be no baby. She spoke calmly, and though he himself felt neither relief nor disappointment, he searched her face, but could not tell whether her stolid expression hid indifference or some fierce exultation.

He felt no desire to rebel against his marriage. He had determined to content himself with the wife he had taken, the girl who, while not comely, was pleasant enough to look upon, and who worked with zest, kept a clean cabin and put good meals on the table. In addition, she came to his arms, soap-smelling and warm and vibrant, the instant he wanted her. It no longer mattered that he had been pushed into the union by an age-old device, for that was done and over, and what remained was for him to build his life.

As winter drew on, his traps began to fill, and his peltries grew into packs, and he knew his initial struggle was over. Whatever came from now on, he had his start. He had his wife, his land, his cabin and furnishings. He had food for winter, seeds for spring planting, and he owed no man.

He was able to buy Massie Ann enough cotton goods and hank thread for two dresses, two chemises, a nightrail. Though she'd been acting withdrawn, she went with him to the shop, looked around it wide-eyed, and confessed that she had rarely entered one before, and shyly selected her cloth. All the way home, she was happy and talkative.

But next morning she cooked breakfast in thin-lipped silence. She moved in a sullen manner. She whacked the bowls onto the table, set Jason's noggin of hot milk before him with such a thud that some of it slopped out.

She dropped into her place at table, mouth drooping.

She took up her wooden spoon, dipped into her mush, laid it down, a look of revulsion on her.

"What's wrong?" Jason asked.

"You ought to know!" she cried.

He stared. "Well, I don't."

"Think!"

Watching her pale, closed face, all he could bring to mind was yesterday's shopping trip. "Don't you like your dress goods?" he asked.

"Ja. I like it."

She was disturbed, even angry, over something. Always, at such times, she reverted to the use of some German words.

"I don't know what else, then," he said carefully.

"Where'll I wear a new dress to?" she demanded. "All we go is to visit Medary and once to see them Davis people!"

"Why—"

"Other men don't just dig and farm and set traps!" she accused. "They take their wives to balls!"

"Balls?" He repeated the word wonderingly. "But I've got to make us a living, Massie Ann. I don't even know how to dance."

"Me neither, but you just watch and do like they do. Pa wouldn't never let me go, and I've waited for you to say we'd go, and they've had balls, but you never said nothing, and you won't take me when I get my dresses made!"

"Nobody has invited us," he said, bewildered.

"I might have knowed you wouldn't do nothing for me!" she wailed. "Not what no other man does for his wife . . . not nothing nice, only the ornery thing!"

"I don't know what you're talking about."

"Babies!" She spat the word.

"You're just angry."

"Ja . . . ja . . . I lose my mush every morning! But you don't see, and you don't care!"

She sprang up, face distorted, and stood glaring wildly down at him. He dropped his spoon, stood abruptly, reached across the table, took her shoulders, and gave her a gentle shake.

"Are you ranting, or is it true?" he asked.

The wildness gave way to a mingle of disgust and satisfaction, followed briefly by the dullness, swiftly replaced by pure viciousness. She glared at him with naked loathing. Then, suddenly, tears were storming down her cheeks.

"Ja, it's so . . . it's so! I won't never get to go no place or be nobody!"

He gave her another, more gentle, shake.

"Now, now."

"Or do nothing but work, work!"

"Why didn't you tell me before?"

"I didn't want it to be s-so!"

"But you knew it was?"

"Ja . . . ja!"

"You didn't behave this way before."

"That didn't come to nothing."

"Are you afraid, is that it?"

"Nein . . . nein!"

"What's so terrible about it, then? Everybody has a family, Massie Ann."

Her tears stopped, and her mean look covered her wet face and twisted her mouth. "Ja, like ma!" she snarled. "Until there's ten or twelve, or twenty! I wanted away from there, and I got away, and I won't be like ma, I tell you, I won't! I'd sooner kill you if you come at me again!"

"We won't have a bigger family then we can take care of," Jason assured her. "You won't be like your mother."

"I've got a good start, ain't I?" she screamed. "Married just two months before . . . and look at me! You're like pa . . . worse'n him! Him and ma was married a year before they had me, a year to the day! And I won't be married a year, even!"

He pressed her shoulders awkwardly. "I can't tell you how sorry I am," he said.

"You ought to of thought about that sooner!"

"Not sorry about the baby, Massie Ann. Sorry about the way you feel."

He saw the stolid look replace the viciousness, saw tears come into her fair eyes. She stared them away, and then she was herself again.

"If you don't take me to a ball now, while I'm my own size," she said dully, "I'll never get to go to one, not in my whole life."

"I'll take you," he promised, "somehow I'll get us invited. And I'll make everything about the baby as easy on you as a man can. Sit down now, eat your mush."

"It'll come up."

"Try."

His hands were still on her shoulders, and he felt a shudder run down her tiny body, and the thought struck him that she was too small to bear a child. He eased her down onto her bench, and she sat drooping while he resumed his own place. He began to eat, and presently she lifted her spoon.

He felt tenderness for her, and desire to protect her from things he could not name. He yearned to tell her how much it meant to him, this knowledge that he was to be a father, that their child would be a true root in this chosen western soil. He wanted to make her understand what a shaking thing it was that, in a few months, he would, for the first time in his memory, behold a kinsman, one of his same blood, who would further be child of his very loins.

He chilled with awe, and resolved somehow to show this confused girl, who had accidentally become his wife and who was now to bear his young, how to look upon the new being with tolerance and affection. He began to speak, groping for the words with which to lead her.

She had never inquired about his childhood, so he told her. He showed her the note found with him on the doorstep of the foundling home. He told of being indentured and apprenticed to Hendrik van Delft, described his duties there, mentioned too the beatings which the Dutchman had intended for his own good. He made it clear that he appreciated her hatred for the filth and poverty of her own childhood, and the longing for cleanliness and plenty which raged within her.

As he spoke and after he finished, she spooned mush into her mouth, the earlier revulsion for it vanished. She said nothing for several minutes and then she told him, "Don't get no invite to no ball. I ain't about to go."

"Why not?" he asked. "What changed your mind?"

"I ain't going to no ball in the family way."

"Why not? You look the same as ever, you're no bigger than a besom straw!"

"They'll know, the women'll know."

"How?" he asked, completely at sea.

"The look around my eyes, that's how!" she spat. "Them old women, they can tell. And now I'll have to make my new dresses big enough to . . . they can tell by the dresses, too."

"Well, I never . . . !" He tried to see things in whatever twisted way she was thinking, failed. "Make one of the dresses to fit now," he said. "I'll buy you goods for another . . . er . . . bigger one later on. When you begin to need it."

"That's the only kind I'll ever need from now on!" she screamed, instantaneously enveloped by viciousness. "What else can I expect from you . . . a doorstep baby?"

Chapter 12

Two weeks later, the middle of December, Medary lost her baby. It was a boy, and for a moment the midwife thought they might save him, but he drew only a few groping breaths and then the scrawny blue little body dangled lifeless from her hands.

"Sometimes," Tench said with aching voice when he came to tell Jason and Massie Ann, "an eight-month baby can make it. But ours was just too little, Mrs. Saugrain says. She says even if he'd been born at the full nine months, he likely couldn't have made it."

"What about Medary?" Jason asked. "Is she all right?"

"She had a hard time," Tench replied, his face dark with anxiety. "She swooned when she found out the boy—we had our work cut out, bringing her to. She's asleep now, looks more unconscious to me than asleep, but Mrs. Saugrain says she'll pull through fast enough. She's of the opinion that Medary tried again too soon, that she ought to have waited at least a year. And she says not to let her try again in under a year, better a year and a half."

Jason nodded. He saw that Massie Ann had her

closed, stolid look. However, she made no comment, but kept her lips thinned in what he hoped would look to Tench like shock.

"Medary wants my name put on the marker," Tench said. "She wants it 'Tench Coghill, Junior.' It's been four hours since— I've already dug the grave, out back where Medary planted the two yellow rosebushes. There's room to set the market between the bushes. I'm having the burying this afternoon, if you folks and Sam and the Davises can make it."

"Sure we can make it," Jason said. "How about a box? When are you going to build that?"

"That's done, too," Tench said, that ache threatening to rend his tone. "It didn't take long. I already had boards I aimed to make a cradle out of after—well, I didn't want Medary to have an empty cradle around."

"Sit down, Tench," Jason urged. "Massie Ann's got dinner almost ready. You look ready to drop."

"I'm going to hunt out the preacher to say the words," Tench replied. "It's short enough notice without me sitting down to eat. Mrs. Saugrain's making stew for Medary . . . I'll have some of that."

He left, but not before Jason had insisted that he do his part by notifying Azor and Annette Davis and Sam of the funeral.

"I hope that squaw ain't coming!" Massie Ann cried the instant the door had closed behind Tench. "If she does, I won't! You tell Sam that, see what kind of a friend he is!"

"What do you mean, what kind of friend he is?" Jason demanded, for the first time angry at Massie Ann.

"If he's any kind of a friend, he'll leave that squaw at the cabin!" she retorted. "He won't bring her around decent women! He won't insult his friends' wives like that!"

"You don't know what you're saying!" Jason told her angrily. "This is a case of death! It's like going to church. There's no difference between people or women—white or Indian—in church."

"What do you know about church?" she screamed. "You ain't never been, any more'n I have!"

"Maybe that's a lack in both of us," Jason said grimly, but his anger was fading. It wasn't just to lose sight of his wife's lack of training. "Medary and Tench go regular," he continued. "Right now, this is our nearest to church, and we're going, both of us, no matter who else does or does not go. We're paying our respects to the dead, to the fourth baby Medary and Tench have had the ill fortune to lose."

"Or the good luck!" Massie Ann spat.

The burying was over, and it had not been attended by Yellow Flower. Massie Ann had become very quiet, and Jason wondered if watching the tiny raw box lowered into the tiny raw grave had in some small degree altered her feelings about her own baby. Later, after they went to bed, she flung herself into his arms and began to weep and storm.

"I don't want to live here!" she sobbed. "It's awful, everything about it is awful!"

"There now," he murmured, to soothe her. "You like the house, you know you do. You like the floors and the glass windows and the fireplaces. It's your own house, and that's what you wanted."

"I want away from here!" she persisted, weeping harder.

"It's just that you're in the family way," he comforted. "Tench says it makes a woman tetchy."

"I wanted away before that, you know I did!" she half screamed. "I want to go to New York and be somebody, not stay where everybody knows I wasn't nobody but Massie Ann Cremer from that hog-Cremer outfit!"

"That would take money, and my money is gone."

"You can sell out. You can get clocks to fix. In New York you can make clocks and sell them and get rich! Promise. Promise you'll take me to New York!"

He stroked her hair, feeling her in his arms as small

and appealing as a child, and her hair was soft and springing. His fingers trailed along her cheek, which was wet with her endless tears.

"There . . . there," he whispered.

"Promise, Jason . . . promise me!"

"You couldn't make such a trip," he pointed out. "You couldn't make any trip with the baby coming. Go to sleep . . . you'll feel better in the morning."

"After, then," she insisted, "after I go through all that suffering! Promise you'll take me after! You've got to, got . . ."

He stopped her words with his lips. He tasted the salt on them and in her mouth when it parted for him, and was overwhelmed by tenderness that was quickly drowned by passionate roughness to which she gave back with abandon.

Afterward, as she slept, the thought fleeted through him that the moment she held their child in her arms love would flood her and they would laugh together in the tenderness of parenthood that it had been he, the father, not she, the mother, who had waited, breathless, for the child. And even as he thought thus, he knew he would never take her to New York or to anyplace but this log house where, though his roots were only newly down, they were going to remain.

But what he didn't know was that never again would Massie Ann, his wife, give him the privilege of her body.

Chapter 13

As winter wore along, they fell into a pattern of living. If Massie Ann never mentioned the coming baby, and Jason, though reluctantly, refrained from doing so lest he throw her into a rage, neither did she complain nor behave in a sullen manner. She talked of household matters, she kept the house shining, she cooked better every passing week, and at intervals she even stitched on small gowns cut from cloth he bought for that purpose.

She didn't appear to mind that he spent hours reading his books on days he didn't trap. She was indifferent the times he tried to share this pleasure and read aloud to her, sighing in boredom or rattling her cookpots until he gave up and did his reading in silence.

She told him he could invite Medary and Tench for supper one night, and they came. Medary looked all red hair and stark white face on which her cat's-mask of freckles blazed. She was so thin her bones seemed almost to show through her skin. By contrast, Massie Ann was filling out, growing definitely plump. She even invited Sam to supper one night, and in return he was careful not to mention Yellow Flower.

Jason made periodic visits to the Cremer cabin. He told them of Massie Ann's condition, knowing her wrath were she to find out, but convinced they should know. Each time they asked, as they always had done, he was forced to admit that she was still estranged from them. Then he would try to explain to their closed faces that once she became a mother herself she would understand the feelings of her own parents. But the German couple, stoic and noncommital, did not respond to his talk, and young Fred, who came to visit his sister now and again, looked surly, and Jason would go home disgruntled.

As spring approached, Massie Ann thickened and fattened unbelievably. She had long since grown heavy-footed and slow. Now, at night, wishing her to feel that he cared about her obvious discomfort, Jason often put his hand on her shoulder or stroked it down her back. Invariably, she jerked away from him as though she believed he was going to demand his husbandly rights.

How long does it take a woman to come back to being wife after childbearing? he wondered. But he asked no one, not even Tench, who was in a position to know. With Medary not too long, he reasoned, as often as she'd lost babies.

Thus he resigned himself to the long wait.

Sometimes, at Tench's cabin or Sam's, he talked with the men who had helped them when they were building. He saw them all at one time or another, the Duval brothers, Pierre Labadie, Gabriel Racine, Jean-François Gascon, William Teper. Once he met Teper's wife, a wiry, sharp-featured, laughing girl with very blond hair, who'd come to the Coghill cabin to visit Medary.

Each day that spring he worked at plowing, at breaking new land, until he was so tired he dropped onto the bunk and into sleep simultaneously. He was putting in a bigger crop and a bigger garden this year, for there must be a great plenty for the new mother so her milk would flow and his child would be fed and strong.

Massie Ann ate mightily as the child within her grew.

She continued to put on flesh until, with her short stature, there came a waddle into her walk. And now Jason began to wonder if this fat would come off as easily as it was going on, or if she would remain obese like her mother.

They had just eaten the first new June peas and potatoes floating together in cream sauce the day Massie Ann was brought to bed. Jason went running wildly across the village to hammer at Mrs. Saugrain's door, then raced back, desperate for Massie Ann, who, now that the time had come, was surely too tiny, her little body too choked by flesh, to bear safely the child of a big man like himself.

When he got back, Massie Ann was between pains, so he stood at the edge of his property and yelled until Tench heard, and then Medary and Tench came running too, Medary to help, and Tench to go for Sam, the two of them to keep Jason company. But when Mrs. Saugrain came trotting up, her plump pouter bosom asurge with movement, he followed her inside, feeling as if he had an iron rod poked clear down his middle, he was so tight and rigid.

All afternoon, the cabin was filled to the rafters with him and his anxiety and the pad of his moccasins. It was filled with green and flower smells and bird twitter, filled with the steaming of water in the fireplace kettle, with the voice of the midwife stroking into Massie Ann's moans and tears and imprecation against her pa, her ma, but most of all against Jason. It was filled with the quiet presence of Medary, her helpfulness, her occasional encouraging glance.

Outside, loyally, Tench and Sam waited.

When darkness came, the candles flickered and made great shadows and wells of blackness in the room. Massie Ann no longer wept or spoke or groaned. Instead, she screamed and every scream pierced Jason like a knife and he cursed himself for bringing her to this. She screamed and pounded the midwife and Medary with her fists, and screamed again and again and at last unendingly out of her contorted and unrecognizable face. The room swelled and pulsed with her shrieks and Jason's ears were riven by them, and they did not lessen but built up until, in the darkest hour before day, a red, fat boy was born.

He began to squawl instantly, taking up where his mother left off, for Massie Ann fell instantly silent, instantly asleep. Jason sat trembling on a bench in the far corner, his head in his hands, unable to move or speak or even to comprehend the clucking and cooing of plump, graying Mrs. Saugrain and Medary as they hovered over the baby.

Medary came to him, presently, with a bowl of mush, thrust it into his unsteady hands. "Eat it," she said. "Then you can see the baby."

"Why can't I see him now? What's wrong?"

"Nothing's wrong . . . everything's fine. Mrs. Saugrain isn't quite finished. She'll be a while. There are things she must do for Massie Ann, then she'll dress the baby, wants to do it herself. Massie Ann had a hard time, it being her first and her so tiny and . . . well, all that flesh. But she's going to be fine. Tomorrow she'll have forgotten all the pain. Women are like that, they don't remember the pain once they hold the baby in their arms. And you couldn't ask for a finer, healthier boy."

It seemed to him that her voice came near to trembling. Then he realized it was probably his hearing that was still on the shaken side, like his hands. He began to spoon the good hot mush into his mouth.

Later, when Medary gave him leave, he walked on unsteady legs to the bunk and looked at the drained face of his sleeping wife, and the near-bald red head of his sleeping son. And the guts within him moved at first sight of one who shared his blood, the only one of his blood he'd ever looked upon. He started to grin, found it too much effort, felt a pang of regret for the hell of suffering he'd put Massie Ann through, gestured helplessly to the women, went out the door, and in the graying and awakening morning told Tench and Sam about his son. And then, scarcely noticing what he was doing, he struck off, walked away through the streets of New Madrid.

When he returned from telling the Cremers that they were grandparents, his news having been received impassively, he was still numbed, unable to capture any of his anticipated elation. Massie Ann, still white-faced, was awake in the bunk, watching the door as he stumbled through it, and she was alone except for the wrapped baby lying between her and the wall.

He looked around in a sudden frenzy that things had gone wrong. "Where is she?" he asked.

"Where's who?"

"Mrs. Saugrain . . . Medary?"

"Them? Mrs. Saugrain went home to fix breakfast for her family. Medary and them went over to their place to eat. Said I need to rest quiet and left me laying here all by myself! I'm sick . . . I'm awful sick . . . I nearly died last night, but you don't care! Nobody cares about me, only about theirselfs."

"I do, Massie Ann, I care."

"You ran off, and now you've come home drunk, that's how you care!"

"I'm not drunk. I've never touched a drop in my life."

"I seen you fall through that door! Don't tell me!"

"I tripped. I'm upset, I guess. It was a hard night."

"Where'd you go, what was you doing, me laying here by myself, dying for all you know?"

"I went to tell your folks about the baby."

"Them! It ain't none of their stuff!"

"They've a right to know, Massie Ann."

"I'll be out of here in a week, no matter what. We can leave then, and I'll be rid of them!"

"Leave? What are you talking about?"

"Go to New York, like you promised."

"I didn't promise, Massie Ann."

She came up on her elbow, pale hair falling around her face. "Ja . . . you did . . . way back there! You said when the baby come, we'd go! Well, the baby's here, and we're going!"

He sank onto a bench, leaned on the table and stared at her. He swallowed. "You misunderstood," he said at last. "Even if I had agreed to such a thing, we couldn't make that trip with a young baby."

"Don't you start that talk, don't you! You worked it on me once, but you don't work it now!"

"Put your head back down, Massie Ann. You'll make yourself sick."

"I'm sick a'ready, and whose fault is it . . . mine? Answer me that, is it mine?"

"No, Massie Ann, no. Go to sleep."

"Nein . . . that's what Medary said! Nein, you don't do that, neither! You don't shut me up! I've looked ahead to New York, and I've planned it, and lived for it! And now you want to back out! Well, I won't let you, I won't—"

"Hush up and listen to me!" Jason heard himself yell.

She fell back on her pillow, eyes burning.

"We may as well settle this here and now, though it's not the proper time," he went on, lowering his voice, speaking wearily. "As you know very well, I was an indentured servant in New York, an apprentice too, which meant that I had to work all those years to buy my freedom so I could go where I pleased and do what I wanted. That is over, and I'm not about to enter into servitude to you, or anyone else. When I left New York it was for good, and I came here and established my home. Now I have planted for the second time, my son was born today on my land, in the house I built, and nothing—not hunger or war or you—is going to make me leave it!"

She lay, white and spent, her eyes locked to him, and then she began to weep, crying aloud, sobs jerking the length of her body, surely, Jason thought dully, causing visible waves in the rolls and swaths of flesh in which it was encased. Tears poured down her face.

Then he was kneeling beside the bunk, trying to

draw her into his arms, to comfort her. Instantly, she was clawing at his eyes, his face, his neck.

"Let me go!" she shrieked. "Don't you touch me, not now, not never! You'll not get no chance to make me like ma, not you, not no brute-beast of a man!"

"Hush . . . hush," he soothed. "This is bad for you, bad for our baby."

She wrenched away, sat up, snatched the bundled baby into her arms, clutched it to her, faced him over it, eyes wild. "Not *our* baby!" she screamed. "*My* baby, do you hear? Mein, mein, mein! If you touch him ever, I'll kill you! He's my baby . . . mein . . . my little Auguste . . . all mein!"

" 'Auguste?' " Jason repeated, stunned.

"That's what I've named him . . . Auguste!" she screamed. "After that Frenchman they talk about, that's so big up in St. Louis, that Auguste Chouteau!"

"Where did you ever hear about Auguste Chouteau?" Jason asked, hardly believing his ears.

"Oh, I've heard talk!" she cried. "He's the biggest, smartest man in all this country, I've heard that, too! Who'd you think I was going to name him after . . . after *you?*"

Chapter 14

She would recover from her frantic ways, Jason told himself. She was young, only nineteen. It didn't matter what she said, or what she named the baby. Auguste Blood was a good name, as good as Jason Blood. The name was fine. Another son could be called Jason Blood.

He and Massie Ann would come to be like other married people, their differences smoothed. Patience was the key. He would be firm but he would be kind and gentle. He would wait. One day she would revert to the friendly girl he had seen standing in his doorway that first afternoon, and develop into the satisfying woman of which the girl had given promise.

But first, he learned, Massie Ann must recover from childbirth. Mrs. Saugrain said she was bleeding too much and must remain abed a bit longer than two weeks.

"She needs rest," the midwife explained, "rest and good rich food to make milk for the boy."

Medary insisted on taking over the cooking. "You've got enough to do, Mrs. Saugrain," she said, "taking care of the baby, washing his clouts, nursing his mother.

The least I can do is put food on the table." She laughed, tossed her hands gently apart. "I have to cook anyway, for Tench and myself. Besides, it gives me an excuse to be around the baby, to see to it that Jason and Tench make the cradle properly! That is, Massie Ann," she qualified, "if it's all right with you."

"I don't care," Massie Ann replied dully.

Her tone implied that hers was the greatest task of them all, that of rebuilding her ravaged body, her strength, to build the baby. Which is true, Jason told himself, observing how carelessly she took for granted that Sam would bring her a fresh-killed turkey, that he would stammer and fall speechless when he looked at the baby.

Jason occupied himself cutting and fitting and smoothing and polishing the cradle. He was fashioning it of walnut, the boards an inch thick. Tench made suggestions, and Jason followed them, knowing that, in a way, Tench was building the cradle he'd hoped to build for his own lost baby. And, though Jason would have taken satisfaction in making Auguste's cradle unaided, he found himself taking satisfaction that it was Tench who helped.

Massie Ann fretted each time she had to nurse Auguste.

"Is it time a'ready, can't he wait?" she'd ask the midwife.

The woman's middle-aged face would hold its calm look no matter what the scowl, the petulance on that of her patient. "He's hungry, ma chère. That's a healthy thing. He'll be a strong boy."

"He hurts me . . . he bites!"

"That's because he's hungry, he's in a hurry, he can't drink fast enough."

"He's got to quit hurting me! It gets worse every time!"

"Take your finger, ma chère, when it hurts too much, push his little mouth apart. He'll loosen, and soon, when he learns there is enough, he won't be so . . . lusty."

Nevertheless, Massie Ann took to weeping, sometimes silently, sometimes aloud, as the baby nursed. Awkwardly, Jason took Medary aside.

"How much of this can she stand?" he asked.

"The . . . skin toughens after a while, I'm told," Medary replied. "It's just that in some women there seems to be more sensitivity than in others, and they do suffer a good deal of pain right at first."

"And she's one of those, one that feels the pain more?"

"I believe so, Jason. The baby has drawn blood. Then, when it's time to nurse on that side again and he chews . . . Yes, he hurts her, hurts her terribly."

With the hurting, Massie Ann seemed to lose interest in the baby. She was indifferent as to how much Medary held him, cuddling and crooning, rocking him gently in her arms, her face beyond tenderness.

Yet, the one time Jason put out his hands to lift his son, Massie Ann turned into a wildcat. "Don't you touch him!" she screamed, with both Mrs. Saugrain and Medary hearing. "He's mein, all mein, I told you!"

"She'll come back to herself," the midwife assured Jason on the third day, when Jason paid her and thanked her for her services. "She can sit up every day until the baby's two weeks and two days old, then she can dress and move around. I've seen many new mothers, monsieur. Sometimes a wildness comes on them, but it's not to worry. They become natural again; they forget the suffering."

Medary stayed in the house by day, caring for Massie Ann and Auguste, cleaning and washing and cooking, openly falling in love with the baby. Tench came for meals. When Jason expressed his concern that Medary was overexerting, Tench waved the concern aside.

"You can look at her," he said, "and see that she's thriving on it. It's the baby. He's the best thing in the world for her."

At night, with Medary gone, Jason slept on a pallet, leaving the bunk for Massie Ann and Auguste. He kept a candle burning so she could see to nurse the baby and change him. The first time Auguste nursed, she wept aloud and stormed at Jason, placing all blame for everything from the discomfort she'd suffered for nine months, through the agonies of birth, up to and including her pain now, inflicted by his biting, hoggish son, squarely on him.

He said nothing. But he wondered, angry in spite of her misery and his sympathy for it, how long a man had to put up with such carrying on. When her weeping and ranting ceased and there was quiet, he went to sleep again.

A shrill scream from Massie Ann brought him off the pallet in one leap.

"You devil . . . you he-Satan!" she was screaming as he leapt across to the bunk. "Bite me, will you . . . I'll learn you . . . !"

Her hand tore at the sucking baby, shoved the bald little head roughly, and her fingers went to the small, hidden neck. "You'll not chew me up, you little . . ."

Jason's hand shot out, tore her fingers loose. As he scooped the baby into his arms, the small, strangled voice lifted and wailed in the halting, chopping newborn sound. Behind him, as he ran from the house and went racing for Medary's cabin, he heard Massie Ann screaming and ranting.

Chapter 15

He pounded up to the door of the Coghill cabin, the baby wailing mightily. He forced himself to knock in a subdued manner, not wishing to alarm Medary.

There was a brief, yet endless pause. The baby caught his breath, wailed again. Surely, thought Jason, he's not hurt too badly if he can make this much noise.

The door opened. Tench stood there, candle in hand, Medary at his back, peering around him.

"Jason!" Tench exclaimed. "What's going on?"

"Let him in, Tench!" Medary cried. "Something's wrong with the baby . . . let me have him, Jason!"

Urgently, in one motion, Jason stepped inside and deposited his now shrieking son in her arms.

"There . . . there," she crooned to the screaming infant, "it's all right, little fellow . . . it's all right! What happened, Jason?"

"She tried to choke him!" Jason blurted, rage and disbelief filling him. "She tried to kill him . . . because he bit her!"

"Oh, dear!" Medary exclaimed. Then, to the baby, "There . . . there . . . it's all right, little darling, it's going to be all right!" She paused in front of Jason,

105

gently swaying the baby. "Did he nurse at all, Jason . . . did he get anything at all?"

"I don't know. She woke me up choking him, saying she'd kill him. Or giving that impression. I don't know if it was at the beginning, when he tried to start, or at the end, when he was nearly through, or when."

"Stir up the fire, will you, Tench?" Medary said. "Set some milk to warm."

It was only a moment before tongues of fire were licking the shreds of wood, then the larger pieces Tench fed it. He set a small iron pot with milk in it on a trivet directly over the first blaze.

The baby's wail quieted to an unhappy and constant mewling. Medary examined his neck, holding him so the candlelight shone on it.

"There's a mark," she said, "but it's not bad. He's not injured, just frightened and, I'd say, hungry."

As if her words had reminded the infant of his ordeal, he began to cry loudly once again. Medary walked with him, patting his back, her cheek against his head, but he wailed on.

It wasn't until she dipped a small teat of clean white cloth into the milk and put this into his mouth that the crying ceased. Now the only sound from him was sucking and smacking, with little warning grunts as she dipped into the milk again, transferring it quickly to him.

"He's ravenous," she murmured. "He'll always be ravenous. He'll be a good eater, Jason."

"Why would she do it?" Jason asked. "She didn't want him, but once he was born, she seemed . . . well, fierce about him. Wouldn't let me touch him, you know that. Why would she all of a sudden try to kill him?"

"He really hurts her, Jason. It amounts to torture."

"But why would she . . . ? Why would a woman try to kill her own young?"

"Sometimes a woman just will, even without the pain. Something happens to her after giving birth, and she isn't responsible. With Massie Ann, it could be only the pain, or it could be both things."

"You mean she's crazy?"

"They ... the women I speak of ... do things which make them appear mad," Medary replied. "But it doesn't last. Whatever it is, it passes, and they make as good a mother as any woman."

Jason sat down, stunned. How many things are there, he wondered, that I don't know about women, never will know?

A sudden fear pulled him to his feet. "I'd better go see to her. She might do something to herself."

"That's unlikely," Medary said. "Be kind to her, Jason, soothe her. Kindness will help her out of this trouble faster than anything. Kindness, and not being hurt anymore."

"But how can the baby nurse without her being hurt?" Jason asked. "How can she heal if he keeps chewing and biting? What do other women do?"

"Grin and bear it, I reckon," Tench put in quietly.

"Tench," Medary chided. "I don't think Massie Ann can bear it," she told Jason. "I think we'll have to give the baby a bottle."

"You can count on milk from our cow," Tench offered.

Jason nodded his thanks, went stalking home, torn between anger and worry. He found Massie Ann asleep, her hands flung up on either side of her fair head as a child sleeps, her face streaked with drying tears. Now and then her breath jerked, and she sobbed softly.

Jason stood gazing down at her. What have I brought you to? he wondered. What have I brought us all to? And then he thought, We'll work out of it. We have to.

When she woke, she was instantly in tears over what she'd done. She wept and berated herself without end, receiving Auguste from Medary's arms as a treasure, sobbing that it would never happen again, never, never. She accepted the plan to bottle-feed with wild gratitude, thanked Medary for the pewter bottle she produced.

"The danger's over," Medary assured Jason on the gallery before she left, "it's done with. She'll be a devoted mother, you can count on it."

And she was. She hovered over the baby, changed his clout at first sign of dampness, kept his bottle as clean as soapsuds and boiling water could get it, heated his milk to exactly the right temperature, washed and ironed for him endlessly. Jason she ignored, except to watch keenly to see that he didn't try to lift Auguste, that he didn't so much as to put a finger on his cheek.

She'd recover from her frantic ways, Jason told himself. Patience was the key. He would be kind, he would be gentle, he would wait.

But summer went into winter, and still she had not permitted him to hold his son. She was always there, hovering, ready to snatch the baby into her own protective arms. She talked to Auguste by the hour, sang to him, and he kicked and cooed and laughed and throve. To Jason she spoke when necessary, and when he was indoors, she moved sullenly about the house, which she continued to keep painfully clean. She cooked bigger, better meals, thumped them onto the table in front of Jason, then sat across from him and ate enormously and in silence.

Unbelievably, she grew even fatter, until, by the time Auguste was three months old, she was a solid block of flesh. Her face was dimpled, and she had more chins than her mother. Sometimes Jason looked upon the wreck of the girl he had married, asked himself if it were his fault, and did not know. If so, forgive me, he thought to the wide face so stolidly and continuously chewing, swallowing. Forgive me. And then he would think, She doesn't have to eat so much, she doesn't have to be so fat.

But even as he pondered, he knew it had not been in him to do other than he had done, or to love this woman, this stranger. The girl, perhaps, if she had taken a different bent or if even yet she would change, but not this lump of a woman. Yet through his resentment rose pity, and with it, determination to help her.

There came the day, with Auguste six months old, that Jason stole a few moments to read before leaving to hunt with Tench and Sam. He was sitting on his bench, his book open on the table. Massie Ann was squatting at the fireplace, vast haunches spread, banking coals around a cookpot, and Auguste was trying to crawl on a blanket on the floor.

Aware of the domesticity of the moment, Jason's attention wandered from his book. Gradually, the actual barrenness underlying the homelike scene struck into him.

His eyes lingered on Massie Ann's back, then moved to Auguste. He was a chubby little fellow, dressed in white, with baby-blond hair feathering his egg-shaped head. While Jason watched, his small mouth pursed and his invisible eyebrows knitted in furious concentration on the wooden spoon which he was gripping in one fist and pounding on the blanket, as if he were trying to figure out why it made no sound. He was staring at the spoon with a look of bewilderment in his fair eyes.

The thought went through Jason, There plays my son, and I don't know him, or him me. It's time to put an end to such foolishness.

In one movement he was kneeling beside the blanket. He put out his hand, gently grasped Auguste's wrist between thumb and forefinger, pulled the little fist over the edge of the blanket, moved it up and down so the spoon rapped smartly on the floor. Smiling, he peered into the baby face to see if understanding was there, and found not that, but confoundment. Auguste stared back at him and his wet little mouth was slack, then it began to quiver, redness washed up his scalp, his eyes squeezed shut, his face convulsed, and the shrieks began.

Massie Ann was there instantly, snatching him up, rocking him in her arms, ponderously moving her body, crooning, eyes stabbing palely at Jason, who remained in consternation upon his knees.

Auguste's cries quieted. Massie Ann patted him, her face assumed that meanness which Jason once had dreaded and now accepted, and her mouth twisted out words.

"*You!* Dirty . . . stinking . . . scaring my baby! He might of died of being scared! You . . . brute-beast, you!"

Slowly Jason rose and stood looking down at his wife, at his sobbing child, and both were strangers. "Shut up," he said quietly. "Shut your mouth, and hear what I am going to say."

Her face kept the meanness. The meanness had entered her eyes.

"I told you once I'll not be your servant," he said, "and that holds. I've waited for you to act like yourself, like the girl I married, but you haven't, and now I'm through waiting. This is my house, you are my wife, that is our son. I am head of the family, and I am to be treated as such. From this moment, you will behave yourself, and when I pick up the boy to hold him, or even to paddle him when he is older and needs it, you will not interfere."

"Ja . . . ja . . . I'm to be your servant now, is it?"

"We're man and wife, and that is how we're going to live, Massie Ann."

"Ja . . . ja . . . like pa . . . like ma, yet!"

"Not like them, but like ourselves, Mr. and Mrs. Jason Blood."

"In New York I'd be different."

"In New York it would be something else you'd want."

"Nein . . . nein! Just to be away from hier, is all!"

"I remember when to run away from home was enough."

"Nein . . . nein!"

"I'm beginning to see that nothing will satisfy you. You didn't like to live with your parents, and I can understand that. But now you don't want to live this way either, which at one time you thought was so fine. You'd better content yourself with it unless you want to leave and fend for yourself."

Her great face had lost its dimples and gone dull during his talking, and now it looked frightened and tears slid down it, but he did not, as he would have six months ago, take her into his arms to comfort her. She was like a child, and if his words were to have lasting effect, he would, at this time, have to treat her as if she were a child.

That was just today, he thought now, sitting behind the log, waiting for a bunch of turkeys to come feeding and scratching and searching through the woods, waiting for even one turkey. Massie Ann liked turkey. It was her favorite meat, beating out deer in her estimation by a hair, though he'd seen her stow away great quantities of both at one and the same meal. That was just today, he thought again. It seemed more like years, because in his mind he'd flashed through all his years, and now he took a few seconds to marvel at how a man's mind can travel, with what swiftness, with what lightning clarity, with what blinding brilliance, forgetting nothing, skipping no event of importance. He looked at the slant of sunlight across a clearing to his left, off toward New Madrid, toward Massie Ann and Auguste and his log house.

No more than an hour had passed.

Chapter 16

The sun was a hot ball bleeding into the western timber when Jason got home, two turkeys slung over his shoulder. Massie Ann stood in the doorway, filling it.

"We're invited to a ball!" she called as if there'd never been a cross word between them. Her voice was alive with the eagerness he'd not heard since their early days.

"That's fine!" he exclaimed. "Who invited us . . . when?"

"Medary brought the in-vite," she replied as he dropped the turkeys to the ground. She seemed scarcely to notice them. Any other time she would have been right at them, intent on dressing and cooking. "It's Azor and Annette Davis, old as they are! They decided at noon, and it's tonight!"

"They go to plenty of balls," Jason said. "I've heard them talk about the ones they used to give, too. But what about Auguste? There's no one to watch him, unless Medary's willing."

"Medary's going, her and Tench. She says we should bring Auguste, Annette told her. She says people take their younguns. And you think Medary knows it all!"

"I didn't realize Medary and Tench had gone to any balls," Jason said.

"They ain't. This is their first one, too. I got it all planned. You carry the cradle and clouts and bottle and I'll carry Auguste. I told Medary to say we'd come." She finished abruptly, a note of stubborn defiance in her tone.

"I warn you," Jason said uneasily. "I've never danced in my life. Or seen anyone else dance, for that matter."

"Ain't nothing to it. You just get on the floor with your partner and hop around in time to the music."

Jason grinned suddenly. "We'll go," he said. "It's a good thing . . . it'll put us out among folks as a couple. And we'll have a good time, a really good time."

Only they didn't.

It turned wrong when Massie Ann struggled into her new cotton dress, made full and ankle long. The blue put a hint of color into her fair eyes, made the whiteness of her skin strikingly fair, and set off her pale, soft hair, but it did nothing to conceal the tremendous girth of her short figure.

She glared down herself. "It's too tight!" she said, spitting the words. "Just look at me, look at what you've done to me!"

There was nothing he could say. He couldn't roughly put the blame on her.

"Lose your tongue?" she screamed. "Ashamed of me?"

"No," he said honestly. "You're my wife, Massie Ann. Auguste is my son. To be ashamed of you would to be ashamed of myself. The dress is a nice color, and it becomes you. In time, you'll get back to your natural self."

"Ma ain't never got back! She used to be as little as I was! Pa don't give her no chance to get back!"

"I'm not your pa," he said quietly. "We're going to live as man and wife, I promise you that. But I promise there'll not be all those children."

"How?" she demanded, her voice shrill. "How you going to keep from it, answer me that!"

"There are ways," he replied. There had to be ways, and he would find them. "You can depend on me, trust me."

It was ten o'clock, the Davises' chosen hour, when they set out, Massie Ann in high good humor, chattering about the evening ahead. Jason suggested that they stop by for Tench and Medary and go in a party.

"I don't want to!" Massie Ann declared. "I want us to go now, right this minute!"

There was already a lively crowd at the Davis house when they arrived, voices making a kind of music of laughter and chatter. The men wore clean rugged garb, the women their best cotton dresses. Children were running about, darting in and out of the rooms, chasing each other, squealing and excited and happy.

Jason and Massie Ann were welcomed with cries and hugs, Azor and Annette themselves introducing them around. Auguste, wakened by the uproar, began to scream. Massie Ann carried him on one arm, shook hand after hand, face blank, eyes shining, saying, "Pleased, I'm sure," over and over, seemingly unaware of her son's screams.

Jason moved along behind her, lugging the cradle, himself nodding and making as friendly a smile as he could in his discomfort. Once he bent to Massie Ann and muttered so only she could hear, "Want me to take the little fellow into another room?"

"I'll take him myself when I'm ready!" she snapped.

Jason felt his mouth tighten and his hands clench on the cradle. It was all he could do to keep himself from grabbing his unhappy son out of the heedless Massie Ann's arms. But he couldn't do that, because if he did, she might very well go into a public tantrum.

Thus, teeth clenched, he kept a grin on his face. He nodded, turned the grin on everybody, both those he knew and those he hadn't met. He saw William Teper and his blond, sharp-featured wife, whom he thought of as the laughing girl. He saw Pierre Labade, nodded, and turned his grin when Pierre introduced his dimpled wife, Marie. He noticed Gabriel Racine and his tall scrawny wife, Yvonne, in a bright green dress. There was Jean-François Gascon and even the Duval brothers, sometime hunting companions of young Fred Bremer. There were others he'd seen on the street and even passed a few words with, and all now greeted him as an old-time friend.

And all the while Auguste screamed.

It was Annette who resolved the situation. "What am I thinking of?" she cried to those still waiting to meet Jason Blood and wife. "This child has a fretting baby to quiet, and her husband needs to get rid of this cradle! Shoo . . . all of you teasers . . . I'll bring the parents back . . . and then the fiddler can strike up and the dancing can begin!"

Auguste was the youngest baby there, Annette told them as she showed Jason where to set the cradle in the room off the kitchen. "He'll have this room to himself," she said. "He'll be as far from the noise as he can get. Used to be, when we gave balls, the little babies slept right through everything in here."

Auguste sucked fiercely at his bottle, fell abruptly asleep. Massie Ann put him in the cradle, allowed Annette to cover him, and they all returned to the main room. Here the fiddler, a very thin little man with white hair, was standing on the table, tuning up.

Tench and Sam and Medary arrived now. Medary's hair looked so red Jason took a second glance, then supposed the soft green of her dress made it that way. Her cat's-mask of freckles hardly showed at this distance and in candlelight. She looked beautiful, in a way.

"Grab yer pardners!" sang out the fiddler in a voice as thin as his body. He scraped the bow across the strings, pulling forth a sharply melodious chord. "Grab yer wife fer the first set, if ye got a wife! If ye ain't, grab yer sweetheart or any girl that'll let ye!" Again he worked the bow, kept it going, building chord after sprightly chord of sound which then skipped into the brightest, fastest tune Jason had ever heard.

Instantly, the room rearranged itself. The walls were lined with watchers, and out on the floor the dancers paired off, standing in two parallel lines facing each other, men in one line, women in the other. Across from Jason stood Massie Ann, vaster than ever in contrast to tiny Annette on one side and a slim young woman named L'Fleur on the other. As far as Jason could tell, husband faced wife down the line, with Azor opposite Annette, Maurice L'Fleur opposite his wife, Tench facing Medary, with her blaze of hair. Sam, the only single man on the floor, had a plump brown-haired girl as partner.

The fiddler began to call the dance in his high-pitched voice, his accent in cadence with the music.

"Swing yer pardners!

"Ladies to the right and a right hand acrosst!

"Look out girls, so ye won't git lost!"

All the others knew what to do, where to move, and how. Jason watched and tried to do as they did. The thud of feet, moccasined and in shoe leather, came onto the floor in a rhythmic beat. Hands met, partners swung, women's dresses stood out from their ankles, swirled, never quieted. The wailing fiddle kept winding on, ever higher, faster, keener, sweeter, the fiddler's voice climbing the music, riding it, the dancers' feet ever quicker, merrier.

On it went, set after set. The women danced with their heads flung back, smiling, hair threatening to loosen and fall. The men matched them step for step, light or heavy on their feet, according to the man, and all the while the fiddler's voice and the fiddle strings sang a high duet, enticing them, luring them, leading them on and on.

Jason kept trying, bumping into others, trying his best to do as they did, but after a couple of sets, when Sam asked to partner Massie Ann, he gave up and stood along the wall and watched. Then it was that, with music and laughter and dancing in his ears, and a misery in his eyes, he watched his wife grimly lope and stumble and flush and try again and again, that stolid, rocky look on her that he knew betrayed tears suppressed.

She was by far the fattest woman on the floor. When she was swung by her partner, first Sam, then Azor, and went loping in her circle, her tremendous bosom rose mightily upward, dropped heavily, rose again. Her buttocks bounced outward so that they moved the back of her skirt, and this movement suggested the accompanying vast surge of flesh along her limbs.

Jason burned in agony for her. Even while he marvelled that one so light and quick of foot at home could be so clumsy on the dance floor, he willed her to catch on, to step with the music rather than in opposition to it.

Unwilling to look any longer at her stubborn suffering, he went into the kitchen, closing the door behind him. Here six or seven men were sitting around the table playing with a deck of cards. He looked in on the sleeping Auguste, pulled that door shut again, watched the card game. Then he went into the yard where a few men were gathered around a jug of whiskey. This, he knew, was because Annette wouldn't allow spirits in her house. When one of the men offered him the jug, he shook his head, remained to talk idly for a time, went inside again.

He'd no sooner got back into the main room than a set ended. Massie Ann turned as abruptly from her partner as her bulk permitted. Spotting him in the place he'd stood before, she made her way to him, her face a blank.

"'I want to go home," she said abruptly.

He glanced at the clock on the mantel. "It won't be over for hours yet," he told her. "It's not even two o'clock. You may be sorry you left."

"Nein. I want away from hier."

"I'll tell Annette," he said, giving in, himself ready to leave, to return to the peace and quiet of home. "While you get Auguste ready, I'll hunt her up."

They made their leave-taking. They walked homeward in silence, leaving the music and stomping and laughter and merriment farther behind until at last it was only a whisper, a faintness in the night. Now came only the stroke of their moccasined feet on the pathway.

"Did you get tired?" Jason asked.

"Ja. I got tired of being laughed at!"

"Nobody laughed at you."

"They laughed, you laughed! You stood and watched me and laughed!" she cried, voice shrill.

"I never laughed!" he protesed. "I only stood. You know that, Massie Ann, know it very well."

"Nein . . . you didn't grin, you didn't go 'haw-haw'! And the women, that cat-faced Medary, all of them, they didn't grin and go 'tee-hee,' but they laughed the worst way, inside, because I'm so big!"

"It's your imagination, Massie Ann. They were all busy having a good time."

"They looked at me and seen ma trying to dance, and laughed! It's all your fault, you made me this way, so's they can laugh at me!"

"Do you think I'd let people treat you that way, Massie Ann?" he asked reasonably.

"I don't know what you'd do!" she shrilled. "Where was you? You was gone, what was you doing?"

"I looked in on Auguste. I watched the men playing cards in the kitchen. I stepped into the yard for a while."

"And drank whiskey! You was outdoors swilling whiskey, and your wife was inside, being made fun of!"

"You know I don't drink," he reminded her. "I don't like the stuff. I went out there to pass the time, and then I came back in to watch the dancing again."

"You should of been dancing with me, not standing against the wall!"

"You had partners. You wouldn't want to be the only woman that had to dance with her husband the whole time."

She had no answer for that, and he breathed a little

more easily. He felt an exasperated tenderness for her. She'd gone to her first ball and it had fallen short of her expectations, had proved to be a torture.

Recklessly, not giving himself time to weigh its wisdom lest he never again dare, he asked, "If you worry about being heavy, why don't you try eating less?"

She surged to a stop. "Now you want to starve me!" she cried. "First you make me like my ma, then you want to take the grub out of my mouth! Well, it won't work! My ma is big because my pa made her that way, and I'm big because you made me that way! What I eat or don't eat ain't got a thing to do with it! Why'd you say such a thing? Tell me that . . . tell me!"

"Well," Jason said miserably, but determined to see it through, "it started with Medary."

"*Medary?*" raged Massie Ann. "You been discussing me with *her?* You been talking to that red-headed, cat-faced strumpet, that fool that don't know no better than to have one baby after another, that—"

"Stop it!" Jason commanded so thunderously that she fell silent and went stomping on. He had to lengthen his stride to keep pace with her. "It's that on the boat downriver, she was so thin. Tench fed her up and she put on weight from good air and good food. Same thing happened when she lost little Tench, you saw that. She ate, and she put on flesh. So it looks reasonable that if a person eats a great deal, he may get heavier than normal, and if he wants to get rid of flesh, he doesn't eat as much."

"That's just a lot of fancy talk!" Massie Ann retorted. "You know you did it to me, and now you're trying to make it be my fault!"

Silent, he followed her along the path, into their yard, into the house. He set the cradle in its place with a thump.

She started in again, weeping now. She raged and berated, she ranted and sobbed. All the while, she was giving Auguste the bottle and settling him in his cradle. Suddenly Jason wished he'd never seen her.

She was rocking the cradle when he stalked out, across the gallery, down the steps. "I hate you!" she screamed after him, "hate you, hate you, hate you!"

He didn't stop until he'd reached the outer edge of the yard. Here he stood, trying to get his mind off their fight by letting the two-o'clock morning chill come through his pores. Maybe it would cool his own rage enough that he could reenter his house in a mood and manner befitting the head of the family.

He turned, stared unhappily toward the candlelit rectangle of open door which looked so homelike but was not. He'd have to shut the door when he went in, even though the December night was almost summer-warm, shut it against dew chill so the baby wouldn't risk the croup of which Medary had spoken.

Even as he stared and thought thus, distant rumbling sounds entered his hearing, succeeded by discharges as if a thousand pieces of artillery were being suddenly exploded. He whirled to look, to locate, to grasp. Simultaneously, the western sky went into a continued glare of vivid flashes of lightning and there came repeated peals of a subterranean thunder, seeming to come from below that flashing horizon. The trees in the yard waved over his head like tempest-tossed spars on the ocean, and the earth trembled and rocked beneath his feet. He felt the tremor and the rocking rise and spread throughout the earth, and it jolted up his legs, jolted and thundered and tore up along his body and threw him to the heaving ground.

As he fell, a sickness came into him at the stomach and a whirling into his head. And as he pushed up a bit, desperately, from the tumultuous earth, its throes jarring up his dancing arms, he saw his house, his home, which he'd hewn and mortised and roofed with his hands, move and sag. He saw the earth on which it stood, caught in still another ear-splitting, blinding crack of lightning, burst open along one end of the house. He saw the whole structure slowly tip and slide toward the fissure in the earth.

Chapter 17

He clawed to his knees, the earth shuddering and rolling in waves under him, clawed into a crouch, inched with maddening slowness on hands and feet toward the house. It now leaned at an angle, ever drifting toward that fissure, open doorway tilted, screams ripping from its candlelight.

"I'm coming!" he roared, but the roar was a whisper in the great cracking, rumbling, subterranean thunder. Sweat sprang from his brow and ran down his face, cords stood out on his neck. He strained along, as the ground undulated in great waves. The waves hurled him onto his side, onto his back, from where he stared upward into the blinding, brilliant lightning. The travail of the earth exploded without end, throwing forth its terrible mixture of noise.

As he fought his way back to hands and feet, he saw trees wave together, lace their branches, remain locked. He saw one tree riven, split down the middle, its upper branches still laced into those of another tree.

The ground beneath him roiled. He fell to his belly, his breath knocked away. He labored back to his crawl, moiled toward the tilted, screaming house. Now a snatch of air returned to his lungs, as piercing as a hot needle, sending pain everywhere. He forced the breath out, pulled in another.

It was then he realized that the wavelike undulations of the ground had been steadily increasing until now they reached a fearful height. Instinctively he tried to veer, to change direction, but instantly the ground ahead, off to his left, burst and a volume of water rose in a geyser as high as the tops of the trees. Offshoots of this vast fountain sprayed over him in tiny, shooting fountains no bigger than a woman's finger, soaking him with water and fine and sodden sand.

He crept toward his moving house, toward its screams, aware that the erupting earth had left a chasm between it and himself. He felt sand under his hands now, wet and hard and thick, blanketing his fertile soil.

The screams were louder, torn and ragged. He pushed to his feet, fighting the heaving of the earth.

A massive figure filled the doorway of the house. "Jason! *Ja-son!*"

And in a sudden split instant of quiet he could hear and be heard. "The baby!" he roared. "Get the baby!"

"No!" Massie Ann shrieked. "You come inside . . . come in here where you belong!"

The earth thundered. The sky flashed. The ground slammed him mightily.

When he could see again, get to his feet in a crouch, the doorway was empty. She might be anywhere, cowering on the bunk, half under the table, unconscious on the floor. The baby could have been thrown from his cradle, some heavy bench crushing his small body.

Somehow he staggered toward the house, squinting against the lightning, defying the roaring, rolling, exploding earth, taking its jolts through legs, body, jaws, teeth. Blessedly, at last, there was the figure in the doorway again, shrieking, and it was holding the bundle that was his son.

"I'm coming!" he yelled.

And then the earth sundered itself, broke suddenly

and deeply all around the house, stood within walls of hissing, geysering soil and water higher than the roof, high as the trees. It opened its great, vicious mouth for the house, for the screaming woman and her bundle. An open chasm fell suddenly in front of the gallery.

"Throw him!" roared Jason. "Throw him to me!"

She shrieked on, sinking with the house as it wafted crazily toward the earth's ravening mouth.

"You damn fool!" Jason roared, his voice rending his ears, riding above the sounds of the clamoring earth. "Throw him, you fool . . . throw him . . . hard. Then jump . . . jump like hell!"

He saw the movement, and then the bundle was hurtling across the widening, deepening chasm. He leapt to meet it, thrusting out his reaching, frantic arms. As the baby landed, thudding against his chest, as his arms tightened and roughly held, as Auguste began to wail in thin, high terror, the earth burst anew and swallowed the house, while Massie Ann stood in the doorway, screaming.

And then the earth burst once again, and Jason, clutching his son, was thrown flat, and water and sand and hard chunks of what felt like pit coal deluged and pelted him.

Chapter 18

Pushing up, the crying infant clutched firmly, he sat witless. He thought of Massie Ann, shrieking in the doorway. The sight of her gulped into the chasm, entombed within the house that once she had loved was engraved in his memory. It can't be, he thought. Things like that don't happen.

Hurriedly, he felt the baby over, and at his touch the wailing quieted into a snuffling mewl, then nothing. "It's all right," he murmured.

It was only then, at sound of his own voice, that he became aware that the awful noises of earth and sky had slackened. And the undulations, which had seemed sometimes perpendicular, sometimes horizontal, had gone into a kind of continuing quiver, so that he got to his feet and found he could walk.

Carrying Auguste, not daring to trust him to any spot of ground, Jason stumbled toward the chasm where his house had stood. He didn't know whether Massie Ann could swim, should the chasm be filled with water. If she could some way have managed to climb onto the roof, she wouldn't drown. Wherever she was, he had to get her out.

There were only distant flashes of lightning now, not enough to see much by. Cautiously he drew to the edge of the chasm, waited for the next flash, and by its light he saw deep, rushing water below.

His breath thickened, stood in his chest as he waited again for lightning. It was long in coming, and when it did, there was only the glint of plunging water. No roof, no door, or scrap of log.

"Massie Ann!" he yelled into the sucking, racing abyss. "Massie Ann!"

The only answer was the run and suck of water. It sounded as if it was dashing headlong away from here, making for the river. But that couldn't be, unless the earth had split a new river from his land to the Mississippi. But then, wouldn't the water be running this way from the river? Suddenly he thought that tides would have something to do with it. Next he wondered if he'd gone out of his head, thinking of new rivers.

"Massie Ann!" he bellowed, and the ground beneath him quivered, but he kept bellowing her name. He walked the edge of the shivering chasm, calling and roaring, disregarding the renewed shrieks of the baby and the sobs that tore his small body.

He staggered back and forth, the earth rocking more strongly now, searching the shore of the chasm, calling her name, peering and looking, for how long, moments or hours, he knew not nor cared. There was no other place to go, to hunt for her. There was only this spot, where she had been engulfed.

He didn't know anybody else was there until the hand clamped onto his shoulder and spun him around. "God a'mighty, man!" yelled a voice, and it was Sam. "You lost yer mind?"

"He ain't that kind," said Tench's voice. "Jason ain't the kind to go crazy. Give him a chance to tell what happened."

"Let me have the baby," Medary's voice said, and her hand came to his arm, restraining him at its mere touch when he would have jerked away and returned to his staggering search. He let her take over, and as his son left his arms a wave of enormous weariness swept him. The thought fled through him how, only yesterday life had been so sure, so settled.

"Massie Ann," he said. "She was in the doorway. She threw the baby to me. But before she could—the house went down."

"Oh, Jason!" Medary cried, and the baby's wailing, which had lessened, grew. "There," she murmured to Auguste, "little boy . . . it's all right . . . there . . . there . . ."

"My God in heaven!" Sam swore. "You ain't got no answer from yer callin'?"

"None."

"We've got lanterns," Tench said, and Jason realized that he was, indeed, able to see their taut faces. "Medary, you sit yonder in the open while we shine the light and see what's there. Don't go near the trees. Now, Jason, show us where your house went down. I can't figure out, the way its torn up, exactly how it stood."

Jason led along the edge of the chasm. "How did you happen to come?" he asked, dazed.

"We left the dance right after you did. We'd taken lanterns to light our way. The dance was still going when we left . . . no telling what's happened back there. The quake caught us just as we came to my place, but somehow we managed not to get hurt. My cabin's wrecked, logs laying all over, but my shed where our supplies are, and yours, is standing. And our cow's there, bawling her head off, but no legs broken or anything. We ain't been to Sam's yet, came over here first as it was nearest and you have the baby."

Sam was following at their heels. "First quake ever to hit here," he said. "Feller told me one day they felt a little shake in the past, but wasn't ever nothin' like this. This was the real shakes."

Jason came to a halt. "I was standing here," he said. "The door was straight in front of me. As far as

I could tell, the house sank down sideways, after sliding a little, which would put it right along here."

They shone their lanterns, and there was nothing to be seen of the house, no projecting edge of log, not even a loose shingle riding the swirling water. There was no way down to the water, the walls of the chasm being sheer.

"I don't see no place where she might of caught hold of anything, a tree root, even," Sam said.

"I'll dive," Jason said and tensed to spring.

"God a'mighty!" Sam yanked him back, held him. "You *are* crazy! That's a whirlpool down there, man! Even a fish'd be sucked out and into the Mississap! If she ain't managed to git out, she's . . . you kin see fer yerself how fast that current is!"

"She might be caught on something," Jason argued. He jerked free of Sam, moved to the edge, looked over again, trying to decide where the front door might be. She might be clinging to the side of the door, even now, catching a breath of air now and again.

Tench grabbed his shoulder, held. "Calm yourself, Jason. Diving in there won't help her. Her only chance was getting out somehow on her own."

"How could she?" Jason asked wildly.

"That water's making for the river fast as it can go," Tench said reasonably. "You can depend on that—the quake has split a channel clear to the river. Which means the quake must have made the river turn on itself, made it flow upstream!"

"Yer right, Tench!" grated Sam. "Damn to hell if you ain't! The goddamned Mississap's turned on itself at last! Yer wife and yer house's both in the river now, unless somebody seen her and pulled her out, you might's well face it, Jase!"

Jason knew they were right. Massie Ann had either miraculously got to safety on her own, or she was dead. It would do no good to dive into this dark, rushing current. It was going to take a search of the territory through which this tide was pushing its way to the river. God willing, he'd find Massie Ann with townfolk who had befriended her.

It was on the heels of this thought that he remembered, with a great sweep of regret, how he had sworn at her in the last moment. "Damn fool!" he had bellowed. "Throw him, you fool!" If she had gone to her death, it had been with his curse ringing in her ears.

"I've got to find her," he said to the others as they clustered on the moving, ravaged earth.

"You will, Jason," Medary said. "If she's to be found, we'll help, and others will help."

They shone the lanterns a last time along the edge of the chasm. It was then Sam spied the moccasin, just a bit of it protruding from the sand, and pulled it forth. He passed it to Jason, who studied it, holding it close to one of the lanterns.

"It's one of her new ones," he said. "She wore them to the ball. Maybe she'd taken them off already."

She could even have walked home barefoot to save the moccasins and accidentally dropped them before going inside. He hadn't noticed, and now regretted that he hadn't.

He shoved the moccasin into his pocket and turned away from the chasm. The four of them walked together to Sam's place, the earth trembling threateningly under them. Here both cabin and storage shed were flat. Only the lodge in which Sam and Yellow Flower had first lived remained.

A figure emerged from darkness, silent as darkness. A quiet voice, which betrayed only a hint of strain, said, "Sam."

"Yeller Flower," Sam said. "Yer all right, then."

"Thank you, Sam."

"I brought my friends. Medary kin use help with the baby."

"Ma'am," Yellow Flower murmured.

"Call me Medary," Jason heard his friend's wife say softly. "And forgive me that I waited . . . for this . . . before I came to you."

Yellow Flower took the lantern Sam handed her, and the two of them settled themselves away from both trees and lodge with the baby. The men waited in silence for the dawn, for the time when they could begin their search. For when they could find out what had happened to others.

Chapter 19

But the dawn that followed the night of terror brought no solace. Shock followed shock. Jason's party huddled in the open, away from the lodge, away from the trees. Sometimes Medary held the screaming baby to feed him with a cloth dipped in milk from the cow they'd managed to bring over, but most of the time Jason held his son against his chest and, with the others, endured.

A dense black cloud of vapor overshadowed the land. It hovered, a vast and somber threatening cover, seeming to hold the devastation which rocked the earth close to its surface, to bear down and make it worse.

There was no chance to leave Sam's land to search. When one of them so much as crossed the few steps to milk the cow, he was thrown to the ground more times than not. The cow herself lay flat, standing only to be milked, and then protestingly.

Later, they were to learn of the scenes of horror in the deep forests where some of the inhabitants had fled in darkest night. Trees about them slashed mightily, split and lashed their great branches fast together over great tracts, inclining in every direction and at every angle to the earth and the horizon. The undulating waves of the earth built in elevation as they advanced, and when they reached a certain height, the earth burst with its own terrible noise in the midst of the quaking underground thunder and the lightning, which seemed to come from below the horizon, and spewed forth vast volumes of water and sand and pitcoal which shot, hissing, as high as the tallest trees. Cabins crumbled, the ground sank, and chasms were formed which swallowed away not only men and animals but houses, even as had happened with Massie Ann.

Large lakes, twenty miles long, were made in an hour, and other lakes were drained. The whole country, to the mouth of the Ohio in one direction, and to the St. Francis in the other, encompassing a front of three hundred miles, was convulsed to such a degree as to create all the lakes and islands, the number of which was unbelievable, and to cover many miles with water three feet deep. When the water left, a stratum of sand of the same thickness was left in places, smothering the soil so that nothing could grow.

The birds lost all power to fly, and came near camps of men for protection. Cattle sought open land, and when the ground convulsed, it threw them into confusion, and they ran about bellowing and bawling. The deer and other beasts of the forests, equally shocked and terrified, would stop suddenly and stand as if fastened to the spot.

A few persons, fleeing from the shakes, sank in the chasms and were rescued. One person died of fright, and one died miserably on an island which kept its original level in the midst of a wide lake left by the quake.

A bursting of the earth just below New Madrid arrested the current of the Mississippi, the river itself becoming a victim of the elemental strife, so that it was driven back toward its source, its very bed elevated by the inner travail of the earth. The vast reflex of its waves sent the river flowing upstream in such manner that, in a little time, a great number of boats were swept by the ascending current into the mouth of the bayou, were carried out and left upon the dry earth, where the accumulating waters of the river had again changed the current.

But though Jason and his party and all other humans, all birds and beasts, crouched upon the undulating, erupting earth, the river would not remain in its course. Now its accumulated waters came booming on and, overtopping the barrier so suddenly raised, carried everything before it with restless power.

Between shocks, Jason and the others scrambled to their feet. But they did not venture away from Sam's place, for the convulsions came not more than an hour apart, and there was no hope of search. During the lulls, they saw people skittering from one point to another, but the only person who came to them was Yellow Flower's cousin, Young Bull, who reported that the Delaware village was partly devastated but no one was dead, and then returned to it as swiftly as he had come. The others didn't so much as look toward Jason's group, so intent were they on finding safety where there was none.

It was after one particularly vicious shock, when Jason and the rest had just pulled themselves into sitting position, that Yellow Flower said quietly, "Somebody comes."

Jason surrendered the baby to Medary and stood, bracing himself for any new tremor. Sam and Tench got to their feet too, and the three of them stood looking toward the north.

Two men were approaching, side by side, square-built and brawny, striding hard, as if in defiance of the treacherous ground below. Their heads were down and forward, as though they were walking into a strong wind.

"God a'mighty!" swore Sam. "It's old man Cremer and that boy of his! How in hell did they ever git this far from their place?"

"The German in them," Tench said. "Let a German set his mind, and nothing's going to stop him."

Jason moved cautiously forward to meet Massie

Ann's father and brother, the horror of what had befallen her descending upon him anew. Tench and Sam moved with him, so they were three abreast when they came face to face with the Cremer men, both of whom were scowling.

"Zo," Cremer grunted. "Du nicht tot?"

"No," Jason admitted heavily. "Not dead."

"Vhy du nicht come help dein vhife's people? Wir hab' kein grub."

Jason looked from Cremer's scowl into that of Fred's, steeling himself to tell them about Massie Ann. Young Fred's eyes were hard and probing.

"Where's my sister?" he demanded.

Jason told them, bluntly, quietly.

They were stricken silent.

"When the shakes let up," Jason said, "we're going to form a search party."

"Vhy?" growled Cremer. "Ein minute du say mein tochter is gone into der ground und der hole ist full mit vater, und next du say du vill search. Du bist ein fool to go on search, mit mein vife und kindern mit nichts to eat."

"There's venison in the shed at my place," Tench said. "Take all you can carry."

"Und how long vill it last?" growled Cremer. "No search . . . ve hunt und fish . . . ve get grub for der living, not search for der tot!"

"We'll manage both," Jason replied. "Is your cabin standing?"

"One room," Fred replied. "Everything else is gone."

Cremer turned and began to slog toward Tench's land. Fred hung back.

"Why didn't you get Massie Ann out of the cabin?" he demanded. "You got the boy, why not her?"

Jason described how there had scarcely been time for Massie Ann to throw Auguste to him. He related how he himself had been slammed to the ground and how, once he'd gotten to hands and feet, the house had disappeared.

Fred's scowl deepened. His fair brows made a wide, bushy vee.

"It's your fault," he said angrily. "If it wasn't for you thinkin' of the boy instead of my sister, she'd be standing here now. You can always get another baby. There wasn't but one Massie Ann! But I'll find her, and when I do, I'll get the truth. You tried to kill her, that's what you done! You was tired of her and you seen your chance to get free!"

"God's sake, feller!" roared Sam. "Jase's bin through hell . . . he 'us huntin' fer her like a madman when we found him!"

"Shut up, Sam!" Jason heard himself say. "This is my mess, and I'm going to take care of it!" He turned on young Fred. "I'm heading up the search party, understand that. You can come along, it's your right to come along. But Massie Ann's my wife, and I'll run this search, not you!"

Fred glowered, his face reddening, darkening. His eyes were like streaks of dirty ice. His mouth went into a sneer.

"I'll be along," he snarled. "I'll be right in front, to see you don't strangle her when we do find her!" He turned and went stomping after his father.

Chapter 20

Tremors continued on subsequent days, though for hours at a time the land lay quiet. During these periods, Jason and Tench and Sam, along with two sturdy young men who had approached their camp, searched for Massie Ann. These young men, Isaac Melon and André Poiriere, volunteered to fetch Fred from the Cremer cabin.

Fred moved into their camp for the search. He accompanied them doggedly, snarling when spoken to, but he was unremitting in his quest, plunging into the wildest bits of woods covered with water to probe and sometimes dive.

"She won't be in the woods," Tench reasoned as they made their way out of a particularly wild stretch of fallen trees, of entangled trees firmly lashed together at the top. "She'd make for houses, people."

"If she ain't dead," Fred snarled, face surly. "If she ain't been kilt and throwed in the water. If she has been, I aim to see fer myself."

No one responded. Jason wondered at Fred's attitude. Had he loved his sister so deeply? he wondered. Or was it the German tenacity of which Tench had spoken, the stubborn determination to grind through whatever he must to prove himself right?

Day followed weary day, filled with unrewarding search, with tremors which rocked the land, with utter weariness. Sitting together nights at their campfire, they talked.

Isaac Melon, eighteen and stocky and tireless, was almost as talkative as Sam. It was he who gave them word of how it had been in the woods during the first tremor the night of the ball.

"André here and me was in the forest at the time, spendin' the night to hunt at first dawn," he recounted. "When the earth was rocking under me, and the tallest trees waving like spars on the stormy ocean, my knees hit together and gave way, and I found myself on them, praying. André yelled, 'Sacré Dieu! Gardez-vous les branches!' And dried limbs from a tree crashed down and we saved our skins by running, or half falling away from there, with the earth still rocking under us and trying to slam us to its bosom!"

Another day came and another, and still they searched, fanning out, each pair taking a specified area, Jason paired with Fred to spare the others the young German's surly behavior. They searched everywhere, stopped at cabins and houses still standing and at camps of people in the open and inquired. No one had seen Massie Ann or a dead body which resembled the description the searchers gave. Every person to whom they spoke was frightened, and many of them were packing what they could salvage, intent on leaving New Madrid for some other place, anyplace where they'd be out of reach of the shakes.

"Where the land won't swallow us up like it done your woman," one thin bent man told Jason. He went on to relate talk he'd heard as to the future of the village. "They say," he said, "that with so much property destroyed, with so much devastation, and the value of what's been lost so great, Congress'll be forced to do something about it."

"What will Congress do?" Jason asked. His own land

and Tench's were not only riven but covered with sand, never to be worked again.

"They say Congress'll pass a law granting to each proprietor whose land was destroyed a section of land somewhere else . . . maybe the Boone-Lick country. The ruined land'll likely be give up to the government, though what it can do with fissures six and seven hundred feet long, and three to four feet of sand on it, nobody can explain."

"There'll be swindles on the heels of that," Tench predicted that night when Jason told of his conversation at the campfire. "Land speculators will come in."

"Why in hell'd they want to do that?" Sam asked.

"Speculators buy cheap. They'll buy up people's rights to Boone-Lick land, watch and see," Tench replied.

"I'd sell mine," Sam declared. "Jest give me the chance!"

While the men went on their search, Yellow Flower put up another, larger lodge to shelter the men. Medary tended the baby, nursing him through the slight cold he'd caught, and, when he slept, salvaged what she could from the wreckage of the two cabins. Sam and Tench had already dug out their rifles and ammunition, but she found additional powder and shot and dried it. She found her iron coffeepot, two iron cooking pots, wooden trenchers and spoons, a knife with a long sharp blade and four of her mother's silver teaspoons. She found also three woolen blankets, washed and dried them and part of her own clothing, which she also washed, tearing some of it into clouts for the baby. There was an ax in the untouched shed, and Yellow Flower had Sam's ax, which he had dug out when he retrieved his rifle.

The days crept on, through Christmas and beyond, and still the men found no trace of Massie Ann. Azor and Annette Davis were safe, their house only slightly damaged. The shocks returned frequently, as they were to do for the next two months. They threw down chimneys, shattered houses, threw up the earth in

some places, sinking it in others. Water continued to
spout up through the cracks and holes in all directions
as the river convulsed with the land.

No wonder, Jason thought, that a people accustomed
to the quiet of a forest, and the peaceful rolling of the
Mississippi, should now feel terror to a degree just short
of madness. The whole populace seemed to be un-
decided. Those who fled felt there was no safety in
flight, that the earth might gulp them down enroute,
and those who remained feared that their cabins would
sink into some sudden, gaping mouth of the earth,
themselves inside. Among those who left were the
Cremers, all save Fred.

There came an evening when the earth was almost
quiet. Jason and the others were sitting around their
campfire. They had eaten deer and cornbread, had
washed it down with hot coffee, exhausted from still another day of vigorous search. There had been the usual
shakes that day, and they had spent considerable time
looking for life and limb in addition to searching.

"We bin lookin' fer two weeks now, Jase," Sam said.
"And we ain't had no luck. None."

"Luck," came Fred's growl, "ain't in it. Work is what
it takes."

"Call it what you want," retorted Sam. "Except fer
that moccasin, they ain't been a sign. We ain't found
a trace of her nowhere's—around Jase's place, or down
that new stream to the river, or along the river no-
wheres. We ain't found her alive, and we ain't found
her dead. Or nobody that's seen hide nor hair of her."

"That don't prove she ain't somewhere, scared to
death."

"Jase, you tell him . . . damn it to hell, tell him!"

"I don't know what to say," Jason responded. "I
don't know what to think. Or where else to look, or
what to do."

"Keep lookin', that's what!" snarled Fred. "Look
where the house was at, look along the stream, go
downriver and look, go upriver."

"We've done all that," Tench pointed out. "A dozen times we've covered that ground."

"Seventeen times," Medary said quietly. "I've counted them, minute by minute, praying you'd all get back, that you'd all be alive."

"We was all right," Fred grunted. "It's Massie Ann's havin' the trouble, the danger. Seventeen times ain't no times at all. We got to keep goin' until we find her."

"We'll find her dead if we find her at all," Isaac Melon said. "Use your head, man. She ain't alive, can't be, or we'd have found some trace of her by now."

"Isaac's right," André Poiriere put in, his deep, keen voice matching his dark-skinned wiry build. "But if you want it, Jase, I'll keep searching."

"Well, Jase?" Sam prodded.

Silence engulfed them. Jason recognized that the moment of decision had come, that all the responsibility lay upon him. It was for him to say, here and now, whether to continue the search or to tackle the future. They were nine souls, one of them his helpless son, in need of a future. Above all, he had to make life safe for Auguste.

"You've done for me all a man could want friends to do, and beyond," he said, choosing his words, intent on speaking truth. "You've looked for Massie Ann when there was hope, and then, when you'd come to feel and know there couldn't be hope, you kept on searching. You've faced truth . . . now I'm facing it. I'm calling off the search. And giving you my deepest gratitude."

"Damn you, Blood, damn you!" shouted Fred. "You want to be rid of her! You don't want to find her, you ain't wanted to!"

Jason made no reply. He had wanted to find Massie Ann, to quiet her terror, to bring her to safety. He had wanted to put their son back into her arms, to go on with their lives.

"We got to plan," Sam urged. "I'm fer gittin' out of here fast and goin' up the Missoura! I'm goin' to git me them eight hundred acres fer forty dollars! How 'bout the rest of you fellers?"

"I'm for it," Isaac said instantly.

"And me," André agreed.

"Where do we get the forty dollars?" Tench asked.

"I've got it all figgered," Sam replied excitedly. "We go up to St. Louis and stay till we git the money."

"How do we get it?" Isaac asked. "Do they pay big wages there?"

"We trap," Sam said quickly. "We barter peltries fer the truck we need fer the trip and after, and the forty dollars. Likely we won't have to pay the entire forty to start, but kin git our land and pay it off whilst we trap and raise crops."

"Traps cost," Jason offered. "You and Tench dug yours out, but the rest of us haven't got any."

"Won't take long, all of us workin'," Sam urged. "We'll all of us git traps, helpin' each other."

"How do we get to St. Louis?" Tench asked. "We can't work our way by boat because the boats aren't running yet. And we haven't got horses or anything to trade for them."

"I got that figgered, too," Sam replied. "They's boats aplenty wrecked, and nobody to claim 'em. Tench, bein' a boatbuilder, kin head us up fixin' one of 'em fer our use. We kin sure as hell bullwhack up to St. Louis. We kin take the cow fer milk fer the youngun, and take our supplies, and we kin hunt fer game once we git a little ways from the shakes."

Jason swiftly considered Sam's plan. It sounded impossible, but to stay here at the mercy of the earth was even more impossible.

"You're out of your mind!" rumbled Fred. "It's four hundred miles! Nobody can fight that crazy current like it is now!"

"It's two hunderd and forty-one river miles," Sam retorted. "I looked into it, before these goddamned shakes begun. I talked to keelers on the way down the Ohio. They said you kin average fifteen miles a day upstream with sail and poles and all."

"That's with a full crew," Jason reminded.

"Hell. Well, say ten miles a day, Jase . . . even five.

I'm tellin' you we'll make it in anyhow six weeks. Even allowin' fer the way the damned river loops and curlicues around so's you have to travel mebbe fifty miles to make five. What you say, Tench? Yer the one's got to boss fixin' the boat."

"I don't see any other choice," Tench replied thoughtfully. "We ain't bettering ourselves here. But Medary," he said, turning to her in the firelight, "I'll give no answer without hearing from you."

"It's our chance," she said. "We have to take it."

"Jase?" pressed Sam.

"I'll go along."

"You young fellers, you ain't changed yer mind?"

Isaac and André shook their heads, grinning.

"Fred?" Sam asked.

"I won't have no part of it," the young German snarled. "I'm huntin' for my sister until I find her!"

"You can't find her," Jason reasoned. "She's gone, she's lost. Your pa's gone now, you don't know where. If you throw in with us, you'll be with friends."

Fred snorted. "You're fools . . . brainless fools! I wouldn't throw in with you if you was the last people alive!"

Chapter 21

Fred, sullen and angry, left at dawn, carrying his rifle and a packet of food Medary had readied. Without so much as a grunt in farewell, he went striding away in the direction of the river.

"It's my bet he'll go down towards New Orleens," Sam predicted. "He's too pigheaded to admit she could've as easy bin swept upriver when the current reversed itself."

"Well, he can't go but one way at a time," Tench said. "We can watch as we go upriver, slow as we'll be going."

Jason frowned. No matter how much looking they might do, Massie Ann had been doomed when the house sank. He'd seen it, he'd known from the beginning, yet had searched and called without letup. There came a time when a man had to accept that what he wanted was hopeless.

"Where did you see that boat you mentioned yesterday?" he asked Sam now.

"Near the Davis house," Sam replied, his voice bright. "Azor Davis says it was abandoned and the fellers went downriver on some stray boat or other. Azor give us a in-vite again to move in with them, but I told him again that we all want to stay in a bunch. The boat's a small barge, and don't look to me like it'll take too damn much fixin'. You got to judge that, Tench. Let's take a look, and if you say the word we kin git right to work. In fact, I say let's make Tench the leader fer the whole undertakin', him bein' the oldest one of us and havin' the most experience with boats."

The others expressed agreement, and Tench accepted the responsibility in his quiet manner. "Since it's up to me," he said, "I'd like you two young fellows—Isaac and André—to stay here at camp whilst the rest of us go to look at the boat. It ain't wise, as I see it, to leave the women alone, now that we don't have to."

The younger men looked disappointed, but agreed to stay.

Tench turned to Sam. "Maybe you can ask Yellow Flower to build a small lodge for supplies and equipment. We can move the stuff over from my shed before dark."

"Wouldn't it save our walkin' time," Sam asked, "if she was to build new lodges down on the river? Give us extry time on the boat job, time we'd otherwise spend fightin' our way ag'in the shakes atween here and the boat."

Tench considered, shook his head. "There's the danger of the riverbank caving in. It's been dropping into the river, taking houses."

Tench was right, Jason thought, but said nothing. He felt it wasn't right for him to enter into a conversation which involved Sam's suggestion to Tench. Now, he saw, Sam was nodding, a look of admiration for Tench on his face. Thus it was decided, and the three friends set out for the riverfront.

The craft was a small barge. Like a flatboat, it was broad and square at the ends, but it was raked forward, fore and aft. It was wider than a keelboat, about twelve feet across, but only about thirty feet long. There was a mast forward, broken near the top, and it had been rigged with a square sail which now hung in mud-streaked shreds. The steering rudder was broken and the oars missing. The small cabin at the stern was fitted with portholes and casements with sliding shutters, broken, mud-streaked and water-soaked. There was a small deck at the prow with a sort of forecastle under it to shelter the crew at night. On this barge, the rowers sat at the prow. Here also was room for an iron cooking grate, and here game shot during the voyage would be hung, along with the two sides of venison they would bring aboard. As on the keelboats, a cleated footway ran around the gunwales.

Tench gave the broken mast and rudder only a passing glance. "This is to be expected," he said. "It's the keel and the hull I'm concerned about. If she'll float, and we can patch her so she'll keep out water, we're on our way."

He went over the boat carefully, examining seams, looking for any weakness. Jason and Sam looked at every inch too, hope building warily. Finally, Tench said he believed the barge would serve their purpose, and they set out immediately to salvage needed materials from other abandoned craft.

The next ten days were filled with work on the barge, with trips between barge and camp, and with the repeated tremors which convulsed the land. These were not as violent as the first quake had been, and did only slight damage to their boat repair, but the ground continued to burst open, with geysers of water and sand spearing skyward, houses continued to fall, and inhabitants and wildlife alike lived in a state of terror. More and more families streamed out of New Madrid on horseback, bound for they knew not where, just away, as far away from the battered river village and its environs as they could get.

Jason applied to village officials and received a document declaring Massie Ann dead by reason of earthquake. One night he gave the document to Medary for safekeeping, and felt the act was, in a way, a burial rite.

That same night a tremor struck, and Jason lay on the ground away from trees and lodges, holding Auguste to him. The others lay around him, and together they endured the onslaught.

The western sky was brilliant with lightning. It was as if a sheet of lightning had been pulled upward and was held without wavering over all the sky, so continued was the vivid flashing. Repeated peals of subterranean thunder boomed and crashed together in a continuous roar. The earth rocked, more chasms opened in the village and in the countryside. The chasms ran from southwest to northeast, occurring at intervals of less than half a mile, and it was while appreciating this utter devastation that Jason became as anxious as Sam to leave it.

He told Sam how he now felt.

"Fine," Sam declared. "Now next thing you need is to git yerself a Delaware girl. You need her fer the youngun. Yeller Flower kin find you one, mebbe she's got a sister. She's goin' to the Injun village afore we shove off. Want her to bring you one?"

Jason smiled, but soberly. Sam meant well, but it was too soon to think of another woman. Though he felt no grief over losing Massie Ann, there was deep regret, and he had no desire to replace her.

"Thanks, but no, Sam," he said. "Medary counts it a favor to take care of Auguste until we go up the Missouri, and by the time we do go, I'll work out something. He'll be older, and I can take care of him myself, likely."

"Well," Sam said energetically, "let's stir up the others and git along to our barge! The faster we work, the sooner we kin git out'n this hellhole!"

Chapter 22

Dawn, that January day, was damp and icy under a northwest wind. The wind swept the village, chilled the inhabitants gathered at the waterfront to see the barge shove off. The wind blew across the deck of the barge, tore at the crew, at the furled sail, buffeted the tethered cow, and made its way into the cabin where traps, rifles, and supplies were stored, and where Yellow Flower sat with the baby. Medary stood on deck waving to those ashore, the wind whipping her skirts fiercely around her ankles.

Jason stood forward at the port, setting pole "tossed." Tench, as patroon, straddled the rudder atop the cabin, his reddened hands on the oar. Isaac and André were ready on the port side, poles "tossed" for action.

Sam, ashore, threw the chain onto the deck with a clatter, then jumped aboard.

"Set poles!" Tench called, his breath condensing in the air. "Back her!"

Jason, Isaac, and André gave a slow, forceful push.

"Set poles!" Tench sang out again. "Back her!"

Now Sam had grabbed a pole, and the four of them shoved to Tench's rhythmic call. The water between barge and shore became a strip of gray, grew, widened. With ponderous slowness, the craft began to swing around.

"Head two!" Tench sang. Jason and Sam sank poles to the bottom of the river. Tench called, "Down on her!" Jason thrust the button of his pole against the thick pad on his shoulder, then leaned forward and crept aft on hands and toes the slow and tortuous length of the gangway. Sam, Isaac, and André did the same. Jason felt the tense and pull of muscle, let it bear and push and strain, for he was, by his own strength and that of his friends, leaving the treacherous earth of New Madrid and making his way into the future.

"Up behind!" sang out Tench, as André and Isaac reached the end of the gangway. Now Jason and Sam leaned doggedly into their creep, taking all the load, as the two young fellows raced forward on the running boards to recommence the slow creep aft.

Suddenly Tench shouted, "Up sail!"

Jason and Sam leapt to the mast. Hands numb, Jason fumbled with the rope, getting it loose. Sam worked too, and now the wind grabbed at the canvas.

Isaac and André steadied the barge with their poles. Tench was hard on the rudder to hold.

With a great snap, the wind filled the canvas so that it stood full and beautiful. The barge began to move upstream, driven by the blessed power of the cold and relentless wind.

From shore came cheers. Jason gave one last look at those he would never see again. Azor and Annette Davis were there, had brought gifts—Azor's rifle for Jason, which meant that every man on the barge was now armed, and needles and scissors and thread for Medary.

Jason regretted leaving them, regretted too that John Denoyer had decided against bringing his wife and sturdy seventeen-year-old twin sons on the voyage. They could have used three more crewmen, and there would have been room in the cabin for Mrs. Denoyer.

But yesterday evening, when Denoyer had helped get

the cow aboard, he still hadn't reconsidered. "I keep backing off," he had said, "can't help it. I admire the guts the rest of you've got, but looking at it the way I do, it'd be foolhardy to join up."

"It's not so much guts with us," Tench had replied. "There's nothing else we can do, is the way we see it."

Isaac and André had tried and failed to locate even one more young fellow who would risk the trip. All the men under twenty had families who objected, or were needed to help at home, and those over twenty were married and had young children. So their crew remained at five men.

Now, at Tench's shout, Jason turned to his pole to help maneuver the barge around a bend, to keep it off the shallows. He put all his strength to his pole.

The crookedness of the Mississippi between St. Louis and New Orleans, made long detours necessary. It was said that the number of times a boat was compelled to cross the river in the ascent from New Orleans to St. Louis was three hundred and ninety. In ascending a bend as they were now doing, Tench observed the accepted upstream travel practice. He avoided the concave side of the stream for the double purpose of escaping the force of the current and the peril of caving banks. Instead he followed close to the convex bank of the bend.

The wind continued all that day. It filled the sail, sent the barge upstream at a rate Tench estimated to be five miles an hour. They saw no other craft, except for an occasional fisherman in a pirogue. They observed and bemoaned the continuing evidence of the havoc wrought by the earthquake.

"Whoops!" shouted Sam once as they shot suddenly faster upstream. "Mannees, effen the wind'll stay behind us, we ain't got a worry! We must of bin livin' right to come out'n the shakes and git the wind at our backs, both!"

"Wind veers," Tench said.

"Sure she veers!" whooped Sam. "But she's goin' to veer our way! Time comes to tie up fer the night, we'll be crackin' our heels together! If she keeps up, we'd best travel all night!"

Tench grinned, shook his head. "Come evening, we tie up," he said. "I'm not about to try going upriver in the dark."

The wind did veer in the afternoon, and in their favor after they'd made a loop. The shore slid steadily past and the day warmed under the sun and the south-westerly wind, so that Medary bundled Auguste up and brought him on deck. His face broke into a smile when he saw Jason, and Jason laughed aloud to see his son.

They tied up well away from any timber which might conceal Indians. Tench assigned chores to each—locating drinking water, tending and milking the cow, cooking and washing up. He assigned each man a time to stand watch during the night.

"You forgot sewing and mending, Tench," Medary said teasingly. "I'll take that over."

"Now, just a minute," Tench said. "You've got Auguste and taking care of the milk. You ain't to work yourself into a decline."

She laughed, and her freckled mask tilted a bit. "I feel fine!" she declared. "One day on the river, and already I'm beginning to feel the way I did on the Ohio! Yellow Flower and I are going to help each other, we've no problem. It's you men who are going to be doing real work, don't ever forget that!"

She was sure right about that, Jason thought more than once, when there was time for thought. It seemed like the wind had meant to give them a flying start, then leave the rest of it strictly up to them. For a time, there wasn't enough wind to make it worthwhile to un-furl the sail.

"We can set poles," Tench said the next morning. "The water ain't too deep here."

At this point the current was sluggish, and it was possible for them to push the barge forward with in-finitesimal slowness by setting and lifting poles, never moving from their places. Jason, sore-muscled from yesterday morning's exertion, threw his strength against his pole.

Sometimes the two on the shoreside used poles while, on the outside, the other two men rowed. Once, all four of them pushed on the same side, each one as he came aft lifting his pole and running around the cabin to take his place again at the back of the line.

In this manner, they toiled upstream all morning. During the rare moments when he wasn't poling, creeping, or running to creep again, Jason felt the reluctant glide of the barge under his feet.

The third day there was still no wind. Jason rolled out from under the forecastle. His body was one enormous ache, one deep, wracking soreness. His elbows were stiff, his back felt like a board. Tench came crawling out next, and he moved much as usual, but Sam and André were grimacing and grinning as they appeared. Isaac, who had stood the last watch, eyed them all, himself grinning.

"Some varmint tied me in knots!" declared Sam. "You fellers sore as I am?"

Jason grinned. He wondered why it helped to know that the others were as stiff as he was.

"I'm goin' ter git some water from that spring," Sam announced. "C'mon, Jase. We're in the same boat . . . sore as hell, but got to lug water fer man and cow!"

He was laughing as Yellow Flower hurried from the cabin with four wooden buckets. Before he took them, he put one finger along her cheek, drew it down to her chin. Jason saw the adoring look on the Indian girl, and then Sam took the buckets and the moment ended. Jason held back to take the gurgling, laughing Auguste from Medary for a moment, and then he followed Sam ashore.

"The river's too deep here for setting poles," Tench told them when they were ready to shove off.

"I've had enough polin' fer a spell anyhow," said Isaac. "What you got in mind, patroon?"

"We'll have to cordelle," Tench replied. "André, take one end of the towline and fasten it to the top of the

mast and pass the other end to the crew on shore.
Jason, you fix the bridle. The rest of you can be swimming ashore. Jason, you join them . . . André the same.
All of you take your knives."

The bridle was a short rope which Jason lashed at
one end to the bow and at the other end to a ring
through which the cordelle, or towline, was passed. The
bridle was used to keep the barge from swinging.

As he worked, Jason heard the others splash into
the water and then a thrashing as Isaac headed for
shore. Sam stayed beside the barge, keeping himself
afloat, and when André tossed out the cordelle, put
the end of it between his teeth and swam after Isaac.

Jason knifed into the icy cold river. André was right
behind him, and together they swam the short distance.

Water cloaked Jason as he slogged onto the bank.
Water hung from his clothes, dripped onto his sodden
moccasins. The winter air came through the wetness and
covered his skin, and he braced himself against shivering. The hilt of his knife was icy when he touched it
to make sure it was still in his belt.

"Space out that cordelle!" Tench shouted from atop
the cabin.

Sam took his place nearest the end of the towline,
then, spacing himself carefully, Isaac stood and waited.
André stepped into position next. Jason, last in line,
gauged his distance and stood nearest the water.

"Get a grip on that cordelle!" shouted Tench.

They gripped the rope, lifted, turned upstream so
that it came up over the left shoulder. This cordelle
was shorter than most, for the barge was smaller than
the normal craft, and the crew fewer in number.

Even so, the towline was going to be awkward for
only four men to handle. It must even, at times, Jason
knew, be thrown over a tree before the boat could be
towed another foot. He waited, with the others, the
rope harsh to his calloused palms, its weight on his
shoulder warning of struggle to come.

"Get set . . . ready!" yelled Tench. "Now . . . *pull!*

All at once . . . upstream . . . every man with even
strength . . . pull even . . . pull . . . p-u-l-l."

They leaned forward, straining, barely creeping.

Surely, Jason thought, the rope boring into flesh
and muscle, surely I'm doing all the pulling. I'm nearest to the barge. The heavy, nongiving vessel held back
on the cordelle, snapped it taut, tried to break it. The
muscles in Jason's legs danced as he strained, and he
was certain that he was pulling on the cordelle alone
and unaided.

But then he became aware, eyes downcast, of the
desperate angle of André's legs in front of him. He
grunting breath and knew that André and the others,
saw André's moccasins dig into the earth, heard his
too, were striving as he was.

"Pu-ll together . . . hard . . . harder . . . more!" sing-
songed Tench's prodding, relentless voice. "Pu-ll . . .
upstream . . . there's a cypress . . . stout one . . . not
bent . . . pull to the cypress . . . to the cypress . . . she's
moving . . . p-u-l-l. . . . l"

Jason's muscles were as taut as the cordelle, as hard
and relentless as the damnable, resisting barge. His guts
tightened, went to muscle, and he strained doggedly on.

Faintly he felt the heavy, reluctant glide back there,
the stubborn resistance. He dug his moccasins into
mud, into soil, into dried growth, and he pulled and
strove until he was a quivering, forward-slanting figure
etched on air, nothing but a slant with a rope gouging
it, pulling, ever pulling, that Tench-voice ever-chanting,
ever-prodding, that heavy, reluctant glide slowly, heart-
breakingly slowly, following behind.

Chapter 23

The following day, too, was spent cordelling. Laboriously, painfully, inch by inch, they pulled the barge upstream. And, though the shore was suitable for towing, Jason quickly learned that did not mean they could expect to find a smooth towpath.

On the contrary, they found themselves fighting brush, cutting their way through with their knives. When the growth was impenetrable, they lashed the towline to some stout tree and went ahead to clear a way with axes. With agonizing frequency the cordelle had to be freed from snags or thrown over trees so they could progress another painful few inches.

The day after that, the bottom of the river was too soft for poling, and the shores on both sides unsuitable for cordelling. "We'll have to warp," Tench decided. "André, man the skiff. The rest of you line up—Jason behind me, Sam next, then Isaac. Stand by . . . stand ready."

Jason took his place. He welcomed warping as relief from the merciless labor of the past days. Warping was essentially cordelling in reverse, pulling the craft upstream to the skiff, and, he realized, was itself a hard task. He'd seen it in operation on upriver craft during his keelboat journey to New Madrid.

He watched André send the skiff upstream, the end of the cordelle fastened to its stern. The line lengthened and straightened in the water as the little craft progressed, until it formed a direct line between skiff and barge. At this point, André lashed the towline to a tree alongbank, turned and lifted his arm.

"Get set, men . . . go!" sang out Tench, and began to haul strongly on the rope, hand over hand.

Spraddled and braced, Jason was ready for the first tight, quivering handhold as it came back to him. He hauled with all his strength, knowing his mates were doing the same, until, with torturing slowness, the line moved for him, and Sam was taking it, then, in turn, Isaac. He heaved and strained, forcing taut rope through his hurting palms, feeling it go to Sam, grabbing the next hold from Tench, and he went deeper into struggle with each clutching, monstrous section. Somewhere, in the endless pull and heave and pass, he felt the heavy, recalcitrant forward slide of the barge.

When they had moiled up to the skiff, André caught the mooring chain Jason tossed down. He lashed the chain around the tree, then untied the towline, fastened it at the back of the skiff and started upstream again.

Jason dropped to the deck, watched his mates drop. His breath was hard and short. "It's a bigger job than it looks, warping."

"It's the hardest method of propulsion there is," Tench said. "Bull Hecker told me that, said six miles in a day is good progress when you warp."

"Six . . . hell's bells!" snorted Sam. "Might's well git down on our hands and knees! We got to toughen up more. Git it out'n our hides, Tench . . . put a lash to our goddamned backs!"

"Blow off all you want," Tench replied. "It's the long run that counts, the taking a day at a time, that'll get us there."

Which is what they did. It was all they could do. They sailed, rowed, poled, cordelled, warped, and even bushwhacked. This was most easily practiced in spots where the river was high and the water flowed among the trees at the sides. Each man in turn, commencing at the bow, seized a branch and, holding to it, walked aft. When he reached the stern, he let go the branch, returned to the bow, and repeated the operation. One man kept an oar plying on the river side.

On the average, they made about ten miles a day. The best days were when the wind was right and they could sail. Then they might cover as many as thirty miles. Always, they watched for sign or word of Massie Ann, but saw neither her nor any other person.

It was on a bright day, their sail filled with sun and wind, scuttling along at a swift six miles, no havoc from the earthquake to be seen, that Medary began to sing. She was sitting out of the wind, the sun across her lap, holding a sleepy Auguste.

Her voice was like the wind, light and true, with a kind of rugged sweetness. And Jason recognized, hearing Medary sing to his son, that music was a good thing, and someday, when he got everything all set, he'd buy himself some books to replace those he'd lost, and he'd manage music somehow in his cabin up the Missouri.

Later, the wind dropped, and they had to bushwhack past one of the many small river islands, cross to the right-hand shore, and cordelle toward a bluff which reared up in the distance. It took them three hours to reach the bluff, three miles in three hours, which Tench said was as good as they had any right to expect.

Suddenly a stiff breeze sprang up, the sun hazed over, and a dark cloud began to form swiftly in the southwest. It's going to blow, Jason thought, and watched the cloud, estimating the speed of its wind against the chances of getting the barge across the river into the cove Tench was set on reaching. They'd make it, he thought.

Tench yelled for Sam and Isaac to run up the sail. The barge went quartering across the stream, roughed up by the current, but keeping her head. She was held steady by the wind and was riding lightly for a barge, and answering to the rudder.

The rain came with shocking abruptness. The wind veered suddenly, and before Tench got the rudder shoved far enough, the wind caught the sail and the barge careened. Jason got one glimpse of the cow as she went sliding and bawling across the deck, over the gunwales, and into the river. Then the current was spinning the barge around and downstream, out of control.

Jason ran to the bow. They were near shore. André and Isaac grabbed bushes to hold the barge, and Sam dropped the sail.

"Get a line around a tree!" Tench yelled, fighting the rudder.

Jason made for the stanchion.

As winds buffeted and rain swathed, the men were hard put to hang on to their bushes. They strained, blinded and choked by rain, holding on to the bushes, first pulled by wind and current to arm's length, then pushed hard against the bank.

Jason grabbed rope from the stanchion, looped it. When there was enough, he lashed the end around his waist and waited until the barge was slammed into the bank again. It was then he kicked off, jumped for the streaming, slippery bank.

He grabbed at bushes, slid back into the water, but hung on to a bush and with painful slowness, sliding back a foot for every two feet gained, pulled onto the bank. Once there, he secured the rope around a great oak, then leaned against it, ducking his head to miss the solid falling rain so that he would not drown.

Chapter 24

Not until the storm ended two hours later could they look for the cow. The only thing they could do was huddle under the forecastle and wait. Medary called from the cabin, trying to get them to come inside. But Tench yelled back that they were dripping wet and the cabin should be kept dry.

Afterward the sky remained overcast, with early dusk promising early night. While Tench and the two younger men made repairs to the barge, Jason and Sam started through dripping bush on shore, under dripping trees, working downstream. They peered into the forest to their right, looked into the shallows to their left, kept a sharp eye on the current.

"You don't actually believe yer goin' to find her, do you?" Sam asked after a time. "Why, she 'us throwed off'n the barge really hard. She likely broke her neck even afore she hit water, way she went over that gunwale."

"I've got to try," Jason said.

If the cow was lost, there'd be no milk for Auguste. And none of them had money with which to buy another cow, even if he could find one for sale, which was unlikely.

"Sure, you got to try," Sam agreed. "We got time to go a few miles afore dark. If we don't see her by then, she's bin swept clean away."

It was well after dark when they slogged their way back to the barge. There'd been no sign of the cow. Their companions were sitting on deck rather than around the customary fire ashore, finishing a meal of cornbread and beans.

"Any luck?" Isaac asked as they came aboard.

"Nary hide nor hair," declared Sam. "The cow's gone fer good."

"The only way out that I can see," Jason said, "is to hunt out a settler's cabin every day and trade fish or supplies for milk."

"That sounds reasonable," Tench responded. "Nobody would turn you down, not when it's a baby involved."

But it wasn't reasonable, Jason thought, lying awake, awaiting his assigned nightly watch. Auguste was an infant, life ahead of him, but presently helpless and dependent, that was true. But the others—Tench and Medary, Sam and Yellow Flower, Isaac and André— they had a future too, and were struggling to make their way to it. If they were daily searching for milk, it would keep them on the river longer, increase all the dangers of travel, and could result in their all losing their lives, Auguste included.

After his watch period, Jason fell at last into heavy, uneasy sleep. Every few minutes, it seemed, he roused long enough to remember the lost cow and think about how to feed Auguste, then he fell again into slumber, with everything unresolved.

When he opened his eyes it was to Auguste's vigorous crying. He jumped up, put his knife in his belt, grabbed his rifle. With any luck, he'd have time to find a cabin and, if they had a cow, convince the settler to trade it for his rifle.

"Hold on," Tench said suddenly. "The women have worked out something. Just wait . . . they're letting it cool, and that boy of yours is plenty mad. He don't want to wait."

Jason moved to the cooking spot, where everyone was gathered. "It's cornmeal mush," Medary told him. "He's seven months old now, and I've known of babies having potato soup. If he'll take this, we'll have no worries."

"It makes sense, Jase," Sam put in. "Hell, my ma, she allus said feed the young from the table, and she done it. I've saw her—and they ain't a healthier bunch anywheres than the Janas younguns. She even spoons cooked greens down 'em, makes a big mess, but they like 'em."

Anxiously, Jason watched as Medary moved the spoon to the baby's eager mouth. Auguste took the mush, and his mouth opened again. When the filled spoon wasn't instantly ready, he began to roar and Jason and his friends to grin. Even Yellow Flower, Jason saw, as a shaft of cookfire struck her usually impassive face, was smiling.

Auguste ate greedily, smacking his lips. Jason's anxiety vanished. It was going to be all right after all.

At dawn a fresh wind came up and they hastened to shove off. Sam ran up the sail, it filled with dewy wind, and they went gliding upriver with such ease they were elated.

"This's too good to be true!" Sam exclaimed at midmorning, "Makes me uneasy as hell!"

Jason, sitting at the bow with Sam, saw that the young Pole was honestly troubled. His almost blond eyebrows looked very bushy as he frowned.

"What's come over you?" Jason asked.

"I've bin doin' some thinkin', rememberin' what I've bin told 'bout river travel. I've bin sizin' up what's happened sence we left New Madrid. Ever' time we've had the wind in our favor, it's bin follered by bad luck, all that cordellin' and warpin' and bushwhackin', and then the storm. Injuns is what I'm thinkin' of now that we're away from where the shakes'd keep 'em busy lookin'

out fer their own hides. Next thing, we'll have them
varmints leapin' out'n the woods and shootin' their
arrers, even rifles, at us. They's a good deal of trouble
with Injuns I've bin hearin' of. The English is stirrin'
'em up, some say it'll lead to war with England, even."

"There was the same trouble when we made the trip
down from Pittsburgh," Jason reminded. "You weren't
concerned then, and we didn't have any Indian trouble."

"Which makes it twicet as liable now. We're one boat
alone, and in wilder country. And it's worse at the other
end now—the English keep impressin' American mer-
chant seamen and makin' slaves of 'em. And settlers
keep pourin' into Injun lands, makin' the Injuns madder and madder, and the English are gittin' more in
cahoots with the Injuns so's they'll fight the Americans,
tellin' 'em it's so's they kin git their land back, when
what the English is after is to keep impressin' our
sailors. The wonder is the Injuns ain't already took to
swampin' our craft on the rivers. Them's the lines I'm
thinkin' on, Jase, and it'd behoove you to think like-
wise, and ever'body in this country, fer that matter."

Jason nodded. There was truth in what Sam said.
Jason, too, had heard much about the situation on the
high seas as well as in the West, before he'd left New
York. Hendrik van Delft had kept abreast of what was
going on in the world, and had spoken to Jason on this
matter.

"War, Jason," he had said bitterly. "We're just past
the Revolution, and we're on our way to a new war.
Napoleon—" He had broken off, then murmured, "War.
Men and war. Somehow they match themselves up,
have done it since the beginning."

"Yes, sir," Jason had said, as was required of him.

He knew nothing of war, but war troubled him. It
was wrong for the English to drag American sailors off
American ships and enslave them on their own ships.
It seemed only right that the Americans should resist,
fight back. And it seemed wrong for the English along
the Canadian border to set the Indians against men like

himself who only wanted to build homes and live honorably.

Now Jason found himself watching the shore more closely than before. He told himself that he was on the lookout for some cabin where they might get milk and also ask for Massie Ann, but he knew that beyond that he was alert for any sign of redskins.

The wind continued for some days, intermittently, and they had less cordelling and bushwhacking. Slowly the miles slipped behind as they passed forest, river islands, isolated cabins, then forest again. They asked for Massie Ann at each cabin, to no avail. Each time they got milk for Auguste, and he drank it greedily from a noggin, but still demanded mush. He was growing almost visibly.

At Cairo, where the Ohio entered the Mississippi, the river was five miles wide. The barge was on the western side, across the expanse from the village. Since they had no need of supplies and no way of buying, they decided not to cross over.

They continued upriver, passing a trading post, an occasional cabin. Day followed day, some of them with the sail filled, others spent in cordelling, bushwhacking, and warping. It seemed to Jason he'd never done anything but haul on a towline in one direction or another or drag a barge along by grabbing hold of bushes. By the time they passed Ste. Genevieve, not stopping to ask for Massie Ann, it being too far upriver, but hugging the far shore, his body had hardened until every inch of muscle was like iron. He knew he was in the best trim of his life and took satisfaction in it, knew that not a man on the barge could best him at any one of the grueling tasks involved in getting upstream.

They were above Ste. Genevieve in late evening and were scudding along under sail. They'd run much later than usual because of the wind, and would tie up when they were safely above the long wooded river island they were now passing. They had crossed to the western side after Ste. Genevieve and were between the western shore of the river and the western shore of the island. When they were about even with the middle of the island, a figure suddenly broke out of the trees and ran along, keeping pace with them, shouting and gesturing wildly.

Tench, at the rudder, cupped one hand at his mouth. "What's the trouble?" he shouted.

"Help!" the man screamed. *"Help!"*

He had wild red hair, redder than Medary's. It stood out behind him, and was long, almost to his shoulders. He was a big man, a chunk of power, and he ran in great vigorous leaps.

"Help!" he kept screaming. "My brother . . . my woman . . . *help!"*

"Don't stop!" Sam yelled at Tench. "It's a trick! It's what river pirates do! Pertend to be wrecked and yell fer help, then kill you and take yer boat!"

"Maybe he was running from the earthquake the way we are," cried Medary, who had come on deck when she heard the shouting.

"It'd be him against five of us," Isaac said. "He'd have a hard time. And pirates ain't never been too bad this close to Ste. Genevieve."

"He ain't alone if he's a pirate!" retorted Sam. "He even names a brother and a woman. There's others hid in them woods, and if we're fool enough to put in there to help, they'll come swarmin' . . . mebbe ten, twenty of 'em!"

Tench, though he was keeping the barge on course, continued to watch the red-headed man. He was running desperately now, screaming out his plight again and again.

"There's wood enough he can build himself a raft," Tench said. Again he shouted to the man, "Got an ax?"

"No . . . nothin' . . . stop . . . *help!"*

"André," Tench ordered, "throw him an ax. Give it a good heave."

"Yer jest throwin' away a good ax that we need!" Sam yelled. "The varmint's a pirate, I know it!"

"We'll gamble he needs this much help," Tench said grimly.

André hurled the ax, hard and true. It fell somewhat ahead of the man. When he reached it he didn't pick it up, but stopped and shook both fists at those aboard the barge, screaming curses.

He was still screaming as the barge slid beyond the island and on upstream. Jason wondered if they'd ever know how the fellow made out, if they'd ever know whether he was himself in trouble or had wanted to give them trouble.

They kept running well after dark.

"I know that fellow claimed he was stranded," Tench told them, "but since we've got the wind with us, I mean to put distance between him and us. The more I think about what you said, Sam, and the more I remember how he acted . . . well, I want to leave him far behind."

It was late when they tied up at the western shore. They stayed aboard to eat the stew which Yellow Flower had made while they ran.

"We'll stand a two-hour watch tonight in place of a three-hour one," Tench said after Medary and Yellow Flower had gone into their cabin. "I'll take the first watch, then Sam, then André, then Isaac and last, Jason. That'll put us into dawn."

It was cold in the forecastle as it always was, but Jason wrapped himself in his blanket. He thought, seems like it's just natural to sleep cold, and even as he thought it, he was asleep.

He roused, still three-quarters asleep, when Sam crawled out to take his watch and Tench crawled in to sleep. The same thing happened with André. And when, two hours before dawn, Isaac put his hand on Jason's ankle, he crawled out a full four-fifths asleep to take his turn. He went at a half stagger onto the top of the cabin, rifle in hand, wondering if the cold wind, which was still strong and steady, would wake him or make him sleepier still.

There was a smell of rain, and everything was so

pitch dark he knew the sky had to be hooded with clouds. He peered downstream and could see nothing but blackness, peered upstream and saw blackness. He peered ashore and toward the far bank of the river with the same result. Then he settled himself, eyes probing ceaselessly, ears attuned for the least sound foreign to the normal, instinctively receptive to any shift of the boat that might be different.

The only sound was wind and water lapping against the barge, against the shore. The only thing he could feel was cold from the wind and the rocking sway of the moored barge. Once he imagined he caught the sound of oars pulling through water but, after listening for what must have been half an hour, the sound was not repeated. He had been deceived by the moving river itself. Nevertheless, he remained alert, rifle at hand.

The first sign of change was a sudden dipping at the bow. Even as he came to his feet, rifle aimed instantly at the thicker blackness now at the bow, he found it hard to believe that danger was upon them.

Chapter 25

He pulled the trigger half a heartstroke before he heard the double crack of rifles at the bow. He fell flat on the cabin roof, propped cautiously on one elbow, reloaded.

They were roaring at the bow. He tried to single out one of those dark moving shapes, but then he didn't know which might be foe and which friend, for his mates had surged onto the deck to defend against the attackers. Rifles cracked.

"Medary!" he heard Tench shout. "Lay low!"

Rifle in hand, Jason sprang off the cabin and across deck. He came onto a roaring man in the darkness, knew from the stench that it was none of his companions, yanked his rifle upward in both hands and brought it crashing down on the fellow's head. The blow sounded dull and deep; the man crashed to the deck.

The barge was aswarm with reeling, grappling, grunting, nearly invisible figures. It was alive with gouging, punching, kicking, swinging weapons, swift knives.

Jason bashed into another fetid shape and swung his rifle up, but this time, before he could bring it down,

there was a battery of rifle fire and something pierced
his calf, bored hotly in, leaving numbness. He felt himself sinking, fought it as he held onto his rifle, then
tried to land so he could reload and shoot at the first
opportunity.

There was still no way to tell, from where he was
half sprawled, which moving, shouting form was friend
and which was pirate. They were all roaring, huge, enraged bellows, bawling killer rage as they struggled and
clouted and got off a rifle shot or two. The black, once-
peaceful world of the river had become a frenzy of
killer rage and murdering fervor.

Jason was staring, ready to shoot, when one rifle
flash revealed a face, one second only, one flying second. He didn't really see the face, but he saw the wild
red hair.

Instantly he pulled the trigger, but even as the shot
cracked he knew it had gone wild, that the red-headed
one had, in that split second, charged a bargeman.
Howling, he thudded mightily into that other body,
the impact of his fists only slightly less audible.

The bargeman crashed down, the pirate surged upon
him, there was a heavy splash overboard.

Ears full of that death-heave, beating with waves of
the bloodthirsty uproar, Jason fumbled shot and powder
into his rifle. He swung it up at the form which had to
be the red-headed one, but another form butted into
the pirate, and he dared not pull the trigger. He swung
his aim slowly, trying to probe the night, searching for
a target.

The roaring, weaving, charging figures were all over
the barge now, fighting hand to hand. Jason held down
the impulse to throw himself into the melee, knowing
his leg would crumple and he would only be a hin-
drance.

Two men were locked in furious battle a step away,
but he dared not bring his rifle down onto either head.
Two figures lay inert on deck with the fighting pair
stumbling over and around them.

There were fewer roars, but the night was crammed with shuddering grunt and groaning, furious curses, with the drive of fist against bone, and the dull sound of rock-hard knuckles murderously pounding into flesh.

"Crow!" roared a voice. "Shove 'er off . . . we're takin' the barge . . . dump the bodies!"

Jason whipped up his rifle, pulled trigger at that red-headed bellow. An outraged howl proved he'd hit, but the flood of curses proved the red-head was alive.

Hurriedly, Jason reloaded for a second try, but the figure had moved, was lost among the others, and again he had no way of telling foe from friend. His breath tore in and out, hot with rage. And he wanted to kill, to pull trigger and reload, again and without end until every pirate lay dead.

He couldn't tell whether the pirate named Crow was carrying out the red-head's orders. There was so much movement, such unremitting slugging and struggle, he couldn't pinpoint anything. He tried to make out the spot where the two inert figures had lain.

A pair slugging murderously at each other weaved between himself and that spot, but he waited. Now, beyond them, a figure took shape in the darkness, moved toward the struggling pair. Jason aimed and waited. The fighters suddenly hurtled apart, momentarily revealing that approaching shape which now roared in a voice not familiar to Jason, and he pulled trigger, the sound of his rifle good to his ears. The shape went down without a whisper, dropped onto the other figures.

At the same time, one of a fighting pair atop the cabin fell leadenly into the water and made no further sound, and the two combatants near Jason came together again, one of them falling under the onslaught of the other. The figure remaining on top of the cabin leapt upon the victor an arm's length from Jason. In terrible silence they fought. Murderously they came together, fell apart, closed again, staggering over the pile of fallen men.

As in a nightmare, one of the prone figures struggled up and lunged at the two fighting so near him, and then there was rifle fire and the boat once more was alive with moving, charging figures.

One of them came at Jason, he lifted his rifle, crashed it down, missed the fellow's head, taking him at the back of the neck. He felt for his knife, and it was gone from his belt.

Now, through the uproar, he heard a voice screaming, a woman's voice. "Jason!" she screamed. "The baby . . . he's got the baby!"

He saw the rushing figure, heard the splash on the river side, went charging for the sound, leg buckling. He kept running, forcing the leg to hold him briefly as he leapt for the gunwale and over it.

The icy water closed over him, shutting out the sound of Medary's voice, swallowing the sounds of battle. He surfaced. The tug of the current was powerful, and he swam mightily away from it, toward the stern of the barge. It would take very little time for this pull of the current to draw Auguste into itself and send him hurtling downriver.

He dived, ears roaring, searching the moving depths for the small form. There was no time, none at all. Auguste wouldn't know not to breathe. He stroked mightily again, turning, following toward the current, sending himself faster through the water than he'd ever swum, and it was not fast enough.

"The stern!" he heard Medary scream.

Her scream cut off, he turned again, stroked violently for the stern, feeling, listening.

Right at the hull, his hands touched the small body and he snatched it from the river. Treading water, forcing the leg, he put the child against his shoulder and whacked it firmly, again and repeatedly. If there wasn't too much water in the small lungs, this would knock it out, knock breath into him.

He heard the activity on the barge as he tried to save his son. As from a distance, he heard the blows, the curses, the commands, heard the splash of body after body hit water. He even knew that the barge was moving, was sliding downstream and away, but it made no difference. He wanted only to get Auguste to breathe.

He gave still another whack to the little shoulders, and it was then that the baby breath caught, came out in a strangling whimper, choked. Then a wail lifted, rose in tiny, jagged peaks, subsided. But the next cry was Auguste's own, and filled with terror.

Chapter 26

Jason scarcely noticed the pain in his leg as he swam for shore, so intent was he on keeping Auguste above water. Somewhere off to the left he could hear another swimmer, maybe two, but he didn't spare a moment to wonder who they were.

When his feet came onto mud bottom, he had an instant of relief. The swimming was ended. But now he had to deal with the slippery underfoot and his injured leg. Water streamed from his clothes, pulling at him, and it was that which gave him the idea of crawling, and this was easier, because he could dig his fingers into the mud far enough to get a bit of purchase.

The mud was cold, the night wind icy against his sodden body. He found himself shivering as he crawled upbank, felt the baby shiver, recognized that it was the cold which put the little catching stutter into his wails.

Jason crawled faster. He had to get Auguste away from the river, find a windbreak. Now there was dried growth under him, and he lunged to his feet and made for a clump of darkness that should be trees.

It was trees, and he half staggered, half fell into their shelter. He sank to the ground and leaned against the rough bark of a big trunk. It cut the wind, but Auguste still shivered and wailed.

Now, out in the darkness, someone began to shout. "H-a-l-l-o-o! Who's there . . . Yeller Flower . . . Medary . . . ?"

"Sam!" Jason shouted back. "It's me . . . Jason . . . in the trees!"

Sam came crashing across the dried growth, someone with him, an old stick or so snapping under their tromping feet. They trod heavily up, dropped to the ground, their breath pulling noisily.

"It's Tench and me . . . Sam," the young Pole gasped. "They throwed us overboard, but we come to."

"Medary . . . is Medary here?" Tench asked.

"Nobody," Jason replied. "Just us."

"Them sons of bitches!" grated Sam. "They've took Yeller Flower and Medary downriver!"

Jason's mind reeled. He pulled it back to his immediate concern, which was for Auguste. He plunged the crying infant into Sam's arms. "Hold him a minute," he said.

Quickly, he unfastened his shirt, wiped his chest as dry as he could with his hands, took the baby and started to strip him. All the while, the stuttering wail never ceased.

"What the hell you doin'?" Sam demanded.

"I can't let him be in wet clothes," Jason replied. He began to rub the naked, screaming baby with his palms.

"You think he's goin' to be better off nekkid?" Sam asked.

Jason put the baby against his own bare chest, briskly rubbed the small shoulders and buttocks and legs. Faintly, he could feel a glow of warmth between his hands and the flesh of his son. The wails subsided to fretting.

"Where are Isaac and André?" he asked.

"André was dumped overboard right at the first," Tench said. "Isaac was one of those laying on deck so long . . . they threw him over later."

"The way we was," Sam growled. "Them bastards!"

"They're dead, no doubt about it," Tench said. "But Medary and Yellow Flower aren't."

"We're goin' after them," Sam gritted. "We're goin' to git Medary and Yeller Flower!"

"Sure we are," Tench agreed. "We'll go first to that island where they tried to waylay us. It may be they've got their headquarters there. They must have come up in a skiff, under sail. If they're not on the island, we'll keep on downriver, because that's the only direction they'll go—they'll not try to get the barge upriver."

"We'll run 'em down, wherever they go," Sam declared. "We'll kill ever' son, and any that's laid hand on Yeller Flower, I'll torture, slow and personal, afore I let him die."

"We've got to consider first, not just start out with no plan," Tench said. "Are you hurt anyplace, Sam . . . have you got any kind of wound?"

"Hell, no . . . nothin' but bruises and maybe a cracked rib. You banged up, Tench?"

"A little. Nothing bad. How about you, Jason?"

"A bullet in my leg," Jason admitted. "Once it's dug out, I'll be all right."

"Anybody got a knife?" Sam demanded. "One of them bastards knocked mine out of my hand and I couldn't find it ag'in."

"I lost mine, too," Tench admitted.

"So did I," Jason said.

"What the hell we goin' to do?" Sam demanded. "I kin dig that bullet out come day, but I got to have a knife. And it'll take time to hunt out a cabin . . . and them bastards is gittin' further away ever' minute!"

"Hold on, now," Tench put in. "You've got the baby to look after, Jason. It's best you don't go with us. I don't like to part company with you, but Medary will be expecting me. Are you able to navigate at all, Jason?"

"I can get along. I swam . . . I got this far . . . I can go under my own power."

"Maybe we'd better wait until dawn, Sam," Tench

said. "We can see Jason to a cabin. It'll give us a chance to borrow a boat and rifle sooner."

"You crazy?" retorted Sam. "We're goin' to have to steal a boat, steal rifles! We ain't got time to explain and mebbe argue we ain't pirates ourselfs! You jest remember I'm sayin' it now, aforehand. We need to start walkin' downriver now, this minute, we ain't got a second to lose!"

"Sam's right, Tench," Jason said. "I can get the baby to some cabin on my own. I figure if I keep moving, the leg won't get a chance to stiffen up too much before I can get the bullet out. I can't be any help to you, so I'll head for St. Louis."

"Medary'll give me her tongue for leaving you and the baby," Tench said. "You with a bullet in your leg, and the baby—"

"Medary's worse off than we are," Jason interrupted. "And Yellow Flower. My regret is that I'm in no shape to help. She'll see Auguste again, you promise her that. I'll leave word at the fur traders in St. Louis, and you do the same when you get there, both of you. We'll come together again,"

"We'll do it, Jase!" Sam said eagerly. "Let's git goin', Tench," he urged. "Jase kin be hobblin' upriver at the same time, gittin' closer to that cabin he's goin' to find!"

Without further discussion, they shook hands, three friends parting in the wilderness. Tench and Sam tramped away into the darkness without rifle or knife, with only the sodden clothes they wore.

Jason remained within the trees. Slowly and rhythmically his hand moved, rubbing and rubbing the naked back of his son to keep life's warmth in it until the rising of the sun.

Chapter 27

At dawn, he left off rubbing Auguste long enough to pull up his right trouser leg and take a look at his throbbing wound. The flesh was swollen and puffed, and darts of inflammation were lancing up from the little hole in midcalf. The pain was getting worse, was shooting up the leg and into the hip, and there was much stiffness. He'd have to start moving or he wouldn't be able to move at all.

Jaw rigid, Auguste clutched in the crook of one arm, he pushed himself up, putting his weight on his good leg. Slowly, his leg like a stick asurge with pain, he hobbled to the edge of the timber, stood just within it, rubbing the baby's back gently, and studied the river.

There was no craft of any sort in view. And if he did spot a boat, he thought, and hailed it, they'd likely think he was a river pirate.

Now red streaks were appearing in the far eastern sky. Jason stood watching, rubbing Auguste, and the red grew until the great ball of sun swam heavily up. Auguste began to scream his hunger cry.

Jason spent the time the sun needed to spread

warmth, to press down over the land, hobbling stubbornly back and forth, baby screaming, schooling his leg to bear his weight the flashing instant he needed to swing the other leg forward.

Later, in full sun, he raked brown leaves and grass and moss, scooping it to the chosen spot, piling it into a bed of sorts. On the bed he laid his howling, naked son, and the yellow heat of the sky covered him. Auguste kicked and flailed, his entire sturdy little body scarlet with hunger and rage.

Jason grinned. "That's it, son," he said. "The harder you cry, the warmer you'll be."

After Jason had spread their clothes to dry, the baby fell asleep, warm in the sun, face tear-streaked and dirty. Jason gazed at him. It isn't right, he thought, that he has to go through so much so young.

It was close to noon by the time he'd dressed Auguste in his dry clothes. The child chewed at his fists, fretted, cried. Carrying him, Jason moved upriver—left foot ahead, drag the right foot along, left foot ahead again. The leg buckled, but when it did he bore down on it harder and the pain kept it more or less straight until he could thrust the other foot forward.

Sometimes he sat down to rest, had to. From time to time Auguste slept, sobs rippling him, but always he roused and cried again. He's too tired to scream anymore, Jason thought, pushing the left foot ahead, dragging the swollen sore leg. He wondered how long it would take a baby to starve, then forgot to wonder, for there was only the endless thrust and pull, the growing pain, the soreness and stiffness, the burning heat of his skin, even as the sun began to sink.

It's not really this hot, he thought remotely as heat entered the pain in his leg, burned down the bone clear through to his foot. It can't be this hot . . . it's winter, and the sun's going down . . . it's just me . . . I'm the one that's hot . . .

He struggled out of his shirt, wrapped it around the baby. Auguste's sobs cut off, his breath jerked a couple of times, his head grew heavy on Jason's shoulder. He is cold, Jason thought, but I am hot.

He kept hobbling, slogging on. Even without his shirt, he burned. He got so he could ignore everything but the heat. Soreness, stiffness, pain, the weight under which the leg buckled—none of it mattered. Only the burning, which was like the fires of hell, which would, of itself, keep Auguste from freezing.

He laid himself forward against the dusk of night, against distance, against heat, stumbled through the hotness, on and on. And when he felt himself falling, he resisted, but when he finally did fall upon the earth, he thought he would rest. Five minutes, and then the heat would let up.

Chapter 28

Before he opened his eyes, he thought, I was right, I'm cooler now. Now I can go on. He tried to sit up, but something pushed him back, and when he would have resisted, the something became hands, one on each of his shoulders.

"He wants to set up, Henry," said a woman's voice. "You'd best come. If he's still out of his head, he may try to leave again."

Other hands came onto his shoulders, bigger and stronger. "Easy, man," said another voice, a man's. "You're one of the strongest fellows I ever seen, but you been sick, you got to take it slow."

With an effort, Jason opened his eyes. He was looking into a wide plain face which was clean-shaven and wore a kind expression. The man had graying hair which had receded to leave him with an unnaturally high forehead. He was thin and dressed in clean rough clothes.

"My son," Jason said.

"He's right here in the cradle," said the woman's voice. "He had a cold and fever, but he's fine. Your fever's gone to. My man dug out the bullet."

She came into view, a slight, thin, graying woman

with hair pulled back to a knot on the top of her head.
Her light eyes were kind.

Jason stared questioningly at the two of them. The
woman seemed to understand.

"Henry," she said, "tell him. He wants to know."

"Well, first," said the man gently, "I'm Henry Johannigmeier. This's my woman, Fan. Our kids are outside playing. Your son's asleep, full of milk and mush.
Fan brung him right out of his cold and fever and she
kept poultices on your leg and spoon-fed you while you
was out of your head. You've been sick some weeks,
but all you need now is to get your strength back
Mr.—"

"Blood. My name is Jason Blood. My son is Auguste
Blood."

"Pleased to meet you," Johannigmeier said, and
smiled.

"How did I get here, to your place?" Jason asked.
"I don't remember seeing a cabin."

"Actually, you was practically on top of us," Johannigmeier told him. "Hank—that's our oldest, he's
twelve—went out to drive the cow in for milking a bit
late that evening, and there you and your babe was.
Lying in the middle of a strip of timber between our
cabin and our pasturage. He wouldn't of saw you if the
babe hadn't of begun to cry, as you was off to one
side of where he was at. He fetched the babe right to
his ma, and me and him carried you in. Slap dark it
was, by that time."

Jason pulled to a sitting position, his leg dully sore.
Fan beat up his pillow and settled it behind him.

"I've got fresh stew," she told him. "You're to eat
before you use strength to tell us what happened to
you and that blessed angel of a baby."

As she bustled away Jason turned to look around the
one-room cabin. It was built of logs chinked with mud.
A fireplace, hung with cranes and pots, filled one end.
An iron coffeepot steamed on a trivet at one side of
the fire, the cradle stood at the other side. He could
glimpse Auguste's fair hair.

A wooden table and benches stood in the middle of the puncheon floor, and a bunk was nailed to the wall opposite the bunk in which Jason sat. Shelves lined the wall on either side of a door opposite the fireplace, which Jason saw was the outside door. There was a small shuttered window above each bunk, around which cold air seeped.

Fan brought stew and cornbread, handed Jason a wooden spoon. "Eat up," she ordered brightly.

He took a few bites of the stew, let its hot goodness trail down into his stomach. He sampled the cornbread, found himself ravenous. He'd meant to talk as he ate, but he was too hungry and too weak.

When Fan took the emptied bowl and trencher, he told her what a good cook she was. She reddened, then hurried away to wash up.

"I come from New Madrid," Jason told them now. "We had a bad earthquake there, so bad that my house was swallowed into the ground. My friends' cabins were leveled."

He wondered, heavily, about Sam and Tench. About Medary and Yellow Flower.

"Word's getting through about that," Johannigmeier said. "We had some strong shakes ourselves, and they did in St. Louis, too. Rattled windows, broke dishes, and knocked down some sheds and the like."

Jason then proceeded to tell how he and his friends had banded together, how they'd been en route to St. Louis when overcome by river pirates. He related how Tench and Sam had gone downriver to rescue the women, and he had started upriver, carrying Auguste.

There was silence as the couple stared at him. They both shook their heads and clucked their tongues over his misadventures.

"I appreciate what you've done for me," Jason told them. "I've put you out enough. I'll be on my way tomorrow. If you'll give me some milk for the boy and direct me to the next upriver cabin, I'll head for St. Louis."

"That's too far to walk!" cried Fan. "You ain't put

us out! Hank's been bunking with you, me and Henry's took two of the younguns in with us, and bedded the rest on pallets. Two of them sleep on pallets anyhow. We'd like the pleasure of your company for a few days while you get your strength. And the joy of a babe to tend—our youngest is four, and won't set still for cuddling!"

Johannigmeier grinned at Jason. "Fan can be a driving woman," he said proudly. "She's purely hungry for company. I've got a way you can get to St. Louis without maybe any walking a-tall."

But before he could explain his plan, the door burst open and the room was filled with stringy-haired, healthy children. Where their parents were thin and work-worn, they were sturdy and red-cheeked. They gathered around Jason and stared at him as though they'd been struck dumb.

He grinned at them, let his look stay on the tallest boy. "You're Hank?"

The lad nodded, grinned. A dimple flickered at his mouth.

Fan shooed them proudly to the table. She gave the smallest boy's bottom a gentle smack, and he pulled away, frowning mightily. She laughed.

When the children were eating, Johannigmeier outlined his plan of travel.

"You ain't going to be in shape to walk on that leg much for a spell," he said. "I sort of figured you was heading for St. Louis, so I pondered and here's what I come up with. It's on the order of riding whipsaw, if you know what that is, only different."

"I've heard of whipsaw," Jason said. "It's when two or three men use the same horse. One of them rides the horse for an hour, then ties it and walks on. The next man, when he catches up, rides the same length of time and leaves the horse for the third man, and so on."

"Exactly. Now. The Weeds live fifteen miles up-river. I'll put you and the babe on my horse two, three days from now, and we'll go to their place, me walking. I'll ride my horse back home. Weed's got two horses.

So, while I'm riding home, Weed'll take you to the next cabin north, and while he's on his way home with both horses, that fellow—Selby—will see you to the next cabin along. And that way you'll get yourself and the boy clear to St. Louis."

Jason stared at Johannigmeier, aghast at his kindness.

This is the only real good fortune, earned or unearned, he thought numbly, that I've had since Mr. van Delft took me out of the home.

Chapter 29

It was March second, 1812, when Jason walked into
St. Louis, Auguste riding his arm, swiveling his little
egg-shaped head, staring at everything. He'd walked
the last lap from the Ryan cabin because he wanted to
strengthen his leg.

He'd seen fruit trees in abundance—apricot, peach,
cherry, plum, early apple—all showing green, ready to
flower. Robins perched in them, and bluebirds and
larks and bunting, throwing all their bright voices into
the early spring day.

The situation on which St. Louis stood wasn't much
higher than the riverbanks, but floods were repelled by
a bold shore of limestone bluffs. The Mississippi flowed
past the bluffs and disappeared into the southern woods.
Back of the village, according to settler Ryan, four or
five springs threw their waters together in a sparkling
rivulet which, a short distance below the village, flowed
into the brown water. Chouteau's Pond lay below too,
a hundred-acre expanse of water, grassy-banked, surrounded by trees and bushes and grapevines.

The village lay between the river and a second bank
which stood forty feet above the level of the plain.

On this bank, Jason saw the line of buildings erected earlier for defense against Indians, and knew that to the north, from Bellefontaine at the mouth of the Missouri to the Kaskaskia river, twenty-two stations or family blockhouses, were being built for defense should war with England come. Along this line, seventy-five miles in length, scouts would pass daily to keep up communications and prevent the enemy from breaking through. Here, on the bank, was a small stockaded fort, used briefly by United States soldiers, but now everything was in disuse except the commandant's house, where courts were held, and the stone tower, which was used as a prison. Some distance beyond were some Indian mounds.

The village had three streets running parallel to the river for about twenty squares, with other streets crossing them at right angles. There was no walkway along the river, as the shops and dwellings that faced Main Street backed up to it.

The residential section was laid out in squares, each divided into four lots with room for each owner to have gardens, fruit trees, and even flowers. Some householders had half a square, and Ryan had said that a few leading citizens occupied an entire square.

Most of the buildings were log, some built like cabins, others in the French style. Many had hand-hewn shingle roofs such as Jason had put on his house. Some buildings were stone and a few were of log and stone combined. All were one story, and were brilliantly whitewashed. A number had their grounds enclosed by stone walls.

Turning onto Main Street, Jason stepped onto the plank walkway and looked about with surprise as he moved along. He never would have expected a village to be so busy.

There were roughly dressed men striding purposefully, their feet shod in heavy Kentucky boots. Two fine-dressed men strolled into a tavern. Long-skirted women with shawls over their heads and baskets on their arms went in and out of shops, past barrels of pungent smelling pickles, aromatic coffee beans and pure white flour. There was a flow of lordly looking Osage men padding the walkway, followed sometimes by their squaws, and there were Shawanese, sober and orderly and quiet. And there were hunters in deerskins and moccasins, merry, dark-skinned French *coureurs* and *voyageurs,* wild as Pawnee, filling the air with their quick voices and laughter. There was a trio of bragging, fighting boatmen, and more than one plain-dressed, steady-moving settler with a pack on his back.

Jason passed the Eagle Tavern, passed a small warehouse, a dwelling with a bakehouse behind it, some small stores, and then, in the middle of the block, spotted the big store with the bold painted sign. The sign read, Griggs Mercantile and Fur Trading Establishment.

Jason turned in and moved through the dimness, the tobacco and spice and fur smells. At a far counter, a gray little man was dickering over some Pittsburgh pigtail with two tall Osage men. There were no other customers.

The little gray man glanced toward Jason, then called, "Amos . . . customer! He's the owner," he told Jason. "Be right with you."

The clerk had hardly finished speaking when a man stood before Jason. He was shaved and shining, and he wore neat dark trousers and coat. He was dressed more like a New York attorney, Jason thought, than a store-keeper. He was almost as tall as Jason, yet gave the impression of being short, perhaps because of his bur-geoning portliness. His hair was thick and dark and covered his eeg-shaped head, which was formed almost exactly like Auguste's fair little head.

"How can I serve you?" he asked in a rather deep voice.

"I'm not in a position to buy," Jason told him. "My name is Blood, Jason Blood, lately of New Madrid."

The man's brows jumped into a faint scowl.

"I'm seeking information," Jason continued, "and an

arrangement by which I can be supplied with rifle and
trapping necessaries to be paid for later with peltries."

"I don't outfit," the storekeeper said. "You might
try Chouteau's and see if they'll outfit this late in the
season."

"Thank you, Mr.—?"

"Griggs. Amos Griggs. Owner and proprietor."

"The information I spoke of has to do, partly, with
friends I'm to meet in St. Louis. We were attacked by
river pirates and separated when they went to rescue
the women of our party. Tench Coghill and Sam Janas.
Have you seen them or heard of them?"

Griggs shook his head. The little gray clerk had
come up in time to hear, and he also shook his head.
"They ain't got here yet," the clerk said. "We'd of
heard. Word of such as that travels along Main Street
like lightning."

"You can ask at Chouteau's and around," Griggs
said. "Make doubly certain."

"I'll do that," Jason agreed. "Other information I'm
in need of has to do with my son here. I'd appreciate
it if you could direct me to some woman who'd look
after him until I find my friends or while I'm trapping
if I don't find them."

Griggs's brows flew up, then dived to his nose. He
turned to the clerk. "Ned, do you know any such
woman?"

The clerk shook his head. "You might go talk to
Granny Grosshart," he said. "She's the only one I can
think of that'd be apt to know. She lives in a two-room
French log house at the south end of Main Street, not
on the river side. You can't miss it."

Jason thanked the two of them and departed. First he
went to the other fur-trading establishments, inquired
about his friends, inquired about being outfitted, and
had no success on either front.

Thus, by the time he knocked at the door of the
French-built cabin at the end of Main Street, Auguste
was fretful. He was wet, and Jason knew he'd have to

put on the spare clout Fan Johannigmeier had given him.

The door opened at last. A tiny wizened creature peered up at him out of a fine tracery of wrinkles with eyes of piercing blue.

"Well," she asked before Jason could speak, "who're you two?" Her voice was as fine and sharp as a needle, and as bright.

"Jason Blood, ma'am . . . and my son, Auguste Blood."

"Come in," she said. "That baby's hungry, or I miss my guess! And he's dripping wet! If that ain't a man for you—stand on the doorstep and let his youngun fret!"

She turned, one gnarled little hand gripping the head of a cane, blue skirt rustling, and led them inside. Her thin white hair was drawn into a bun at her neck.

"Set," she ordered, nodding toward a wooden armchair near the fireplace. "Give me the boy . . . he is a boy, ain't he? I thought so," she continued when Jason nodded. "He looks all boy. I can manage him on my left arm, rheumatics or not, the day ain't come when I can't clout a baby, and feed him. When that's done with, then you can tell who sent you here and why. Folks are always sending folks."

She took the dry clout Jason proffered and went into the adjoining room, leaving the door open. He could see a walnut bedstead and the corner of a dresser from where he sat.

The room he was in was comfortably equipped. The board floor was spread with a braided rug, curtains hung at the windows, there was a substantial table for eating with two chairs drawn to it. There was a second wooden armchair with a small table beside it which held the Bible and a wooden candlestick. The fireplace was generously equipped with iron cookware, and shelves on either side held both wooden and china bowls.

When Auguste had fallen asleep and the old woman had washed out his wet clout and hung it to dry at the

fire, she sat down in the other armchair and shot that piercing look at Jason. "Now," she said, "talk."

Briefly, Jason told her everything that had happened, including the fact that Tench and Medary and Sam and Yellow Flower had not yet reached St. Louis. "You can see," he concluded, "how it leaves me in need of someone to tend the baby."

"Ain't but one thing a man in your fix can do," Granny said. "That's get married, and get married fast."

Jason frowned, started to reply, remained silent.

"I know," the old woman continued, sewing that needle of a voice through the ticking of the clock on the mantel, "you ain't been a widower three months yet. That's a luxury to feel like that, and you ain't in a position to pamper yourself."

"I don't know any women," Jason pointed out.

"There's women in St. Louis I know of—one or two that's never married, and there's a widow that wants a man. She'd make a good wife, too, and she'd mother your boy. If you want, I can send you to her, and you can look each other over."

Jason stared openly.

The thin little mouth smiled, displaying new wrinkles. "You're shocked. This's raw country, son. We do what we've got to do when it comes to hand. When a man's left with younguns out here, he ain't got a choice. He's got to get himself a woman fast. The women understand, they know. Because it's the same for them. If a woman's left with younguns, she's got to get herself a man to provide. Don't anybody hold it again' them."

Jason thought of what Sam had told him. Sam had said, Get a squaw. Get one like Yellow Flower.

"If I could hire an Indian woman," he said now. "Yellow Flower, the Delaware girl I told you about, helped with Auguste. If I could find one like her who'd be willing to be paid later . . ."

He saw the blue eyes sharpen, saw mischief come into them. "There is an Osage woman," she said, "but she lives in the Osage village. You'd have to send him with some of the Osages that's been here to sell their furs. If she'd do it, that is."

"How do I find out?" Jason asked. He didn't like the idea of sending Auguste to an Indian village, but he needed to explore every possibility.

"I'll direct you to where you can find out," Granny replied, and he would have sworn that the mischief was a-dance in the blue eyes. "Go up this street to Chestnut, then to the finest stone house in Barn Street. Ask for Lillian Dusard. She's the only one can know if the woman'll do it—it's her mother. Leave the baby here," she added, "let him get his nap out."

The house, when Jason found it, presented a very long front and was unusually deep. It seemed to be divided off into more and larger rooms than any other he'd seen in the village. There would be the central rooms, one for sitting and one for eating, and each end of the house was divided into smaller sections for sleeping. One of these, however, would be a kitchen, he thought.

The grounds were surrounded by a stone wall on which vines were greening. He looked beyond the wall. The house, situated on the westernmost street, abutted the fenced miles of common fields where each householder had a grant measured in arpens on which to grow food. To the south lay the grazing commons, where the villagers drove their cattle every morning. Beyond was timber, some of it already timidly green, later to become a blaze of greens.

He pushed the iron gate open, went up the stone path, onto the gallery, across it, and worked the iron knocker. The door was opened so swiftly that he stepped back, surprised.

A girl stood there, tender as spring, as those delicate green shoots he'd seen coming to St. Louis, and with that same inlying hardiness to sustain the tenderness. She was rather tall, lissom, and she was clothed in soft and falling brown. Her hair was black as night, very straight, and wound into a gleaming braid. Her black eyebrows were arched against the near-dusky complexion of her oval face.

Her eyes, near-black, were long and shining, and they were on his face, searching it over in amazement, in wonder, even in awe. Her features were classic, mobile. Her lips were shapely, not too full, and now, as she gazed, the lower lip was quivering, almost invisibly, but quivering.

Her voice was like music, quiet music, as she asked, "Who . . . are you?"

Amazement filled him and Jason could not speak. And I thought I had to go to New Orleans to find her, he thought. The wonder beat through him, swelled into his ears, his throat, and lay there, beating.

Gone was every vestige of his dream of that dark-eyed girl with silken petticoats. Fled was any memory of earthquake or lost wife or river pirates.

There was only now, there was only this moment. And this girl.

Chapter 30

He couldn't speak or even breathe. He didn't want to ask her about some Osage woman to tend Auguste, not now. But he had to say something because she was waiting, her face a tender, eager quest for him, his voice. He had to tell her.

"I'm Jason Blood," he blurted. "Granny Grosshart sent me. I've got a nine-month-old boy without a mother—she was lost in the earthquake. That was in New Madrid."

"I'm sorry," she breathed. Then, "Granny told you that my mother once took care of an orphan child?"

He nodded, swallowed, unable to say what he wanted to say. No matter how Granny Grosshart had put it, a man couldn't ask a girl like this to marry him, penniless, without rifle or traps to his name.

"I've got to outfit myself," he blurted on. "Trap and pay my debts later."

"I'm Lillian Dusard," the girl said. "My mother is Young Doe, half French, and she lives in the Osage village with her husband, Swift Foot. Her father is Eagle Feather, a chief. Any child brought into her lodge is held in honor."

"Is there . . . would she . . . ?"

"Please come in, Mr. Blood," the girl said. "The family is away at the moment, and we'll have privacy." There was a throb in her voice, as if she were excited, and when she stood aside for him to enter, her eyes were downcast.

She took him into a sitting room. There was a mirror on the wall, he noticed that, and a silver candelabrum on a table near the fireplace, with a short-armed rocker drawn close. She sat in the chair, motioning him to another chair opposite. He reached it in one stride and sat down, all the things he wanted to say choked inside and hammering at him.

"Now," she said with that throb, that excitement. "The two little Griggs girls aren't due home from school yet, so they'll not come running in. I live here to teach them French and music and help with their numbers."

Music, the thought swept through him; he'd have to have an instrument in his new cabin, a pianoforte. But she was waiting with that tender touch of eagerness, so, not presuming to ask if this were the home of the Amos Griggs he'd met earlier, Jason plunged into his account. Somehow, though his heart had balled up in the middle of his stomach and was beating like a heavy hot rock, he told his story. When he'd finished, she knew about the home and Hendrik van Delft, she knew about New Madrid and Massie Ann, the river pirates, everything. By the time he got to the point where he'd talked to Granny Grosshart, he felt he'd known this girl all his life.

The way she looked, she felt the same about him, but he couldn't be sure. He could only see that eagerness on her, feel the eagerness in himself.

"So," he finished lamely, searching futilely for a way to say what he really wanted to say to this girl, "I came here to ask about your mother. And if she'd be willing. And if she'd wait for me to pay her after I've trapped."

"She didn't take payment before," Lillian Dusard said. "It would offend her. It was a gift of her heart for a child in need. Later, the child's father gave her a fine horse, which she wouldn't keep, but gave to me."

"A gift, then," Jason said. "If she'd do it."

He looked at Lillian Dusard searchingly, wanting to know all there was to know about her. As though she sensed his want, she began to speak.

"My father, now dead," she said, "was Thurlow Dusard, only son of an English mother and a French father. He became a trapper, and he married my mother in the white man's way. I was born in the Osage village and learned Osage ways; white ways I learned here, in school. I am twenty-two years old."

"I'm twenty-two years old, like you," he said, and his eagerness sounded in his tone.

Her face was very still. Her star-bright eyes roved over his face. "I've never told a man such things before, Jason Blood."

"I want them," he said, his voice roughening, somehow managing to hold it low so as not to alarm her. "Out here . . . in the West . . . when a man . . . or a woman . . . Granny Grosshart . . ."

She understood, because she nodded, and there was no need for him to stumble on, to explain that which defied explanation. But, despite her understanding, he dared not say that he loved her, when he'd only just met her. He dared not say he'd gone beyond wanting some woman to care for Auguste, that now he wanted her, Lillian, for his wife. That his heart cried out for her now, that it would always cry out for her from this moment until the end of life.

"Granny knows," Lillian said now, with that throb of voice "she's lived, and she knows. In this country, things come without warning, as your earthquake did. Your life changes overnight, in the wink of an eye. You have to make decisions suddenly or you have no chance. It's . . . I suppose you could call it the wilderness way . . . for white men, for Indians, for animals and birds. You have to . . . adapt. Which means you do what you can do at a given moment."

Suddenly he found himself telling her of his hopes

and aspirations, of the eight hundred acres of land he meant to get, up the Missouri. He told of his drive to root himself into the land.

Then, somehow, she was telling him of her childhood, explaining about her parents. "My mother didn't want to live white, and my father didn't want to live Osage, so they dissolved the marriage. They wanted me to learn, so I spent much time in St. Louis with my father, and my mother married Osage. She has other children now. My brothers and sisters are three-quarters Osage . . . Singing Lark is the oldest."

"Singing Lark," Jason repeated. "And you are Lillian. You don't have an Osage name?"

"No, I'm named after my English grandmother. I'm spoken of in St. Louis as Osage, even as a squaw. I want you to know that. Actually, I'm one-quarter Osage, one-quarter English, one-half French."

"I don't know what blood I am," Jason said. "My son is German from his mother."

It was as though they were trading vows, he thought. And wondered if he dared blurt out what was on his mind, if her telling him so much about herself wasn't, come to think of it, pretty bold encouragement on the part of a girl.

Not knowing if he was half out of his mind, he grabbed his courage and plunged. He asked, "In view of my situation and the way of life here in the West, are you willing to hear me out? I've got a thing to say."

She nodded, star-shine eyes on his face.

"I've got a strong body, and a will to work and make something out of life for myself and my family," he began. "I know how to hunt and trap, I know how to farm my land, when I get it, and I know how to build a tight, good cabin. I've got a nine-month-old son who needs a mother. I've got affection, the kind a man holds for a certain woman, that woke in me when you opened the door."

He came to a stop. Her star-shine remained steady, and he thought dazedly that this was the maddest, most hopeless way any man could go about what he was trying to do.

"I haven't even got a cabin now, or a rifle or a trap. Or a place to lay my head tonight."

She said, "Nine months old."

"He isn't walking yet." He waited. "I'm not a timid man."

"No."

"I need someone for Auguste. But more than for him, I want you for myself. I'd want you if he'd never been born. You know what I'm asking?"

"I . . . think so. Only . . ."

"I'm asking you to marry me before the parson."

The star-shine deepened.

"I know it's hard for you to say yes or no so suddenly."

"It is . . . a shock. And confusing. Seeing you at the door, feeling that I actually recognized you, that I'd been . . . waiting. Then such a proposal. I can't think."

She looked at her hands in her lap. She thought of Quick Knife, who was also waiting for her decision, waiting impatiently to make her his number-two wife. She thought of the young settler who had come up from Ste. Genevieve to trade and remained to court. He had a four-room house, grain in his shed, two strong horses and he'd never been married. But she'd told him no.

She recalled what Rhoda Griggs had said only yesterday. Always Rhoda Griggs said, no matter who the man, "You can do better than that Indian. Nobody could tell you've got Indian blood, you look more French than anything."

What can you say when someone is so well meaning, so determined? she thought. How can you say, I'm not wanting to hide my Indian blood. If I feel right about a certain man, if he be Indian to the bone, I will marry him in the Indian way. I'm not looking for a white man. I'm not looking for a husband, but I want the right one, and if I meet him and he wants me, I'll marry him. And no amount of white blood or Osage blood or education or fur trading or trapping or farming or money or power can put into my man the thing I must have.

It wouldn't be easy to tell this man, this Jason Blood, no today or any day to come. She was so precipitately drawn to him. He was a tawny god, strong from what he'd already met in life, ready for what must yet come. If he were to reach out and put his hands on her arms and lift her from the chair, she'd go, here and now.

But he wouldn't do that, he'd know it to be unfair. He'd let her make her own decision, swift though he demanded it to be. "We've talked of the past," she said quietly, "and have become acquainted a little. I'd like to exchange opinions. To learn more of each other."

"I'm willing," he said. "What do you want to discuss?"

Suddenly she smiled at him. He saw her lips curl and only then noticed how red they were. Her smile made her whole lovely face glow.

"That did sound serious," she said. "But I am serious. What do you want in life . . . do you want a fortune?"

"If you mean money, no."

"You spoke of much land."

"It won't seem so big when I give out a hundred acres to each son when he's ready to marry. So he'll have a roof over his head, land to grow his food."

She nodded, watching him.

"I want my sons educated," he continued. "And my daughters. So they can enjoy reading . . . music, too. I want them to have the will to work, respect for the Bible and for man."

"Position . . . do you want position for them . . . for yourself?"

"If you mean like Colonel Chouteau, no. If you mean to be held in respect by family and neighbors, yes."

Her voice was quivering. "You want the same things for Auguste and for the children we will have, you and I, if we marry?"

"Exactly the same."

"Our children, if ever they are born, will have Osage blood," she pointed out.

"They will know, from birth, to be proud of it."

"If I say yes, Jason Blood, there is a thing I would want, really want."

"You have only to tell me, not ask."

"I would want you to go with me to the Osage village and live Osage for a year."

He watched her face, waited.

"For two reasons," she continued. "One of them is practical—we can live off the land as the Osage live, and when the winter trapping starts, you can trap with the Osage and get the money for your land when you sell the peltries. The other reason is practical too. By yourself living Osage, you will know Osage ideals and Osage thinking and through this will understand the Osage in our future children."

Frowning thoughtfully, Jason pondered. Now she, in her turn, was requiring a swift yes or no from him, even as he was asking the same from her. They were demanding, each from the other, a basic readjustment of life. The amazing part, he realized suddenly, was that the two readjustments would fit, would meld into an unshakable whole.

"It suits me," he said. "I'm for getting married tomorrow."

As she started to reply to that, hurrying feet crossed the gallery. The front door banged.

Lillian jumped up from the rocker and started across the room, but before she could reach the door it was flung open and Amos Griggs entered. He rocked back onto his heels to avoid crashing into her.

"What's going on here?" he demanded. "Ned went to deliver some meal to Granny Grosshart, and she had that strange fellow's baby there and told Ned she'd sent the fellow—Blood's the name—to you! He didn't actually show up, did he?"

Jason, who had risen, advanced to the center of the room. "I did come, Mr. Griggs," he said. "I'm sorry if it displeases you, but I'm glad I'm here."

"You're *glad?*" thundered Griggs, his brows knit. "This happened to me once before and I'm damned if I'll stand still and let it happen again, in my own house, in the same room!"

"I don't know what you mean," Jason said. "The reason I'm here—"

"Jason," Lillian put in, "let me. I know what happened with your sister, Mr. Griggs . . . Mrs. Griggs has told me."

"And this is the same thing!" Griggs raged. "Don't tell me it isn't! That time a fellow walked out of the woods with a pack on his back. He'd come to buy himself a cow to feed his twins and to find himself a wife to mother them. He found my sister, Devora . . . as fine a woman as ever walked the earth. And right in this room he talked her into walking off into the woods with him, with a pack on her back, and there she's stayed. Four years, and not a word from her, don't know if she's dead or alive!"

"She did write, sir," Lillian reminded quietly. "You read it aloud to us, and Mrs. Griggs cried. Your sister sounded very happy in her letter, very content."

"Think she'd be likely to admit she'd made a mistake?" Griggs retorted. "Well, it's not going to happen again! I forbid it, and by God, this time, I'll call the marshal to prevent it! You're in my house, young woman, you're employed to educate my daughters, and you're not going to leave to marry this . . . river rat . . . who hasn't even got a rifle! Not from this house, you're not!"

"Then, sir," Lillian told him very quietly, "I'll do it from Granny Grosshart's house."

And she came to Jason and slipped her hand into his.

Chapter 31

Two days later, on March fourth, Jason Blood married Lillian Dusard. She wore deerskin dress and moccasins, he wore his rough clean garb, both ready for travel. They stood up before Parson Blalock, whose voice was so old it trembled on the marriage words. The parson's aged and palsied wife was there to witness, and Granny Grosshart, whose cabin it was, and Auguste, and no other.

Before the words, the parson made sure all was in order. "You're a widower, young man? You so declared and showed proof?"

"I so declared," Jason replied. "My document was lost when river pirates took our boat. Medary Coghill holds it for me, and when she gets to St. Louis she'll show it to the proper ones. I've left instructions in writing at Chouteau's place."

The parson proceeded with his words, and they murmured their responses, all of it a daze for Jason. Toward the end a silence held them.

Then the parson said, "The ring, please."

And Jason had none. He had no ring, hadn't thought

of a ring, either this time or the other. He shook his head at the parson.

When the kissing was finished and the farewells, Jason and his bride started north along Main Street, heading for wilderness. He led Lillian's fine black horse, which was loaded with their possessions. Auguste, in his Osage cradle, was hung to the saddle bow turning his fair little head as usual, giving an occasional howl.

"He doesn't like the cradle," Jason said, and smiled down at his bride, thinking how it was going to be tonight.

She laughed, a rippling song of laughter, and in that moment Jason sensed that laughter was a part of her. She linked her hands through his arm, pressed tenderly. She walked easily beside him, as if she'd always done so.

Suddenly Auguste gave a crowing chuckle. They looked back in time to see his whole face break open in that way it had.

Lillian laughed with the baby. "You see!" she cried. "He likes the cradle well enough! It's much easier to carry a baby this way. When we stop, the cradle can be set on end, out of harm's way, or even hung to the limb of a tree where he'll be safe and can see what is happening.

"How long does an Osage baby have to be strapped up?" Jason asked, not liking the idea overmuch, though he himself, following Lillian's instructions, had made the cradle.

It was simple, consisting of a plank about a foot longer than Auguste. He had been laid flat on its blanket-padded side and secured by strips of blanket beginning at the feet and ending under the arms.

"Until he's old enough to walk," Lillian replied. "Which won't be long now, for Auguste. We'll take him out of the cradle at night. He may learn to walk before we reach the village."

Auguste chortled again, eyes on Lillian.

"He's taking right to you," Jason said.

"He's a friendly baby," she smiled. "I'm glad he's like that. It makes it easier for me to win his love."

In that moment, walking into their future, with their possessions, including traps and rifle bought with gold Granny Grosshart had demanded that Jason borrow, he was overwhelmed by the magnitude of his good fortune.

Past the shops of the village they moved, aware of citizens, trappers, Indians from many tribes, of women and children, of boatmen. Past the Griggs store they went, with never a glimpse of Amos Griggs or his clerk, Ned. And Chouteau's place, where Jason had left a letter for Medary. Past the blacksmith shop they went, past houses and cleared land, along a small road and eventually into the timberland.

When they hungered, they stopped beside a running stream. Lillian stood Auguste's cradle against a hickory while Jason put the horse to graze and drink. Lillian opened the packet of food Granny had given them. They sat on the ground to eat, but before she served either of them, Lillian broke off a soft chunk of cornbread and put it into Auguste's impatient little fist. She laughed when he tried to cram it all into his mouth, took his wrist in her fingers and restrained him until he began to chew at the bread less fiercely.

She kept laughing, a low ripple of contentment. Jason thought it was the most beautiful sound he had ever heard. He wished he knew how to tell her how he felt about her. He watched how tenderly she regarded his son, how careful she was that he shouldn't choke on the bread. He watched how daintily she herself ate, and how little.

"We mustn't walk too far in a day," he said. "I don't want you to tire."

"We need to walk a substantial distance every day," she replied. "I've done it before, I don't tire. It's close to four hundred miles to the village, across the Missouri border into Kansas land. The sooner we get there, the less chance we run of meeting a war party."

He felt hair stir on his neck. On the trail this way,

one man with one rifle would stand little chance of defending wife and child against marauding Indians.

"I didn't hear about war parties in St. Louis," he said, frowning.

"Nor I. But you never know what the Sacs will do. Or the Foxes. Osage want peace, but the Sac chiefs say they can't restrain their young men from joining battle parties from other nations."

"Is your village ever attacked?"

"It used to be, but not for a while. A party of Osage came down with peltries last week, and they said it's been quiet and peaceful."

Jason breathed more easily, somewhat relieved. Now, as they shared their first meal, he found courage to ask her something that had puzzled him.

"You're one-quarter Osage," he said.

"Yes, Jason."

"And your mother is half Osage, half French."

"Yes."

"And Eagle Feather, your grandfather, is full Osage and your grandmother—"

"Flying Bird."

"She's full Osage, too?"

"You wonder how my mother can be half French when both Eagle Feather and Flying Bird are full Osage."

"I started figuring. And I wonder."

"Eagle Feather isn't my mother's natural father, Jason. In the Osage nation there is a custom, one of kindness and courtesy, by which an Osage man permits an honored visitor to enjoy the favors of one of his wives. Eagle Feather once had a French trapper friend who saved the Osage from a great and costly war with the Sac. In gratitude, he loaned his number-one wife, Flying Bird, to the Frenchman for as long as he remained in the village. My mother, Young Doe, was born of this union. As is the custom, she became Eagle Feather's acknowledged daughter, as dear to him as any other daughter. It is a beautiful thing. There is no dishonor."

Her openness about her origin, her pride in it, awed
Jason. He could find no words with which to express
the depths of what he now felt, could only nod, hoping
that she would sense how proud he was of Lillian
Blood.

It was evening when at last Lillian took the cradle from
the horse and stood it against the trunk of a walnut
tree. They were inside a clearing ringed with hickory
and walnut. Beyond, through one thin stand of trees,
lay a small valley. At their feet a stream ran its stony
bed, making its way toward its river.

Lillian got the ax off the horse, saying, "Whoa . . .
Jet . . . whoa," as he moved restlessly.

"If you want firewood, I'll cut it," Jason said. "Then
I'll unload Jet."

She moved to the edge of trees and began to chop,
in a businesslike manner, at a small green hickory.
"This is for our lodge."

Already, by the time he leapt to her side, she was
starting on the second hickory. When he tried to take
the ax, she resisted.

"The Osage woman builds the lodge, Jason."

"In the village, maybe. But here, a day's walk from
St. Louis, we're where the man does the man's work.
When we get to the Osage village, we'll live Osage.
Away from there, we're married white, and we'll live
white."

Lillian surrendered the ax.

Thus they built together, made their fire together,
ate together. Jason watched as she readied Auguste for
the night, as she cradled him in her arms, listened as
she sang, her voice a throbbing which got into him,
surged along his veins, and set him aquiver and impatient, and, strangely, in awe of what was to come.

He wished, he yearned, he ached and pained to draw
her here and now into his arms, to enfold her, to par-
take of her, to whisper how wonderful she was, and
how she blessed him to become his wife. Instead, he

could only sit, that quivering through him, streaking his marrow, and wait.

After the fire was banked so the embers would live, after Auguste, nested in his blanket, had fallen asleep, Lillian came to Jason on their blanket. She was naked, the skin of her body soft and fragrant and warm in the coldness of the night. And when he would have reached out for her and could not because of the great shuddering emotion which swept him, which threatened his ability to hold back, to wait, it was she who took the initiative.

"I will undress you, my husband," she whispered. "I know how it is with a man; I have been told by my mother. When we are both natural, we are as nature itself, and nature is neither anxious nor shy, not in its heart."

She undressed him, and Jason found that his haste had been stripped away with his clothing. He took her into his arms, and bore her down upon their wedding blanket and his body entered hers, and there came to pass such glory as shook his soul.

And he thought, This is joy.

Chapter 32

The days passed like a song as they walked through the forest, the plain, along the bank of the Missouri. The nights were glory in their own lodge, in a friendly Indian village, or in a settler's cabin, and Jason could not count them, for they fled, lost in the wonder of Lillian.

He thought of how it had been as he walked from New York to Pittsburgh, how long the miles, how weary the way. He recalled how time had dragged when he was building his house, how slow the time while Massie Ann carried Auguste, the heavy creep of it in the months that followed his son's birth. He could feel again the standstill of time during the earthquake, and the arduous and hopeless search that followed. And the endless struggle up the river.

And now time was speeding by!

The day they reached the point where they must leave the Missouri to bear south and west they picked a rolling, river-bordered spread of land for their future home. They marked the location on the map Jason was making, and stayed there while he paced off his eight hundred acres. He drove his stakes into the ground and carved his name on every one, J. Blood, so that anyone else, discovering the beauty and fertility of the section, would know it was already spoken for.

It began to snow as they resumed their journey. The flakes were big and feathery and the whitest Jason had ever seen, and they drifted against the face in a kind of benediction. One big flake settled on Auguste's little nose and he chortled. Lillian laughed too, the sound low and songlike, weaving into the falling snow.

It was late afternoon, April sixth, when they came in sight of the Osage village. It was situated in Kansas land some fifty-six miles west of the Missouri line, about on a parallel, Jason conjectured, with Ste. Genevieve, on the Mississippi. The village was filled with lodges, with children and dogs, with tall men, and with women.

"The Neosho River, where you'll trap, flows about a quarter of a mile west," Lillian said.

Jason looked west, but the river was hidden by forest. "How far does the timber reach?" he asked.

"From either shore, about three or four hundred yards. I used to spend days roaming there. It's got splendid oaks and walnuts and hickories and mulberries. I love to eat the mulberries, though many say they're not fit to eat."

Jason gazed beyond the forest. Extending as far west as the eye could see, the prairie rose gradually and evenly, unbroken by abrupt descents or elevations.

"The land lies so evenly," he remarked.

"Yes. The village is situated ideally. In the summer months, the prairie breezes cool it, and sometimes at night you need a fire and must cover yourself with a blanket. In winter, moving the lodges into the nearby woods provides enough shelter for the Osage and feed for the horses. In summer, the prairie is covered with grass. See . . . over there." She gestured.

Jason looked to where horses in number were grazing in the short tender new grass. Small boys were at play along the edge of the pasturage, their shouts coming thinly across the distance, a few of the older ones not playing, but moving among the horses as though to make certain they were all as they should be.

As they looked about, Jason and Lillian kept moving. They came to the edge of the village, Jason leading the horse, Lillian nodding and smiling to some girls they passed.

He estimated there must be some two hundred lodges here, standing fifteen to twenty feet apart, rising in every direction, with little regard to the order of their arrangement. Children and dogs were thick, and off at a distance a group of men were playing a game with a ball.

"Some of the lodges are very large," Jason commented, estimating that one they'd just passed looked to be a hundred feet in length.

"Each lodge," Lillian explained, "holds one family. An Osage with five wives must provide five different fireplaces, one for each wife. She places her bedding and personal belongings—clothing, cooking utensils, and such—whatever he allows her."

"He's head of the lodge, then, the husband."

"Not exactly." She laughed softly. "Every man is a chief, according to his wife—outside the lodge. Inside, she berates him for all sorts of things—for not killing the biggest buffalo, for not winning a race, for not trapping the prettiest fur. It's because she wants him to be the best in the village, and she lets him know about it when he isn't the best, to encourage him. But outside, she boasts to the other women of the prowess of her husband, making him sound like the best in the village."

Jason grinned, studied the lodges as they moved deeper into them. They varied from seven to ten feet in breadth and from twenty to a hundred in length. They were built in the fashion of Lillian's overnight tents, but with stronger hickories secured more firmly in the ground in their two parallel lines, their ends lashed together above to form a continuous arch. They were covered with more grass matting than the overnight tents, and had more holes in the roof, according to the number of fireplaces. Over these holes, dressed buffalo skins were thrown loosely to prevent rain from entering. Dirt was heaped against the matting at ground level to secure the matting from violent gusts of wind, and a few feet off from each lodge a deep trench was dug to carry off water when it rained.

"This," Lillian announced at last, "is Eagle Feather's tent. We'll greet him first."

Jason dropped Jet's reins, and the horse stood. Lillian took the cradle off him, hung it on her back, pushed aside the blanket that hung over the opening of the lodge, and entered, Jason following.

There were three cookfires, with women and children gathered to them. There was the aroma of cooking. The floor was spread with buffalo robes and bear skins. Jason noticed hunting accoutrements, horse trappings, kitchen utensils, and clothing ranged along the sides of the lodge where they would not interfere with the movements of those inside. Then his attention was drawn by a slow and powerful movement at the first fireplace, and one of the tallest men he had ever seen came to his feet. He held out his arms and Lillian hurried into them and laid her cheek against his shoulder.

For a heartbeat, she remained there, then moved to stand beside the tall man and spoke proudly. "Oh, Eagle Feather, father of my mother, accept our affection. I have brought my husband, whom I married before the parson in St. Louis. I have brought Jason Blood."

The Osage man's hair was glittering white and fell in two long braids over his chest. His body, clad in deerskin, was powerfully formed. His countenance was noble and comely, with a high forehead and wide temples and his black eyes were so deep set they appeared to be small. They were lustrous and searching, and at the edge of friendliness.

Jason made a slow, respectful nod. "I am honored to have your granddaughter as wife," he told the chief.

Eagle Feather's eyes gleamed. "You are welcome

in Osage village," he said. His voice was deep and, like Lillian's, made a kind of speaking music. "Lillian's village, the village of her birth."

"I have come to trap, to take my furs to St. Louis to sell, to buy land on the Missouri."

"Trapping is best in land of Osage," the chief said. "Hunting is best."

Lillian stepped to the fire and drew a white-haired woman to her feet. "Flying Bird," she said, speaking slowly, "here is Lillian's husband. Ja-son. This is mother of my mother," she added, glancing at Jason.

Flying Bird smiled, her coarse-featured face breaking into so many wrinkles that Jason thought of Granny Grosshart. She spoke a flow of Osage that caused Lillian to smile.

"She speaks no English," Lillian explained, "though she understands. She says we will make fine babies, and wants to know . . ." She turned in sudden confusion and hugged her little grandmother.

Jason didn't know which way to look. Eagle Feather remained impassive.

Lillian banished the moment by urging Jason to the next fire. Here she presented the middle-aged woman and her half-grown children. "This is Busy Fox, Eagle Feather's number-two wife." She took him quickly to the last fire, where a woman of less than forty stood, proud and graceful, a cluster of younger children about her. "This is Pretty Bush, number-three wife."

All three wives, Jason noted, had coarse, irregular features. The ungainliness of feature, however, was atoned for by a well-knit and graceful form, even in Flying Bird, who must have been almost comely when she was young.

When they returned to the first fireplace, the chief asked, "Ja-son. Do you honor the lodge of Eagle Feather or that of Young Doe?"

Jason glanced at Lillian.

"My husband would have me speak," Lillian said. "We would have our meal at the fire of the chief. We would then go to the tent of Young Doe. Tomorrow, I shall build a lodge for my husband."

Eagle Feather settled himself at the fireplace of Flying Bird. Lillian shrugged the cradle off her back, sank down on a bearskin, propped the cradle against her arm.

"This is Auguste Blood," she said. "He is the once motherless son of my husband. Now he is my son as well."

Auguste promptly sounded his hunger cry. Flying Bird murmured in her own tongue, gave Lillian a horn ladle, then gave one to Jason.

"You dip in first," Lillian said, "you're the guest. There'll be only the five of us. Flying Bird's children are grown and in their own lodges."

Jason dipped into the family bowl of what proved to be boiled pounded corn. It tasted good, somewhat like mush. There was no meat in the bowl, would be none, Lillian had told him, until the spring hunt.

When they had finished, and Flying Bird had patted and stroked the sated Auguste, murmuring like a flowing brook until he slept, Eagle Feather brought forth his big pipe, filled it, lit it with a fiery ember, puffed deeply to make it draw. He then dipped it ceremoniously in the four directions, then toward the floor and toward the roof, took a long draw, and handed it to Jason.

Jason, who had never before smoked, took the pipe with what he hoped would look like confidence. He put the stem between his teeth, tried to disguise his distaste for its bitterness, took a shallow cautious pull. Crushing the need to cough, he passed the pipe back to Eagle Feather, then, jaw stiff, sternly and deliberately he expelled the smoke.

Very shortly, the pipe was in his hand again, and the process had to be repeated. Before he'd had to suck on the pipe too many times, however, somehow managing never to cough, it was finished.

Lillian rose, hanging the cradle on her back.

*   *   *

Before they'd taken a dozen steps away from the lodge, a figure seemed to spring out of the dusk before them. Jason took it in with one swift, comprehensive look, and his blood gave a vast, heavy thump.

It was a man who stood there, at least five or six inches over six feet. Neither the dusky light nor the deerskins he wore concealed the fact that he was muscled and hardened into a bold sword of manhood. He had lean, strong legs and arms, broad, big chest, narrow, slim waist, hard stomach. His hands and feet were small, his wrists and ankles finely boned.

His head was boldly shaped and, in the warrior fashion, shaven except for the scalp lock. This was of a blackness exceeded not even by his deep-socketed, intensely bright eyes.

The racial characteristics were strong in him. He had the high forehead, the wide temples, the strong, aquiline nose, a little curved and beaked. He had the flat upper lip and the more protuberant lower lip and a wide, stern mouth. His chin was cleft. If his body was a sword, his face was a broad blade, as beautiful and as murderously ready as any sheathed weapon. His expression, at this moment, was serious, dignified, almost soldierly. He was a superb man, a magnificent man, a burnished god of a man.

"So," he said to Lillian. "You have come." He used English as if it were an insult. "As Quick Knife said you would come."

"Don't jest," she replied.

"Quick Knife never jests."

"Nor do I evade. I made no promise."

"You came back." He was arrogant now.

"I always do. I come to visit my blood."

"It is different this time. You will be Quick Knife's number-two wife."

"Have you changed so much?" Lillian asked quietly. "Do you now speak of private matters in the presence of others?"

"Quick Knife spoke with Eagle Feather. That was private."

"Sometimes," Lillian told him, "it isn't easy for me to keep to Osage ways. I know, without being told, of what you and Eagle Feather spoke. It no longer is possible. For this," she continued, drawing close to Jason, "is Jason Blood, my husband. He has sat at the fireplace of Eagle Feather's number-one wife, he has eaten from the common bowl. He has shared the pipe with Eagle Feather."

The warrior's eyes met Jason's eyes.

"What she says is true," Jason told him shortly. He was angry, and his instinct was to order Quick Knife to stop badgering Lillian. Instead, to avoid violating some Osage protocol unknown to him, he stood quiet, his clenched fists the only outward sign of his anger.

And of his shock that Lillian might seriously have considered becoming wife to an Osage warrior.

"It is known," Quick Knife said, arrogance rising, "that the white man comes where he is not welcome. And now this white man, this Ja-son Blood, has taken that which is not his. He has taken Quick Knife's chosen wife, leaving him second choice—the sister of Lillian, Singing Lark."

Abruptly he turned and was gone.

Chapter 33

Jason moved to plunge after him, but Lillian caught his arm. He stared at her in the dark light.

She looked so reasonable that he had an impulse to shake her. Then, as quickly as it had taken him, the impulse vanished. She smiled and led on.

At the opening of the lodge stood another tall Osage, also handsome. He was perhaps forty years old, as magnificently built as Eagle Feather, though not as tall as Quick Knife, being only two or three inches over six feet. His head was shaven except for a jet-black scalp lock.

Lillian introduced them quickly. The warrior extended his hand, Jason took it, and they exchanged powerful grips. "Swift Foot greets Ja-son, husband of Lillian," he said. "Peace."

"Peace," responded Jason.

"Is peace upon you, husband of Young Doe?" asked Lillian. "Is peace upon your lodge?"

"Peace is ever upon this lodge. The wives of Swift Foot do not quarrel among themselves."

"And the village? Are the Osage at peace with the nations?"

"The daughter of Young Doe still asks questions?"

"Yes. Swift Foot has always answered the questions. There is talk of white man's war in St. Louis, and fear of attack by Indian nations."

"The Osage are at peace. Yet there are always young warriors who want to go to war. It is not for Swift Foot to speak of these matters. It is for Eagle Feather, the chief."

Lillian bowed her head in acceptance. Swift Foot stood aside and she drew Jason into the lodge.

There were three fireplaces in this lodge, too. A tall and comely woman of perhaps forty was standing in the light of the first fire. She looked much like Lillian, though with blacker eyes and a duskiness of skin that Lillian did not have. Around her were her children, and beyond, at the other cookfires, waited the other wives and their children.

Lillian embraced her mother, drew her forward, presented Jason.

"Ja-son," said the mother in the softest voice he'd ever heard, and he wondered if her French blood had not graced her voice, even as it had marked her features with beauty. "Young Doe hap-py. Wel-come, Ja-son."

Jason bowed, smiled.

"My sister, Singing Lark," Lillian continued, "daughter of Swift Foot and Young Doe. She is fifteen."

Singing Lark stepped forward, a lithesome girl with skin duskier than her mother's. Her resemblance to Young Doe was remarkable, even though it barely missed the coarseness of feature common to the Osage women. Jason conjectured that the one-quarter French blood she bore had softened her beauty. She looked hauntingly like Lillian.

Singing Lark gave him a warm, openly adoring look. "Ja-son," she said in a voice that he expected to be like Lillian's, filled with music, or like that of Young Doe, exceedingly soft, and that was neither, but a rich velvet caress of sound. "Ja-son." She smiled, became even more beautiful.

Now Lillian brought forward brothers, each younger

than the one before. "Six of them, besides Singing Lark
at this fire," she declared. "You'll learn their names or
not, it doesn't matter. There are so many children in
this lodge, I doubt if Swift Foot himself can tell them
apart."

She slipped the cradle off her back and into the eager
arms of her sister. She led Jason to the other fireplaces,
presented the other wives, both younger than Young
Doe. They were coarse-featured, graceful-bodied, surrounded by waves of children. All told, Jason estimated,
there must be twenty children in Swift Foot's lodge.

"Eighteen," Lillian whispered, later, lying in his
arms at the side of the tent. They were opposite Young
Doe's fire. Everyone was asleep around the individual
fires. "My mother has seven, Hot Sky has six, and Diving Fish has five. Most are boys, and Swift Foot is
proud of this."

"Why don't you have an Osage name?" Jason whispered.

"Because my father was a white man and didn't wish
to name me in the Osage manner. The Osage father,
when his child is born, steps outside his tent and the first
thing he beholds becomes the baby's name. The first
thing Swift Foot saw when my sister was born was a
lark singing."

Thus they whispered until they fell asleep.

When Jason awoke, he gazed across the darkness of
the lodge at the fireplace, where a few coals glimmered.
Lillian slept on, close against his back. There was no
stir among the blanket-wrapped figures around the fires,
no sound from any child or even from Auguste. Jason
lay motionless, listening to the wilderness village for
whatever sound, whatever vibration, had stolen into
his sleep and broken it.

There was a far restlessness, he imagined, in the
buffalo robe on which he lay, a hint of life which he
felt in his arm against the robe, in his thigh, along the
side of his foot. It seeped through skin and flesh and into
his blood, went quivering down his blood, and into his

ears, and brought, very faintly, the muted and distant throb of drums.

Indians . . . Sac . . . he thought. And he leapt to his feet, grabbing up his rifle.

"It's all right!" Lillian was up too, holding his arm.

As though her whisper were a signal, or the drum sound, soft but rising insistently, had called them, those in the lodge wakened. Moving as one, they arose from their blankets. From beyond the front wall of the lodge came a moan, low at first, then rising, climbing above the drums, soaring. In answer, a hysterical cry came from beyond the opposite wall of the lodge, and simultaneously from some other distance sounded a lifting, wailing sob.

A shrill, rending cry rose from the number-three fireplace, and at this every soul in the lodge of Swift Foot, down to the least child, the startled Auguste with them, began to wail and keen. Now those in the lodge moved out through the entrance, loud and lamenting, moved into the drumming throb, into the growing wails, their own cries blending into those others. The chorus swelled, drifted away from the lodge for some destination not known.

Now Lillian had Auguste on his cradle and on her back. "It's the Osage hour of mourning," she explained swiftly, her voice the only sanity in the throbbing and the wailing that filled the wilderness. "At dawn, at the time for rising, we go into the woods, and we mourn. Together, as a nation, we mourn, each for his own."

Jason felt the hair on his neck stir. "Mourn for what?"

"For whatever loss each has suffered. A loved one who is dead, an evil, great or small, which has befallen us, even the loss of a favorite horse or dog. Or some ancestor we have never known, have lost the privilege to know. It is a good thing, Jason. It keeps an understanding in us for others, all the Osages together, mourning as one."

"How long does it last?"

"Less than half an hour. Afterward, when we have mourned, we enter into our day and laugh and sing and do what comes to hand. There is no need to brood, for we have washed away our troubles, we have cleansed ourselves. I would take Auguste, if you do not forbid. I was taken by my mother with my father's consent."

Osage blood and Osage custom were what had gone into making Lillian what she was. He would not change her.

"I don't forbid," he said.

She left, carrying his son on her back, and he was alone at the lodge, alone in the village while the nation mourned. And their united cry became a song rising out of the timber, rising above the Neosho.

Chapter 34

Lillian, with the help of Singing Lark, set about building their lodge right after breakfast. She chose a spot off to one side of the newer lodges of the village, as, she said, was custom. Then she and her sister began to cut down their hickories.

Jason, honoring Osage custom, didn't try to help, but did permit himself to step off the measurements after the hickories were set into the ground. The tent was to be ten by twelve feet.

He next made his way, through shouting, playing children and leaping dogs, toward the lodge of Eagle Feather, hoping to become acquainted with the old chief. Out at the pasturage, he saw men and boys moving among the horses, rubbing them down, examining an occasional hoof. He passed a number of women carrying water in wooden buckets, a few with skin buckets.

A group of young men were playing a sort of ball game. Another group of men were sitting under a tree, conversing. Though he caught snatches of their talk, Jason could not divide it into anything which sounded like words. The Osage tongue was a mystery to him, as it was always to be, as French had been in New Madrid. One or two of these conversing warriors looked directly at him and he nodded soberly and they returned the nod almost imperceptibly.

He did not see Quick Knife anywhere.

Jason found Eagle Feather sitting on his haunches at the sunny side of his lodge. He was looking across a distance, watching some young warriors engaged in racing. Most of them were lined up, while two ran like the wind from one point to another, heads thrown back, scalp locks standing out.

Eagle Feather now looked up at Jason. "You may sit," he said.

Jason squatted, and, when the chief made no conversation, himself remained silent. He watched the ball players, the racers, the conversing ones. Finally, unaccustomed to seeing grown men disport themselves in this manner, he frowned, trying to figure it out.

"You have question?" Eagle Feather asked.

"Well . . . yes. Is this some holiday?"

"Holiday?"

"A day of special celebration. Of games and races."

"It is no such day. Why do you ask this question?"

"When they work, what do they do?"

"Work?" repeated the chief reflectively. "Why should Osage man work? His wives build his lodge, clean his rifle, sharpen his tomahawk, cook so he eats many times each day. His wives make his moccasins and clothes. Osage man goes on spring hunt, he goes on fall hunt, he takes care of horses. He keeps body strong with races and games. He makes war. Osage man has no thing white man calls work. Osage man has no need to tire himself in such manner."

Jason considered. With some wonder, he recognized that the activities with which the Osage men filled their time was a sort of work. In their own manner they provided food for their great families, and kept themselves fit so as to defend their village against enemy nations, and to protect their hunting grounds.

"You speak of war," Jason said. "You know of the white man's war which may come?"

"Eagle Feather knows. In St. Louis the white man has scouts. Young warriors speak of it. Quick Knife has spoken most. He warns that white man has taken country from nations east of Mississippi River, and that white man will spread until he takes all on this side of river, coming even into Kansas country."

And he will, Jason thought, astonished to find himself in agreement with Quick Knife about anything. The white man will come, he's here now, I'm here.

"What do you think about the situation?" Jason asked.

"Eagle Feather is old man, old chief. Osages have lived on this land all my days, all the days of my father and his father. There have always been white men who tell Osages many things, and Osages have believed perhaps too much. Quick Knife does not believe.

"At first, Osages welcomed white men, French men. They lived Osage, married our daughters, put French blood into Osages. They did not want Osage land, to rip it apart for 'crops,' or to fasten cabins to land, ruining land. They hunted prairies and trapped rivers with Osages. It is open to you, Ja-son, how Osages liked French?"

"I understand," Jason said thoughtfully.

"Quick Knife speaks that Americans are not like French. He speaks truth. Americans ruin land with ugly lodges, tear land with iron and wood and kill natural growth with 'crops.' Osages do not want this done to their land. In past, when president in Washington did nothing to stop Americans, Osages went to war with Americans and took many scalps. Eagle Feather helped this war when he was young warrior, to protect Osage land.

"Then white men in Chouteau's town called chiefs together in council. They scolded chiefs, as chiefs' wives do in their lodges, as wives scold wind for blowing their cook fires, and water for coming in at fireholes. White men spoke that Osages had taken American scalps and stolen Americans' horses, and must pay much money.

"How can doing as Osages have always done mean Osages must pay money? Quick Knife asks this, and Eagle Feather asks. Osages have always gone on warpath, they have always taken scalps and taken horses from their enemies. Osages are not women, they are warriors and hunters. What must warrior do? Sit as today Eagle Feather sits at the door of lodge while Americans take his land? Osages have fought Cherokee, because Cherokee want our hunting grounds and make war on our villages. Osages have never made war on Cherokee, they do not want what Cherokee have, but Osages will not let Cherokee hunt on their lands, and this is right."

Jason nodded, absorbing, considering.

"But now Quick Knife and other young Osages want to enter into white man's war if it comes, and this fills Eagle Feather with trouble. For white men in Canada—men who are English and will fight on side of England—are telling nations along Canadian border that they must fight white soldiers to keep them from taking land which belongs to Indian nations. They have made Indian nations believe that this is what this war is about—white man pushing Indian further west until one day he will push him off surface of earth. And that is not what causes this war. It is war between white men—English and American—and Indians, Osages with them, should not enter into it.

"I ask, Ja-son, husband of my granddaughter, if you wish to fight in this war. You are white man, and many white men enter white man's armies."

"As I understand the trouble," Jason said, "it's caused by England's determination to keep America from trading in certain lands across the ocean, to keep America from growing as rich and powerful as England. I heard a great deal about it in New York, where I used to live. If there had been a question of defending our shores while I was there, I would have fought, yes."

The chief nodded solemnly. "Ja-son thinks as Eagle

Feather. But Quick Knife and other young warriors listen to white man in Canada."

"Does that mean the Osage will fight if war comes?"

"Quick Knife and others will attack American cabins. They will not go into armies far away."

"Can't you stop them? You are the chief."

"Chief is not like white army general," Eagle Feather explained. "When general gives order, it is obeyed. There is no argument, no council sits in discussion. To be chief in inherited. My father was chief, and his father. It is position of honor and prestige and some power. But power is limited, and can be set aside."

"How can that be done?" Jason asked.

"Osage government is simple. Eagle Feather is called great chief and presides at councils, speaks of any subject requiring discussion, entertains important guests. Next, after great chief, come subdivisions, each with its own chief, who is elected for victorious deed or appointed by great chief. This too is honor only; they have no power.

"Last come braves—warriors who number more than chiefs, who hold real authority of government. They are men who earn position by great deeds and victories on battlefield, as white man calls it. A brave is favorite of Osage nation, and his counsel will be followed where word of chief above him would not be listened to."

"Does each subdivision have a leader?" Jason asked.

"When village goes on hunt, hunt is led by one chosen Osage man. When war party is raised, it chooses warrior to lead. In neither time does Eagle Feather have power. Hunting party follows elected leader, war party follows its leader. You know now, Ja-son, why Eagle Feather cannot force the young warriors to refrain from scalping. He can only counsel. They will do as they decide."

"Has a war party been raised?" Jason asked, alarmed that he may have brought Lillian and Auguste into danger.

"Not yet," Eagle Feather replied. "And will not be,

not before spring hunt is ended, because all Osage, young and old, wait for hunt. Yet Quick Knife speaks of warpath more hotly every moon, and some young warriors listen. At this moment, though he knows none will go on warpath at once, he holds councils in forest with youngest and most impatient of our warriors."

Chapter 35

The lodge was ready before nightfall, and Lillian cooked
their supper over her own fireplace. Singing Lark ate
with them, insisting upon being the one to feed Auguste,
who chortled and patted her cheeks, his fat little hands
very white against her skin.

When they had finished, when Auguste was asleep,
Singing Lark sprang to her feet and went dancing about
the tent. The firelight showed her to be smiling, eyes
alive and sparkling and, when they came to Jason, adoring.

"There will be song in this lodge this night!" she
cried. "Ja-son, your number-one wife, Singing Lark's
sister, sings as another lark! Would you hear us, would
you listen, Ja-son?"

"Why, sure," Jason replied, a grin taking him.

The girl was so eager, so young. Lillian was smiling
at her, smiling at Jason, lovelier than ever before. She
put up her hands and drew the younger girl down onto
the bearskin beside her.

Thus they sang, sisters momentarily so alike they
might have been twins. Their voices came together in
Osage words, twined into one velvet, angelic tone.

Listening, there was again awakened in Jason a love for music, and again he resolved that Lillian must have a pianoforte, and so fill their cabin with music.

It was Singing Lark who ended the songs. "Are we going to the dancing, Lillian?" she damanded. "Will you take Ja-son?" Her great black eyes were sparkling. She was looking lovingly at Jason.

Her open adoration made him uncomfortable. The mention of dancing worried him. He'd never attended frolics, and after the ball he'd taken Massie Ann to on the night of the earthquake, he had less inclination than ever to join any group merrymaking.

But Lillian might want it, he thought guiltily. And indeed, when he looked at her, she was watching him hopefully.

"I've always liked the dancing," she said.

"Then we go," he told her.

He was amazed at the speed with which the sisters bound Auguste into his cradle, never waking him. In no time, they were walking the labyrinth of dark lodges, going toward the sound of drums.

"Quick Knife once stayed with Lillian at the dancing," Singing Lark said teasingly. "When Lillian went to St. Louis, he stayed with Singing Lark. What will he do tonight?"

"Quick Knife isn't a brave you can tease," Lillian said warningly.

"He's the handsomest warrior in all the Osage!" cried Singing Lark. "He knows it . . . he tells it . . . the way he walks, dances, hunts, rides. All the Osage girls want to be his number-two wife!"

She gave a little skip, which put her ahead of them, and then she turned and waited. Now she walked very close to Jason, as did Lillian on his other side, his son riding her back.

They arrived at the place of the dance, a little apart from the lodges. All the Osages had thronged to the spot, and most were sitting on the ground, ringing the dance area. A few were moving about at the edge of the watchers, two or three were feeding the fire in the center of the ring, which flared high, lighting the scene. The drummers, three of them, squatted over their drums at one end of the dance ground.

Jason saw Quick Knife at once and knew the warrior saw him. He was standing beside the drummers, towering over all the Osage men. Lillian and Singing Lark sat down at the rear of the Osages, and Jason sat, cross-legged, between them.

The drums kept a low and heady beat, the men, glitter-eyed from the fire, playing them. Now the first dancers, warriors, came leaping into the circle, as lightly and breathlessly as the flames themselves. They went into the dance, forming a circle. Blending movement into drum music, they circled, lightly stepping, bending forward almost to the ground, straightening lithely, faces to the sky. The drums slowed, grew heavier, and singers wound their voices into the dancing and the drums, and along the rims of the watching Osages, the younger ones now were swaying to the music of the dance.

Now Quick Knife made his way boldly across the dance ground. He came toward Jason, who got to his feet and waited. This was a potential enemy, and he wanted no enemy. He would establish a peaceable if not friendly relationship with the warrior. Quick Knife spoke English; they could at least trade ideas. If he could avert trouble with Quick Knife, others might be friendly, and Jason wanted friends.

"Quick Knife," he said clearly as the warrior stopped before him. "Greetings. Peace."

The black eyes glinted coldly from their deep sockets. The arrogant Osage visage turned to Jason.

"Quick Knife comes for Singing Lark," he said, using English, as he had done before, as if it were an insult.

"Quick Knife is certain Singing Lark wishes to go with him!" cried the girl. "Perhaps he is too certain!"

"Singing Lark will come. She will sit in high place."

"Will Quick Knife dance for Singing Lark?" she teased. "For Singing Lark and no other?"

"It is so. Come."

With unexpected decorum, the girl rose and, without a backward look at Jason or her sister, followed the warrior. A moment later she was seated on a high rise of ground, so that her head was higher than that of any other watching the dance.

Jason wondered at her abrupt compliance with Quick Knife's wishes, wondered how it would be for her, should she become his number-two wife. As though she sensed his speculation, Lillian murmured to him.

"All the Osages know now that Singing Lark is Quick Knife's choice for number-two wife. He has singled her out for honor. She is sitting beside Sucking Bee, his number-one wife, and her two sons. Sucking Bee will show kindness to Singing Lark, for she was my dearest friend when we were children. You can see, even from here, that there is kindness in her face."

Jason studied the number-one wife of the warrior as best he could. She had strong and stocky shoulders, which was all he could see, and coarse, blunt features. Her skin looked very dark. When she turned to answer something Singing Lark had apparently cried out to her, she smiled.

He wondered if Singing Lark had committed herself, had made a promise, by going with Quick Knife, by sitting with Sucking Bee. Again, in that way she had, Lillian answered his unspoken question.

"My sister is as proud, in her way, as Quick Knife. In all the nation she couldn't find a husband to excel Quick Knife. But she is young . . . she is the most beautiful girl in the nation . . . she is willful. Quick Knife would not, after tonight, take refusal by her."

"He's not concerned about her being a willful wife, then," Jason said.

"Singing Lark won't be willful, not after she's a wife," Lillian replied quietly. "She is warm and loving, and will become wife to no man unless she wants to be."

They fell silent, watched the dancing, listened to the drums and the intermittent singing. Jason enjoyed the music, but was relieved when Lillian suggested they return to their lodge.

He sprang up immediately. "What about Singing Lark?" he asked.

"Quick Knife will take her to Swift Foot's lodge," she replied. "We are free to go."

The days vanished. Though Quick Knife's arrogance and open dislike for Jason never relented, Jason, made friends with some of the young Osages. He raced with them, learned their game of ball, became proficient. He fished, hunted small game, tended Jet, keeping him as glossy and groomed as the horse of any Osage. He conversed fluently by the hour with Eagle Feather and Swift Foot, but haltingly with the younger Osages, who knew little if any English.

He lamented, one day, to Lillian that he was making no progress in learning Osage. "It was the same with French," he told her, and not for the first time. "I never could make any sense of it. And you speak all three languages—English and French and Osage. And will want to teach it to your children."

"*Our* children, Jason," she corrected gently. "I promise that only English will be spoken in our home. My husband is not to wonder what is being said."

"That's too much to ask," Jason protested. "You want our children to know their blood, all their bloods —French, Osage . . . and whatever I am. American, let's say."

"They'll know their blood. And they'll know the languages when they're older. But English will be spoken within the family."

He stared at her, benumbed with love. "You're the only unselfish person I've known," he said humbly. "Except for Medary."

"You know many of them now, Jason," she responded. "The Osage are taught from birth to be unselfish. If what you say is true, unselfishness was given me as Osage heritage."

"It's an uncommon thing," Jason said.

"Not among the Osage. They consider ingratitude and selfishness mortal sins. The most frightful personal danger, the most painful starvation, the most tragic sufferings, cannot excuse a selfish act, nor will the most powerful excuses be accepted to justify an ungrateful one."

Her voice was shaking a bit. Jason loked at her, concerned. Her mouth wasn't quite steady, and this was the only time he'd seen it like that.

"Why are you so upset?" he asked.

"A terrible example of it happened in my own lifetime, Jason. It happened one winter when I spent a month in the lodge of Swift Foot and my mother. I will tell you of it, and perhaps, when I repeat over and over to Auguste the things he must believe to grow into an unselfish and never ungrateful man, you will know my reason for doing it, and will not be displeased."

"I'll never be displeased," he assured her. "Tell me what happened."

"An Osage family, Great Tree and his wife, Diving Duck, and their two small sons and Great Tree's son, Brown Water, from his dead number-one wife, strayed from the village in search of game. Great Tree told of this when he returned, told it in my hearing.

"They were in the woods for two days, and they found no game of any kind, and were very hungry, as you can understand. They tried to return to the village, but took the wrong way and were lost. They wandered for some days, without a morsel to satisfy their hunger. Worse, there came a heavy fall of snow.

"It was then that Great Tree found and killed a woodcock. Without hesitation, he passed the bird to Diving Duck. She seized it, and after barely warming it over a fire, served it to her own children, each with its share. Then, leaving out Great Tree's first son, Brown Water, though he cried and wanted meat, she herself greedily ate the remainder of the nearly raw bird.

"All the while, Great Tree sat opposite her, on the

other side of the fire, watching her closely and fiercely. When she had eaten, he motioned her to him. He then spoke to her quietly of what she had done. She had deprived his eldest son, her stepson, of life when it lay in her power to restore it to him. He had himself felt as severely as she the pains of hunger, but, with the hope of serving her and the children, had willingly given up his share of the food the Great Spirit had thrown in his way. She should have done the same, should have at least treated his son as well as she treated her own. She was very selfish, he told her, and she had brought her doom upon herself."

"Doom?" Jason repeated.

"Yes. As he finished telling her that, he seized his tomahawk and, one after the other, butchered her and the three children. He didn't make an exception of the son by his number-one wife. Then, leaving the four in the positions in which he had sacrificed them, and taking only what would protect him from the cold, he resumed his sad and wandering journey. By accident, he was picked up by a party of hunters, among them Swift Foot, and it was to them, gathered in Swift Foot's lodge, that he related all that had happened."

"What did he do after that?" Jason asked.

"He wasn't blamed, as a white man would be under the same circumstances. A council sat, with Eagle Feather presiding. It was a grave offense, even though necessary, and he had to atone for it in private. He was later scalped by the Cherokee. With the Osage, as you have now heard, a selfish trait, and an ungrateful one, is quickly noted and dealt with. Even if comparatively slight, it isn't so considered by the Osages, and for years after will be reproached."

Jason found himself pondering this tale in the days to come. It impressed him deeply, caused him to watch the Osages, to recognize their spontaneous unselfishness. Even Quick Knife, with all his prowess and arrogance, committed no act which bespoke selfishness or ingratitude.

Jason found himself now in tune with the life-rhythm of the village. Racing and ball playing and hunting kept his body hard. For relaxation, as night approached, he sometimes joined the men as they congregated in numerous parties at the largest and most convenient lodges. There, encircling a little fire, they would remain perhaps until dawn, engaged in social conversation. The sole topics of conversation with the men, he learned, were women, war exploits, hunting, and horses. The night was rarely allowed to pass without several dances, accompanied generally by singing and the beat of the drums.

But he was really content when he was in their lodge with Lillian and Auguste. And he knew that, much as he had come to admire the Osage and their ideals, it would be a relief to him to live as a white man in his own cabin.

Chapter 36

On June second, the morning of departure for the spring hunt, the dawn chant in the woods was sung earlier. The sounds were different today, with excitement in them, and there were prayers that Jason could identify. He couldn't himself pronounce the Osage word, but he knew that in their own tongue they were crying over and over, "Buffalo . . . buffalo!"

Moments later, in the village, there was incredible activity as the nation made ready to leave. Almost every living thing was to go—men, women, children, infants, horses, dogs—and the village seethed like a disturbed colony of ants.

Warriors charged here and there on horses, little bells tied to the horses' manes ringing and tinkling. The young men were painted red and green and were handsome in their fine blankets, which liftd behind them in the wind their riding created, bronzed torsos bare to the sun, eagle feathers dipping and lifting.

As Jason saddled Lillian's horse and cut out the riding horse and pack horses allotted him by Eagle Feather, riders milled about the pasturage, herding pack horses to the village. And when he returned there, most of the lodges had been disassembled. Dogs yipped and yelped, children squealed and tumbled on the ground, and women scolded incessantly as they hurriedly disassembled their lodges.

Caches had been dug, and now Lillian buried the separate parts of their lodge carefully, as the other women were doing. She also buried things not necessary to the journey, such as extra cooking pots.

Then, working with incredible swiftness, she loaded some matting, two buffalo robes, and two blankets onto one pack horse, along with clothing, hunting accoutrements, and cooking utensils. The second pack horse would be used only every other day on the trip out and hopefully would be, on the homeward trip, loaded with buffalo meat. She strapped Auguste into his new larger cradle, hung him from her saddle bow, and mounted.

Auguste, now almost a year old, grinned at Jason, who grinned back. He might really be walking by the time the hunt ended, Jason thought.

Now a young warrior came dashing around on his horse, bells jingling, feather dipping, blanket flowing. "All make ready to leave!" he was crying out. "Swift Foot, leader of the hunt, tells all to make ready to leave! The time has come!"

The heralding, of course, was in Osage, which Lillian interpreted for Jason, but he'd taken in its import already.

Instantly, the women were in their forked-stick saddles, children were caught up and tucked in among the various bales and bundles, and the babies in their cradles were tied onto the saddles.

Except for two lodges, one sheltering an old warrior and his old wife, and the other an old woman alone, the village was abandoned. It was almost as though two hundred lodges had never stood beneath today's early sun. There were left only the fire pits, the ground around them clean and bare.

Jason, looking here and there toward spots he knew very well to be caches of family belongings, where he'd seen the women digging and burying and covering, could not identify the spots. "It's so clean, so natural," he said, kneeing his horse over to Lillian.

"As it should be, Jason. The Osages hold the earth and the sun and wind and rain—everything they enjoy —as a gift from Wah-kontah, a gift to be used with gratitude and cherished and left, when finished with, unharmed and unmarked."

Jason watched the milling camp as they waited their turn to line up. Swift Foot, with Eagle Feather beside him as honored chief, was far ahead, he knew. The warriors named as wayfinders and scouts trotted out ahead of the village, which fell naturally into its long line. The wayfinders rode together, but the scouts went fanning out across the prairie on either side, even in these first moments. Each of these lookouts, Lillian said, carried a mirror which he could use for signaling should some enemy be sighted.

One group of warriors stayed far behind to make sure no one fell out and perished or was lost. As the last horse took its place, and the long line moved out of the village on the first day of the six- or seven-hundred-mile journey to the hunting ground, the women began to sing. Lillian, riding beside Jason, sang with them, and her voice lifted and fled into the sunlight like some graceful, airy, golden bird spun of melody.

The children, elated to be on the way at last, screamed, and some of them cried. A number of the high-spirited younger warriors raced back and forth along the line, bells ajingle. Even the youngest already wore the painted eagle feather in their hair, the right to which they'd won by stealing horses. They must be the finest horsemen in the world, Jason thought. They rode as if they'd grown right out of the horse. They yelled and whooped at the horses, at those in the plodding line, at one another, at the sun and wind, whooped for the joy of the hunt to which they were bound.

Jason and Lillian kept as far behind the others as they could, to avoid dust. The warriors riding in the rear were some distance yet behind them.

"This isn't your first hunt, is it?" Jason ventured.

"I went once before," Lillian replied. "I wanted to go, and my mother and Swift Foot were eager to take me. My father said it would be a good thing. He believed if I did what is natural to all my bloods, there would be no warring in me among them. So I went, and learned how the hunt proceeds. Lodges are built every night, but the men don't talk and dance until dawn at this time. Their one thought is the hunt, so they rest longer hours. I saw them bring down buffalo on the plains and deer and elk and antelope in the timber. I was twelve years old, and had never been able to accept that the spring hunt needed to be for meat alone. I saw for myself that the summer coats aren't what they'll take at the trading posts. Only then did I understand why it was just the fall hunt that was for meat and skins and fur which has grown thick and warm for winter."

"And you were gone the whole eight weeks, you didn't get tired of it?"

"Nine weeks that time, and I was sorry to come back," she said, smiling. "Then Swift Foot himself took me to St. Louis by horse and when I got there I was happy to start my lessons and music and be with my father again."

Jason smiled with her, thinking of the eager young girl so at peace with her bloods that she found happiness in either life. His own sense of well-being deepened as they rode through the hours.

When the nation was four days on the trail, an elderly woman, enormous with child, fell to the rear of the train. It was only an hour after the tents had been struck, and she was walking laboriously and doggedly along under the morning sun.

When she faltered, then went on, Jason asked, "Where is her husband? Why is she back here, alone?"

"It is the Osage way," Lillian replied.

"If she can't keep up with the train, she should have a horse," Jason insisted. "We could put her on our spare pack horse."

"No, Jason," Lillian murmured. "Let's stop for a time . . . under that tree yonder. That way, we'll put ourselves too far behind to watch her. She doesn't want to be watched. Please, Jason," she repeated when he failed to turn his horse.

At the real concern in her tone, he complied. Consequently, after the train had gone far ahead, and the trailing old woman was but a dot on the earth, they remounted and walked their horses along behind the far-flung procession. So long had they waited that the rear-riding warriors were now in sight behind them.

Somewhat later, having lost sight of the old woman, they were passing a small copse of wood. Groans were issuing from it as they were about to pass on, and Jason, hastening in the direction of the groans, found the old woman on the point of giving birth to her child.

"I'll go for help," he told her, heedless of the fact that he couldn't speak her tongue. "Lillian can look after you until I get someone . . . the medicine man . . . somebody."

"The medicine man has nothing to do with this," Lillian told him as she came up. She knelt, spoke to the laboring woman in the Osage tongue, and the old creature objected strenuously to what she had said, waving her arms about, then doubling to her travail.

"What did she say?" Jason asked.

"She wants us to leave."

"We can't just ride away," Jason exclaimed.

With a gesture, Lillian spoke again to the woman. Again came great protest, accompanied this time by no little anger. And then, at Lillian's further words, a frantic, enraged gesture, followed by deep and tortured groans which seemed to tear their way out of her throat.

Swiftly Lillian produced a piece of blanket with which she had once wrapped Auguste, laid it on the ground near the laboring woman, remounted, turned her horse, and rode back toward the trail. Jason followed reluctantly, acceding to what might be Osage custom, but privately, he determined to come back later. He was not going to abandon an old woman and newborn infant to die.

They resumed the march, riding easily into the sweet prairie wind, the sun warming them so they began to perspire. The prairie rolled ahead as far as the eye could reach, rolled to each side into infinity, it seemed, tenderly green, grasses moving under the wind.

In something over an hour by the sun, the old woman overtook them, walking briskly and to all evidence in excellent health and spirits. They reined in, she held up a fat, bright-eyed infant for them to see, folding away the blanket Lillian had left for her.

She spoke proudly in Osage, and Lillian smiled and responded.

"The child is a boy," she told Jason. "She says her husband will be very proud."

Then the old woman went on ahead of them at a pace which would, within a reasonable time, bring her up to the rest of the train. Jason stared at her progress, hardly able to believe.

"She'll build her lodge tonight," Lillian told him. "She'll cook supper for her husband and her other children. And she'll have milk for the baby, and he'll grow and thrive on the hunt. Her husband, who is a good hunter and respected in the nation, will name the child for whatever he sees in the moment his wife appears before him. And he will raise the boy to be a great hunter because he was born on the hunt."

"The Osage women . . . are they always like this?"

"Yes," she said. "The Osages are healthy, not subject to very many diseases, which is fortunate, for their practice of medicine is primitive. They—we—have certain roots for the cure of snakebites, and we're always careful to keep the injured part of any wound very clean. These things I trust, but not the medicine man."

"I've noticed that the one in the village is treated with great respect," Jason said. "I've nodded to him. He wasn't exactly cordial."

"Red Horse is a very important man," Lillian explained, "too important to make idle talk. There are other medicine men in the nation, but he is the most distinguished. However, what I witnessed in the case of Sucking Bee, who is now Quick Knife's number-one wife, makes me hold him in doubt. And with him his ... colleagues."

"What happened ... or can't you tell me?"

"I can tell you anything, my husband. It was the summer when I was thirteen, as was Sucking Bee, my dearest friend. She got a wound at play and it filled with a very bad and poisonous pus and caused her great distress. Red Horse was called. Because she cried out for me and was hysterical, I alone was allowed to remain while he treated her.

"He was accoutred in the most fanciful clothes, face and arms coated with red and green paints. He was received by Sucking Bee's family with profound respect."

"Like a doctor always is," Jason put in.

She nodded, and continued. "After they had gone, he began his treatment. He threw his hands aloft, abjured the evil spirit that possessed Sucking Bee, in a supplicating yet threatening manner, to leave her. Then he lay at her side, applied his lips and teeth to the wound, pulled the skin violently from one side to the other, all the while making a nasal grunt, now and then crying out a threat. This went on ten or fifteen minutes, with Sucking Bee holding back any cry or moan. Finally Red Horse pulled the flesh violently, jumped to his feet, and spat from his mouth a small frog. This was the evil spirit which had possessed Sucking Bee. Pointing to it, he said, 'Rejoice, my daughter! You are now cured! Behold the bad spirit that infected you! You suffered because he is large, but have no fear, for he is now harmless.' Then he scattered a pinch of aromatic root over the fire. The rest of the disease would be carried away on the smoke. Then he left."

"And Sucking Bee?"

"Two days later, her little brother had the idea of pricking her arm with his knife. This way, the pus got out. He did this several times, and Sucking Bee recovered. Red Horse, however, had full credit for the cure. He was feasted and courted by Sucking Bee's family, and they gave him a beautiful hunting horse."

Jason frowned. He hadn't considered sickness until now, for there had never been any contact with it in his life.

Lillian seemed to know what he was thinking. "This is a healthy country," she told him. "I know how to deal with snakebite and cuts and broken bones and quinsies and fevers. I have a book of treatments among the books I left at Granny Grosshart's. We have no need of a medicine man, or a doctor."

Chapter 37

Days flowed as the nation rode westward. For Jason they were a swift, sunlit, blowing prairie of fleetness. As they traveled, passing each gentle rise, swelling endlessly one after another, softly green, freshly blowing, Jason felt the lure of the hunt come to birth within him and rode with it throbbing in his blood.

Each night Swift Foot went among the lodges and told them all that the day's journey had been good. No danger now threatened. They could rest at peace. They could bathe and cook and eat, and the young men could play their games, and they could hold the dances.

When they were something over two weeks on the trail, the long file assumed a different look. Ahead now, Quick Knife, arrogant and competent, led a solid bank of warriors, and very close to the rear came the warriors who before had stayed far behind.

There was now no straggler, no distance between lodge families. The scouts rode farther out, reported more often. Close-ranked the Osages moved, and there was an awareness, down to the smallest child, which

Jason had not seen before. They had entered into the dangerous territory where, on nearly every hunt, the Osages had had to fight enemy nations who challenged their right to pass through.

Riding this lap of the journey, time crept. Jason became restive the first day, unwilling to ride with the lodges, and he spoke of this to Swift Foot.

"Ja-son could ride scout with Plunging River," Swift Foot said. "Ja-son knows Plunging River."

"We've raced together. He speaks English. Is it settled?"

"Not settled. Can be war. Quick Knife is war leader. Quick Knife must say."

Jason went directly to the lodge of Quick Knife, separated from his own only by that of Swift Foot. The warrior met him at the entrance, towering above him, presenting the impassive Osage visage which, as he regarded Jason, gave off cold arrogance.

Jason put his case bluntly, steeling himself. "I would ride scout with Plunging River. Swift Foot sent me to you."

"You have been scout?" Quick Knife demanded.

"No. I've got a quick eye, a keen ear."

"Scout is often first killed." The words were biting.

"I'm handy with my rifle."

"You are not Osage. Plunging River is chief scout."

"I won't try to take his place. Unless he's killed."

The deep-socketed eyes glittered. "Go with Plunging River." The glittering tone revealed Quick Knife's hatred, his wish that Jason be killed.

Thus Jason rode out each day with Plunging River, searched the prairie for signs of an enemy. Day after day they found no sign. At last they traveled out of the dangerous country, and now the scouts, Jason with them, were on the lookout for buffalo.

The seventh day after enemy danger ended, in the middle of the morning, Jason, riding with Plunging River, saw the changed motion of the scouts to their right, which signified that they had sighted something.

They rode fast to the scouts, and coming to the top of a rise saw the buffalo herd, which was moving at a ponderous pace along the flat, grassed bottom between the swells.

Jason looked at the sea of enormous, humped, shaggy animals, some with calves beside them, and tried to estimate their number. Two or three hundred, he thought, maybe more.

Plunging River gave a low-voiced order to one of the scouts, then said to Jason, "Go. Tell Osages."

Jason raced his horse nose to nose with that of the scout. They galloped to the moving train, reined up before Swift Foot and Eagle Feather, and gave their news. Immediately, Swift Foot sent heralds among the people, spreading the word, telling the size of the herd and its position.

"Make ready for the hunt, make ready for the kill," Lillian later told Jason was what the heralds had cried. "Women, sharpen knives, get horses ready for men, keep all children quiet. No one to shoot a gun, no one to walk upon the prairie or whisper! All is quiet for the death of the buffalo!"

Swift Foot named the warriors who were to hunt, and they threw off their blankets and put aside their guns because this was the first day of kill, meat was needed by the nation, and the sound of guns would scatter the buffalo. They took up their quivers of arrows, tested their feathered bows, and waited, alert for the signal to press forward to the front. The women, faces placid, made ready the horses for the men who were to hunt.

Jason noted there was no grumbling, no expression of disappointment on the face of any warrior not called to hunt. They were ready to take their turn. What mattered was that there should be meat for the nation.

The signal was given, and the hunters pressed to the front. Quick Knife was among them. Eagle Feather, though not chosen to kill, stayed in the front, as did Jason and his fellow scout.

The rear-marching warriors now became the officers of the Osages. They stationed themselves about, with long whips, to keep order if needed, and excited children watched them and moved carefully.

When the hunters had moved forward, the women began to sharpen their sharp knives. "Buffalo have ears, they hear and run," the guarding warriors told them. Jason, though he did not understand the words or even hear them, saw how the children respected the warriors and were instantly quiet for them as they were not quiet for their mothers. And he saw how quietly the women made the needed preparations, with never a breath of scolding.

Swift Foot now lifted his hand above his head, let it drop. He pressed his heels against his horse's flanks, and went trotting toward where Plunging River and the other scouts waited, watching the herd. The hunters and warriors, the women and children, the Osage nation, went cautiously and slowly so that the many horses would not set up a tremor in the earth which would rise into the buffalo and send them running.

At the top of each rise, Swift Foot halted the party, waited to move on until Plunging River signaled for them to advance. They came at last to the trough beneath the final swell.

Here Swift Foot told the women to make camp, to wait until he sent messengers for them. They were to keep their axes silent as they built their lodges; they were to allow no infant to cry.

He now deployed his hunters, sending them in a wide circle around the herd, keeping only Eagle Feather and Jason and the second scout with him. The excitement through all the nation was high and silent, tense with waiting and discipline.

Swift Foot urged his horse cautiously to the top of the swell, Jason and the others following. Here they waited until the encircling hunters were in place. The herd had moved very little. Dull-witted, unknowing beasts, they kept grazing, not on the alert for danger as would be so many deer. Ponderously they moved, inch by inch, their great shaggy bodies blocks of ugly stupidity.

Swift Foot lifted his arm, gave a high and lasting cry, and the hunters thundered in from all sides, rushing down the slopes, riding head-on into the herd, scattering it and encompassing it. Dust enveloped herd and riders, but Jason saw Quick Knife on his horse, saw others picking their buffalo, riding mercilessly down upon them.

Quick Knife was riding down a great and murderously ugly bull, bow tensed, arrow ready. He raced and thundered until he came alongside the bull, then let fly his arrow.

It tunneled deep into the great chest of the beast, which ran on a little way, blood spurting from its nostrils. The bull plunged to a stop and stood, legs wide, ponderous head hanging, its blood surging forth, and then the dust enwrapped it and Jason could see no more.

The breeze moved the dust, and before it swirled thick again, Jason saw that the flat shallow trough of prairie was strewn with dead cows and bulls and even calves. Yet the hunters rode after the herd, which was running now, making a noise like thunder in the earth, and kept running beyond the far rises, its thunder fading.

The women were now signaled to approach, and each family of wives came onto the hunting ground, scrambled off their horses, and claimed the cow or bull or calf its man had killed. Jason watched as Sucking Bee, with Lillian and Singing Lark helping her, dealt with the great bull which Quick Knife had killed.

With a keenly sharpened butchering knife, Sucking Bee rapidly slit the skin of the bull's belly, ripped it down, spread it on either side. Then the three women turned the bull until it lay on its crumpled legs in such manner that the hide shielded the meat as they swiftly butchered it.

The hunters and all the other men rode back to camp, leaving the women to their work. Here they gathered outside various lodges to smoke and talk of the hunt.

Jason, with Plunging River and others, squatted outside the lodge Lillian had built, identified by the red and blue blanket at the entrance. In front of the lodge immediately across from him, Quick Knife was speaking proudly and arrogantly to the men gathered there. He threw a murderous look at Jason, then turned his back and continued his boasting, making an occasional grand gesture.

"Quick Knife says his bull is the biggest ever killed by Osage," Plunging River interpreted. The others in the group nodded and discussed the bull, using a few English words along with Osage.

Presently the women whose men had not hunted today came riding in with their children. They started fires in readiness for the feast to come, and the children cut sharp sticks for roasting the meat. The other women began to return, hearing the kill.

Lillian, Auguste's cradle hanging from her saddle horn, rode in later with Sucking Bee, whose small sons were on her horse, and Singing Lark, who led the two pack horses laden with red, bleeding meat.

They helped Sucking Bee unload the meat, then, leading their horses, came to Jason. Auguste was roaring his displeasure at the cradle board, and Lillian quickly freed him and set him on the ground, where he began to stagger determinedly back and forth, grinning.

Lillian started to build her fire at once.

"I didn't kill a buffalo, remember," Jason warned.

"When one Osage kills one buffalo, all Osages feast!" Singing Lark announced. "Many buffalo were killed today. There will be tight bellies in all the camp tonight!"

And so it was that they feasted, and after the feast the young men held their games, and after the games, as darkness came, the drums started. And the girls moved forward, each choosing a man, and the dance about the big central fire began in a weaving, circling pattern. And Jason saw that Quick Knife sought out Singing Lark before she could come to him or go to another, and he noted the toss of her head and the young quickness of her body.

He watched the dancing idly, murmuring with Lillian. They were talking of the cabin they would build on the Missouri, overlooking the river, and they decided to start with one room only and add a room each year until they had enough.

While they were still planning, Singing Lark came running to them and stood. "Quick Knife," she announced breathlessly, "asked me to be his number-two wife!"

Jason looked at the girl, standing rigid against the light of the fire. Then he stared at Lillian, but couldn't quite see her expression.

There was dismay in her voice when she spoke. "What did you tell him, little sister? You should not forget that you are lovely enough to be number-one wife to the greatest warrior in any of the Osage nations."

"Singing Lark told him," the girl said, "that if she is number-two wife to any man, she chooses to be number-two wife to Ja-son, husband of her sister."

Her words slammed into Jason, even though he thought she was jesting. But Lillian's rigid silence told him this was no jest.

"I'm honored," he managed to say. "But it isn't white man's custom to take a number-two wife. Your sister is right—you should be number-one wife."

He felt the relaxation in Lillian, knew he'd found the right words.

"Singing Lark," murmured the girl, "is sorry about white man's custom. Quick Knife is very angry, Ja-son. He will try to kill you."

"The Osages don't revenge themselves so," Lillian

said gently. "It isn't the nature of the Osages, little sister."

"Quick Knife is different. Ja-son must not trust Quick Knife. He is very angry because two Osage girls he wanted have chosen Ja-son when Quick Knife offered himself."

Chapter 38

It was after Singing Lark had gone and Lillian had stepped inside to tend Auguste that Quick Knife came striding boldly through firelit shadow. Jason got to his feet.

Quick Knife surged to a halt. "The hunt," he said, "is the time to kill."

"That's right," Jason responded. He was taut, ready.

"It is the time for Quick Knife to kill. To kill the biggest bull and cow. It is the time for Quick Knife to kill the white man who steals wives."

"I have stolen no wife," Jason said coldly.

His every muscle waited.

"You stole Lillian. Now Singing Lark. Without you, Quick Knife would have both."

"And if you kill me you will have them."

"Singing Lark at once. Lillian after the year to mourn. Quick Knife will grant the year."

"Just how are you going to kill me?" Jason was icy with anger.

The knife which slashed out at him was the warrior's answer.

247

Jason sprang aside, but not before the tip of the blade opened the skin of his forearm.

The knife yanked back, came stabbing down, this time for the neck. Jason threw himself to one side, felt the knife's bite again, then jerked headlong back and forward. He grabbed the knife arm, wrenched it to his chest and pinioned it. Shoving mightily, lips skinned back, body straining, he forced the warrior backward. They crashed to the ground, Jason imprisoning that arm, going for the knife.

The Osage twisted free, sprang to his feet and, as Jason lunged up, drove the knife murderously toward his face. Jason darted his hands above the knife wrist, chopped the edges of them murderously down.

With a howl, the Osage leapt back, knife flying away. He dived for it, and Jason sprang after him. The warrior was touching the weapon; Jason kicked the knife wrist powerfully.

Again the Osage howled, his great voice rending the night. There was the silent movement of watching, wordless Osages drawing closer.

Now Quick Knife recovered his blade and hurtled at Jason. Jason again leapt aside, and as he landed, an object skittered into his foot and a high feminine voice cried, "Knife . . . Ja-son . . . knife!"

There was no time to snatch it up. Quick Knife was attacking, faster than before. Jason dived for the warrior's knees, hit them with such force that the impact jolted his bones. Quick Knife shot across Jason's back and landed on the ground.

He was on his feet and coming by the time Jason got his own knife. The Osage's breath, hot with near raw buffalo meat, hit him, and then he felt the hotness in his shoulder, a numbness that sliced to the bone.

Swiftly, before Quick Knife could yank the blade free, before he could move, Jason drove his own blade high into the bronzed and sweating chest. They hung together, each holding to the haft of his own knife buried in the flesh of the other.

Unexpectedly, the warrior let go. He hurled his

forearm under Jason's chin, rammed the windpipe, increased the pressure, and they staggered, free arms grappling bodies, Jason trying to pull his knife out of the warrior's chest, the warrior throttling him.

Jason let go his knife, yanked free, staggered back. They circled, drove at each other, knives aquiver in their flesh. This time it was the warrior who danced aside, Jason who plunged on.

Before he could turn, Quick Knife was on him, on his back, legs clamping his waist, riding him as he would his steed, chopping one fist onto Jason's head. The blows thundered into Jason's skull; he bucked and heaved, trying to unseat the warrior, but he was not to be shaken. He lunged forward, carrying his rider, numb pain in his shoulder, shattering blows in his head.

Now Jason threw himself headlong onto the ground, smashing his rider's great body, panting in relief when it rolled off him. He pushed up from the ground, arms dancing.

Quick Knife lay on his back, that haft pointing to the sky.

And then Lillian was at Jason's side, and Singing Lark. And they were helping him up, walking him, sobbing, arms quivering but strong.

Chapter 39

Not until the hunt was ended, until after the drying racks had been hung with the stripped and bloody meat and the meat had dried, did the two wounded men heal enough to make the journey back. Neither was able to join the hunt again.

After the women had rebuilt their lodges on the original sites near the Neosho, Eagle Feather called a council in final meeting to deal with what had taken place that first night of the hunt. Swift Foot was called, and Plunging River and the others, all men who were wont to deal thoughtfully and wisely with such problems as arose within the nation. They had met the night of the affair and agreed to ponder, each in his own mind, until their lives resumed in their permanent village.

Thus, when the council ended and the members had departed, Eagle Feather sent for Jason to come to his lodge. When Jason arrived, the chief was standing outside in evening dusk. Swift Foot and Quick Knife were both with him. Quick Knife appeared less arrogant than ever before.

"Eagle Feather will tell council decision," the chief

said. "It is hope of Eagle Feather that Ja-son and Quick Knife accept."

"It is my hope that I can," Jason said.

Quick Knife stood impassive.

"Young men bear hot blood," Eagle Feather continued. "Young warriors, young white men. They are alike."

Jason waited, searching the face of the old chief.

"It is not Osages' custom to seek revenge within nation. Ja-son is part of nation now. Trouble between Quick Knife and Ja-son came over women. To fight over women is not tolerated by Osages. No more fight between Quick Knife and Ja-son. They have proved they are both best fighter, that they are same. From this moment they go in peace. If enemy attacks Osages, they fight enemy, side by side."

Jason frowned, looked at Quick Knife. A trace of arrogance showed beyond his impassivity.

"If Quick Knife agrees," he said, "you can rely on me."

The young warrior gave no sign.

The chief said, "Council agreed that Ja-son has Lillian for wife, that Singing Lark cannot be number-two wife in white man's marriage. Swift Foot told that his daughter, Singing Lark, is yet without wisdom to choose husband. She must wait. Thus Quick Knife may yet take Singing Lark for number-two wife. Council agreed that this is honorable to both Quick Knife and Ja-son."

"I agree also," Jason said.

In stately manner, arrogance invisible, Quick Knife gave his word. Then they separated, each to his own lodge.

Jason reported to Lillian what had taken place.

"Quick Knife will be a fine husband for my sister," she said, smiling, the firelight tender on her face.

"Then you think she'll take him?"

"Probably—when she's older. She couldn't do better, and he'll be good to her. He's very kind to Sucking Bee, and she wasn't—" She broke off, suddenly confused.

"She wasn't first choice," Jason said, "because you were. And she wouldn't have been second choice if Singing Lark had been older at the time."

"Jason," Lillian murmured, drawing him down, pulling his arms to hold her in the way she best liked. "Maybe we'd better build two rooms in our cabin right away. Because, about the time you finish the winter's trapping, we'll have a new baby in this lodge."

He couldn't speak, he could only hold her, his blood thundering.

His second son was born after the maize was reaped and pounded, after the fall hunt, after the winter's trapping, after some of the hotheaded young warriors had gone on a scalping expedition.

It was before dawn on the first day of March, 1813, that Lillian woke Jason with a touch. "It's time, my darling," she said. "If you'll go for my mother and Singing Lark. Swift Foot's number-two wife will take Auguste at her fire."

Jason leapt up, scrambled into clothes, wrapped the sleepy Auguste in a blanket, went for the opening. There he paused. "You'll be all right . . . with me gone?"

"Of course, darling."

As he plunged past lodge after lodge, Jason felt the same miserable urgency he'd felt before, when Auguste was born. Any minute now, any breath, Lillian would come to that extremity when her screams would tear forth, when her anguish would ride the sky.

Young Doe and Singing Lark woke at his first low call. They ran ahead of him, and when he came into his lodge, they were setting water to heat, even as Mrs. Sougrain had done in New Madrid. Lillian was breathing audibly, breath catching now and again, but she told Young Doe where to find white cloths which would be needed, and the blanket in which to wrap the baby.

Jason squatted anxiously at the far side of the fire, watching her fiercely. She saw him, motioned, and he moved to sit beside her. Her hand came into his and remained, gripping when her breath caught, holding and squeezing, until it quivered out.

He wondered, as she caught her breath more frequently and held it longer, and her hand squeezed harder and harder, if she might have the strength to break the bones of his fingers. But he did not move his hand, for anguish was upon her.

It ground her visibly, bored the length of her once lithesome, once-tender body. She was straining, the cords of her neck standing clear and hard. Sweat was pouring off her face, dampening her hair.

Now Young Doe set her hands against the swollen belly and pushed, crushing a moan out upon the air, a sound which fluttered past the thinned lips and went into a thread of travail. This continued without end, until suddenly Young Doe was holding the newborn infant by the ankles, freed at last from its own travail, and she was crying, "Boy-child, Lillian—boy-child!" She slapped the baby smartly on the back and the lodge was filled with an abrupt, high-pitched mewling.

And from beyond the lodge, from down in the timber, came the mourning chant of the nation. And a wisp of apprehension stirred along Jason's spine.

Into the chant, banishing the apprehension, Lillian asked, "What is your full name, Jason?"

"Jason Blood. Just Jason Blood."

"That's what we'll name our son," she whispered. "Jason Blood."

Now Young Doe and Singing Lark took the baby to their lodge for a week as was the custom. Jason, watching Lillian fall into exhausted sleep, sat holding his love in his heart—love for her, for Auguste, for the new Jason Blood. And he wondered if ever a man had been so blessed. After that he wondered if such fortune could last, then roughly put the doubt from him.

Chapter 40

In exactly one week, Lillian strapped baby Jason into his cradle board for the trip to St. Louis. Against Jason's protest, she had dressed the day after the birth and the next day was walking to her mother's lodge to nurse the child instead of having him brought to her. She spent time, on these occasions, playing with Auguste, who appeared to think his new brother was a toy to pummel and lavish with bump-head kisses.

"You can't make the trip yet," Jason argued.

"I'm perfectly strong," Lillian declared. "Waiting is out of the question. Swift Foot and the others have to go down with their furs and get back in good time for the spring hunt. And you and I need to go now so you can sell your peltries and pay for our land. After that, we still have to make the trip back to our land, get some food crops in, and build our cabin."

Indeed, she bloomed as they rode toward the Missouri, traveling in their small caravan. The wind was strong, with ice in its teeth, and it swept without letup across the prairie. The cold litted color into her cheeks, reddened her lips, and she grew vibrant before Jason's

254

eyes and he ceased to wonder if she could withstand the trip.

Swift Foot led the way, four young warriors rode scout, and Jason and Plunging River saw to the pack horses laden with peltries. Two of these loads, most of them prime furs, belonged to Jason.

When they reached the Missouri, they camped at the spot where later Jason would build the cabin. His stakes were still in place, weathered and a little crooked, and he straightened them. Then, while Lillian put up temporary lodges, he set to helping the Osage men build the pirogues in which they would take their pelitres down the charging, tumultuous river.

They cut down two big trees, then gouged and burned out the inside of each log into a thin wooden shell. The beam of each vessel was necessarily less than the thickness of the log, and its length corresponded with that of the original log.

Swift Foot fashioned them so that they would accommodate two oarsmen each, leaving bulkheads at intervals to strengthen them and to provide compartments in which to stow the peltries and transport Lillian and the babies. Each had a square undercut stern without a rudder, and a rounded bow with a hole burned through it to receive the mooring rope.

Such a wooden canoe had solid advantages, Jason knew. Though heavy and sometimes awkward to handle, it was sturdy enough to survive snags and gravel. However, since it could be upset, they fastened the two pirogues side by side, using hewn poles, at a distance of almost eight feet. Such a vessel, Swift Foot said, could carry their peltries and would not be easily overset.

They embarked at dawn. Three of the Osages would remain in the lodges and care for the horses until Swift Foot and the two oarsmen returned. Then the party would ride together back to the village.

Even though they had as solid a craft as could be taken down the bucking, wild Missouri, Jason helped push off almost reluctantly. He jumped aboard with all speed. The current grabbed the canoes, tossed them aloft, dropped them, yanked them downstream with instant, breathtaking speed. That uneasy feeling Jason had had before took him full force.

He had Lillian, he had Auguste, he had a new son, who bore his name. He had untold wealth in the form of peltries with which to establish himself on the delectable land of his choice. He had everything a man could want. And it wasn't natural, in his experience, for everything to fall to his favor.

He gripped his oar, grimly fought the river. He stared at the heaving, rushing water, too deep for poles, too swift for oars, too crooked for sails. He knew its reputation. It was always rising unexpectedly, lifting logs and driftwood off hundreds of bars, hurling them downstream. It wedged logs in its mud bottom so they stuck upward, leaning with the current, often hidden, and these were what boatmen called snags because they could pierce a boat. The Missouri tore sturdy trees out of the forest edge, anchored them in its mud by their roots or branches, giving them freedom of movement so that they surged up on the current, fell under with a tremendous vibration, jumped out of the water again, and these the boatmen called sawyers, and they slapped and crushed any boat they could, destroying it.

This devil river would be his undoing, Jason thought. But still he fought it with his oar, his body, his will.

The Missouri yanked its current this way and that; at times the current even leapt upstream. It whirled and spun the lashed canoes, and it reached them with not one but three sawyers, and yet, somehow, they survived. Stubbornly Jason and his companions fought the current, the oars, rushing and plunging ever downriver in spite of all the river could do.

They tied up at St. Louis at noon one bright and blowing April day. The sun was warm, but the wind was cool, and Lillian kept both babies wrapped. She had never looked more alive, or lovelier. Jason had never felt more exultant.

"I'll go to Granny Grosshart's," she told him. "Take

as long as you want with the peltries and the inquiries about your friends. I hope they're here, safe and well."

"Medary'll be anxious to meet you, if she's here," Jason said. "The two of you'll be friends the minute you see each other."

She smiled, delicately fashioned a kiss with her lips. And then she turned and moved along the plank walk of Main Street, Jason in his cradle on her back, Auguste on her arm.

He watched her with pleasure. She was as slender as the first day he saw her, and he noted with what grace she nodded to folks she passed, as was the custom in river villages, whether a person be inhabitant or newcomer.

A sense of well-being descended upon him. They'd conquered the devil Missouri. They were here. It was good, really good to be back in the white man's world.

He helped unload the pirogues, taking the peltries to Chouteau's establishment. When they'd deposited them along the river side of the building, the three Osage men wandered off to do some sightseeing. Jason went inside to sell the peltries, not only his own, but those of his companions and of the Osages back in the village who had sent down their winter trapping.

He felt in his pocket to make sure of his list. It was a record of how many bundles of beaver, how many buffalo robes, bearskins, and bales of other peltries, along with an estimate of their excellence and condition.

The only people inside the store were some trappers and a sandy-haired balding clerk, who was busy examining the peltries they'd brought in. Jason recognized the clerk as the one with whom he'd talked before he left St. Louis for the Osage village. His name was Will Ford.

Now the clerk excused himself to the trappers for a moment and came to Jason.

"You brought a lot of peltries, I see," he said.

"Yes. From up along the Neosho, best kind of furs."

"I'll deal with you after I finish dickering with these

men," Ford said. "That's what you're here for, I take it."

"That, and to ask after friends of mine," Jason replied. "If you recall—I'm Jason Blood. I spoke to you before I went from here a year ago, about friends of mine who'd gone after river pirates—"

Ford nodded. "I recall, I do recall. Thought you looked familiar, but then I see everybody. Yes. Coghill, that's the name. And a young Pole. They went to rescue a woman and a squaw. Did it, too."

Relief hit Jason so hard it was all he could do to keep from going into a tremble. "They're here, then," he exclaimed, "they're in St. Louis!"

"Nope. I gave them your note, though. Coghill and his wife went on up the Missouri somewheres or other. The Pole and his squaw, they're in and out. Trapping. He asks about if you've showed up yet."

"Mrs. Coghill," asked Jason, still agape at the wondrous news, "did she leave word for me, any paper or letter?"

"Never laid eyes on her myself. Gathered she'd been sick. Coghill didn't leave nothing, and like I said, the young Pole, he's in and out, asking."

"Maybe I could talk to Mr. Chouteau," Jason ventured. "See if Sam spoke to him."

"Chances are he never did," Ford said. "Anyhow, Mr. Chouteau's been out of St. Louis more than he's been in. He's got this war on his mind, and keeping the Indian villages where we get furs friendly to us. That's where he is now, in Indian country."

"St. Louis . . . is it in danger of attack?"

"Unlikely, not by the British, anyhow. We've got military for defense, but unless English agents out of Canada foment the Indians against us, there's not real danger. We're lucky we've got Mr. Chouteau, the Indians liking him the way they do." He glanced toward the trappers, who were waiting and beginning to shift restlessly. "We have some isolated murders, some young hothead braves taking a scalp here and there. I'll have to finish with them fellows," he added hastily, "and after that look over your peltries, Mr. Blood, and make you an offer. Sorry I can't help more on the other matter, but that's it."

He went hustling to the trappers.

Sam, Jason thought warmly, he's stayed behind to meet me. And he felt rich in friendship.

By the time he'd waited for Will Ford to finish his transactions over three bales of second-rate buffalo robes, it was late afternoon. Ford paid the trappers cash, they departed, and he turned again to Jason.

He studied the list Jason gave him, tapped it with one square-tipped finger. "Got some prime fur, eh? If it's what you say on the list, I'll give you our best price. It isn't often I make a statement like that. But it isn't often a man comes in with a businesslike list either. I notice you've got one second-to-third-rate buffalo robe, which saves me time arguing later on. If your whole lot is that accurately rated, all I've got to do is check, and it won't take near as long as it did with those other fellows."

"I think you'll find that the peltries and list match," Jason told him. "I've got other lists for the pelts belonging to the Osages."

In something over an hour Ford had offered Jason almost four hundred dollars for his furs, and he had accepted. Now his zealous, tiring winter work was forgotten. His head felt thick from the wonder of being a rich man, able to get his land, free and clear, to pay Granny Grosshart what he'd borrowed, to buy window glass and anything else Lillian might take a notion to for their cabin. She should have materials for sewing, he thought, for dresses and for the boys, who would be growing fast. And they should have a cow.

"I can credit you the amount," Will Ford said. "You can take it out in barter if you want."

Jason explained his immediate need for cash, and Ford produced the amount named. Jason put the gold carefully into his pocket, and they began to examine the peltries belonging to the Osages.

Swift Foot and the other two returned, and Ford gave them their credit papers so they could do the bartering they'd been commissioned to do by various Osage women. Only when they had begun to look at blankets and iron cook pots did Jason permit himself to make his triumphant way along Main Street to Granny Grosshart's cabin.

He was surprised that the sun had gone and all was gray and chill with coming night. The hours had fled, had seemed, after waiting his turn at Chouteau's, to have melted. So this was how it felt to be successful, how men made fortunes to give a woman like Lillian a proper cabin.

He walked faster, began to hurry.

There was no premonition, none at all.

Chapter 41

He rapped smartly at Granny's door. "It's me," he called. "It's Jason—finished at last!"

"Well, come in!" a voice replied, and it startled him a bit. He didn't remember Granny's voice being querulous.

But he pushed open the door to candlelight, a grin on his face, glad and excited to be seeing the old lady again, to pay what he owed her and then some. He stepped inside, arms out to sweep her up, cane and all, and whirl her about the room, anticipating how she would squeal and laugh and scold and demand to be set down. "Hello, Granny!" he cried, and took one long step toward the figure at the fireplace.

And then he surged to a halt.

This wasn't Granny Grosshart, or even Lillian, but a strange person, a scrawny girl-woman who reminded him, somehow, of someone. Not Granny, he thought in that bewildered instant, not Medary, not Mrs. Johannigmeier or any of the other settlers' wives on the way up to St. Louis. Not anyone he could think of anywhere, not even Mrs. Allis, back at the home.

He stared at the girl-woman.

She was the only one here. The door to the other room was wide open; there was no one inside.

Maybe Granny didn't live here now. Maybe she had moved in with one of her sons, or even died, and this bone-thin, pale-haired, pale-eyed being had taken her place.

He gazed at the bone face, and his mind, curiously, fleshed it out, padded, then padded again. And the body the same until it became mountainous. All these things—with the pale hair and the venom which flared in the pale eyes—did it, lanced the first awful flash of suspicion through him.

But that couldn't be . . . it was impossible . . . he had searched without letup, searched until it was hopeless. The authorities had even given him a legal document. . . .

"Why'd you do it, Jason Blood?" she demanded. "Why'd you run off and leave me? Where's Auguste . . . where's my baby?"

It is, Jason thought groggily, it really is.

And it was. It was Massie Ann.

Chapter 42

Lillian, he thought, Lillian.

"Well," demanded Massie Ann, "why don't you answer? Doing what you done to me!"

"I searched," he told her. "We all did—Tench, Sam, two young fellows, Fred. We had to give up. We couldn't stay there."

"Fred didn't give up. He stayed. He found me, and followed you to St. Louis, right to this cabin! This very minute he's down the street looking for you!"

There was no answer. No excuse, because she'd been alive, and he'd given up.

"Don't stand there deaf and dumb! Fred's right— you took advantage of me, had to marry me! You wanted to get shet of me, and you seen your chance and took it! Ja . . . and now look! Where's my baby, you can anyhow answer me that!"

"He's safe. He's in good hands."

Lillian, he thought, oh, God, Lillian.

"Don't you want to know where Fred found me?" Massie Ann asked, her voice rising, thinning. "Ain't you even that interested?"

"Of course I am," he said numbly. "It looked impossible that you could have lasted even five minutes, the way the ground swallowed the cabin up, you inside it."

"Well, it didn't, not really" she cried. "I fell out of the door, and when I hit water, I grabbed on to a piece of wood and held on for dear life. The water was swift as anything, and it took me along fast! It was all I could do to get a breath of air and keep hanging on to that wood. Forever and forever, it went on and on! You just don't know what I went through, Jason Blood! If you'd of jumped in there like a real man, you could of saved your wife all that misery and suffering! But did you? Nein . . . nein! You took my baby and run, that's what! My brother was the one had to come searching all down the river, halfway to Natchez! If it hadn't of been for Fred, I never would have remembered who I was or where I was from! But one look at him when he showed up—and he was killing mad the way you run out on me, still is—and I remembered everything!"

"I'm sorry, Massie Ann. If I'd believed there was the slightest chance—"

"Sorry!" she interrupted, the word coming in that spitting way he remembered. "You didn't do nothing! It took strangers to pull me into their boat, half drowned and out of my head! Strangers in a strange cabin had to put me in a bunk and nurse me! I was sick, I was awful sick for a long time, and I'm still skin and bones, and if it wasn't for Fred— Ja . . . you'd like it if I hadn't never remembered who I was and where from, because then you could keep my baby, and you wouldn't have to take care of a wife you was glad to get rid of!"

"I wasn't glad, Massie Ann. I thought you were dead, and I wasn't glad."

"Aber you ain't glad I ain't dead!" she accused. "You ain't telling me how happy you are I'm here! You ain't breaking your neck to give me my baby, my Auguste I ain't seen in sixteen whole months! But he'll know me, he'll know his ma! I want him, Jason Blood, I want him this second!"

She was screaming now, and into the screaming came the sound of the door opening behind Jason. He turned, and it was Lillian who stood there, baby Jason in his cradle on her back.

Quietly, she closed the door, quietly faced them. "What is it?" she asked, puzzled. "Is something wrong, Jason?"

Chapter 43

He stared from Lillian's bewilderment to Massie Ann's rage. Tried to swallow, to push back the roar in his ears.

"Who is she, Jason Blood?" screamed Massie Ann. "What's she doing here? With a papoose on her back? She ain't nobody named Granny Grosshart, she ain't no old woman on a cane that took you and my baby in!"

He saw alarm spring in Lillian's eyes, saw it dim their shine, and then they went quietly stricken. "You're Auguste's mother," she said, the words barely audible.

Massie Ann's pale eyes shot their venom. "You the squaw Jason got to take care of Auguste?" she asked sharply.

"He came looking for someone to care for Auguste, yes." There was no quiver to her voice, no hint of how she felt, aside from the deepening dismay in her eyes.

"You see!" Massie Ann shot a triumphant look at Jason. "Fred was told you'd been in St. Louis looking for Tench, and for a woman to take care of Auguste. We just got this far, Fred had to stop and work our way. The minute we landed, Fred asked at a tavern, and they said this Granny Grosshart had took in a man and a baby a year ago. So we came to see her, only she wasn't here and she ain't showed up. I waited, kept the fire up. Some may look down on the Cremers," she continued, "but when it comes to figuring things out, nobody's smarter than my brother." The pale eyes stabbed at Lillian. "Where've you got my baby at?"

"He's with Granny, at her son's house," Lillian said, addressing her words to Jason. "When I found she wasn't at home, I went over there to inquire. And we stayed to visit. I came back now so you wouldn't . . . so I'd be here when you arrived."

"Where's this house at?" demanded Massie Ann wildly.

"There's no need for you to go there," Lillian said, and now her voice held a tremor, though very slight.

"Oh, yes there is!" screamed Massie Ann. "That old woman's got my baby! You take me, take me this minute!"

Lillian shook her head. "There's no need—"

But Massie Ann, giving her no time to finish, sprang to the attack, claws out. Before he knew he was going to move, Jason had grabbed her by the shoulders.

She began to struggle like a wild thing. "Let go of me!" she shrieked. "You ain't keeping me away from my baby!"

She fought him. She shrieked and kicked and clawed, and Jason held her, waiting for her to quiet, even a little. Lillian moved away from the door and stood to one side.

At that moment, Fred Cremer burst in, throwing the front door violently open. He jumped across the room, toward Jason to fling him away, but Jason let go the clamoring Massie Ann with one hand and gave the burly young fellow a vigorous shove.

Fred caught his balance, made as if to charge, rocked to a spraddle-legged halt. He put his eyes boldly at Lillian, then glowered at Jason.

"Massie Ann!" Fred bellowed. "Shut up your screechin' . . . I got something to tell you!"

Her screams stopped abruptly. She ceased to struggle, but every line of bone showed she would make for Lillian the instant Jason let her go.

"We've got him!" Fred shouted. "Got him by the balls! Know what he done when he hit St. Louis, know what he went and done?"

"He found a squaw to look after my baby," Massie Ann cried, "and that's her, and she won't take me to him!"

Again she tried to spring at Lillian, but this time it was her brother who stopped her, roughly. "That ain't the way!" he bawled. "I told you . . . we've got him! Sure, he went lookin' for a squaw, but I just found out he married the squaw, married her in front of a parson and went and lived Injun with her, took Auguste along, made him live Injun, and now he's got a papoose for a brother, or maybe a sister. And there she stands, like the squaw she is, with her papoose on her back, brazen and shameless!"

Murderous fury took Massie Ann, but when she would have sprung again at Lillian, her brother still held her back.

Lillian went into the other room, closed the door.

Lillian, Jason thought, staring at Massie Ann, oh, God.

"How could you do that to a white woman?" Massie Ann demanded, spitting the words. "How could you do it to me? Marrying a squaw, having a papoose by her!"

There was no answer. He was riven by her plight, by that of Lillian, his heart. The flood tide of his need for Lillian swept away Massie Ann's needs, her rights, as surely as had the earthquake swallowed her home.

"She's three-quarters white," he heard himself saying.

"She's Injun," Fred snorted. "You was mighty quick to marry for a man that'd just lost his wife, and in such a way."

They were forcing him to defend himself, and there

was no defense. He was completely in the wrong. Fred had proved that by finding Massie Ann.

"What you going to do about it?" Fred pressed. "You going to kick the squaw and her papoose out, and do right by my sister? You going to get down on your knees and beg her to take you back?"

It wasn't right to desert Massie Ann. It wasn't right to turn from Lillian. When there are two rights, Jason asked himself, how can a man choose?

"I'm not the kind to beg," he said, out of a nightmare. "I married you, Massie Ann, in good faith. Then, after the earthquake, when I was convinced you were lost, I started upriver on a barge—"

"My sister don't want to hear your troubles," Fred cut in.

"When I found Lillian Dusard," Jason continued, "I married her in the same good faith. She's been a mother to Auguste, and now we have a son together."

"You can't be pa to a papoose!" Massie Ann shrilled. "My baby can't be brother to a papoose! You ain't married to her . . . you're married to me! Send them off where they belong . . . send them to the Injuns!"

Jason was married to both of them, but he wanted only Lillian. And both his sons. He couldn't let Auguste be brought up by Massie Ann, couldn't sentence him to having mind and life twisted by her furies, her changes of mood, her graspings.

"Say it!" Fred commanded. "Tell mein schwester you're going to face your duties!"

"Much has happened to both of us, Massie Ann," Jason said slowly, making every effort to speak truth. "It wouldn't be easy under any circumstances to take up our marriage and go on. We're not the same people now."

"We're exactly the same!" she screamed. "I'm Massie Ann, you're Jason Blood! How can you stand there and say we're not the same people?"

"Our bodies, yes," he agreed, and felt pity for the girl he remembered from that first day, the almost pretty, eager girl who had been entranced with his new house. "But our minds—what we want and mean to have—those thing are different. You've gone in one direction, and I've gone in another."

"That's easy to say!" she cried. "You always could say things fancy! Things out of them books you read! You just want to get shet of me, and I ain't going to let you!"

Now Jason heard himself say what he'd had no conscious thought of saying. "I'll give you everything I own," he heard the words say. "I'll sign over my rights to the land in New Madrid—the government will make some kind of trade there—and give you all the monies except what I owe Granny Grosshart from the peltries I sold today. There's better than three hundred and fifty dollars. You can have it all if you'll give me a divorce and let me have Auguste."

She started for him, ready to claw, and he didn't blame her, not really. But Fred grabbed her, shook her until she quit struggling. She stood within his grasp, hair fallen and floating, and stared wildly at Jason.

"You don't want much, do you?" Fred snarled. "This ain't ended, I promise you that. I'm taking mein schwester away now, but we'll be back, with folks behind us!"

He started for the door, forcing Massie Ann along.

"Auguste!" she shrieked. "I want Auguste!"

"You'll have him," Fred told her viciously, yanking her, never missing stride. "When we get back, you'll have everything Jason Blood owns. And you'll have him, too—there ain't no way he can get shet of you!"

"It's all your fault, Jason Blood!" Massie Ann screamed as her brother pulled her through the door. "Everything that's happened is your fault! If you'd took me to New York, things wouldn't be like this! Now you'll have to take me to New York . . . have to . . . have to!"

Chapter 44

They were gone.

Lillian came into the room again, softly.

"You heard it all?" he asked.

She nodded.

"The offer I made . . . is that what you want?"

"It isn't my decision," she said. "It isn't my right. She . . . has the rights."

There was no tinge of self-pity in her words, only the statement of fact.

He tried to read her dark eyes. There was no shine. Her face was as impassive as that of any Osage.

Is she thinking Osage? he wondered. He felt like a dying man, fighting what was right, fighting what was wrong, for no reason but that he must survive. Is she thinking she can go to the Osage with my son Jason, knowing I'd never take him from her? Is she thinking —oh, God, is she thinking that she can in all honor become number-two wife to Quick Knife? Or is she thinking white, panicked that she's not my wife at all, that her child is bastard?

Because he had to know how things stood between them, he blurted out his instinctive solution. "If I do

271

what I offered her," he asked, "if I give her all I own, will you marry me?"

She gazed at him, impassive, Osage.

His inward agony ripped and tore. How he must appear to her, how feckless, selfish. And the Osage had taught her to abhor the selfish. And he was asking her to marry him, and he was tied to Massie Ann.

"Osage, I mean," he plunged desperately on. "Say she won't divorce me, say she takes all I have, all but Auguste—will you marry me Osage? Will you live another year in the nation while I trap again? Will you go with me, Osage-married, to our land on the Missouri? And if she still won't divorce me, ever, will you live with me all our lives Osage-married?"

A silence fell. She stood motionless, impassive.

He dared not defend himself, dared not put the thought of selfishness in her mind if it hadn't got there of itself.

"You must think before you make this offer," she said at last. "You must measure and weigh."

"Do I think, do I measure and weigh before I breathe?" he asked. "No—my body must have air and I take of it, freely, without ever a thought. You are my life, Lillian. I need no thinking, except how to keep you. I will give Massie Ann all I own, give her more later, when I get it, but I will not live with her, under any conditions. Not even if you take Jason and leave me."

Now she's bound to know, he thought, that I suffer the selfishness of love.

She made a bewildered gesture. He could see that she was trembling. He moved to her, but when he would have put his arms around her, she seemed to shrink from him, though actually she did not move.

He let his arms drop. "It's too much," he said miserably, "coming at you of a sudden. You need time to sort things out. Our children will bear the name of Blood, don't let that worry you. I'll adopt them legally, beginning with Jason. I know I'm asking things of you

I have no right to ask, but there's no way for me without you."

He stood close as she trembled, and now he was trembling with her. The enormity of their situation overwhelmed him as the earthquake had overwhelmed him, rendering him so that he could do only what came to hand.

"Let's lie on Granny's bed," he murmured, "so you can rest."

"We haven't the right," she told him, her voice sounding dim and shadowy, like the corners of the room where the candlelight didn't reach. "Not now . . . not yet . . ." The voice evaporated, was gone.

"Then you lie down, and I'll go after Granny. Maybe you can talk to her. She's a wise old woman."

Anxiously, he waited for Lillian's response.

"It would be kind of you, Jason," she whispered. "Granny has lived, and she's seen things and observed . . . as you said, she's wise. She's at her son William's home. It's on Barn Street, the third house from the corner of Rue Bonhomme. Please . . . hurry."

As he went striding for Barn Street, Jason thought desperately. Lillian didn't know what to do. Oh, God, he thought, or prayed, or demanded, she's got to know! She's got to stay with me! Granny's got to tell her it's the only thing to do!

Chapter 45

After Jason reached the house on Barn Street and introduced himself to the bearded middle-aged man who answered his knock, he was promptly invited to come inside. There, in a solidly furnished sitting room, he acknowledged his introduction to Grosshart's middle-aged chunky wife. Then he asked for Granny.

"She's back in the south chamber seeing to Auguste," said Mrs. Grosshart. "He's alseep, and she's made up her mind to leave him for the night. Your wife was willing, and Martha—that's our youngest daughter, she's sixteen—will bring him back in the morning."

Now, as Mrs. Grosshart turned to fetch the old lady, Granny came in, cane clicking on patches of bare floor. She stopped, peered up at Jason, those piercing blue eyes shining keenly from their tracery of wrinkles. Her needle-fine voice came at him, wasting no time in greetings. "Something's the matter," she said. "Something's happened. Is it Lillian . . . the baby . . . ?"

"If you could come with me," he replied, "I could tell you on the way."

"I'll get my shawl," the old lady agreed. Then, ac-

cepting it from her daughter-in-law with a nod, she
went to the door in her sprightly cane-tapping manner.

Outside, she led him to a bench under a tree within
the walled grounds. "Set," she ordered. "Whatever it is,
I don't want to be stumbling along a dark path when I
hear it. If I'm to be any good to you, I don't need to be
breaking a hip."

He sat beside her, tried to calm his breathing.

"You're shaking!" she exclaimed. "Out with it . . .
what's wrong?"

Bluntly, he told her. He described how Massie Ann
had been swept to the river and downstream during the
hurricane, how her brother had brought her to St.
Louis. He told what had happened in the cabin between himself, Massie Ann, Fred, Lillian.

He told what he'd asked Lillian to do.

"She hasn't said whether she will or not," he finished.
"She was trembling, and could hardly talk. I don't
know, maybe it seems to her I'm dishonoring her, but
I don't know of any other way . . . anything else I can
do."

He waited. There was a small, chilly breeze, and it
ruffled the foilage in the tree above them gently, a sort
of green and breathing sound. There was the scent of
some flower on the breeze, but he didn't know what it
was.

"There ain't no way for you and Lillian but the
Osage," said the old lady at last. "This same thing's
happened before, and right here in St. Louis, though
hardly nobody knows. It'd create an awful scandal if
folks ever did find out . . . they're fierce again' bigamy.
But it did happen, and it involved a leading family,
respected folks. Yet they carried it off, are to this day.
In your case, you're going up the Missouri and nobody'll give it a second thought, if you act fast enough.
Them that know'll forget, and folks upriver won't know
to commence with."

"I don't care what people think, or what they say,"
Jason told her, "except for Lillian's sake. I want her

any way I can get her. These people you mention—how did they manage?"

"To be honest," Granny said wryly, "because hardly nobody got suspicious but me. And I never talked, not till now, for your benefit. I ain't being mean in my thoughts again' your legal wife, but even if she was a saint from above, coming back from the dead like she's done, you thinking her lost and marrying Lillian, loving her like you do, it'd be more than you could do to put her aside. And from what little Lillian told me about your first marriage, that was the wrong woman for you, likely the wrong one for any man. I've known her kind. The main trouble, if you go Osage, is your keeping Auguste . . . the mother having a mother's rights."

"I'll just—take him," Jason said. "If it comes to that. Once I get him up the Missouri it wouldn't be easy for her to get him away from me. I've got to put his needs first. I've got to straighten this out in the best possible way."

"You're in a fix," Granny agreed. "I figure learning of others who done the same thing you're thinking on—circumstances are different, but underneath it's the same—and came out fine, should encourage you."

"I appreciate your help," Jason murmured.

"Well. It's the Chouteaus," Granny related, her voice weaving in and out of the breezy darkness like a fine, flashing needle. "Grandma Chouteau is still living here, never did go back to New Orleens. It begun when she married Auguste René Chouteau of New Orleens about the middle of the seventeen hundreds, and had a child by him. That's our Colonel Auguste Chouteau, who's so important in St. Louis.

"Her husband mistreated her, and she took her son and went back to her family. Nobody blamed her a bit. After that she met Pierre Laclede—his name was really Pierre Laclede Liguest, but he adopted the form Pierre Laclede. You've maybe heard of him. He picked out the site for St. Louis, got a monopoly on the fur trade about 1760 or so. Anyway, him and Madame Chouteau took to each other real hard. The rules of the Catholic church made divorce out of the question, except under certain circumstances, which they couldn't establish. So Madame, with the advice and consent of her friends, just like I'm advising you, made a civil marriage with Laclede and went to live with him.

"She had four children by him, all of them bearing the name of Chouteau, because that was the French law. Then, when Auguste was thirteen, Laclede brought him upriver and established a fur-trading post that was the beginning of St. Louis. Pierre Chouteau, Laclede's son by Madame, was six years old at the time, that's the same Pierre Chouteau that lives here now. Madame reached here in the spring.

"A house was built for her, Laclede was nearly always away, spreading the fur-trading operations in every direction. Young Auguste was forever going from one post to another in Indian country, collecting furs and seeing to trappers.

"He grew into a man, grew up with the village, known to everybody. He got property and is one of the heads of the Missouri Fur Trading Company today. There's not a more important man anywhere than him. After Laclede died, when everybody had forgotten him, much less remembering that he was married to a Chouteau, Auguste came to be considered the founder of this village.

"I've even heard folks claim that no such person as Laclede ever lived here at all. So you see, what was bigamy then was forgotten while it was still going on. I'll venture I'm the only one knows this story, which is true and I personally know it to be true, because I came here as a bride myself. I was acquainted with one woman at the time who'd known the first Auguste Chouteau, knew firsthand he'd made Madame so miserable in New Orleens that she left him."

She ceased to speak, and they sat in silence. The tale of successful bigamy which he'd heard lay heavy in Jason. Would Lillian, when she learned this story of St. Louis's leading citizens, be encouraged and emboldened? Would she decide without hesitation to follow in that other woman's footsteps? Or would she turn from the whole situation in distaste, turn away from him, convinced that he offered not honor, but dishonor?

Granny suddenly shot up from the bench. She jabbed her cane at the ground. "Come on, Jason," she said, "I want to get home to Lillian."

She went through the gate and along the pathway so fast he had to lengthen his stride to catch up with her, so rapidly did she move, cane going.

"I hope," he said once, "that she'll listen."

"She will!" Granny promised fiercely. "I've known that child since she came here to go to school. She's never been unreasonable, always been thoughtful beyond her age. She's got a level head on her. She's bound to realize that, everything considered, the Osage way is the only choice!"

Chapter 46

Jason thought of Massie Ann as they walked, of her tribulations and needs, and the thoughts were burned away by his fever for the life which he could not give up. He wondered what a monster he must be, and then they were at Granny's cabin, and there was only Lillian and his sons in the world.

"You stay here," Granny said when they were inside.

She hastened into the other room and closed the door, leaving him to the fire-whispering silence, the candlelight. He paced, tried to think, could only wait. Wait for the sound of their voices, for the cry of baby Jason. Wait for the door to open, for knowledge of what Lillian thought, felt, decided.

An hour passed, then another. Silence and pacing continued. Once he mended the blaze, handling the wood carefully, making no sound to disturb the emotion-torn silence.

Then a knock sounded at the outer door, and he took up a candle and went to send away whatever intruder might be there. Three men stood outside, grim-visaged in the spill of light.

One of them stepped forward. He was tall, yet appeared short because of some portliness. He was neatly, almost fashionably, dressed, and his thick dark hair was properly combed over his egg-shaped head.

"Amos Griggs, if you recall," he said shortly.

"I recall." He remembered every instant of that day in Griggs's house, the feel of Lillian's hand as it slid into his, the sound of her voice as she said she would go with him, with Jason Blood, that she would marry him.

"We're a delegation," Griggs continued. "We need to come in."

Frowning, Jason stepped aside and Griggs entered, followed by the others. They stood in a row and faced him.

"So you'll know who you're dealing with," Griggs said, "this is Cat Reardon, and this is Bawley Crowe. Reardon's a blacksmith, village couldn't do without him. Crowe's proprietor of the Riverside Inn and Tavern, known to keep an orderly place and uphold the law."

The men looked steadily at Jason.

Reardon was broad, rough-boned, rough-dressed. His hair was tan and unkempt and his rough-featured face hard as the iron at his smithy.

Crowe was tall and thin and held his fashionably clad body like a knife ready to slash. He was black-haired and black-eyed, his features sharply honed.

"Whatever you're here to say," Jason told them, "say it."

"It has come to our attention," Griggs replied bitingly, "that a certain young woman, a Mrs. Jason Blood, has arrived in the village under the protection of her brother, one Fred Cremer. This young woman has been through hell—yes, hell . . . I hope you understand—in the New Madrid earthquake, torn asunder from her beloved husband and her son, her helpless infant. By God's divine intervention she was rescued, nursed to life, and eventually restored to her brother, who had never ceased to search for her."

"You can stop right there," Jason said in cold anger. "I know they're here. I've spoken to them."

"We're a delegation, sir," interposed Crowe keenly. "When a delegation waits upon a man, he hears it out. If he is a just man, and a wise one."

Jason felt his mouth go hard. But he waited.

"The young wife and the brother," Griggs continued, "set out to find her husband, who had too lightly given her up for lost, for dead, and for her infant. Their travels brought them to St. Louis, and their inquiries uncovered the information that the husband had departed from here to trap but that very likely he would return to sell his furs. Further inquiry uncovered the fact that he had actually arrived, with the child, and that the Indian girl who'd been seen with him was known to be a friend of Granny Grosshart's.

"Consequently, the young wife came to this cabin. Here she found her husband, who did not open his arms to her. Instead, even as she was being so cruelly rebuffed, her brother brought the dire word that her husband had 'married' the Indian girl, that he'd had a child by her. The husband, when confronted with this accusation, brazenly admitted his guilt and demanded a divorce from the woman who is his wife in the sight of God and man. And she was forced to leave, after complete repudiation by her husband, without so much as setting eyes on her child, her own flesh and blood!"

He fell silent, glared. Reardon's iron face endured, Crowe's features cut and slew.

Jason's pulse surged, deep and cold with rage.

"Can you deny what I've said, Blood?" demanded Griggs.

"It's true enough," Jason said shortly. "Why are you butting in?"

"We're doing what upright citizens anywhere would do if they find a bigamist in their midst," Griggs retorted.

"My first wife was declared legally dead by New Madrid authorities," Jason told them, his rage deeper, colder. "They gave me a legal document. When I married the second time, the document not being available, I declared myself, in truth, to be a widower."

"Produce the document," Reardon growled.

"I entrusted it to someone for safekeeping. We were attacked by river pirates, lost everything, perhaps the document as well. I've only learned of this. I'll write to New Madrid for a copy."

"There ain't time for documents," snorted Reardon. "We're going to set things straight, here and now."

"How do you figure to do that?" Jason challenged.

"We're giving you the opportunity to do the right thing," Griggs replied. "We're warning you that the people of St. Louis won't tolerate a bigamist."

"There's a good many men down at my place," Crowe said. "The woman's brother is there, and so is she. They've told the story, and the men don't like it, none of them like it. Cat and others came in, and men are still drifting in to find out why such a crowd's there and what they're so hot about. Some wanted all of them to come over here after you. I persuaded them to send a delegation. Cat offered to come."

Reardon's great tan eyebrows were set in a frown. "They're tetchy," he growled, "tetchy as all hell. Crowe, he suggested consulting Mr. Griggs, see what he thought. The two of us went to Mr. Griggs's house."

"You interrupted a fine evening of music my daughters were providing," Amos Griggs said testily, "just as you interrupted their musical education when you lured Lillian Dusard, who, until that time, was as fine and talented a girl as lived, in spite of her Osage blood, from under my roof. What we're here for, as a delegation representing some very angry citizens, Blood, is to demand that you immediately return to your legal wife, restore her son to her, and forget about your rash move in regard to the Osage woman."

"And what of Lillian, what of the girl you say is so fine?" Jason asked evenly. "What becomes of her?"

"She had her opportunity when she lived in my

home. She tossed it aside. She can return to her people."

"And if I refuse your demand?"

"Then whatever happens is on your own head, not ours. The men at Crowe's establishment are willing to give you until morning. Think it over. Let them know, at the tavern. Don't disturb me with this matter a second time."

"I'm not going to think it over," Jason told them. "I'm going to stay with Lillian. If she'll have me."

He saw the crimson wash up Amos Griggs's face and lose itself in the dark hair. He saw Reardon's features go beyond iron, those of Crowe infinitely keen.

And when they departed, without another word or glance, he knew that he had made three implaccable enemies. And that they would carry anger back to those who waited at the tavern.

Chapter 47

They could demand that he abandon Lillian and cleave to Massie Ann, the law could so decree. But no man, no gathering of men, no court, could force him to take Massie Ann again into his arms, to lie with her, to live with her, to cope with the complaining, the demands, the viciousness. Even if there were no Lillian, he would not again endure Massie Ann.

No one, not God himself, could force him.

He would choose. And his choice was Lillian, and if he couldn't have her, he chose to go on alone with Auguste.

He paced to that closed door, listened. There was no sound within.

He prodded the fire, quietly. He paced again, not thinking.

At first, when he heard the subdued knock, he was confused, believing that it came from the other room. But then it sounded again, insistent, and he went to the front door and opened it.

Sam Janas was outside, rifle in hand, hair mussed, sharp features sober. He strode in.

"Jase," he demanded, "what the hell you got into?

They's a mob forming down yonder, they're all stirred up. I like to never found out who it was they're so het up over bein' a bigamist. I was way to the back, and then I seen Massie Ann and Fred up front—they didn't spot me, thank God—and then I knowed it was you, the very one I went in there to in-quire about, like I always do!"

"Then you know I married again."

"Married Osage, way I hear it. A squaw."

"She's three-quarters white," Jason explained wearily. "She's in the next room with Granny Grosshart, deciding whether she'll have me. One thing sure, I'm not going back with Massie Ann."

"That's what's causin' the trouble," Sam warned. He leaned his rifle against the table, faced Jason. "You hangin' on to the squaw, claimin' she's yer wife, makin' yerself a bigamist with yer own mouth. I ain't saying one way or the other, it not bein' my affair."

"That paper declaring Massie Ann legally dead," asked Jason, "do you know if Medary took it up the Missouri?"

"Hell, no, she didn't. She didn't have nothin' when we found her, she was stark nekkid and so was Yeller Flower, except fer a rifle."

"What happened . . . how did you find them?"

"We stole a boat, stole rifles. Not long after we left you that morning. We went down that river faster'n hell, caught up with them sons-a-bitches that day at the island, took them by surprise. That island we passed that day and that son-a-bitch tried to hail us down.

"They lost the barge. It sunk on 'em, struck a snag. They took the little boat and made fer the island. It was four pirates left, is all. Well, they had some likker, and begun to hit it. They was whoopin' and hollerin', workin' up to rape the women. They'd rip off some of the women's clothes, like a dress, and throw it into the river and dance around, yellin' at the current to go faster with it, and then they'd rip off another piece and do the same, until they had 'em both bare to the hide.

"They divided the women out—one woman to each

two of theirselfs. Medary's two raped her, one holdin', the other performin'. But when the first 'un tried on Yeller Flower, she'd somehow got holt of a knife, and she put it in his back, clean to his heart. When the other 'un come at her, she stabbed him in the balls, sliced his thing half off, and then, with the first two still busy with Medary, she stabbed the one holdin' Medary down right in the belly. The one on top of Medary come up like he 'us shot out of a rifle and he went fer Yeller Flower, got her and was chokin' her and bless God if Medary didn't grab up a rifle and shot the bastard in the back!

"Time me'n Tench got there, they'd buried them four bastards. They 'us still nekkid 'cause they couldn't bring theirselfs to take clothes off of dead men.

"Medary 'us on her last pins. She swooned away when she seen us. Yeller Flower was bad off too, but she never did swoon. And she'd took off all the gold them bastards had wore in money belts, so me'n Tench not only had our women back, bravest kind of women, but we had us a stake. Shared it out in three parts— one fer Tench, one fer me, one fer you."

"I don't need it," Jason said. "I got close to four hundred dollars for my peltries today."

"Hell, I sell furs, too. More money the better, more land. Yer takin' yer share."

Jason wondered if the pirate gold would be enough to maintain Massie Ann in New York, dismissed the wonder. That could be determined later.

"Will Ford told me Tench had gone up the Missouri," he said.

"Sure did. Reason we didn't git here sooner, Medary was like dead, clung to Yeller Flower like she was a sister. We made it to Ste. Genevieve, but there we had to stay. First, Medary was all tore up by them bastards, then before she could travel she come up in the fam'ly way from one of 'em. It couldn't be Tench, account of the earthquake and our time searchin' and riggin' the barge and travelin' upriver. Couldn't of bin Tench. Then she took the notion she might be carryin' the baby of the bastard she'd shot in the back and the idea she might of kilt her own baby's pappy done her more harm than bein' raped. But she lost it, thank God. She was holler-eyed yet when they left here."

"I've been up the Missouri and back," Jason said. "I didn't see any sign of Tench."

He aimed to settle off the Missoura, some quiet branch. Figgered they'd be that much further removed from the war if fightin' should break out. They want a quiet place to live anyhow, not so much comin' and goin'. Tench figgers there'll be lots of traffic on the Missoura in time, and he don't want to be bothered."

"Lillian and I picked a place on the river," Jason said. Just to speak her name was a comfort, made her seem closer.

"That her name . . . Lillian?"

Jason nodded.

"Likely her and Medary'll hit it off. Yeller Flower, too. Me'n Yeller Flower waited here, knowin' you'd come back. We've trapped in and out, even with her in the fam'ly way. That's how Delaware squaws are, havin' a baby is nothin'. She's give me a fine boy, born on the trail, and I married her last trip in. Can't have a boy named fer me—Sam'l she calls him—without right to his pappy's whole name."

Jason nodded. "Medary will be pleased," he said.

"She sure will. We'll be able to locate their place without no fuss. Tench worked out a sign fer where they turn off, said he wouldn't go too awful far from the Missoura, so's we won't have too hard a trip to visit each other. That is, if you still aim to go after . . ." He gestured, fell silent.

Into the silence came Granny Grosshart. She closed the bedroom door, nodded to Sam, who murmured his name, then whispered to Jason.

"She's finally fell asleep, poor little thing. She ain't ready yet, son. I've told her about Madame, I've told her how you feel, and she says she knows how you feel. We talked and we prayed and then we talked some more. She nursed the baby, thought he had a fever for

a while, but he didn't, was wrapped up too warm. At
the last, before she went off to sleep—and it ain't a
easy sleep—she asked me to tell you that her regard
and her feeling for you ain't changed. But she asks for
the night, she asks that it be morning when she sees
you, when she decides."

Despair struck heavily through Jason, but this was
what Lillian needed. So he nodded.

"If she rouses," he told Granny, "if she wants to see
me sooner, tell her I'll be waiting."

Chapter 48

When the old lady had gone back into the bedroom, Sam turned urgently on Jason.

"You ain't got till mornin', Jase!" he exclaimed. "That's a lynch mob buildin' down at the tavern! If you got yer head set to stick with yer squaw, you got to git her out'n that room, do it now, and git out of St. Louis while the gittin's good! I'll help you, I've got me two horses. You kin have both of 'em and take up the river here and now fer Tench's, and me'n Yeller Flower'll foller in a week or so and bring ever'thing to outfit both of us. I got the pirate gold and I got my own gold. We kin act and act now!"

"Thanks for the offer," Jason said decisively. "But I won't be run out of St. Louis by anybody."

"Looks like you've been around Injuns enough by now to know when to quit. You lived Osage, didn't you?" At Jason's nod, he plunged on. "Injuns quit when things go agin 'em, then come back at whatever it is when things are in their favor."

"I couldn't go now, even if I wanted to."

"Because of what the old lady said?"

"Exactly."

"Hell, man—yer Lillian's a woman! Walk in there and drag her out, if you got to, and slap her onto a horse and git goin'! If you don't, the way them jackasses at the tavern's ravin' about bein' decent citizens and bigamy, they'll come here and stick you into a barrel of hot tar in no time!"

"We're living in modern times, Sam," Jason said, considering. "Talk is cheap, threats are easy to make, not so easy to back up. I don't doubt that the crowd at the tavern is ugly, with Fred there to stir them up, but the men wo came in delegation to see me—"

"I heard what Crowe and Reardon said when they reported back," Sam interrupted. "That's how I know the mind they're in . . . one feller was sayin' that lynchin's too good fer the likes of you. Accordin' to me, it ain't but a matter of time until all hell'll break loose!"

"I'll take my chances," Jason said, after a moment. "Griggs and the other two gave me until morning."

"And what'll you do then?"

"I'll take Lillian and the boys, if she'll go, and we'll leave," Jason said grimly. "If she won't go, I'll divide my money between her and Massie Ann and I'll take Auguste to Medary. Make my start alone. This is a free country. A man can't be forced to stay with a woman he doesn't want."

"They won't stand fer it," Sam muttered. "I tell you, Jase, they won't stand fer it!"

They had been staring at each other, at total cross-purpose, for some time, when the sound began. It was the sound of voices, the muttering growl of many people. The sound grew and deepened, drawing nearer and nearer, and then it thickened outside the cabin, enriching itself, swelling. Suddenly it lifted into a roar. And Jason knew that it was, at last, an entity, a great, dangerous animal of vengeance.

"My God, Jase!" Sam whispered. "Grab yer rifle!"

Jason's rifle leaned against the wall where he'd put it earlier. He left it there.

"Open up, Blood!" bawled a voice, soaring above the continued roar. "Let her in!"

Jason took two strides, yanked open the door.

Massie Ann stood on the step, her brother looming and glowering beside her. Behind them, massed black against the night, was the now silent crowd-animal, formed of twenty people or thirty, Jason could not estimate.

Massie Ann stepped into the room, Fred with her. Immediately the doorway was filled by Cat Reardon, a big smithy hammer in hand; behind him pressed Bawley Crowe, and behind him faceless others.

Massie Ann stood, bone-thin and young-old and angry-pitiful. Her pale eyes defied Jason, begged, demanded. "I'm here to ask you for the last time, Jason Blood," she said, whining. "Are you going to do the right thing by me or not?"

The crowd-animal pulsed with silence. It had heard her question, her plea, her demand. It waited for Jason's reply, acceptance, refusal.

Cat Reardon said, "We're treating you downright gentle, Blood—so far. For the sake of your wife. We're giving you a second chanct."

"You gave me until morning."

"Things has changed. You said you wasn't going to think. She wants your answer, Blood. She wants it now."

Jason spoke slowly, so she could understand, so the mob could hear and know. "The offer I made you stands," he said. "The land in New Madrid is yours, all my money is yours . . . better than three hundred fifty dollars from my furs and money I don't know the amount of that Sam has for me."

"Five hundred," Sam put in. "Gold."

"You can go to New York on that," Jason said. "You and Fred both."

"And what do you do—stay with the squaw?" Massie Ann spat.

"Either that, or I take Auguste only, and we go up the Missouri."

Everything he said sounded wooden, abrupt, brutal. But he was unable to give less than truth.

"No!" Massie Ann screamed. "It won't do! I've got a right to everything—the land, the gold, going to New York, my baby, my husband! That's what I want, and that's the only way!"

"I've told you how it is," Jason said. "I won't change."

Now the growl of the crowd-animal resumed. It had brought Massie Ann here to force an answer from Jason. It had got the answer, the one it could oppose, the one it wanted. The tension of violence rose.

"You're crazy!" Massie Ann screamed on. "You're raving crazy to say such things to me, your legal wife, the mother of your lawful son! Taking my flesh and blood away from me! Why, even in the Bible, the judge wouldn't let the baby be taken from it's mother— next thing you'll want to cut my flesh and blood in two! Now—for the last time—you ready to do your duty by me, or not?"

"Not your way, Massie Ann," Jason said, from between his teeth.

She whirled—to her brother, to Reardon, to the mob beyond. And she screeched, her shrill voice shooting like some wild night bird through the darkness, "Come and get him! Tar and feather him . . . ride him on a rail . . . kill him!"

Chapter 49

"God!" yelled Sam above the roar and surge toward the cabin. "Grab yer rifle, Jase! We got to stand the sons-a-bitches off!"

Jason snatched up his rifle. Massie Ann leapt aside as a burst of men filled the room. Ten of them there were, fifteen, more, and banks of them outside. They were armed with rifles, iron bars, clubs. One man threw his rifle up and pulled off a warning shot which crashed into the edge of the mantel.

Sam took aim at him, and Jason slammed his rifle barrel down on the barrel of Sam's rifle, sending the bullet into the floor.

"Hold off!" Reardon yelled. "We got a lady present!"

"Give up, Blood!" bellowed Fred Cremer. "Come quiet!"

The men growled, and the growling mob-animal outside built its sound into a roar. This rolled like rough thunder.

Reardon's eyes were slits. "You had your chanct and turned it down, Blood. That don't set well with the citizens of St. Louis. Mr. Griggs himself'd agree to that, if he was here. Now you got a choice. You can come

with us on your own two feet, like a man, and take
your tar and feathers and come out of it to be husband
and pappy. Or you can hang back and be drug and
nobody'll give a damn if the tar's hot enough to stew
you on the hoof!"

He jerked the big iron hammer which he gripped
in one hand. The hammer must be one he used in his
work, Jason thought, and was amazed that his mind
would slip onto such an irrelevant matter. But the
mind defied him and wondered how human flesh would
feel under the swing and impact of that hammer.

Even as these thoughts crawled or passed or fled
through his mind, he knew he'd never go with this
mob of his own volition. He'd not walk tamely to the
death which this roiling crowd, this animal, had deemed
in its frenzy was his proper due.

Before he moved to fight, he had to get them out of
the cabin, out of the grounds, away from Lillian, from
Jason, from Granny.

"Watch out, Reardon," Fred bawled now. "He's up
to something! Grab him now, like mein schwester said!
She don't mind, what she's been through! Don't hold
back for no squaw. We better take her too—and the
papoose!"

Massie Ann sprang forward, eyes wild. "Ja!" she
screamed. "Take the squaw, take the papoose! Boil
them in tar, get rid of them!" She went on screaming,
not in words, but in mob-craze which sparked in her
maddened eyes and stood in hot points of insane fury
on her voice.

Now fear took Jason, terror for Lillian, for his son.
The law, he thought, the law.

"The marshal," he muttered to Sam. "Get the
marshal!" Then, as Sam moved, shoving between two
men, trying to shove farther on, he turned to Cat
Reardon. "I'm ready," he said. "Let's go."

"It's a trick!" shrilled Massie Ann. "I seen him
whisperin' to Sam Janas . . . he's a squaw man hisself!
Grab him, too!"

The men closed in around Jason, a slow closing as

of water coming to a boil, weapons ready. Among them, caught in their tide, Sam was borne near to Jason. He saw Sam's rifle lift to crash down on a head, any head, and lunged at him, again crashing it downward with his own rifle.

"Not here!" he shouted.

A hairy hand shot out, wrenched at his rifle, and Jason let it go.

"Outside!" he shouted, swept by need to toll the mob away. There, in the open, away from the cabin, he'd deal with his own extremity. "Sam!" he prodded.

"I'm goin'!" Sam howled, and threw himself against the tide surging in at the door, and the tide pressed him back as if he were a bit of flotsam, a straw. Someone tore his rifle away from him, and when he began slamming with his fists, Reardon and another man grabbed him and held him, though he lunged and grappled without end.

Instinctively, Jason hurtled at them. He was yanked backward so violently that his head jerked and his teeth cracked together. Again he charged, but the hold on him—there were three of them at arms and knees—was iron and he couldn't move. He tensed again, gave one great, abortive twist.

Now a mighty arm clamped his chest, another crushed his throat, forcing his head back, cutting his breath. They were still holding his arms, his knees, so relentlessly that, though he tried again and again, he could make no move.

They began to drag him backward, toward the door, and he let them. He'd lost sight, in heat of rage on Sam's behalf, of the fact that he wanted to get out of the cabin and away.

Massie Ann, suddenly, was in his line of vision. Her face was twisted, her pale hair straggled across one eye, and she was screeching and pointing at him, at the bedroom door.

And now that door opened, and he saw Lillian, still in her travel dress, standing there, Her glance flew across the roiling men to him, a look of tenderness, alarm, terror.

"Go back!" he shouted, even as she came running toward him. "Go back!"

Out of the end of his eye, he was aware that Massie Ann had snatched up a rifle. He saw it swing, heard the sound it made when she pulled trigger.

And then Lillian stopped running, stood for a heart-beat, then wilted to the floor. And a flower of red, shaped like a wild rose, showed on her back, moved, bloomed, grew.

The red flower drew silence over the men within, over the mob-animal outside. Jason lunged toward Lillian, but the men held him, though no voice growled.

Only an instant had passed, for Massie Ann was just lowering the rifle, her face ashen, her mouth fallen open. Now Granny was darting, faster surely than any old woman with a cane had ever moved, and she dropped the cane and knelt beside Lillian and gently, ever so tenderly, turned her onto her back, hiding that vicious flower of red.

Granny's wrinkled face was stiller than the grave. Her fingers went to Lillian's throat, rested lightly there, and a listening came onto her.

And it came upon the men inside, upon the mob-animal out in the night, upon Jason and Sam, and even on Massie Ann. All were listening and silent, so silent that when Granny's whisper came it was like a shout.

"She's gone," Granny whispered, looking at Jason. Then her blue eyes pierced around the room, once through the open door to the mob. "You've got no reason now," she whispered on. "There is no bigamy. Not anymore."

Massie Ann screamed, once, the sound sharp. She fell suddenly to the floor, unconscious before her tiny body smacked down, and Jason saw, in the next heavy lunge of pulse, that one hand was touching the hem of Lillian's skirt.

Chapter 50

"Damn you, Blood, damn you!" bellowed Fred Cremer. He lurched to Massie Ann, lifted her against him, shook her, slapped her face, roared at her to come to. Even as her eyes fluttered open and blinked, wild as never before, the young German turned on Jason, still supporting her. "Dein trouble has been ended for you . . . by dein wife! Let him go, you fools!" he howled at the men still holding Jason, and their hands fell away from him.

"Now!" Fred roared. "Mein schwester got herself in trouble for you . . . she'll go to jail . . . she'll hang! Unless you get a lawyer for her . . . stand by her . . . stand by the mutter of dein sohn!"

And Lillian, mother of my son? Jason's blood surged.

He stared numbly at her still face, at the staring dark eyes. It couldn't be true, it couldn't have happened. Yet there she lay, she who, a moment ago, had been running to him, there she lay, stilled for eternity.

Life had become an ache, a festering wound. He stared at her staring eyes from which starlight had died.

"Now," Sam said loudly, "the marshal'll have to be

gone after." He gave a yank and Reardon and the other man let him go, faces blank.

"She wasn't but a squaw," Reardon muttered.

"Even if that was true," Sam snapped, "it's still murder."

One or two of the men inside nodded, expressionless, the stillness yet upon them. The ones outside, crowded to door and window, were as still.

Fred lifted his half-swooning sister into his arms. "I'm takin' her to the inn," he said. The crowd opened, let him pass through the door and out into the street. "Get yourself down to the inn fast, Blood!" he bellowed and tromped away.

"I'll go after the marshal," Sam told them, lifting his voice so all outside could hear. "Jase, leave her be, right on the floor. The marshal'll want to see how she fell. You fellers better stay here, all of you, and tell yer story straight. Yer involved in a murder trial now, like it or not."

Again the men inside the cabin fell back, letting Sam through. They followed him out, but Jason was aware that they stopped outside and stood, with the others, in silent clusters, here and there.

Jason and Granny were alone with the dead Lillian. In the bedroom baby Jason slept; on Barn Street, in the home of William Grosshart, Auguste slept.

"Can't we . . . put her on the bed?" he asked Granny.

The old woman shook her head. "The young man was right, son. The marshal's a particular man. It won't take long for him to walk it. Go outside, breathe some fresh air."

He turned, but at the door he hesitated. Then, not to be influenced by the men who had mobbed against him, he went into the grounds and walked among them, head bent, seeing nothing.

He was aware that someone had approached him and stood blocking his way. A dim light fell through the window, enough that he could recognize the man as Cat Reardon.

"You'll get no more trouble from us," Reardon said.

"Granny was right. There ain't no bigamy now. What you do regardin' your wife—whether you stand by her—ain't none of our concern. Nobody can force you to hire her a lawyer, I reckon."

Get a lawyer, Fred had demanded, and now Reardon had brought up the same thing. Jason reflected numbly on this. Pay a lawyer to defend Massie Ann, who slew Lillian, and with her his life?

It was as if Massie Ann were some stranger, not his wife, neither his first wife nor his only wife. He didn't feel married to her, had never, he realized, felt husband to her. It was as if she had come out of nowhere, or rather from Hell itself, a weapon to cut down and destroy.

If he didn't hire a lawyer, and she was found guilty in a court of law, she would be hanged by the neck until she was dead, and in a manner he would have killed her. He would have been granted revenge, of a sort. If he did hire the lawyer, and she was acquitted, ah, then what?

Stunned, unable to feel grief or hatred or love or remorse, he faced the alternatives.

Massie Ann would hang. Or, acquitted, she would demand her place as his wife. If refused this, she would demand custody of Auguste.

Jason was standing alone, in the darkest corner of the grounds, when the marshal arrived.

Chapter 51

The nightmare hours crept. The marshal, a bull-built man named Johnson, made his examination, ordered two men to carry Lillian's body to another house, started asking questions.

Johnson's face was broad and heavy, with sideburns to the jaw. His eyes were mud-color, overhung with black brows. His voice boomed like a bass drum.

Woodenly, Jason answered Johnson's questions. He told what had happened, from the time of the earthquake until tonight, through the moment in which Massie Ann had snatched the rifle and fired it. Even if he wanted to shield her, and he was too numb to want or not, it would do no good. There had been many witnesses.

He told the marshal that he would be responsible for burying Lillian and responsible for the child she had left. And he agreed to pay for a lawyer. He would stay in St. Louis for the trial.

They buried Lillian at noon. Jason and Sam had dug the grave under the willow tree at the rear of Granny's property, and Sam had seen to getting a stout oaken box. Granny had dressed Lillian in blue and had personally lined the box with her own best quilt.

Only Granny, her son and his wife, the Reverend Blalock and his palsied wife, Jason and Sam, were at the graveside. As the old preacher droned his words, Jason thought how gay Lillian had been yesterday, bringing his sons to see Granny. He thought how, on the day he first met Lillian, they'd spoken of the quickness with which things in the wilderness could happen. He saw Granny weeping, and wondered why now he had no tears.

When it was over, when Granny had laid a spray of summer blossoms on the mound and Sam had set a marker, they scattered. The Grosshart couple went to their home where their daughter, Martha, was tending Auguste and the baby, the reverend and his wife moved, on their uncertain old legs, toward their home, Sam left to hurry back to Yellow Flower and their son, saying he'd rented a cabin near the river.

Jason followed Granny indoors. His body was heavy, his legs hard to move. He sat and stared into the cup of coffee the old lady set before him, listened to the sound of the mantel clock measuring time which had, now, no measure.

Not unexpectedly, Fred Cremer came knocking at the door. Granny let him in.

"They got Massie Ann in jail," Fred snarled. "The marshal come to the inn in the middle of the night and drug her off."

Jason waited, unblinking, for Fred to continue.

"She don't belong in jail. She don't belong there."

"It's the law, when . . . it's the law."

"To hell with the law!" raged Fred. "There's other laws, too . . . laws that say a man has one wife! There's got to be a law says it's right for a woman to fight for what's hers, like mein schwester done, there's bound to be! I've been busy with her troubles all morning, and I've hired a lawyer, Archer Black, told him you'd pay."

Jason nodded.

"She wants out of that jail. She wants out right now!"

"I can't do anything about that. You'll have to discuss it with Black."

"She wants to see the boy. Black fixed that. I'm to fetch Auguste to the jail here and now. It'll go again' you if you try to stand in my way."

Jason looked at Granny. He was still so bereft of emotion he didn't know whether he was against exposing the boy to Massie Ann or not. And he didn't know what to do.

She seemed to know. "It won't take long, Jason," she said. "They don't let a visitor stay long at the jail. That is, if you feel so inclined."

A dull resignation took Jason. He wondered if a man has the right to deny a woman, even one like Massie Ann, one sight of her child. He wondered if he was being a fool even to consider such a visit.

"I'll be the one to take Auguste there," he heard himself saying. When Fred started to object, he moved his hand impatiently. "If he goes, that is."

Fred scowled, but gave no argument.

The jail was located in the old fort. It was inside the stone tower, presided over by a fat jailor with a belly overhang. Auguste kept up his prattle, saying his new word, learned on the downriver trip, over and over: "Boat . . . boat . . ."

"One visitor at a time," the jailor said gruffly, when Fred explained why they had come. "Jest one of you goes in with the kid."

"I don't want to make no trouble," Fred told him, his tone friendly. "This is my sister's man . . . always will be, can't get shet of it. It's their baby . . . he can go in."

Puzzled at Fred's unprecedented friendliness toward anyone other than his sister, Jason followed the jailor, wanting to get the next few moments behind him. Auguste left off his prattling and stared about in the way he had.

The cell was a half-circle, the one straight wall being that formed by the iron bars. Massie Ann was sitting, thin as a wraith, on a quilt-covered cot.

Before the jailor had the key in the lock, she was at the door, gripping the bars, trying to shake them, to hurry him. Her eyes were on the child, never seeing Jason. Her pale lips had fallen apart, the lower lip fluttering under her breathing.

As he swung the door open, the jailor put his hand against her shoulder and held her back. "Mein kind!" she screamed at him. "Ich will mein kind habe . . . stop pushing mich!"

"Give yer husband a chance to git in," the jailor snorted. He stepped aside, still holding her back, and Jason entered.

Even as the jailor escaped and was locking the door, Massie Ann flew at Jason, snatched Auguste from him, clutched the instantly screaming boy to her, and herself began to scream and keen. Auguste's face went beet-red, his head reared back, and his screams rose louder than those of his mother. He screamed, drew breath and held it, screamed again, stringing his screams one to another, and Massie Ann strung her shrieks and keening to them so that together they made a stridor of rage, misery, terror.

Jason put his hands on the child, tried to lift him free. Massie Ann clutched him tighter and screamed, "Get your hands off of mein kind!" There wasn't a tear in her eye, for all her lamentation. "What've you done to him, what've you done to my baby, you and that squaw?"

"Nothing's been done to him!" Jason shouted, had to shout or not be heard. "He's scared, that's all!"

"Scared of his own ma?" she shrilled. "If he is, you made him scared, you and her! Scared of his ma, his own flesh and blood!"

"Quit yelling!" he shouted. "Quiet down! The longer you carry on, the more he'll cry. He's not used to noise!"

"No," she raged, but she dropped from screaming to

loudness, "I reckon he ain't! He's used to sneaking Injun ways!"

He almost struck her. Then he stiffened his jaw and stared, amazed at her brashness, her ruthlessness even now, after what she had done. It was incredible, that absolute change from the shy-eager girl who first had come to his house, filled with admiration and longing.

Would she have been different with some other man? he wondered. And knew, in the next breath, that she would not have been, that never would there be an end to her wantings. She would do anything to set her way. Including murder.

"Aren't you sorry for what you did, Massie Ann?" he asked. "Aren't you even upset?" Later, when he could feel again, he might hate her, despise her. Not now. He could only endure, wait, get Auguste away.

"Of course I'm upset!" she snapped, jigging the shrieking child in an effort to quiet him. "What woman wouldn't be, her husband turning her baby again' her, keeping him from her so he don't know her?"

"Your being separated couldn't be helped," he reminded her. "Doesn't it bother you that you . . . killed? That you're in jail, that you're going to be tried, and maybe . . ."

"It's your fault!" she accused, shrieking again. "If you hadn't of taken up with her, I wouldn't of had to do it! If you'd of acted like a natural husband when you seen me . . . Anyhow, she wasn't but a squaw." She dropped the screaming, spoke only loudly enough to be heard above Auguste's crying. "That lawyer, he says her being a squaw and standing in my way, taking my husband and turning him into a bigamist, makes it something about the sanctity of the home."

"Does he think he can get you acquitted?"

There was no point in accusing further. There was no defending Lillian to this vicious, half-crazed woman in the presence of the hiccoughing, sobbing Auguste.

"He says, if we get the right jury. If he gets men that didn't know the squaw when she was growing up and so ain't got the notion she was some kind of lady. If he can show that she drove me out of my mind, stealing my life. But I don't like it . . . I don't like that kind of lawyer-talk . . . it's too risky!"

Before Jason could respond, she made one of her quick changes. "I want a different lawyer!" she demanded. "This one'll get me hung! Get me out of here, take me away!" She was pleading now, a vicious, threatening sort of plea, but plea it was. "Just you and me and Auguste . . . we'll be a fam'ly again! It'll be different, Jason . . . you'll see . . ."

"It could never be just the three of us, Massie Ann," he told her. "Because I've got another son now."

"Not him!" she screamed so ardently that Jason thought her throat must split. "'Don't think I'll ever take your papoose in," she screamed on, "don't you think it, not for a minute!"

Chapter 52

It was another half hour before he got the sobbing, hiccoughing, vomiting child away from the jail and into Granny's arms. Auguste lay against the old woman's bosom, a convulsive sob wracking his sturdy little body now and then.

"Not again," Jason said. "She'll not see him again."

"Couldn't her brother quiet her down?"

"One visitor at a time is the rule. Fred's with her now. She quit screaming the minute he went in. Before I got out of the cell area, they were whispering together. Whispering!" he repeated, marveling that Massie Ann had calmed herself to that degree.

"Well, let them whisper," said Granny. Gently, she began to undress Auguste. "I'm going to give him a bath, and then feed him mush and greens, and when he's full, he'll take a long nap. I've sent word for them to sure keep the baby overnight. I had a feeling Auguste would need all the quiet he could get. He's been through more than a baby's got a call to go through."

Jason watched the clever old hands at their tending, read the kindness of the old face.

"As for you," Granny continued, "I'd appreciate

it if you'd cut me some firewood. My woodpile's getting low . . . well—" she smiled soberly, "lower than I want it right now. I'll cook you up a hot mess of cornpone and pork to go with the greens."

"Later," Jason said. "I want to go down to Chouteau's and look at merchandise, start picking what supplies I'll take up the Missouri when I go."

"Fine, good for you. And you ain't to worry about the babies while you stay in St. Louis. Between me and Will's folks, we'll manage fine. We've already talked it over."

Eased by Granny's kindness, by her gentleness, Jason set out for Chouteau's. As he walked, he puzzled over how he and Sam and Yellow Flower were going to manage the trip up the Missouri with three babies. Well, it wasn't a thing he had to figure out this minute. Yellow Flower must know the Delaware way; Indian women went anywhere with any number of children.

Now and then, as he neared the shops, he passed a man, once two men walking together. All of them nodded soberly to him and he nodded in return, wondering if they'd greet him so if they knew his identity.

At Chouteau's, the sandy-haired clerk he'd dealt with before came directly to him, there being no other customer. "Can I help you, Mr. Blood?" he asked, his tone open and friendly.

"You know what happened," Jason said bluntly, waited.

"I heard . . . the whole village is talking. It's a tragic fix, all right. Those hotheads last night—don't get the idea that everybody in St. Louis is like them. And they've cooled down, though it took a tragedy. They're ashamed, can't meet each other's eyes, not a one of them, Cat Reardon included, and he's brazen as they come. Bawley Crowe's as usual, and Amos Griggs. I understand the two of them came on the delegation only, didn't join the mob later."

"No. I didn't see them there."

"I can't tell you how sorry I am about . . . everything . . . Mr. Blood."

Jason nodded bleakly.

"There's one thing," Ford offered. "You'll find as you walk the street nobody looks down on you. They're sorry you're in this fix. Only way they'll show it is they'll speak when you pass."

"I've run into that already."

"Fine, fine. Now, what can I show you? The best of everything is right here, and I'm at your service."

Over an hour later, when Jason left the trading post and started for Granny Grosshart's cabin, he felt satisfied with the things he'd had put aside to take upriver. He'd return every day or so and add to his purchases, he decided, until he was sure he had everything he needed.

The occasional man he passed on the street looked him in the eye and said a pleasant good day, or did not quite meet his eye and nodded and hastened past. He returned their greetings soberly and knew, by the time he'd gone two squares, that Ford had been right about the changed attitude of the villagers.

When someone hailed him from the rear, he turned. Sam was hastening toward him.

"I was comin' over later on," Sam told him. "Thought I wouldn't horn back in too quick. I heard that Fred blabbed all over that he 'us goin' to take Auguste to see his ma or know the reason why. I figgered you had enough on yer hands without me."

Briefly Jason told of the visit to the jail. They walked on as they talked.

Sam shook his head, then brightened. "Say, I've met up with a fam'ly that's goin' up the Missoura, Jase! They want someone to travel with, and we've talked on it since I left you today. Name of Franklin . . . man and wife and a good stout son of sixteen. Thurlow—that's Franklin's name—and me'll git pirogues ready, and soon's the trial's over, we kin all git started.

We'll make room so's if Massie Ann's let go and you take her along, there'll be a place."

"Thanks," Jason said. "I'll want to go, and the boys, that's sure."

But after Sam took his leave and he walked on toward Granny's, Jason felt impelled to put his mind to what he was going to do about Massie Ann, should she be acquitted. She'd never hear of going up the Missouri, even if he were willing to take her, which he was not. However, once acquitted, she'd demand and do everything in her power to force him to abandon baby Jason and take her to New York.

He shied from the thought that she might be hanged, but then forced himself to face that possibility. As far as he could tell, she had not herself fully recognized what her end could be, was concerned only with getting out of jail, going to New York with himself and Auguste.

When he reached Granny's woodpile and threw himself into the work, nothing had been resolved concerning Massie Ann. He grabbed the ax and began to chop, swinging the ax with all his strength, stacking the wood along the back of the cabin, handy to the door. On he worked, into dusk, into dark, not thinking of the grave under the willow tree, not thinking of Massie Ann, or of his sons. There was only work and later, exhausted to the core, the hasty eating of hot food, and falling onto the pallet Granny laid near the fireplace.

He was sitting at the table at daybreak, Auguste trotting around the room as if yesterday had never been, Granny at the fireplace cooking eggs, and still nothing was resolved. Into this, came an abrupt, thunderous knock.

Before Granny could call out for the person to enter, the door was yanked open. Sam charged in, came to the table, stopped.

He looked like the world had come to an end. His breath was short and fast, his sharp features were bleak with surprise or shock or concern, Jason couldn't tell which. He watched Granny urge Sam into the other chair, saw how heavily he dropped into it, how absently he pushed aside the coffee the old lady had brought. For an instant, Jason was sure something had gone wrong with little Sam'l or with Yellow Flower.

Before he could think how to ask, Sam said, "Jase . . . nerve yerself. I got the damndest news you ever heerd . . . and I don't know if it's good or bad. Last night, about nine o'clock, that Fred Cremer broke his sister out'n jail!"

Chapter 53

"I can't believe it," Jason heard himself say.

Like that, just like that, Massie Ann was gone. Again. Swallowed up, this time in flight. What that would mean, whether the end of trouble or the start of worse trouble, he had no idea.

"Well, Fred done it," Sam assured him. "Yeller Flower was feedin' Sam'l, which woke me up, and then I heerd a commotion . . . men runnin' past . . . and I follered. They was a crowd outside the jail. And I found out about Massie Ann and Fred. The marshal's sendin' deputies over here, I seen them fixin' to leave and then I got the hell away, run ever' step to let you know, so you wouldn't be took by surprise. You look out towards the shops, and you'll see them, that I know."

Jason went to the door at once and indeed, only a square away, two men were hastening in this direction. He stepped into the yard, met them as they arrived.

One was almost as bull-shaped as Marshal Johnson himself, with hair the color of the morning and a face like rock. The other was taller and slimmer, with an unkempt red beard.

The bearded one was spokesman. "Marshal's deputies," he said. "You Jason Blood, husband to Massie Ann Blood?"

"I am," Jason replied.

He was aware that Sam had followed him outside and was standing behind and slightly to his left. He could hear Granny, in the doorway, saying something to Auguste.

"You know she broke jail last night?"

"My friend here, Sam Janas, just brought the word."

"We've got a paper says we can search the house and premises of Granny Grosshart, where you're known to be staying, to see if she is harboring this fugitive from justice."

"My . . . Massie Ann's not on the premises, not to my knowledge. It's wrong to disturb Mrs. Grosshart. She's law-abiding and innocent of any of this."

"She's known to be a woman who does what she wants. Anyhow, we got to look. Orders."

"I heard that, Ralph Stuart," Granny called. "Come on in, you and Pos Abadie both. You won't find no fugitives in my home or around it."

They learned this firsthand, tramping through the cabin, looking under the bed, opening the armoire, walking every inch of the grounds. They went into the shed, around the woodpile, even tramped past the grave under the willow tree as if, perhaps, Massie Ann lay stretched on the far side of the girl she had slain, using her as cover from the law.

When they had finished, the bearded one turned to Jason. "Marshal wants you to come to his office," he said shortly.

"What fer?" demanded Sam. "He think Jase's got her hid in his pocket?"

"Let's go," the deputy said, "we've got a lot to do."

"I'm comin' with you, Jase," Sam announced and took his place beside Jason.

Granny called after them that Jason wasn't to worry, that his babies would be safe.

"Sounds like she thinks they're goin' to lock you

up," Sam muttered. "They can't do that, can they, Jase?"

"I wouldn't think so," Jason replied. "Unless they could prove that I helped Massie Ann escape. Then they might."

They walked on, Jason and Sam in front, the deputies at their heels. As they came to the old fort, numbers of people were standing about, presumably discussing the jailbreak. Jason caught snatches of talk, and knew that more than one curious glance was directed at him, though he kept his gaze straight ahead, avoiding causing anyone the embarrassment of having to speak or not speak to the husband of a murderess. He knew, further, that speculation would now begin as to why he was here and what might be the outcome of his appearance on the scene.

". . . posse . . ." he heard as he passed a clump of men.

A thrill of dread flashed down his spine at the thought of armed men pursuing a terrified Massie Ann, dragging her back. And they would have to drag her, now that she'd got free.

And in that instant he knew he wanted no vengeance on Massie Ann, no pain inflicted on her cringing, desperate flesh. But the noose, the rope which might eventually circle her screaming, struggling neck, which would snap it suddenly and clean, did he want that? Or did he want her to walk free, as though she had never blasted death into Lillian's heart?

What do you do if the law says the mother of your one son must hang by the neck for the murder of the mother of your other son? he thought. How do you decide?

So far gone was he in despair over his unanswerable questions that it took Deputy Stuart's heavy clamp on his arm to bring him back to the moment.

"I've reported to the marshal," Stuart said. "Go on in. He's waiting."

Jason stepped alone into the marshal's office.

There was a plain board table behind which sat the

marshal. He was scowling, his big black brows dipped like awnings over their muddy eyes. He looked so big-shouldered that he dwarfed the ledger-laden shelves behind him.

"Pull up a chair," he boomed. "This'll take a while."

Jason complied, bringing one of the three straight chairs to the front of the table. He sat down and waited.

"Before I start my questions," the marshal said, "I'll state what happened here last night. To set the record straight. So you can't shilly-shally about answering."

"That suits me," Jason said.

"This Fred Cremer was a slick one," the marshal began. "From the minute they locked Massie Ann Blood up here, he got on the good side of this one jailor—Jim Covey his name is—friendly and anxious about his sister. Po-lite. That's how he worked it.

"About nine o'clock last night, he came to the jail, bringin' his sister some special soup. And Jim, thinking Cremer was just a thoughtful brother, tryin' to make things a little easier for his sister, agreed to let him take the soup into the cell himself, and visit.

"While Jim was unlockin' the cell, Cremer brought that bowl of hot soup down on the back of his head and dropped him. He's burnt all over the back of his head and neck besides sufferin' from the poundin' Cremer gave him. Cremer then tied Jim up and gagged him and locked him into the cell, and him and his sister lit out."

Jason waited. There was nothing he could say.

"When did you last see your wife?" the marshal asked.

"When I took my son, Auguste, to visit her in jail. Yesterday afternoon."

"What did she say to you at that time?"

"She wanted a different lawyer."

"Why was that?"

"She thought a different lawyer would get her out of this trouble."

"What else did she say?"

"She wanted out of jail."

"What was your response?"

"I . . . in effect . . . told her it was impossible."

"What next did she say?"

"It was personal."

"She's broken jail, Mr. Blood. She's a fugitive. Personal or not, I have got to ask you to give me answers."

"She wanted to resume our married life."

"What did you say to that?"

"I . . . indicated . . . it was out of the question."

"What was her attitude then?"

"She became very upset . . . she'd been upset the whole time . . . and screamed and said things a woman will say at such a time . . . in her anger. And in her fear, marshal."

"She was afraid she'd be hung?"

"She was too upset by everything to fully appreciate the hanging part of it."

"But she did tell you she wanted out of jail?"

"Yes, she did. And her brother told me."

"She told you she had plans to break out. And her brother told you."

"No. She did not. And her brother did not."

"You were told the plan. And you helped."

"She told me nothing. You can ask the jailor. He was just outside the cell. He heard everything we said, couldn't keep from it. She was screaming, and when she wasn't screaming, we still had to raise our voices to hear each other over the baby's crying. The jailor will bear me out, marshal."

Johnson grunted, and Jason knew the marshal had already learned all this from the jailor.

"The brother. Cremer. He came to you. You planned it together. He broke her out. You helped them make it away."

"Fred never came to the cabin after Lillian was killed. You can ask Granny Grosshart. I slept the night on the floor at her fireplace. She saw me there, she was up and down with my baby, moved around, said she couldn't rest."

The marshal grunted.

"Where did your wife and her brother head for?"

"I haven't any idea, marshal."

"You're bound to have some notion, whether she'll go to family or friends."

"I don't believe she'd go to her family, even if she knew where they are. They left New Madrid after the earthquake, and unless she found a letter waiting when they passed through New Madrid on their way to St. Louis, which I doubt, she has no idea where they are."

"That still leaves friends."

"She has no friends, marshal. Only her brother."

"How about his friends?"

"He has none either. He used to hunt with a couple of young fellows sometimes."

"Names?"

"Anton and Pierre Duval. They're brothers. But they wouldn't be apt to hide Fred and Massie Ann, even if Fred knew where they were. The Duval family was among the first to leave after the earthquake."

He couldn't bring himself to mention the people who had rescued Massie Ann, or the family which had taken her in and nursed her. He didn't know their names, had no idea where they lived, except that it seemed to have been downriver.

"We know that some folks in a boat picked your wife out of the water during the quake," the marshal said. "And that a family down toward Natchez took her into their cabin when she was out of her head, and Cremer found her there. The jailor heard all that, heard her talking to her brother about it at the top of her voice. I want the names of those folks from you, Mr. Blood."

"I don't know the names, never heard them."

"Where do they live?"

"I never heard that, either."

"You think your wife and her brother could've gone there—to the folks that nursed her?"

"I suppose they could. If they had a way."

"They got a way."

"What way is that, marshal?"

The muddy eyes slammed at Jason.

"Won't hurt to tell you, I reckon. A pirogue was stolen last night, sometime after ten. We figure they hid out at the fort until everybody was off the street, then stole the boat . . . it belonged to Will Routsong . . . and he'd chained it up about ten."

"They don't know much about boats, marshal."

"I aim to capture her and bring her to trial, Mr. Blood. I've already sent two men downriver, which is the logical direction. They've got a head start, but they'll be laying up now, hidin' during the day, riding the current at night. My men won't lay up at all, so they'll overtake them. Now that I know she wasn't hid out with you, I'm going to send two more men downriver. What I want from you now, Mr. Blood, since you don't seem to know for certain, is where do you think they might logically head?"

Not for New York, Jason thought, because they couldn't take the pirogue upstream on the Ohio. Further, they had no known money for keelboat fare, and Fred couldn't earn both their passages as one of the crew. And Massie Ann could never survive the trip afoot, and they had no way to get horses, short of theft. They wouldn't go to New Madrid both because of danger of further earthquake and Massie Ann's hatred of the place. That left only the family that had nursed her, or some downriver town or city, such as New Orleans. But these things the marshal could reason out for himself.

So Jason shook his head.

The marshal scowled. "You wouldn't say if you did know. Man don't want to inform on a woman he's lived with. Well, my deputies'll go to every cabin and settlement on the way to New Madrid, and then to New Madrid itself. If she's there, which I think is logical, they'll bring her back. If not, they'll try downriver cabins and towns, go as far as New Orleans, even."

"You're not sending a regular posse?" Jason asked, recalling the bit of conversation he'd overheard.

"What for? I'll have four good men on the trail. Now, here is something you can answer me. You're not fixin' to leave St. Louis right away, with her on the run, are you?"

"I was leaving immediately, as you know, before all this happened. I'm still going as soon as possible. I've got land up the Missouri."

"Stay here a spell, say a month. If they don't run your wife and her brother down in that time, it's going to take longer for authorities along the river to help and spot them and take them in custody. In that case, we'll send you word up the Missouri, and you can come back for the trial."

"All right," Jason agreed, "I'll stay the month."

"That's all then," the marshal said. "You can go."

Sam fell in step with him the minute he came out. They started walking in the direction of Granny's cabin.

"What happened?" Sam asked. "What's the marshal want . . . what'd he say . . . how'd they manage to break out?"

Jason told him, briefly.

"You goin' downriver with the deputies today?" Sam asked when he'd heard everything.

The thought hadn't occurred to Jason but now, as they walked, he considered it. The first time Massie Ann had vanished, when the earth had opened and taken her, he'd searched long and painfully to bring her back to living. This time she had vanished by her own act to escape punishment, and if he were to find her, protect her, he'd be aiding and abetting in the slaying of Lillian. If he helped the deputies bring her back and she hanged, he'd be dragging her back to death.

"No," he said to Sam. "I can't do that. I'll stay here, I'll wait the month.

"Is it always like this," he wanted to ask his friend

and did not, "is there always a flash of doing, then an eternity of waiting?"

He thought of Massie Ann's son, of Lillian's son. And he thought, dully, God help her, not knowing what he wanted done, or in what form. God help Massie Ann.

As for himself, the only capacity of his heart was to cherish Jason, son of Lillian's flesh and his other son, Auguste.

Epilogue

In the year after the events herein recounted, up to and including April 4, 1814, the following developments took place:

The War of 1812 was still in progress, though St. Louis was not seriously touched by it.

Granny Grosshart had been dead some four months, having succumbed to pneumonia, though tenderly nursed by her family.

Hendrik van Delft was also dead, and his Dutch nephew was expected any day to take over the New York estate.

The Cremer family, back in their crudely repaired cabin, were living in filth and had two more babies.

Quick Knife was courting a more mature Singing Lark.

Sam and Yellow Flower Janas, happy over the birth of their second son, Tench, were building a new room onto their cabin up the Missouri.

Azor and Annette Davis, in New Madrid, were planning a ball.

The settler family which befriended Massie Ann after the earthquake was moving to Louisiana.

Marshal Johnson's deputies had found not the first trace of Massie Ann and Fred, and he was relentlessly determined to apprehend them, sooner or later.

Five hundred dollars, the share of pirate money given Jason by Sam and Tench, was on deposit at Chouteau's for Massie Ann.

The two fugitives were in the neutral ground of Texas, that strip of land which neither Texas nor Louisiana could claim, where lawbreakers were safe.

Tench and Medary Coghill were living six miles up a tributary of the Missouri, Medary lonely for Jason's sons.

Thurlow and Auwina Franklin, with their son, Emo, were living in a cabin on the Missouri. Franklin was convinced, from his family Bible and old letters, that his father had been a connection of Thurlow Dusard, Lillian's father.

Jason Blood was living in his new house on the Missouri, his sons cared for by the fifty-year-old widowed sister of Auwina Franklin. He was reasonably content with this arrangement and was standing ready to build his life, ready for what was to come next, whatever that might be.

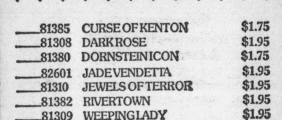